IG

A sudden gust of wind engulfed Mara, and she looked up to see Tajarez entering her tent. He stood silently, watching her, his dark eyes resting on the gentle swell of her creamy white breast.

Mara would have covered herself against his intense stare, but her heart pounded so forcefully against her ribs that she could not move.

Stepping toward her, Tajarez spoke no words. Instead, he reached out raising her head to his own. Then he took her lips with his, soft and searching—soon hungry and devouring.

"Mara, beloved," he whispered, glorying in the feel of her precious, silky body. Then he tasted of her honeyed lips again before savoring her eyelids, the lobes of her delicate ears, and her throat. And all the while, he never stopped murmuring "Mara."

# HISTORICAL ROMANCE AT ITS BEST!

Savage Splendor

CONSTANCE O'BANYON

**ZEBRA BOOKS**
**KENSINGTON PUBLISHING CORP.**

ZEBRA BOOKS

are published by

KENSINGTON PUBLISHING CORP.
475 Park Avenue South
New York, N.Y. 10016

First printing: December, 1983

Printed in the United States of America

*This book is dedicated to someone I watched face life as a challenge to be met. When life became hard, you only grew stronger. I watched with great pride and love as you reached for the sky, knowing anything you wanted out of life you would obtain. When I was teaching you about life, I learned from you. When you were small you gave these words to me, I now give them back to you.*
*I love you more than all the leaves on all the trees, in all the world: my son, Rick.*

## LOST ENCHANTMENT

Speak to me of yesterday when we laughed and loved in the sun.
A gentle touch, a soft caress as our love had just begun.
Reveal to me a time gone by when my world was free and light.
Whisper to me of the love we shared on a bright, star-filled night.
My tortured mind reaches backwards to a not too distant past,
To a soft-spoken word and a gentle kiss and a time that could not last.
I am now lost in a faraway place, not to hear your voice or to see your face.
I cry out for a time gone by, and the abiding love that will not die.

# INTRODUCTION

The many tales and legends of the Seven Cities of Gold have long held a fascination for me. What was it about the legends that caused such outstanding explorers as De Soto, Friar Marcos and Coronado to search so diligently for the cities without ever finding them? Were they driven by the promise of riches that the Seven Cities were said to possess? Was it in search of a highly advanced civilization, ruled by a mighty king who lived in a magnificent palace?

Come with me now as we journey back in time to a virgin wilderness that had not yet felt the destructive scars the white race seems to leave on the land it populates.

Come with me to a secret place, an Eldorado, an Eden . . . the Seven Cities of Gold.

It is a land rich in silver and other wealth. And has great cities; the houses are of stone, and terraced like those in Mexico; the people have weights and measures, and are civilized. They marry only once, wear woolen clothes . . . and are ruled by a king.

—Friar Marcos

# One

We dwell in an Eden beneath a bright starlit sky.
We dwell in an Eden, my love and I.

The tall Indian dismounted silently and quickly ducked behind a pine tree. The evening breeze stirred his long ebony-colored shoulder-length hair. He wore white buckskin trousers with a white vest to match. His handsome face creased into a frown as his senses became alert. He could hear the splashing sound coming from the pool that was barely visible from where he stood.

The soft leather moccasins made no sound as he stepped to the side of the pine tree so he could have a better view of the pool. His dark eyes moved over the rippling surface and he watched quietly as a woman surfaced and with swift strokes swam toward the bank.

He slipped behind the tree once more to conceal his presence from her. His eyes fastened on her golden hair that streamed down her back to her waist as she emerged from the water. His eyes blazed when he noticed that she wore nothing. Her beautiful body was perfect. Her waist was tiny and her hips well rounded. Her breasts were full and firm. On her lovely face was a smile, as if she were having private thoughts known only to herself. The white woman slipped into a soft robe and stood gazing off toward the setting sun.

The tall Indian noticed the way her robe clung to her wet body, emphasizing her soft curves. He was close enough to see the deep green of her eyes. His heartbeat accelerated as he stepped from behind the tree and grabbed the woman. She did not scream, but her eyes widened as she tried to wriggle out of his arms.

"You are my captive, it will do no good for you to struggle, white woman," he said in a deep, passionate voice.

There was still no fright in the emerald-green eyes she turned up to him. "You would do well to release me. My husband is a fierce warrior and it is said that he guards his wife jealously."

"Should I fear this man who is your husband? Perhaps you would prefer me to him?"

"I prefer no one to my husband. Men have died for touching me," she told him, struggling for her release.

"Silence, woman. I would hear more about this man who is your husband," he told her, tightening his grip.

The woman's struggling had caused her robe to slip from her shoulder, revealing a creamy white breast. The Indian resisted the urge to touch the satiny skin.

The woman gave him a look that said she knew what he was thinking. "My husband is Tajarez, King of the Lagonda tribe and ruler of the Seven Cities of

Gold," she said proudly.

"It is right that a woman such as yourself belongs to a king. If he is a king, are you then a queen?"

"I am his queen, yes."

His hands slid around her shoulders and down to her tiny waist. His eyes blazed as he looked at her parted lips. "I would see what it feels like to kiss a queen." His lips descended and the woman did not pull away but met his descent halfway. His mouth seemed to scorch her tender skin, and he felt her arms move around his shoulders. The hands that rested about her tiny waist pulled her tighter against his long, muscled body.

When the Indian raised his head, his eyes were passion-laced, and the white woman smiled, recognizing her power to move him.

"Tajarez, it has been so long. I have missed you so much! When Jeffery brought me word that you wanted me to meet you in our Eden, I lost no time in getting here."

He lightly touched her golden hair. "Two weeks is a long time to be parted, beloved. I wish we did not ever have to be separated, but as king of the Seven Cities, my duties must often take me away from the palace."

"How long can we remain here?"

"I can spare no more than seven days, then we must return home."

Her lovely face eased into a bright smile. "If seven days are all we have, should we waste time talking?"

He laughed and picked her up into his arms, carrying her toward the white tent that had been erected for their comfort. It was dark inside the tent, but Tajarez did not bother lighting a torch. He laid her onto the soft fur robe and lay down beside her, pulling her to him so her head rested on his shoulder.

"I rode to the palace to see our son and daughter before I came here. It seems they have grown since the two weeks I saw them last."

"Little Hamez is trying to walk. He has no patience with crawling as his twin sister does. He is like his father in many respects."

Tajarez smiled. "In what way?'

"He takes a few steps, and when he falls he gets very angry, but he stands up to try again."

"He is worthy to be called the prince royal," Tajarez said proudly.

She snuggled closer to him. "You may not be so pleased with him when I tell you what he did two days ago. Vista was rocking Tamera so she would fall asleep while Hamez played on the floor. After our daughter had fallen asleep and Vista laid her in her bed, she could not find Hamez anywhere. She alerted the guard and a thorough search was made of the second floor, but Hamez could not be found, so then the ground floor and even the gardens were searched, but we could not find Hamez anywhere. I do not mind telling you I was frantic until Jeffery discovered him in the antechamber curled up in your chair fast asleep."

"He is anxious to sit on his father's throne," Tajarez said. "But how did he get downstairs?"

"I suppose he crawled. I told Vista that she was to watch him more closely. He could easily have been injured."

"I do not see the harm. I will not have him coddled."

"But, Tajarez, he is not even a year old."

"Nonetheless, I think it is time to assign a man to see to his needs."

"No, he is my baby. I do not want him to be turned over to a man just yet. Could we not wait another year?"

Tajarez smiled. "Perhaps, but you must understand that as the prince royal he will be raised differently from any other children we might have."

"I know, and I accept that, but I want to keep him with his twin for as long as possible. Let him be a baby for a while longer."

Tajarez's hands moved over her soft curves, and all thoughts of her son left her mind as he bent his dark head. "I do not wish to talk of my son. I have missed you, beloved."

Mara parted her lips and surrendered herself in the arms of her husband. A week, she thought. A week away from everyone, alone with Tajarez, no one but herself and her tall, dark husband.


It was the hour just before sunup when the world is quiet and the eastern sky is lit with a soft, rosy glow. Mara looked at her sleeping husband beside her. He seemed tired. It would be good for him to have a week of rest, she thought. Tajarez had so many demands on him, for he ruled seven cities. He was absolute ruler, and it took up most of his time.

She brushed a dark strand of hair lovingly from his face, and he flinched at her gentle touch, but did not awaken. She had never thought it possible to get as close to another person as she had to Tajarez. He was as arrogant and as unapproachable as ever to others, but she knew the man behind the king, and she loved him so deeply. He was loving and kind, sharing his problems with her and telling her at night when she lay in his arms how he had spent his day, often asking her advice about some small matter. On important business he made the decisions alone, without counsel from anyone, with the exception of Sagas the Wise.

Mara lay back against his shoulder and studied his handsome face as her mind reached backward to the time when she had first met him. She had been sixteen when she was abducted by two Indians in the woods near her home just outside St. Louis. The two Indians had taken her far into the wilderness, where she had been rescued by a tall, beautiful Indian, who, it appeared at the time, could not speak. It was not until much later that she learned that he was the prince of an as yet undiscovered, highly advanced Indian tribe. Tajarez, after rescuing her, took her to a fort to be returned to her family. But by that time she had fallen in love with him and had begged him to take her away with him. He had ridden away and she had thought she would never see him again. It was a year after he rescued her that he found her again in her home in St. Louis and took her to his home in the hidden valley where she became his bride.

Their courtship had been a long and stormy one, and when Mara learned that Tajarez had come for her because of the old Indian prophecy, her anger had been renewed. She quoted the prophecy to herself:

When the Golden One comes
There will be peace and plenty
The past will be revealed
To the few and the many
One man will die
Another shall weep
There will be love
Where the Golden One sleeps.

At the time she had not believed the prophecy, but as time passed she had come to know that it was indeed true. The palace of the king had gold sheeting on one wall, and on that sheeting were drawings and ancient hieroglyphics, which Mara could decipher because her father had lived for some years in Egypt and had mastered the hieroglyphics. He had passed that knowledge on to her.

Her brother Jeffery had traveled with her to the hidden valley and was now married to Tajarez's lovely cousin, Sasha. Tajarez had made Jeffery the head of his guards. Mara and Tajarez now had twins, a son and a daughter, and Mara was deliriously happy.

Tajarez opened his eyes and stared into her face. "How long have you been awake?"

"Not too long. I was just remembering the past."

He drew her into his arms. "Let Sagas the Wise dwell on the past. You and I will look to the future."

Mara snuggled up in his arms. "What are your plans for the future?"

He smiled at her. "My plans for the future are no different than my plans right this moment." His eyes blazed and he looked deeply into her eyes. "I want

15

to love you every day of my life. I hate when my duty takes me away from you. These past two weeks I have been so lonely, even when I am surrounded by others. I fear I have become too dependent on your love. Sometimes I become frightened at what my life would be like if you should leave me."

Mara was startled by his revelation. He was such a commanding figure, strong and self-assured, it was hard to think of him having any weaknesses.

"Tajarez, I want only to stay by your side forever. I love you so much."

He grinned wickedly. "Prove it."

Her arms went around his neck and her mouth sought his, and soon they were transported to a place where the two of them had been many times before.

# Two

I followed my love to a far distant land.
I followed him blindly as he took my hand.

It was the day Tajarez set aside for judgment. The people of the Lagonda tribe brought him their problems, and he tried to help them reach just solutions.

A beautiful young Indian maiden stepped forward and bowed her head. When she raised her head, she looked into the eyes of her king and smiled boldly. "My name is Nina, my king."

Tajarez smiled at her. "How may I help you, Nina?"

"I am very distressed, my king. I am pledged to marry Matio, and yet my heart is engaged to Matio's older brother." She gave Tajarez a seductive smile, and her knees felt weak as her handsome king looked deeply into her eyes.

Tajarez was dressed in a white wrap that was fastened about his waist and fell midway to his knees. Golden sandals crisscrossed halfway up his long, powerful legs. His broad chest was bare but for the golden neckpiece that fastened about his neck and fell to his waist. A golden crown of double cobras circled his ebony hair. Many a young maiden had lost her heart to the handsome king, but he had eyes only for the woman who was his queen.

Mara entered the room and the group of people who had been gathered to receive judgment from their king moved aside to allow her to pass. Palomas, her personal bodyguard, kept a watchful eye so no one would attempt to approach her. Instead of climbing the dais to sit beside Tajarez, she chose to sit on one of the white cushions so she could observe the proceedings without herself being observed, as she often liked to do. She noticed how the lovely Indian maiden was looking at Tajarez, and he seemed to be enjoying himself. Mara felt jealousy burn in her heart as Tajarez gave the girl a warm smile.

"How long have you been pledged to Matio, Nina?"

"Since birth, my king."

"When was it that you first knew you wanted to marry his brother, Harset?"

"This last summer, my king." She gave him a helpless look and Mara wondered what was going on inside her husband's mind.

"A pledge to marry is not easily broken, Nina. What do your parents say?"

The girl ducked her head. "They say I am pledged by honor to marry Matio, my king."

"Are the two men present?"

Two young men moved out of the crowd and approached Tajarez, bowing their heads. "I am Matio," one of them spoke up, "and this is my brother, Harset."

"How say you, Matio? Will you release Nina from her pledge of marriage?"

The young man looked at his king with earnest eyes. "I would not like to give Nina up, my king, for in spite of her fickle way, I love her."

"I am not fickle, my king," Nina spoke. "I love only Harset."

"What say you, Harset? Do you, too, love Nina?" Tajarez asked.

"It is so, my king. I did not mean to, it just happened. If you will give her to me I will give her a better life than my brother can. This past month I have been made apprentice to Drexal, the farmer, who has no sons of his own and has taken me as his heir. On his death I shall be very well off."

Tajarez's eyes narrowed. "Matio, when did Nina become dissatisfied with you as her pledged?"

"It was just after my brother received word that he would be Drexal's heir."

Tajarez leaned forward. "I see. What is your profession, Matio?"

"I am keeper of my father's horses, my king." The young man stepped forward. "I have applied to the royal guards many times but have been turned down because of my youth. But I am very strong, my king, and have won many tournaments. If I could become one of your guards, I know Nina would like to be my wife. She is very conscious of social standing."

"Is that the only reason you would like to be in my guard?"

"No, I would like to serve you, my king."

"I see. I am going to do something you may not

understand at the moment, but I believe with the passing of time you will come to see that I have made the right choice for you. The three of you step forward and I will render my decision. Nina, I have decided to overturn your pledge to Matio and give you to his brother, Harset."

The young girl smiled brightly. "You have made me very happy, my king."

Matio looked crestfallen and prepared to leave. He bowed to his king and stepped back a pace.

"Hold, Matio, I have not yet dismissed you. When you leave here, I want you to report to Jeffery, the head of my guard. Tell him that beginning tomorrow I want you to begin training to become one of my royal guards. It will be hard work, and many times you may wish you had never wanted to become a royal guard, but I see in you the makings of a good man, and I would like to have you in my personal guard."

Matio's face lit up and his smile seemed to brighten the whole room. "I cannot believe my good fortune. I am most grateful, my king," he said, beaming happily.

"After you have reported to Jeffery, return home to tell your parents of my judgment. Then bring your belongings and prepare to move into the palace with the other young men in training."

"I cannot believe this, my king. It is what every young man hopes for but does not think will ever happen to him."

"You do not yet have the position. You must first prove your ability and there will be many who will vie for the position. Few ever succeed."

"I will succeed, my king."

"I do not doubt it. I expect to see you wearing the silver and turquoise before too long."

Tajarez's eyes moved to rest on Nina's face, which had lost its color. "Are you not happy with my decision, Nina?"

"I may have been a bit hasty, my king. On thinking about it, I believe I would like to be Matio's wife after all." The young girl smiled prettily.

Tajarez leaned toward Matio. "You can see that I have rendered you a favor, Matio. Would you like me to reverse my decision and allow you to marry Nina?"

The young man looked into the eyes of his king with a fresh understanding of Nina's character. He could now see what his king had seen from the beginning. Nina was ambitious and calculating, and now that he had been offered a chance to try for the royal guard she had switched her loyalty once more, for the wife of a royal guard lived in the lower portion of the palace and was looked up to by all the populace. "No, my king, I would not like you to reverse your decision."

"But Matio, you said you loved me," Nina said, reaching out to him pleadingly.

"I am sorry for my brother, but grateful to him all the same, for my eyes are now open," Matio stated.

Tajarez looked at Harset. "You may withdraw. I trust you will be happy with the decision which was rendered here today. It does not speak well when a man tries to take from his brother. I fear you may live to rue the day."

Harset looked shamefaced and grabbed Nina by

21

the hand, leading her from the anteroom. Tajarez smiled, thinking the fickle Nina would not have an easy time of it.

Mara sat, thoughtful for a moment. Tajarez had learned well from his wise father, for he had looked below the surface of human nature and detected the truth as she had seen Hamez do on numerous occasions. Tajarez was a man worthy to rule in his father's place. He would be a great king, and she was the fortunate woman he had chosen as his wife. She rose to her feet, thinking it was time for the twins to awaken. Tajarez saw her and gave her a special smile that told her he would join her later.

Palomas cleared a path through the crowd so Mara could pass. The people looked on her almost with reverence on their faces, and she smiled brightly at them as she passed. No one dared approach her, however, for it was forbidden to do so without her permission.

When Mara reached the steps that led up to the second story where the royal chambers were located, she saw a woman sitting on the bottom step, holding a young child who seemed to be about the same age as the twins. The woman was startled when her queen sat down on the step beside her. "What a lovely child. I judge her to be about the age of my children," Mara said softly.

The woman would have risen but Mara reached out and touched her arm. "Sit with me for a moment. I rarely get a chance to talk to anyone who has children the age of mine."

The woman tried to speak but seemed speechless from the honor which the queen bestowed on her by talking to her. She was further startled when the queen reached for the baby and held her in her lap.

"What is her name?"

"T . . . Tinka, my queen."

"Tinka. That is a lovely name. Is she teething?"

"Yes, my queen. You must have care or she will dribble on your lovely gown."

Mara laughed and planted a kiss on the child's fat round face. "I can assure you that I am used to being dribbled on. You must remember that I have two babies, so I have twice as much of everything."

The woman looked at Mara in awe, and the look was one of worship. She knew her friends would never believe that she had spoken to the queen, and indeed that the queen had held her daughter in her lap.

"What is your name?" Mara asked as she cuddled the child close to her.

"I am known as Denes, wife of Sanco, the herdsman."

"Tell me, Denes, is Tinka having any pain with her teething?"

Palomas smiled. Trust Mara to do the unexpected. She was so warm and loving that she could not help but reach out to people. How young and unqueen-like she looked at the moment with the Indian child curled up in her lap. It was his honor to guard her, but her unorthodox behavior sometimes made it very difficult for him.

Mara had not noticed that the crowd of people in the anteroom had moved around her, staring at the sight of their queen sitting on the step talking easily with Denes and holding her daughter in her arms.

"Yes, my queen, I find she has pain sometimes and will cry excessively."

"Palomas, go into the nursery and ask Vista to give you a container of the salve the medicine man gave me for Hamez."

Palomas snapped his fingers to summon the guard who stood near by, and sent him for the salve.

When would Mara learn, he wondered, that he was her protector and could not leave her side when she was among the people.

"Little Hamez seemed to suffer greatly from his teething, while his sister did not suffer in the least. The medicine man gave me this salve to rub on his gums and it seems to help a great deal," Mara said.

"I could never take the medicine of the prince royal, my queen. The honor is too great."

Mara laughed delightedly, and the woman stared at her as her baby drooled down the front of the queen's gown. Mara did not seem overly concerned as she hugged the child.

Mara was startled as she looked up to see the crowd of people that by now surrounded her. She had been so deep in conversation with Denes that she had not noticed that she had become the center of attention. Her eyes widened as she saw the crowd move aside and Tajarez stood over her frowning.

Smiling, she stood up and held the baby out to him, and anyone could have heard his heartbeat as the mighty king took the herdsman's baby in his arms.

"This is Denes, and her daughter, Tinka," Mara informed him.

The woman, Denes, scrambled to her feet and

bowed before the king.

"Tinka is having trouble teething. I have sent someone to get a container of the salve the medicine man gave me for Hamez," Mara told him.

Palomas folded his arms across his wide chest and smiled. Trust Mara to upset the judgment proceedings. He watched as his king's frown turned to a smile. Palomas knew his king was no more immune to Mara's loving kindness than anyone else.

"A pretty child. What is her age, Denes?" Tajarez asked the woman.

"She was born not a week before the royal twins, my king."

Tajarez handed the child back to her mother. "I trust the salve will be of help to her." Then he lapsed into English so only Mara could understand. "You have a way of disturbing me even when I sit in judgment."

She smiled sweetly. "I am sorry," she answered him in the same language.

"I doubt that you are. If it is not asking too much, could you refrain from dispensing medicine while I am sitting in judgment?" His words were spoken harshly but the soft look in his eyes told their own story.

By now the guard had returned, carrying the container of salve. Mara took it and handed it to the woman. "I would not give it to her unless her teeth are really bothering her."

"I thank you, my queen, and may I say that I honor you as my queen?"

Mara took her hand. "It is I who am honored, Denes. Now if you will excuse me, I believe my children may be awake and wondering where their mother is.''

"We will talk of this later, Mara," Tajarez said as he turned and made his way back to the raised dais where he conducted his business.

Many eyes watched their lovely queen as she climbed the stairs, but none more adoringly than Denes. Word would spread that she had talked to the queen, and she would find favor as a result.

"Tajarez did not seem well pleased that you made a shamble of the morning's judgments." Palomas was one of the few who was allowed to speak so familiarly to the queen. He adored her and had once even saved her life when she fell over a cliff. He had been chosen as her protector by Tajarez's father, Hamez, and had undergone an operation that had rendered him impotent so that he could be her guard. He had never regretted giving up his manhood on her behalf, for his happiness lay in seeing her happy, and Mara had indeed found great happiness with his king.

Mara smiled. "It was not my intention to disrupt the proceedings. I merely wanted to talk to someone who has a baby so I could compare how my children are progressing. I live such a restricted life here in the palace, shut off from the people. Do you really think Tajarez was angry?''

"I believe he was not overly concerned."

Mara sighed. "It is very difficult at times to be a queen. I do so like the people of the Lagonda tribe and wish to get to know them better."

"You are the queen whom they all adore. I, myself, would have you no different than you are."

They had reached the top of the stairs and Mara looked at Palomas. "Do you really feel that way?" He smiled at her fondly. "It is so, my queen."

Mara spent the rest of the day with the children. She laughed and played with them, and when it was time for Vista to put them to bed for the night, she kissed each of them and went downstairs, where she had promised to meet Sagas the Wise. When she reached the chamber, she saw him across the room looking at the gold sheeting on the wall. His long robe was the same color as the white of his hair, and he wore no ornaments of precious metals, but he was a man who wielded a great deal of power and commanded respect. He was somewhere over a hundred and twenty years old. No one, not even he, knew for sure what his age was.

Mara was helping him decipher the hieroglyphics, and the two of them had become very close. Everyone, including Tajarez, was amazed at the way Sagas had warmed to Mara. His fondness for her was apparent. When she was with him his eyes would light up. He was thoughtful and considerate of her, two qualities Sagas was not noted for.

To Mara, Sagas was as beloved as her own grandfather, who lived in Philadelphia. She and Sagas would have long conversations, and Mara found him to be, with the exception of Tajarez, the most fascinating person she had ever encountered, although Sagas's powers and insight often left her feeling apprehensive. He had predicted Mara's coming to the Seven Cities even before she had been born, and to many she was still referred to as the Golden One.

Sagas smiled brightly as Mara approached, and she gave him her hand. "I understand you caused some excitement this morning while Tajarez was holding judgment," he told her.

She sighed. "It seems when I do the simplest things they turn into a disaster. I fear Tajarez was not too pleased with me."

The old man released her hand. "When I spoke to him he was indeed pleased with you. Never change, Mara. You will be a great queen, and the people love you well."

"Are you speaking as my friend who wants to comfort me, or have you seen into the future and know I will be a great queen?" she asked, knowing that Sagas could indeed see the future, but very rarely revealed to anyone what he had seen.

"I speak merely as one who has grown to know you and to see the effect you have on the people around you. Have I not seen Tajarez turn from a man seeking happiness that always eluded him to a man who has found love and contentment?"

Mara smiled at the old man. "You would make a great diplomat, Sagas. I wonder why my husband has not considered using you in that capacity."

"I am too old. I want to live out the rest of my life here with you as you reveal the secrets of the past."

Mara looked at the gold sheeting on the wall. "We have already discovered that an ancient pharoah fleeing death at the hands of his brother found the new world and was aided by the Lagonda tribe. They migrated to this hidden valley and began to build a

28

great city. The Egyptians began to intermarry with the Lagonda tribe and produced the race of today. I have been working on the next part and have unraveled some of it," Mara told the old man.

His eyes gleamed brightly. "Tell me what else you have discovered."

"It seems the pharoah was ailing and feared he would die. He called his council around him and declared that his rule would pass to his daughter and not his son, who he feared was weak and would be unable to rule. He then ordered his daughter to wed the chief of the Lagonda tribe."

Sagas looked at Mara in disbelief. "He handed the rule to a woman, when he had a son?"

"So it would seem, Sagas."

The old man knotted his forehead in concentration. "Imagine, a woman ruling the Seven Cities."

"You will have to remember, Sagas, there were not then seven cities. The construction had barely begun on one city."

"This is truly a revelation. I must talk to Tajarez about this development. Perhaps he will want to change the charter to read that if a king has no male heir his rule can then pass to his daughter instead of to his brother."

"Do you feel that you should do that? This was written many hundreds of years ago. I suspect the law was changed for a good reason."

"Perhaps. I will think on it."

Mara kissed the old man's cheek. "I am very fond of you. I have enjoyed working with you on the hieroglyphics, and you have infected me with your enthusiasm."

Sagas tried not to show how pleased he was by her words, for he, like everyone who knew her, was her devoted slave. He had seen visions of her throughout the years, and had even seen her birth in a dream. He knew how surprised Mara would be if he told her how much he knew about her life before she came to the hidden valley. "I am going to bed now. I have much to think on," he told her as he strolled away from her with his hands clasped behind his back.

Mara watched him fondly for a moment, then she climbed the stairs to the third floor of the palace where her brother Jeffery and his wife Sasha lived.

Sasha greeted Mara with a hug. "I was hoping you would come to see me today. I have been bored doing nothing," her lovely sister-in-law told Mara. Sasha was expecting a child, so Mara had insisted she take it easy. In the past Sasha had been chosen to wait upon her, but Mara had gradually made Sasha more of a companion than a servant.

"Where is Jeffery?" Mara asked.

"As a matter of fact, he is with Tajarez. I believe they have ridden into the city."

"How are you feeling, Sasha?"

"I am in good health. I heard about the commotion you caused at the judgment today."

Mara sighed. "Word gets around fast. It was nothing more than a harmless conversation with a young mother. I am afraid Tajarez was not well pleased with me. I fear I shall hear all about it tonight."

"Was he angry with you?" Sasha asked, knowing she would not like to be the one to incur her cousin Tajarez's displeasure.

"I believe he was."

"Have you eaten?" Sasha asked, turning the conversation.

"Yes, I ate with the children. I believe I will leave now. I find I am very tired."

As Mara descended the stairs to the chamber she shared with Tajarez, she was frowning. From all that was being said about the incident in the anteroom she feared she would have to face recriminations later that night when Tajarez came home. She had convinced herself that he would be very angry with her. She removed the soft white robe and climbed into bed, thinking she would pretend to be asleep when Tajarez came in. That way he would have a whole night to sleep on it, and perhaps his anger would ebb by morning. She had faced his anger on numerous occasions in the past, but not lately. Tajarez could be very formidable and every inch the king when the occasion called for it. Hearing the door open softly, she cringed on the inside and closed her eyes tightly, hoping he would think she was sleeping. She heard him remove his double crown of the cobra and place it on the stand beside her own crown. Tense moments passed and she knew he was removing his clothing. She felt him lie down beside her and she resisted the urge to peep at him through her eyelashes to see if he looked angry.

She felt his hand close over her arm, but she did not respond.

"Mara," he said in a deep voice. She willed herself to feign sleep.

"Mara, I know you are not asleep. Palomas told me you just entered our room moments ahead of me."

She opened her eyes, trying to see if he was angry with her.

"You have been in the city," she said, unable to think of anything else to say at the moment.

"What is wrong, beloved? Are you not feeling well?"

She hesitated, not wishing to bring up the subject of this afternoon. "I am feeling fine."

"Are you worried about something?"

"No . . . yes. I am sorry about this afternoon, truly I am," she said in English.

"Ah, I see," he said in the language of the Lagonda. "You think I might be angry with you."

"It occurred to me," she said, lapsing into the Lagonda language.

He shook with laughter, and pulled her into his arms. "I am not angry with you, and I would have you behave no differently than you do. My people love their kindhearted queen. I am convinced that the Seven Cities have never known a queen such as yourself. And where my people adore you, I, myself, worship you."

"You are sure? You are not just saying that?"

He raised an eyebrow. "Would I say it if it were not so?"

She laughed and peppered his face with soft kisses. "I am so relieved. I was frightened that you were displeased with me."

"Indeed, I am well pleased with you, and you know I could never stay mad at you for any length of time." His hands moved over her body in the most sensuous way, and Mara drew in her breath. Tajarez had the power to make everything right with his

32

lovemaking.

Mara closed her eyes as his lips descended. She heard him groan as his lips covered hers, and knew she could also move him, as her hand slid along his rib cage to rest on his hip.

"You are a seductress," he murmured against her lips, in English.

"Do I please you?" she asked, in Lagonda.

"Never have I known such pleasure until I took you to my bed," he told her moving his head and staring into her green eyes. His forehead wrinkled into a frown. "Sometimes I will be talking to someone, and you will flash into my mind, like the other day with Sagas. I did not hear half of what he was saying to me."

Mara smiled. "What did Sagas say?"

Tajarez wound a strand of golden hair around his finger and gave her a heart-melting smile. "He told me to quit wasting his time and go bed my wife."

"Tajarez, that's awful," she said in mock anger. "What did you do?"

"I took his advice. Sagas is a very wise man," he said laughing deeply.

"I will never grow accustomed to the easy way the Lagonda treat the act of love," Mara said turning her back on Tajarez.

Tajarez rolled her over and laughingly crushed her in his arms. "It is a natural thing, not something to be spoken of in hushed tones, as the white man does. Do you not find our love beautiful?"

Mara could not resist his inquiring look. "I find everything about you and me beautiful."

His dark eyes fastened on her satiny breast, and he

33

reached out his hand to circle the rosebud nipple with his finger. Lowering his dark head, his mouth settled on the creamy peaks.

Mara groaned as his hands moved over her flat stomach to her thigh.

Tajarez raised his head and looked into her eyes, and she thought she saw pain on his face. "What will I do when I cannot reach out and touch you at night, beloved?"

Mara's legs opened to his gentle pressure, and before she could ask Tajarez what he had meant, he entered her body, reaching deep inside of her, and she was incapable of speech. Tajarez knew all the right places to touch her to make her mindless, while his lips assaulted her mouth. His lovemaking was different somehow. It was as if he was frantic in his desire. Mara writhed beneath him as he drove his manhood into her with urgency. Pleasure coursed through Mara's body. When he raised his head, she sought and found his lips once more.

Never before had Tajarez been so rough with her. Usually he was very gentle, but tonight he seemed to be driven. Mara felt tears in her eyes, but they were not tears of pain. Her body had never known such desire, such fulfillment. Mara felt Tajarez's body explode and she moaned as her body answered his.

Rolling over on his back, Tajarez kissed her tears away as he murmured softly to her.

"I am sorry, beloved. Forgive me, are you hurt?"

"No, my love. I do not cry from hurt, but because of the beauty of our love."

He pulled her on top of him and ran his hands over her back and hips, then he crushed her to him so tightly that Mara did feel pain. He was troubled about something, she could feel it.

"Tajarez, is there something bothering you?"

He lifted her head and gazed at her intently. "How can you know?" he asked as he studied every detail of her beautiful face.

"I love you, and I can sense when you are troubled about something."

His mouth outlined the shape of her face. "Mara, Jeffery received a letter from your brother David today."

"How?"

"I sent one of my warriors to David's home to inform him of the birth of the twins, and he sent a message back by him."

"What was in the letter? David is not ill, is he?"

"No, but he asked that I allow you to visit him and Linda, reminding me of my promise to him before we were wed."

Mara missed her brother David, but she was torn. She did not want to be away from Tajarez.

"You think I should go?"

"I gave David my word before I took you away from his home that after the birth of a son you would be able to visit him."

"Will you and the children go with me?"

"I cannot go, Mara. I am needed here, and I cannot allow you to take the children."

"Then I will not go. I do not want to be parted from you."

His arms tightened about her protectively. "I cannot bear the thought of you not being beside me, but I gave my word and my word cannot be broken."

"Even if I do not want to go?"

"Even then, Mara. To let you go will be to tear my heart from my body."

Understanding the kind of man he was, she knew how much it meant to him to honor his word, and she as his wife must not make it more difficult for him.

"I wish you would allow the children to go with me. It will be very painful leaving them behind."

"It will be hard enough for me to let *you* go. I could not bear it if the children were gone, too. When I made the promise to David I was the prince royal, and had my father not been killed I would have been able to journey with you to your brother's home. But as I have the responsibility of my people to consider, I cannot leave just now."

"When will I leave?" Mara asked, becoming resigned to the thought that she must go.

"It should be as soon as possible. I would like you to return before winter sets in."

"Oh, Tajarez, I want you to be proud of me, and I want to be the kind of queen who is strong and does what is expected of her, but I fear I will not be able to leave when the time comes."

His hands moved over her body as if trying to burn the feel of her into his mind. He swallowed a lump in his throat, wishing they did not have to be parted. "You will tell David that I will not allow you to visit him again. I cannot bear to think of you being gone from me."

"Tajarez, what if little Hamez and Tamera forget about me? I will not be here when they begin to walk. I will miss so much. And how will I sleep at night without you beside me?"

"As for the babies, you must not concern yourself on their account. I shall spend every free moment with them, and I will speak to them of their mother each day."

She buried her face against his wide chest, hoping she would not cry. Closing her eyes, she let his nearness fill her heart. She loved him so deeply and wanted nothing more than to remain beside him. "Will Jeffery go with me?"

"No. He does not want to leave Sasha while she is expecting the child, but I am sending fifty of my best warriors to look after you. I have not forgotten how the Kiowa chief tried to take you from me. There will be no danger this time. My warriors will care for you."

"Will Palomas go with me?"

"Of course, as well as your serving women, Falon and Minet."

"When will I go?"

He was quiet for a moment. "In two days' time. I will ride with you for the first week, but then I must return."

He kissed her lips softly, and when he made love to her he was so gentle it brought tears to her eyes. How would she ever be able to leave him when the time came, she wondered.

# Three

I need you, I want you. Do not send me away.
I am begging, I beseech you, allow me to stay.

Mara kissed Hamez and Tamera and handed them back to Vista with tears in her eyes. "Watch over them carefully, Vista," she said turning away quickly and rushing from the nursery before she broke down completely in front of her children. She found her brother Jeffery waiting for her in the hallway and went into his outstretched arms.

"It is almost April, honey, you should be back by the end of August. Time will pass quickly," he told her, knowing what she was feeling.

"Jeffery, look after Tajarez for me. He will . . . he is going to be lonely. Try to see that he does not miss me too much," she told him, leaning her head against his shoulder to hide the tears that blinded her.

Jeffery tilted her chin up and gave her a reassuring smile. "I will, Mara, there is no need for you to worry about Tajarez, just take care of yourself."

Knowing that Tajarez was waiting for her, Mara smiled bravely. "I hope I shall be home before Sasha has your baby. I do so want to be with her when the time comes.''

''I am afraid that will not be possible, but hopefully you will be in St. Louis in time to witness the birth of David and Linda's baby.''

Mara's eyes sparkled. ''We Goldens seem to be populating the world lately, do we not?''

Kissing her brother on the cheek she rushed quickly down the stairs and through the huge anteroom where she found Sagas waiting for her. He reached for her hand and placed something in it. Mara saw it was a heavy golden chain with a disk in the shape of a pyramid. The face of the pyramid was engraved with tiny hieroglyphics.

''What is this, Sagas?'' she asked as she read the markings out loud. ''It says: 'I will seek where I belong.' What does it mean?''

The old man looked deeply into her eyes. ''Put it on, Mara, and do not take if off for any reason. It will help you find your way home.''

''I do not understand.''

A veil seem to cover his eyes, turning the black circles to smoky gray. ''Heed my words and never take it off,'' he warned as he turned his back on her and hurried away, leaving Mara to wonder about his words. She slipped the gold chain over her head and felt it nestle between her breasts. It felt warm against her skin, almost as if it were alive. Knowing by this time Tajarez would be wondering what was keeping her, she forgot about the chain and walked out into the bright sunlight.

Mara's heart was warmed as she noticed the people of the Lagonda tribe were lined up along both

39

sides of the roadway to see her off. Smiling proudly, she raised her hand to them and received a rousing tribute. How she had grown to love the people of this hidden valley. This was her home and where she belonged.

She felt rather then heard someone beside her and did not need to look up to know Palomas, the ever faithful watchdog, was standing near by. He would be with her on the journey, and for that she was grateful. Mara was dressed in white doeskin. The fringe at the neck and hemline of her dress were beaded with gold. White doeskin moccasins fit snugly about the calves of her legs. Dressed as she was, she had a freedom of movement she had never enjoyed in the conventional clothing she had worn before coming to the Seven Cities as Tajarez's bride. She had long ago abandoned her side-saddle and now rode astride as any Lagonda maiden would.

The crowd became strangely silent as she descended the wide stone steps that led up to the palace. With one last final wave to her people she joined Tajarez, who was waiting for her at the bottom of the steps. She dared not look at her husband as Palomas helped her mount her horse. Mara did not look back as she rode away with Tajarez at her side, Palomas and the guard following closely behind. She was leaving everything that was dear to her, and she almost resented the fact that Tajarez had given his word to David to allow her to visit him.

As they rode across the bridge that spanned the river, Mara looked at Tajarez. He had not spoken to her nor did he look in her direction, and she knew he was also wishing that he had not given his word to David. She knew he would be very lonely without her and would suffer until she was with him once more. Mara made herself a promise that she would not add to his unhappiness by crying, if she could help it. He would try to hide his feelings, but she knew him so well, he would never be able to fool her. The face he presented to his people was not the real Tajarez. In many ways he was very vulnerable, at least where she was concerned, and she knew she must be strong for both of them.

It was warm and cozy inside the big white tent as Mara lay in Tajarez's arms. She thought how different it was from the journey when she had first come to the Seven Cities. On that journey she had not been allowed to be with Tajarez. Even though they had been married in a ceremony at her home in St. Louis, the marriage was not recognized by the laws of the Lagonda tribe. Mara, as the intended bride of Tajarez, the prince royal, had to be pure and untouched until she reached the Seven Cities, where Tajarez's father had joined them as man and wife. It had been a long journey for both Tajarez and Mara.

The mink robe felt soft against Mara's bare skin. She turned to face Tajarez, who had not spoken a word to her all day.

He picked up the golden disk that hung about her neck. "What is this?"

"I am not sure. Sagas gave it to me and told me not to remove it."

41

"It has writing on it. What does it say?"

"It says 'I will seek where I belong.'"

Tajarez frowned. "What does it mean? What did Sagas say?"

"He said very little. I do not know why he gave it to me."

"I asked him if it would be safe for you to make this journey, and he said all rests with the Great Father. If I thought for one moment that you would be in danger, I would not allow you to go."

"I cannot see what harm could come to me with the army of warriors you have surrounded me with, but I would much rather return home with you."

"Mara, do not ask it of me. I am half out of my mind dreading the day we must part. Do not ask me to break my word to your brother."

"I could go another time."

"No, it would be just as hard later. I will fulfill my obligation to your brother, and then I will have kept my word."

That night they made love frantically, as if trying to fill each other with the love they felt. Long after Mara had fallen asleep, Tajarez held her in his arms and whispered words of love in her ear. Fear nagged at the back of his mind. He fought against the urge to take her back home with him, but honor ran deep in his veins, and once he had given his word he felt bound by it.

On their last day together Mara was teary-eyed. When they stopped that evening to make camp, Tajarez took her hand and led her to the top of a small hill. He did not look at her as he spoke.

"Mara, will you think of me?"

"I will think of little else."

"The hand of the warm season is upon the land. The season of growing is not too distant, then there will be the harvest season, before the time that wild geese fly you will be home."

Mara laid her head against his shoulder. "Did you ever wish that time could stand still?"

He turned her to face him. "For now I wish time could fly on golden wings, and you would soon be back with me."

The breeze stirred his long ebony hair and Mara saw the sadness in his dark eyes. "Oh pray, my love, that time does indeed fly on golden wings," she whispered.

"Time has had very little meaning to me in the past, but now each day you are away will seem as one of your years, beloved." He bent his head and kissed the tears from her face, then he took her hand and led her down the hill and into their tent.

Neither of them wanted to sleep. It was the last night they would have together in a very long time.

Mara was determined that she would not cry again, knowing how Tajarez felt about tears. To him tears were a form of weakness. She remembered the one time she had seen him cry. It had been when his cousin Anias had abducted her and Tajarez, bound by a leather strap, was forced to watch what he thought to be her death at his cousin's hands. He had despised himself that day for his weakness, and Mara knew that he had not forgotten that she had witnessed his shame. To her it had been final proof that he loved her, but to him it had been a sign of weakness and shame.

Mara must have fallen asleep, for she felt Tajarez's hand on her shoulder as he shook her gently awake.

"Beloved, it is almost sunrise," he whispered.

She threw her arms around him knowing they were approaching the time of parting.

"Mara, do not forget to leave St. Louis no later than the end of July in order to be home before the first snowfall."

"I will not forget."

"Mara, you will let no other man touch you," he said in an agonized voice. "I know you will see many of the men who have admired you."

She cupped his face between his hands. "You know Palomas would never allow any man to touch me. What about you? Will you smile at all the pretty maidens while I am away?"

His dark eyes looked deeply into her green ones. "I will look at no one," he whispered. "You have my word as king."

"You have my word as queen, that I shall be too busy thinking of you to look at anyone else." The tears she had willed not to fall washed freely down her face. "Oh, my dearest love, my heart is breaking at our parting," she sobbed.

Tajarez grabbed her and crushed her tightly in his arms as he smothered her face with kisses. They remained in each other's arms until the sun made its appearance for the day; then they both arose and dressed.

Mara went into his arms, knowing it would be the last embrace they could share, for the king could not make a public showing of his feelings.

"I will miss you each moment, Tajarez."

He traced the outline of her face with his finger, then he lowered his head and kissed her passionately. They stood locked in each other's arms for a long time, but at last Tajarez raised his head.

"It is time for you to leave, beloved. Oh, I almost forgot."

He led her over to a chest and raised the lid. Mara saw it was filled with gold. "This is so you will be able to purchase whatever you need."

She laughed up at him. "Oh, Tajarez, what could I possibly need with all that gold? Besides I already have everything a woman could want."

"You will purchase a large quantity of the tea and coffee that you like to drink."

Mara knew it would do no good to tell him that with such a large amount of gold she could buy several coffee and tea plantations.

"Come, it grows late," he told her.

They walked out into the morning sunlight, and as soon as they had vacated the tent it was dismantled and loaded onto the back of a packhorse.

Tajarez raised his hand and the warriors gathered around to hear what their king had to say. "I charge each and every one of you with the queen's safety. When you reach her brother's home you will set up camp in the woods, awaiting the time for her to return home. I do not want her left alone. When she is in her home, Minet and Falon, as her servants, will attend her. You, Palomas will not leave her except when she sleeps at night."

Everyone nodded in agreement.

Palomas led Mara's horse forward and Tajarez

45

lifted her onto its back. His hand lingered about her waist and she knew by the look he gave her that he was reminding her she was the queen. She touched his face softly and he stepped back a pace.

"Until I see your face again, beloved," he whispered so only she could hear his words.

Mara urged her horse forward as the warriors closed ranks around her, each knowing he was charged with her safety, and each willing to stand in the way of anything that would harm her.

Looking over her shoulder Mara saw Tajarez raise his hand to her. She was too far away to see the expression on his face. Was his heart breaking as hers was, she wondered? She resisted the urge to turn her horse around and ride back to plead with him to allow her to return home with him. When she rode up the hillside he was still standing where she had left him, with the view of the tall mountains that hid the Seven Cities rising majestically behind him.

Mara had a feeling of deep foreboding as she rode down a deep gully and could no longer see her husband.

Palomas, who was riding beside her, spoke. "It seems to be a warm day, Mara," he said, and she silently blessed him, knowing that he, who never talked much, was making small talk so she could think of something else besides Tajarez.

"Yes, it is a lovely day." Tajarez would be proud of her she thought, if he knew the tears that were in her heart did not reach her eyes.

"Look to the left of us, my queen," Falon said. "I see the king."

Mara looked toward the hills and saw Tajarez

46

sitting on his horse. How alone he looked, Mara thought. She nudged her horse on to a faster pace, knowing she must not weaken. Tajarez would expect her to act as his queen.

They rode hard all day and Mara could feel every mile that separated her from the man she loved.

That evening Mara sat on the fur robe while Minet brushed her golden hair. Minet and Falon had been trained by Sasha, and Mara found them to be very sweet and even-tempered. They both watched her now, apprehensively, knowing she was sad at being parted from the king and her children.

"Tell us about the white man's world, my queen," Falon encouraged her.

"You will find it very different from our home, Falon, bigger but less densely populated. It in no way compares to our hidden valley."

"Do all of the people have the golden hair and the green eyes of you and your brother Jeffery?" Minet asked.

"No, you will find many different shades of hair and eyes. There are people with red, black, brown, and, of course, golden hair such as mine. Then the color of eyes could be green, blue, gray, or brown."

"How wondrous," Falon said in an awed voice.

"Will your brother David welcome Falon, Palomas, and myself into his home?" Minet asked.

"Yes, you will find you will be a very welcome guest, although the housekeeper Tess might frighten you at first. She sounds very gruff at times, but hers is a loving nature."

"Does your brother live in a big house?" Falon wanted to know.

"Yes, it is very large, but not on the scale as the palace." Mara stood up and stretched her arms over her head. "I will dress for bed now. It is a long way to my brother's home. I need my sleep, as do both of you."

"Can Minet and I go for a walk, my queen?" Falon asked as she helped Mara into her robe.

"Only if one of the guards accompanies you. I have assured both of your parents that I will look after you, and it is not wise for two unattached maidens to be alone with so many men about."

"None of the warriors would harm us," Minet spoke up. "We are in your service."

Mara smiled. "I was not thinking that anyone would do you harm. I saw the amorous looks you both received from some of the young men."

Falon smiled. "We are considered to be quite a catch since we are in the queen's service."

Mara's laughter bubbled out, and her two servant girls exchanged glances, glad they had caused her to forget her sadness for the moment. "I shall have to keep a wary eye out for potential bridegrooms for the two of you."

"I have my eyes on the new guard who has been assigned for this journey. He is very handsome, and his name is Matio," Falon said.

Mara frowned, thinking the name sounded familiar. Was that not the young man who was allowed to try out for the royal guard on Tajarez's orders, she wondered. Tomorrow she would ask Falon to point the young man out to her so she could see if he was the same one.

Mara lay down on her bed as Minet and Falon left

the tent to go for a walk. She was so lonely. Never had she been without Tajarez and her babies at the same time. She did not fall asleep until the two girls returned.

Minet and Falon slept near the tent entrance, and they were aware of the queen's restlessness. They felt sorrow in their hearts that she was so sad, for she was kind to them and they loved her well.

Many times during the night Mara would reach out for Tajarez and find he was not beside her. In the stillness of the night she listened to the hooting of an owl and the lonesome sound of a howling wolf. Mara prayed for forgetfulness in sleep.

The next morning Mara tried to give the appearance of lightheartedness. But the ever watchful Palomas knew that she was putting forth an effort, and he talked to her as they rode along.

When they made camp that night, Mara climbed up an embankment and looked at the glorious colors of the sunset. The red and purple colors were streaked across the sky and for the moment she was lost in the beauty of it. She wondered if Tajarez was witnessing the same sunset.

She was startled when she heard Palomas come up behind her. "You are wondering if Tajarez is watching the sunset," Palomas said with his usual perception. "A Lagonda warrior will always look at the sunset when he is out in the wilderness."

"How do you know this?" she said, smiling.

"Because we want to know who wins the battle."

"What battle?"

"Has Tajarez never told you of the sun battling with the moon?"

"No."

"Ah, my queen, then you do not know why the sky is splashed with color at the beginning and end of each day."

Mara smiled as Palomas sat her down on a rock and sat down on the ground beside her. It was not like him to talk of such things, and she knew why he was doing it. He is such a dear man, she thought.

"Tell me about the battle, Palomas," she said softly.

He braced his back against the rock she was sitting on and she followed his gaze up into the heavens where the sun had turned the sky to a bright red and soft pinks.

"When the Great Father created the earth there was only day. The sun was supreme ruler of the sky, bathing the earth in its brightness. The Indian children would frolic and play until they would become exhausted. It was a happy time, but soon they became discontent, and the Great Father looking down from his heaven saw this, and wondered why his children were becoming listless and unhappy. He asked the king the reason for the discontent and the wise king answered him: 'The people have nothing to look forward to. Everything is always the same.' The Great Father thought and thought, how could he change the world so his children would have something to look forward to? He went to the sun, who shone brightly with its golden colors. Now the sun was very vain, since he was the only source of light for the earth, and he had begun to think he was more important than the Great Father. He had become arrogant and pompous.

'How would you like it if I allowed you to have someone to help you watch over the earth?' the Great Father asked. The sun answered, 'I need no one to help me. The people love me more than they do you.' This made the Great Father very angry. The sun needed to be taught a lesson, but the Great Father did not want the earth to be entirely in darkness. He went to the moon, who was small and dark, and asked him, 'How would you like to do battle with the sun? If you win I will allow you to cover the earth with your darkness.' The moon became very excited, for he was small and insignificant. 'But how can I who am so small take on the mighty sun, who is so powerful?' he asked. And the Great Father answered: 'With courage. You must do battle with the sun, and if you are brave you can win many victories.' And although it was true that the moon was small, the Great Father had chosen well, for he was indeed courageous. The heavens trembled as the battle began. The battle lasted for a very long time, but soon the mighty sun began to tire and lose some of its light. It needed to rest for the moon was draining its power. In one final burst of glorious color the sun faded, the moon won its first battle, and the earth became dark. The sun knew it was not defeated, for it would rest and regain its powers to wage a battle for supremacy once again. After the sun had rested he began the battle anew with a blast of wonderful colors. Each day the sun battles for control, but each night he loses that battle to the tiny, courageous moon.''

Palomas had finished talking and stood up and offered Mara his hand. She looked into the sunset

51

and smiled up at Palomas. "The moon has almost won another battle."

"It will always be so, Mara. I was told that story as a child and each day at sunset I find myself looking to make sure the dark wins over the light."

"I doubt that I will ever think of the sunset without remembering your story. Do you know what my father told me about the sunset?"

By now dark had covered the land and many stars had covered the ebony velvet sky. "I can not guess," Palomas told her.

"My father said that each sunset is unique. Once you have seen a sunset you will never see the same one again. Think of it. The world must be thousands of years old and yet no two sunsets are ever the same."

"Yes, just as the leaves on the trees and the flowers are alike and yet none of them are the same," Palomas said.

"We could carry it one step farther. No two humans are ever the same."

Palomas laughed softly. "I do not know about that, but you are unique. There has never been one to equal you."

"Is that meant as a compliment, Palomas?"

"Indeed, my queen, it is so," he said leading her down the hill toward the camp.

That night Mara slept the night through and the next morning awoke feeling refreshed. Falon braided her hair, and Minet served her breakfast. Mara ate the dried meat and sweet corncakes that would be her diet until she reached David's home. There was little time to kill and prepare fresh meat, since they were moving at such a fast pace.

When they stopped at midday Mara refused the dried meat Falon served her but ate some of the sweet corncake.

"Falon, ask the young man Matio to attend me," Mara said wiping her hands on a clean napkin.

Falon's eyes lit up as she smoothed her hair into place and rushed to find Matio. She found him standing beside his horse, and he smiled at her as she approached. When she stopped in front of him he held his breath. Falon was a lovely young girl, and although Matio had admired her from a distance, she never seemed to notice him.

"It is a fine day, Matio," Falon said, smiling coyly.

"You know my name," he replied in a surprised voice.

"Why should that surprise you?"

"I never thought you noticed me. I have often received a smile from Minet, but you hardly look at me."

"Perhaps you would prefer it if Minet had come to you," Falon said in a haughty manner. Minet was precocious, and she flirted with many of the young warriors, but Falon was shy and could not show her feelings. She looked up at the tall, handsome Matio and wished she could be more like Minet.

"Oh no, I did not mean to imply that I preferred Minet, I admire you greatly. I am well pleased that you should stop to talk with me."

Falon became angry. How dare he think she had sought him out on her own? "I did not seek you out, Matio, I come with a message from the queen."

"The queen sent you to me?" Matio asked in disbelief.

"Yes, she asked that you attend her at once," Falon said dryly.

Matio could not believe he had been summoned by the queen. He had never been allowed to get within ten horse lengths of her. He had often observed her from afar, and he had lost his heart to the beautiful golden-haired goddess who was his queen. The older warriors spoke of her in awe, and each of them was ready to defend her with his life if the need arose, but actually to speak to her was too much to hope for.

Matio straightened his silver and turquoise head-band and stood up to his full height. "Why would the queen ask to speak to me?"

"It is not your place to question, but to obey," Falon replied, wishing she did not feel so intimidated by the handsome Matio.

His eyes blazed angrily. "You would do well to learn some social graces from Minet. Does your queen ask you to insult me?"

Falon wondered why she had acted so superior to Matio when she wanted him to like her. She supposed that she was jealous of Minet, who was so lovely and could smile at a man without feeling shy. Matio felt crushed that Falon did not appear to like him. He had watched her for many days, and while he liked the maiden Minet, she did not compare with the lovely and distant Falon.

"Come, the queen awaits," Falon said. Matio looked past her to where the queen was talking to Palomas, and followed Falon.

As Matio approached he saw the formidable Palomas fold his arms over his powerful chest and give him a guarded glance. Many of the warriors were impressed by the queen's personal guard. He was second in command only to the queen's brother Jeffery, and he answered to no one but the king.

Mara smiled at Matio as she recognized him as the young man who had received Tajarez's judgment.

"You may approach the queen," Palomas said in a soft voice. Palomas never raised his voice, there was no need to. All that was needed was one look at his powerful body and his dark eyes that seemed to see right into the soul of a man. Matio pitied anyone who would try to cross him. Palomas was not a handsome man. His nose had been broken in battle and was slightly crooked. His features were irregular, but his strength and courage could be challenged by no one.

Matio bowed his head and when he looked up he saw the most beautiful face he had ever seen. Before he had only observed her from afar, but, being close to her now, he wondered how anyone could be so lovely. Matio was aware he was staring but he could not tear his eyes away from her beautiful face.

"I am told your name is Matio. I recognize you from the day you sought my husband's judgment."

Matio felt the fool as he tried to reply and the words seemed to stick in his throat. How was it possible that the queen had ever noticed him? He had the feeling he was drowning in her beautiful green eyes, so he lowered his head.

Mara could see that Matio was uncomfortable, so she tried to put him at ease. "How is it, Matio, that you became one of my husband's guards so quickly?"

Matio raised his head, and saw the queen smiling at him. He tried to return her smile but he felt as if his face was frozen. "It would have taken much longer had the king not needed extra guards to accompany you to your brother's home," he blurted out, hoping she did not think him a fool. He could not seem to concentrate on anything with her looking at him.

"You are far too modest, Matio. Palomas tells me you proved yourself and earned the right to become a royal guard. He said many were passed over who had been trying for the guards for much longer than you."

Matio was pleased that she had learned how quickly he had been accepted. He himself could not yet believe he now wore the silver and turquoise. He had tried very hard to prove himself, and he had defeated the royal teacher in hand-to-hand combat, a feat that had not been accomplished since Palomas had done it. If a warrior could defeat Lagno he automatically won a place in the royal guards.

"I am pleased with your accomplishment, Matio. Tell me, do you like your duties as a royal guard?"

"Yes, my queen," he replied, not daring to look into her beautiful eyes again.

"I am curious. Do you not wish you had married the girl you were pledged to?" Mara asked, looking at Falon and smiling slightly.

"No, my queen. I have come to know that I was fortunate that she chose my brother over me. I hope my brother will find happiness with her."

Mara laughed, and the sound of her laughter was so beautiful to Matio's ears. "Take care, Matio, that your duties in the guard do not take up all of your time." She smiled at Minet, who was looking boldly at the handsome warrior, and then her eyes rested on Falon, who stared wistfully at Matio.

"Matio, I would like it if you would join my personal guard. Would that please you?"

His eyes widened in disbelief and he went down on his knees before her. "I would gladly die in your service, my queen."

Mara stood up and motioned for him to rise. "I do not ask that you die for me, Matio. Rather, I would ask you to live."

Matio stood as if frozen to the spot as he watched the queen walk away from him. He was startled when Palomas's voice sounded beside him.

"If you are to be in the queen's entourage, should you not mount your horse?" Palomas said, thinking Mara was up to matchmaking. He had observed the proceedings, seeing the way Falon and Minet had looked at Matio. He smiled inwardly, wondering which of the maidens Mara had picked out for the unsuspecting Matio.

"She is so lovely. Her voice is as the wind whispering in the trees. Her eyes seem to draw one's heart from one's body. There has never been such a queen. There is no woman living or dead who can rival her."

"It would be wise if you kept such feelings to yourself," Palomas warned.

Matio realized he had spoken aloud, and, worse yet, that Palomas had overheard him. "I meant no disrespect. I spoke foolishly," he said quickly.

"Watch your tongue or you will find yourself walking among the spirits. I suggest you look to your duties and not at the queen."

"Is it not permitted to admire the queen?" Matio asked.

"It is permitted to admire her silently," Palomas answered him.

"It will be as you say, Palomas," Matio said. "I will not forget," he added.

The days that followed fell into a familiar pattern. They would ride hard most of the day, stopping only to rest the horses and to eat. They would make camp early while there was still plenty of light.

Mara's tent was set apart from the rest of the camp. It was huge and made of white doeskin. She had every comfort. There were soft fur rugs to cover the ground and a bed of white ermine skins, soft white cushions to sit on, and golden plates and goblets for her to eat and drink from. She was pampered and looked after in a way that might have spoiled anyone of lesser character than Mara. She was of such a loving nature that those who knew her well adored her. She was known for her kindness, and her bravery was legendary.

Often they passed Indians from different tribes, but the Indians never attempted to communicate with them in any way and let them pass over their lands unmolested. The legends of the power and strength of the Lagonda tribe had reached far and wide, and none wanted to meet with their displeasure. The few Indian tribes who had dared come up against them in the past had faced defeat. It was said that they were ruled by a great king and lived in a hidden valley. Anyone who would dare harm a Lagonda warrior met a swift death.

It had been three weeks since Mara had parted from Tajarez. There was an emptiness deep inside of her, but she did not allow the others to see it. She pretended to be happy and lighthearted. Mara missed her twins. She resented the fact that Hamez and Tamera would grow and develop while she was away. She would miss all the cute things that babies do, and she would not be there when they started to walk. If only time would pass quickly. If only it was not such a long journey to St. Louis and back, she thought.

They had left the prairie behind and were now traveling in a heavily wooded country. Although it was early May, it was often cold at night. Several times it had snowed, and Palomas had told Mara that spring would be late this year. She knew when they reached the mountains that the snowfall would probably be heavier.

On this particular day, Mara was dressed in a fawn-colored gown that was beaded with gold. Her hair hung down her back in a single braid and was encircled with a leather and gold headband. Because of the cold weather Minet had unpacked Mara's fur-lined cape, which Tajarez had given her before she left the city. It was a beautiful cape of white doeskin lined in ermine, and Mara treasured it because Tajarez had had a woman make it for her as a going-away present. She had thought it much too grand to wear on the journey and she had told Tajarez so. He

59

had laughed and told her nothing was too grand for his queen. She was now grateful for the warmth of the cape. There was an icy wind blowing and the smoke-colored sky hinted that it would snow before they made camp for the night.

Mara saw that they were approaching a river and dreaded the delay. The rivers they had crossed were always tested by Palomas, and if he thought it unsafe to swim the horses across many rafts would have to be built to take them across, which sometimes caused them to lose a whole day.

Mara halted her mount while Palomas tested the waters. She watched as he entered the water and rode midway across. He then returned to her side. "It is safe to cross here," he told her.

Mara sighed. She dreaded the thought of crossing in the icy waters. The current was swift and she did not relish the possibility of falling from her horse into the icy water. She gave an involuntary shiver as her mount balked. Palomas took the reins and led her forward.

"Do not despair, I shall see you safely across," Palomas said.

She gave him a half-smile as she pulled the hem of her cape up and tucked it about her waist, not wanting it to be ruined by the river water.

The icy winds seemed to intensify as she guided her horse into the river. She gave a grateful sigh when they reached the opposite shore.

Palomas held up his hand for the others to halt. "We will camp here for the night," he ordered.

# Four

While I seek a haven, I find a hell.
My eyes reach upward, while downward I dwell.

Mara walked away from the camp and sat down on a fallen tree trunk. She wrapped her robe about her for warmth. Looking up over her head, she thought how strange the branches looked. They had already started to bud, and the tiny unfolded leaves were covered with a light layer of snow.

She looked in the direction of the setting sun and smiled as she remembered what Palomas had told her about the battle between the sun and the moon.

"The moon wins again," she said to herself.

It was that time of day that can be called neither day nor night. The mountains in the distance, which were snow-covered, took on a rosy hue. It was peaceful sitting alone, Mara thought. Privacy was such a luxury to her. She seldom got the chance to be alone. Palomas was always beside her unless she was inside the tent, and then Falon and Minet were her constant companions.

Mara had stolen away from camp hoping she could enjoy the peace and serenity of her surround-

61

ings. She knew at any moment someone would discover her absence and she would have to return.

What was Tajarez doing at this moment, she wondered. Did he miss her as much as she missed him? "My dearest love, being parted from you is so painful," she said to the now darkened sky. She was so overcome with homesickness she could feel an ache deep inside her. Standing up, she walked over to a small incline and stood with her back against a tree. She tried to think of something else. She was almost nineteen years old. A wife, and a mother of twins. Surely she could act like an adult instead of like a child who was away from its mother for the first time.

Transferring her thoughts, she tried to think about Sagas's predictions about the white man's moving into this wilderness, cutting down the trees and destroying the land, pushing the wildlife further north. Mara smiled. She was already beginning to think like an Indian. She hardly thought of herself as white anymore. Her people were the Lagonda, and her husband their king.

She thought of Jeffery and Sasha. She was sorry she would not be home when Sasha's baby was born. The baby was due in June and there was no way she could be home by then. Mara had already decided she would spend no more than two weeks with David and Linda; that way she could be home by July instead of August as was planned. Mara smiled to herself. Tajarez would be surprised when she returned early.

Suddenly Mara sensed a change in the atmosphere. The birds that had been nesting in the tree over her head took wing and flew into the sky. She frowned. It was not her presence that had disturbed the birds. She had been standing under the tree for a long time and the birds had not been disturbed by her. Fear made the back of her neck tingle. She had the strongest feeling of danger. Her hand automatically strayed to the golden medallion that Sagas had given her. It felt warm in her hand, almost as if it were alive. It seemed as if Sagas's face appeared before her and she could plainly hear his voice: *"Run, Mara, Run!"*

In her fear and confusion, her feet would not obey the command to flee. Suddenly she heard a deep growl coming from somewhere in the darkness in front of her. She strained her eyes in the near-darkness, trying to see the animal that threatened her.

She drew in her breath as she saw the wolf. He was crouched not twenty yards from her, ready to spring. The animal inched closer, and the deep growling that issued from his mouth made Mara feel the strong taste of fear. She took a step backwards and found her back against an overhanging cliff. There was nowhere to run. The wolf stood between her and the safety of the camp.

She tried to call for help, but the only sound that issued from her mouth was a soft groan. She kept her eyes glued to the wolf, which was not much more than a furry blur. The animal seemed to sense her fear as it edged closer, giving her a better view of it. It was huge, she thought. Its coat was gray matted fur, and its ears stuck up in a point. It flashed through Mara's mind that the wolf did not look much different from a large dog. Looking at its bared teeth she knew she could easily be ripped apart by them. White foam covered the wolf's mouth, and Mara watched fascinated as it ran down the gray shaggy coat and onto the snow-covered ground. She had not known that a wolf foamed at the mouth. How could she, she had never seen a wolf so close up before. She observed the animal as it leaped to its feet and lunged toward her.

Mara heard someone screaming Tajarez's name and realized it was herself. She was going to die, and no one could prevent it from happening. Palomas would have to return to the Seven Cities and tell Tajarez she was dead, she thought in horror. She closed her eyes tightly, wishing she had brought a weapon with her. She waited to feel the sharp teeth tear into her skin. A new sound made her open her eyes, the sound of the wolf attacking. But it was not she who was the victim, but one of the Lagonda warriors who had seen she was in trouble and had come to her rescue. She could not see who the man was, it was too dark. He was rolling in the snow with a grip on the wolf's throat, and by sheer strength was holding the wolf's sharp teeth away from him. The animal was making horrible noises, and Mara could see its fangs rip the man's arm open. She ran toward the man, but strong arms went around her waist and she was lifted up into Palomas's arms.

"Help him," she sobbed. "He will be killed!"

Palomas was grim-faced as he looked down at her. "It will be better if the wolf kills him."

"What are you saying! Are you mad?" Mara looked at Palomas in disbelief, thinking she had not heard him correctly.

"I order you to help him, Palomas," she shouted so he could hear her above the horrible sounds the animal was making. She closed her eyes when she saw the snow was covered with blood. She noticed the man now, his name was Unat, keeper of the horses. He had a death-grip on the wolf's throat.

Mara shuddered as she saw Unat being ripped apart. It was his blood she saw on the snow. She buried her face against Palomas's chest. By now others had gathered around. What was the matter with them? Why did they not help Unat?

"You know what to do, Matio," Palomas said as he tightened his hold on Mara and started walking back to camp.

"What is Matio going to do, Palomas? You are acting very strange," Mara said, not understanding anything that was taking place.

"It is best you do not know. I do not want you to see," he answered.

"I asked you what Matio is going to do, Palomas, and I expect an answer. As your queen I demand to know."

"Mara, Unat is a dead man already. Were he to survive we would have to slay him," Palomas told her softly, wishing he could spare her the horrible truth. He did not feel guilty for being relieved that it was Unat who must die, and not Mara.

Mara tried to wriggle out of Palomas's arms. "You told Matio to slay Unat. My God, are you such a monster that you would order a man killed just because he might lose his arm? I never have been ashamed of you until now, Palomas. I order you to stop Matio, and if you do not, Tajarez will hear of this.'' She tried to sound strong and authoritative, but the horror of what she had witnessed and the unwillingness of the others to help their companion was too much for her.

Palomas paused at the tent opening. "Mara, the wolf had rabies. Unat will not want to live. Matio is performing an act of mercy."

His words hit her with a force that took her breath away. Now she could understand why everyone was acting so strangely. "Oh, dear God, say it is not so. Is there nothing we can do?'' She pleaded as her body shook with pent-up emotions.

"Mara, by now the deed is done. Unat walks among the spirits. He knew when he saw the wolf that it was rabid. It was his choice to die."

"It is my fault," she sobbed, overcome with grief. She remembered Unat as always laughing, and his eyes had always lit up when she spoke to him. It was hard to believe a man so strong, so alive, was now dead.

"It was not your fault, my queen," Palomas said, as a way of reminding her that she *was* the queen and that she must act the part. He placed her on her feet inside the tent and she sank down on the soft robe, knowing her trembling legs would not support her. She buried her face in her hands, and wept. Minet and Falon came to her immediately and took her in their arms.

"Look after your queen, I will return shortly," Palomas told the two young maidens.

"We saw what happened, my queen," Falon told her sadly. "Palomas was right, it was not your fault.

If Unat had survived he would have gotten the fear-of-water sickness, and he would have died in agony."

Mara raised her tear-stained face. "Does it matter? He is dead, and death is so final."

"No, my queen, by now he walks among the spirits. He will tell the Great Father that he died so his queen might live, and he will know great honor," Minet said.

"I did not want him to die," Mara said in a pitiful voice. "So many have died because of me," she said remembering the Kiowa raid, when the Kiowa chief had tried to take her away from Tajarez.

"You are the queen," Falon said, as if that justified so many dying on her behalf.

Mara's mind was tortured, and she tried to think what Tajarez would do in this situation. That gave her the courage to do what must be done. Rising to her feet, she walked over to the jug of water that stood by the tent opening and washed her face. She then ran shaky hands down her gown. A golden strand of hair had come loose from her braid and she tucked it behind her ear. Squaring her shoulders, she removed the cape Tajarez had given her, and carrying it over her arm, walked out of the tent.

The warriors were gathered in a circle, and when they saw Mara they moved aside to let her pass. She tried not to close her eyes when she saw Unat lying bloody and mangled upon the snow-covered ground. She could see where an arrow had pierced his heart, and she swallowed the bile that rose in her throat. Kneeling down beside him she saw that, despite the fact that his body was a bloody mass, somehow his face was mercifully untouched. Mara touched his face, knowing he had given his life without hesitation to save her. There was a gasp from the crowd of warriors as she leaned forward and kissed Unat on the forehead. Standing up, she placed her fur-lined cape over him, and then spoke to the group of warriors who watched her to see what she would do next.

"Let it be known that Unat died the death of a brave warrior. I, as his queen, decree on this day that his name shall be honored. Did he have any family?" Her voice was clear and did not show the sorrow she was feeling.

"He had a wife and a small daughter," Palomas said.

"Listen to me, my people. I want it known that a brave man has forfeited his life. Palomas, it is my wish that Unat receive great honors. Let him be buried with this symbol of my esteem," she said as she removed the golden armband that spanned her upper arm and placed it down beside Unat's dead body.

The crowd of fierce-looking men bowed their heads in silence knowing Unat had received the greatest honor a warrior could hope for, to be buried with the gold. It was a symbol to be carried to the spirit world so all would know he was honored by his king and queen.

Palomas stood with his arms folded across his broad chest, feeling very proud of Mara. She might look weak and fragile, but inside her beat a heart of courage, and she was wise beyond her young age. Once again he thought the Great Father had created the perfect woman in her. Looking around him he saw the adoring look on all the faces of the fierce Lagonda warriors, and knew they were wishing they could be honored by their queen as Unat had been.

"Palomas, I want you to select one man to return to the Seven Cities to take the news of Unat's death to his family. Instruct him to go first to the king and tell him what has occurred so he can bestow the honor on his wife and daughter. Then I want Unat laid to rest in a manner befitting his courage."

"It will be as you say, my queen," Palomas said.

Matio watched as the queen walked into her tent. Never had he seen such a woman. He envied Unat his opportunity to choose to die for her. Her kindness was well known by all, and her bravery was legendary. Everyone knew she had once slain a great chief to save Tajarez's life.

Unat's body was wrapped in Mara's fur-lined cape for burial. Mara lay down wearily, knowing she would not sleep, fearing her dreams would be haunted by the sight of Unat in his death struggle with the rabid wolf. All night she longed to be held in Tajarez's strong arms, so she could find the comfort that only he could give her.


The days followed each other with no change except in the country they were riding through. Where before they rarely saw another human being, they now saw scattered cabins. The crude cabins appeared to belong to trappers. On rare occasions, they would see a small farm that had been carved out of the wilderness. The weary travelers never slowed their pace. It was now the end of May, and the weather was much warmer.

They were now nearing a wide river, and Mara looked at it with a feeling of dread. It appeared to be a river that they would need a raft to cross. As they reached the bank she knew Palomas would insist they build rafts, and that would cost them a whole day. Mara had worked herself into a fevered state wanting to get to St. Louis so she could quickly return to Tajarez and the children. Her heart seemed to grow heavier with each passing mile, and she wanted nothing better than to turn her horse westward and return to the Seven Cities.

Mara halted her horse at the edge of the river, not allowing him to drink since he was lathered and had been running hard. Matio was beside her and she glanced up at him. "What do you think, Matio, will we need a raft to cross?"

His eyes grew soft as they always did when she spoke to him. He could not yet believe that she had chosen him to be among the personal guards who surrounded her. She had chosen him over older and more experienced warriors. "I do not know, my queen. Palomas is checking the depth now."

"It does not look to be too deep, and yet it is a great distance across and it is swift," she said knowing that most probably Palomas would want to build rafts. "I believe the horses could easily swim this river," she added hopefully.

"I hope it is as you say, my queen," Matio told her.

Mara dismounted and bent down to bathe her face and hands in the river. She then cupped her hands and drank until her thirst was quenched. Standing up she led her horse forward so he could drink.

Minet appeared at her side and handed her a piece of dried meat. "I have spread a robe under the shade tree for you to rest upon, my queen," the girl told her.

Mara waved the dried meat aside. She was not hungry. Lately the thought of food had made her feel nauseous, and she had begun to wonder if she might be expecting a baby, but had decided that her upset stomach came from the sameness of her diet. She thought how good a piece of deer meat that had been roasted over a campfire would taste. She would even settle for a rabbit, she thought wistfully.

Mara made her way to the robe and sat down wearily. Falon offered her a corncake, but Mara shook her head. "You look pale, my queen. Are you feeling well?" Falon asked in concern.

"It must be the heat, Falon. I will be fine once we reach the other side of the river."

The two girls sat down beside Mara and looked at her with concern written on their faces. Seeing this, Mara laughed.

"Please, I am fine. Do not concern yourselves and please do not say anything to Palomas. You know how he fusses. He would only insist we camp on this side of the river."

A shadow fell across Mara's face and she glanced up to see Palomas standing over her.

"What is it that they were not supposed to tell me, Mara?" he asked.

"Your hearing is too keen. Some things are not meant for your ears, Palomas."

71

"Am I to take that as a compliment?" he asked smiling slightly.

Mara's laughter bubbled out. "Of course. How else would I mean it?" she replied, giving him a mischievous grin and hoping he had not overheard that she was not feeling well. "Tell me, will we be able to cross without making rafts?"

Palomas lifted his head and stared at the river. His craggy face was in profile to Mara, and she felt love for this man who always stood in harm's way for her. He was as dear to her as her brother Jeffery. She knew he would not cross the river until he was sure there would be no danger to her.

"I have sent some of the warriors across the river to determine if we shall need a raft. There is something that is causing me some concern and I will want to wait and see what happens. I think we should camp on this side of the river."

"But why? There are still several hours of daylight left."

"Mara, look to the mountains. There are rain clouds hanging over them. If it has been raining in the mountains, there could be a heavy run-off that will swell the river, making it impossible to cross until the river recedes."

"I do not see—"

"Mara," he interrupted. "The river may look calm at the moment, but within moments it could become a raging torrent, with the run-off."

"If that is the case should we not cross now? I do not want to waste any more time than is necessary," Mara said.

"We shall see," he told her absentmindedly, and

72

Mara knew from experience it would do no good to press him. Palomas would cross the river when and only when he thought it safe for her. It did not matter to him that she was queen. He always had the final decision concerning her safety.

Mara looked toward the mountains and could tell it was indeed raining hard. She stood up, knowing if they did not hurry, they would be caught on this side of the river, losing perhaps two or even three days before the swollen river would recede. She set her chin stubbornly. This time she would take the decision for crossing the river out of Palomas's hands. She walked purposefully toward her horse, took the reins from Matio and vaulted onto her horse's back.

"We cross the river now," she told a startled Matio, who quickly mounted his horse. It would never occur to him to disobey his queen.

Palomas did not see Mara's intention until it was too late. By the time he mounted his horse, Mara and Matio were already in deep water. Palomas urged his mount into the water, fearing he would not be able to reach Mara in time.

Mara turned her head and gave him an impish smile. But the look he gave her in return clearly showed his displeasure. Matio kept a wary eye on her, ready to help her if she needed him. There were warriors on both sides of the river, watching them make the crossing. Palomas's anger was boundless as he urged his mount onward. Looking upriver, he was the first to see the wall of water that rushed toward them.

Mara and Matio were midway across the river

when she heard the sound of rushing water. Looking up, she saw the swollen river water as it rushed downstream toward them at unbelievable speed. The churning torrent carried with it debris and uprooted trees. Mara chided herself for acting with such foolhardiness. It might be possible for her and Matio to reach the safety of the other shore, but what about Palomas? Would there be time for him to escape the destructive wall of water that was sweeping everything along in its path?

Mara pulled her horse up and turned back to look at Palomas. Matio, seeing it was her intention to go back to Palomas, grabbed her reins and pulled her forward. Time seemed suspended as Mara glanced at the opposite shore, which was still a great distance from them. She saw the warriors plunge into the water and swim toward her with powerful strokes.

The roar of the water was deafening, and Mara realized none of them would reach shore before the floodwaters were upon them. Her old fear of water returned. In a flash she remembered the time she would have drowned had not Tajarez saved her. After they had married he had insisted that she learn to swim. She was not a strong swimmer and she knew she would never be able to swim in the raging floodwaters. She was aware of the effort Palomas was making to reach her but she knew he would never reach her in time.

Mara saw Matio plunge into the water. He swam around to her side and held his arms up to her. "I will save you, my queen," he shouted. "Come to me."

She had a firm grip on her horse's mane and did

74

not intend to let go. "I cannot, Matio, save yourself," she yelled to make herself heard above the noise of the raging waters.

Matio grabbed her horse's bridle, which was trailing in the water, and pulled himself up. He then pried her hands loose from the horse's mane, pulling her into his arms, and Mara felt the water close over her head before she was lifted up by Matio.

Mara felt great fear, which she knew she must overcome if Matio was to save them both. She had no time to think as the full impact of the floodwaters hit her and Matio and tossed them end over end. Mara could feel herself being dragged under, and she felt her lungs would burst from want of air. Even in her fear she thought of the many who might die because of her stubbornness and willfulness. She thought of Tajarez, and knew she must fight to live. It would destroy Tajarez if she were to die. In so many ways he needed her, and this gave her the courage she needed to fight to live.

She felt Matio's arms about her waist as he swam toward the surface with her. She kicked her feet to help him all she could. When they cut through the surface Mara gulped in a deep breath of air. The current was so swift that they had been carried a long way from the point of impact.

Matio strained his muscles to the limit to keep Mara's head above water. The strain on him was great and he could feel his strength ebbing. He knew if he did not find something for them to hang on to he might not be able to keep her afloat for much longer. He saw an uprooted tree not five feet behind them. With his last ounce of strength he pulled Mara out of the way just as the tree swept past. Grabbing onto a branch with one hand while his other hand encircled Mara's waist, he pushed her against the tree and pinned her body against the rough bark with his own body.

Mara leaned her head against his shoulder, too exhausted to even speak. The danger was not over, but for the moment they were safe. Mara raised her head and searched for Palomas. She strained her eye, but could see no sign of him. Her spirits plunged as she saw his riderless horse. The animal was dead and was bobbing up and down in the churning waters. Hot tears scalded her water-soaked face.

"I have killed him. I have killed Palomas," she cried, only to have her cry carried away by the sound of the raging floodwaters.

Matio knew he would have to get Mara to shore quickly, because the swift current was tearing at his arm muscles. He feared he could lose his hold on Mara at any moment.

"Do not despair, my queen, I shall save you," he said against her ear. He could feel her slight body tremble and he felt great love for her at that moment. He knew it was wrong to love the wife of the king, but no one would ever know but himself. Looking up, he saw a point where the river narrowed, just before it emptied into a larger river, and he knew he must save her before they reached that point. He noticed several large trees growing beside the river, their branches extending across the river at its narrowest point. If he could grab one of the over-hanging branches he might be able to pull Mara to safety.

Matio pulled Mara away from the tree she had been clinging to and swung her around to his back. "Grab on to my neck and hold on tightly," he yelled, hoping to make himself heard above the churning waters.

Mara grasped his neck as her only lifeline. She could see that his intention was to grab the low-hanging branches and tried to relax so he could swim more easily.

Matio thought his arms would be torn from their sockets as he extended himself and reached for a branch. His hands were slippery and wet, and the bark of the tree cut into the palm of his hand. Mara's weight was slight, but now she was twice as heavy. He felt his grip slipping and swung his body around so he could grip the branch with both hands. Moments passed as they were suspended above the floodwaters. By pure strength of will, Matio knew, he would save her or lose his life trying.

Mara reached over her head and grabbed on to the branch, relieving Matio of some of her body weight. He was then able to swing his legs over the branch and pull her to safety. The branch dipped drunkenly with the combined weight of both their bodies, and Matio knew he must get her to the ground before it snapped. Holding her tightly in his arms, he inched toward the trunk of the tree.

It seemed to Mara that it had been hours since the whole ordeal had begun, but in truth it had been only the space of a few minutes. She could not bear to think that she had caused the whole thing, that because of her, many must have lost their lives this day. A dark curtain seemed to descend over her mind. Matio had jumped to the ground and held his arms up to her.

"Come to me. I will not let you drop," he said.

Mara did as he asked and she landed in his arms. He held her tightly in his arms and could feel the trembling of her slight body. The ground they were standing on was a good six feet below the cliff bank. It looked as if at some time in the far distant past a giant earthquake had broken this part of the land away from the rest of the shore. They would have to find a way to reach the top.

Mara raised her face and looked at Matio sadly. She knew the only reason she was not dead was because he would not allow her to give up. "You saved my life, Matio."

"Would that I could always stand between you and harm, my queen."

She touched his face softly, and saw the look of adoration in his eyes. "Oh, Matio, I fear because of me many lost their lives this day."

"I do not think anyone has lost his life, my queen. A Lagonda warrior is taught to swim and to survive under much worse circumstances."

"You are only trying to make me feel better. I saw Palomas's horse and it was dead. I could not bear it if . . . if he . . ."

"Palomas knew as I did that to stay on his horse would mean his death. The flying hoofs would have been very dangerous. He would have gone into the water as we did."

"I pray it is so, Matio."

"Look, my queen! I see Palomas! There he reaches for the branch that overhangs the water,"

Matio said excitedly.

Mara watched as Palomas grabbed for the tree branch and hauled himself up out of the water. Her heart was racing and she wanted to run to Palomas as he dropped down beside her.

"I was frightened you had drowned," she cried as she threw herself into his arms.

He dislodged her hands and pushed her roughly away from him. "I am very angry with you, Mara. You acted unwisely, and are fortunate that you still live. Take heed that I will not tolerate such behavior in the future."

"You dare to speak to the queen in such a manner?" Matio said, not knowing that on many occasions Palomas had shown Mara how displeased he was with her, and no one had dared object, least of all Mara.

Palomas's face became a mask of fury as he faced Matio. "I charge you with the fault, Matio. You should have prevented her from trying to make the crossing. You knew it was dangerous."

"I obey my queen, which is more than I can say for you. I will not stand here and listen to you insult her as if she were a child," the daring, foolish young warrior declared.

Matio had no time to defend himself as a strong hand shot out and grabbed him by the throat.

"I should kill you for what you did," Palomas hissed.

Mara, knowing Palomas's strength, tried to wedge her body between the two men. "Release him, Palomas. It is I who am at fault."

Suddenly Mara heard two gunshots ring out simultaneously. She saw Palomas release his hold on Matio with a look of disbelief on his face. "Mara," he whispered as he reached out to her and then stumbled backwards to fall into the churning waters below.

"He has been shot, Matio. Did you see the blood on his chest?" she screamed, but when she looked back to Matio, she saw that his face was covered with blood. Reaching out her hand to him she watched as he crumpled at her feet, face down.

On the inside Mara was screaming in agony, but no sound issued from her mouth, and she could hear nothing above the raging floodwaters that carried Palomas's body downstream. Her beloved Palomas was dead. She dropped to her knees and tried to turn Matio over. She heard him groan and knew he was badly injured.

Matio tried to rise, and, getting halfway up, fell backwards. Through a haze of pain he saw the two white men making their way down the side of the bank. Mara was making whimpering sounds as she tried to pull him to his feet. "Get up, Matio, get up," she cried. Clasping her hands together she saw they were covered with blood.

"Oh, God no!" she screamed. Darkness was closing in around her and she tried to hold it at bay. Her mind could not accept what she had just witnessed. Palomas and Matio were both dead and she, who was the cause of their deaths, was still alive. "No! No!" she screamed and her voice echoed and reechoed around the surrounding canyons. Something inside Mara's mind snapped and she fell to her knees.

She reached for the golden medallion that hung about her neck and pulled on it until it came loose in her hand. She felt as if a dense fog was closing in on her and everything was spinning around in her head. She slumped forward in total darkness, thinking and feeling nothing. She was surrounded by shadows, and her mind retreated behind a dark curtain.

# Five

I seek who I am, I cried out in despair.
My cry went unheeded, as it danced on the air.

The two trappers made their way down the embankment and stood over Matio's body.

"Damned thieving redskin," the eldest of the two replied as he kicked Matio with the toe of his boot. "He ain't gonna cause anyone no trouble no more."

The other man was examining Mara. "Lookie here, Jake, she is passed out cold, but she don't seem to be hurt none."

"Lucky for her we came along when we did," the man called Jake spoke up. "She sure is a pretty little thing, ain't she?"

"Damn me, Jake we done went and saved her from the two savages that were fighting over her. We best get her out of here before any more of them red-devils shows up."

Tajarez looked around the anteroom and motioned for the wife of Unat to come forward. "I know you have been told of how bravely your husband died. Nothing we can say can bring him back to you, but I share your grief. I have known him since he and I were young boys, and I shall miss him."

Unat's widow raised her head proudly and looked her king steadily in the eyes. "I, as his wife, feel pride in the way he died, my king. I know if he could speak to us from beyond the grave he would say to us that he lived the way he died, with honor and bravery."

"It is so, Balon. I am told that he was buried with gold that the queen gave him," Tajarez told her.

The woman bowed her head, and when she looked up Tajarez saw tears sparkle in her eyes. "I had not been told that he was buried with the gold, my king, I thank you for the honor."

"Balon, I know that it was difficult for you to come here today, but, as a friend of your husband's more than as your king, I want you to know you will be provided for. The queen has sent word that there was no fear in Unat's heart when he met his death. As the widow of a brave warrior who found death protecting his queen, you shall receive the death duties, which should keep you and your daughter in comfort for as long as you live."

Balon dropped to her knees and lowered her head. "It is good, my king. I am honored."

Tajarez stood up and offered the woman his hand and helped her to her feet. "May the Great Father comfort you in your sorrow, Balon," he said as he led her over to Sasha. "Sasha will find a woman to go with you to your home and see that you have all that you need, Balon."

Sasha led Balon away and Jeffery moved to Tajarez's side. "My lord, Tajarez, did I hear correctly? Was Unat slain protecting Mara from a rabid wolf?"

"Yes. It seems he died in her stead."

"I wish she were safely with David now; anything could happen to her. No matter how good the protection is something can always go wrong."

Tajarez tried to close his mind. He did not want to hear his own fears spoken aloud by his brother-in-law. When he had been told about Mara's experience with the wolf, he had died a thousand deaths thinking she had almost lost her life.

"It does no good to speak of this, Jeffery. Is there not something you should be doing now?"

"You sent for me."

Tajarez looked beyond Jeffery to the gold sheeting on the wall. His footsteps were soundless, the golden sandals made no noise as he walked across the room. When he reached the stairs that led up to his room he turned back to Jeffery.

"I did send for you, but I have changed my mind."

Jeffery watched Tajarez climb the stairs, wondering what he had wanted with him.

Tajarez walked toward the nursery, glad that his common sense had returned. When he had first heard about the rabid wolf, he was prepared to send out a large party of warriors to guard Mara on her return trip. Seeing Balon, who had just lost her husband, standing so bravely before him made Tajarez feel shame. He, like his father before him, must appear above such weakness. At least outwardly.

When he reached the second floor where his apartment was located, he opened the door of the nursery and saw Tamera toddling toward him on unsteady legs. She laughed gleefully when she saw her father and held her arms out to him. Tajarez lifted her into his arms and smiled at the kiss she planted on his cheek. "Do you miss your mother, little Tamera?"

Tamera nodded her head. "Mother," she said in her brand of baby talk.

Tajarez handed her to Vista and picked up his son, Hamez, who had been named for his father. Lifting him over his head, Tajarez was rewarded with a happy giggle from his small son.

Little Hamez fixed his father with an intense gaze with his green eyes. It was almost painful for Tajarez to look into Hamez's eyes, since they so closely resembled Mara's. Mara's and Hamez's eyes were a clear emerald color, while Tamera's were green with brown flecks.

"Are the children eating well, Vista?"

"Yes, my king," she answered with a smile on her face. It was not for her to tell the king that he had asked that very same question only that morning when he visited the nursery.

Tajarez kissed Hamez on the cheek and placed him back in his bed. Ignoring his son's loud protest, he walked to the door. "I will be back to see the children later this evening, Vista."

She smiled. There was no need for him to tell her he would return. He was a most devoted father, and Vista thought the people would be surprised if they could witness the many occasions on which their king sat on the floor playing with his offspring. He was a very loving man, and since Mara had become his wife, he showed his affection openly to those who were close enough to the family to witness it.

To his people he appeared a commanding figure, but many were the times that Vista had seen the soft look of love in the king's eyes when he looked at the young queen. It was a special look that warmed Vista's heart.

Vista's brother, Palomas, was protector of the queen, and their family had been honored to have two members serving the royal family. The positions she and Palomas held were coveted by many.

She picked up the young prince royal, trying to soothe him. The two infants missed their mother greatly, and Vista would be happy when the queen returned. It seemed the young queen could brighten up a room just by entering it, and Vista, like many others, had been the recipient of the queen's kindness on many occasions. The queen had insisted that Vista's own baby daughter be brought to the nursery so she could have her near her. There were two other women assigned to help her with the twins, but Vista preferred to do most of the personal things for the young prince and princess herself. Her husband, Naras, had been given a position in the royal stables so the family could be together.

"Do not cry, little prince," she soothed. "Your mother will be home soon. Until she returns Vista will speak to you each day of her, so you will not forget she loves you."

* * *

Tajarez entered the anteroom and found Sagas pacing the floor. He watched the old man in silence for a moment. Sagas stopped in front of Tajarez and glared at him.

"You took your time coming. Did not Jeffery tell you that I sent for you?" Sagas demanded.

Tajarez smiled slightly. Sagas had the habit of addressing the king as if he were *his* subject. But Tajarez took no offense. It had been no different when Tajarez's father had been king. Sagas the all knowing, the sage, was a very dear and trusted friend and advisor.

"Had I known the summons was an order, I would have rushed to you, Sagas." Tajarez told him lightly.

Sagas waved Tajarez aside. "I have to go away for a while," the old man said wearily.

Tajarez saw nothing unusual in this. Sagas was always going into the mountains where he would disappear for long periods of time, and no one knew what he was doing or when he would return.

"Where are you going, my old friend? When can I expect you to return?"

"I am going to the mountains, and I do not know how long I will be away."

Tajarez was thoughtful for a moment. "Did you hear about Unat's death?"

"Of course," Sagas said impatiently.

Tajarez raised his eyebrow. "You are in a rare good spirit."

Sagas favored Tajarez with a look of disgust. "I have no time to pass pleasantries with you."

"I was not aware that Unat's death and the danger

Mara escaped was pleasant," Tajarez snapped. "Do you care to tell me why you are going?"

Sagas avoided Tajarez's eyes. "I go into the mountains because I have seen a vision that disturbs me, and I need to be alone where I will not be distracted."

Tajarez did not press Sagas. His long experience with the old man had taught him to ask no questions. Sagas would only tell him as much as he wanted him to know, and no more.

"Can I reach you should the need arise?" Tajarez said, trying a new approach, hoping Sagas would tell him more of his plans.

"You cannot reach me. When the time is right I shall return. There are black days ahead. Do not always believe the worst, but keep the faith," the old man said, looking inward. Tajarez watched as Sagas walked away from him with his white robe flapping against his bony legs.

"Wait, Sagas, what do you mean about dark days?" he asked, feeling fear. Sagas was never wrong. If he said something would happen, it would always come to pass. "Sagas, is Mara in danger?"

Sagas turned to Tajarez as he reached the door. He saw the worried frown on his king's face. There was no need to worry him unless he could not find Mara. "Be at peace, my king. Mara was caught in a flood, but she was saved."

The color drained from Tajarez's face and he rushed across the room to Sagas, and grabbed him by the arm. "What are you saying, Sagas, tell me about my wife!"

Sagas knew he had already said too much. He had

not intended to upset Tajarez. It was just that he himself was upset. The spirits had been unable to locate Mara since she had been taken away by the two white men. Mara must have removed the golden medallion.

"There is no need for you to be concerned, my king. As I told you, Mara survived the floodwaters." He shrugged Tajarez's hand off his shoulder. "I must leave you now. Keep good thoughts."

Tajarez wanted to call him back to make him explain about Mara being caught in floodwaters, but he knew Sagas would say no more. Wild thoughts kept nagging at Tajarez's mind. That night as he tried to fall asleep, his thoughts were still troubled.

Sagas climbed the high mountain, not needing the bright moonlight to guide him. His footsteps were sure and accurate, for he had made the trip many times in the past. It was near morning when he reached the huge cave. The entrance was hidden by the thick foliage that grew along the rock wall. Across the opening of the cave there was a large boulder. With superhuman strength Sagas rolled the stone aside and entered the dank, dark cave. The first thing he did was to light a torch, which he placed in a metal holder that was attached to the stone wall of the cave. Sagas did not need the light. He knew the inside of the cave as well as a mother knew the face of her own child.

He sat down on a rough buffalo hide, the only comfort he allowed himself. Closing his eyes, he looked inward to where his true sight could be found. No one knew it, but Sagas was almost completely blind.

His voice was but a whisper as he rocked back and forth. "I am searching for you, Mara. I told you not to remove the medallion. How can I reach you? How will I guide you home?"

Sagas saw only darkness. He was silent for a long time. Suddenly he saw a pinnacle of light, and Matio's face flashed before his eyes. "Ah, I have a tool. I will use the young warrior, Matio. He will be my eyes and my legs," Sagas said loudly. "I will find you, Mara," he said in a voice that shook with emotion.

The Lagonda warriors searched both sides of the river thoroughly, desperately, hoping to find their queen. They found Palomas washed up on the shore. He was gravely wounded and they feared he would not live. For many days they continued to search, but they found no clue to lead them to their queen, and the young warrior Matio was missing. They did not find his body. It had been raining for some time and the downpour wiped out all footprints. There was no clue for them to follow.

Miraculously, no one had thus far lost his life because of the flood, unless the queen and Matio had drowned, or unless Palomas died from his wounds.

Palomas was taken back to camp and examined by the young medicine man who was traveling with them. It was discovered that his wound had been made by a white man's bullet.

Falon knelt down by Palomas with tears in her

eyes, while Minet nervously clasped and unclasped her hands.

"I wish Palomas would awaken. Perhaps he has some knowledge of the queen," Falon cried.

The medicine man looked from one maiden to the other. "I fear Palomas will not recover. I doubt he will ever open his eyes again."

It was a week after the queen's disappearance that the weary, dejected warriors returned to camp. Each man dreaded the thought of returning to the Seven Cities to tell the king Mara was missing, probably drowned.

Jantu, who was next in command after Palomas, sat beside his gravely ill leader, wishing he would awaken and tell him what to do. He did not want to face the fact that if Palomas did not regain consciousness he would have to give the order to return to the hidden valley.

Matio regained consciousness as the heavy rain fell on his face. He looked about him in a daze, not remembering where he was, or why he was lying on the ground. His head ached painfully. Reaching up, he tested the painful area and found his hand covered with blood.

Suddenly he remembered! He and Palomas had been shot by two white men. He remembered trying to warn Palomas, but pain had exploded in his head and he had fallen into darkness.

He rose unsteadily to his feet and staggered

weakly forward. "Mara! My queen! Where are you?" he shouted. He dropped to his knees and examined the ground about him. It was no use, the rain had washed away every trace, every footprint. He remembered seeing Palomas fall into the water, but surely the white men had not shot the queen. They must have taken her, he reasoned. They would not harm her, would they? No, they would have made her their prisoner. He tried to think clearly, but his head was aching painfully. He could return to camp, perhaps Mara had been found and taken back there. No, if she had been found he would have been found as well, and taken back to camp. If he were to return to camp he would only waste valuable time. Perhaps the others were searching for her as well and he would meet up with them on the trail. He tried to pull himself over the high cliff, and he fell backwards many times before he finally succeeded.

Matio had no way of knowing how long he had been unconscious, but he calculated it had been at least two suns. He was extremely hungry and thirsty. He could do nothing about his hunger for the moment, but he could drink from the river to relieve his thirst.

Once his thirst was quenched he started moving in a northerly direction. Some unknown force, some instinct, was driving him, guiding his footsteps. He did not question the instinct's origin. He merely followed where it led him. He would push on until he found some clue that would help him locate his queen. Many times he fell to the ground in total exhaustion, only to rise again to forge on. When at last he fell to his knees, too weary to go further, he slumped over and slept, unaware that the rain had begun to fall again.

Mara awoke and looked about her in total confusion. Where was she? She sat up slowly and tried to remember. She seemed to be lying on a blanket with a crude structure over her head to protect her from the falling rain. It appeared to be some kind of animal skin stretched across four stakes that had been driven into the ground. It was no more than a camp. . . . She frowned. She was in the woods, and apparently alone. Her mind was a blank. She felt unbridled fear. What was she doing here? She looked down at her hand and saw some strange object she was holding. It appeared to be a golden medallion of some strange sort. She turned it over wondering where it had come from. There was some writing engraved on it, but she did not bother to read it. It was heavy and she did not want to slip it over her head. Looking down at her legs, she noticed she was wearing leather moccasins. Without thinking she slipped the medallion into one of the shoes. She stood up slowly, testing her legs to see if they would support her weight. She felt shaky and weak, so she leaned against the trunk of a tree.

She had the strongest feeling that she did not belong in her surroundings. It appeared she was in some kind of a camp. There was a campfire, but it had evidently been put out by the rain that was falling. Mara looked upward and noticed the rain had ceased and the clouds were moving away leaving a bright, sun-kissed day. She circled the camp, looking for something that might appear familiar to her. There were several animal traps hanging from the branch of a tree, and many animal pelts lying against the tree trunk giving off a not too pleasant odor.

Mara spotted a leather pouch, which she hoped would contain water. Lifting it to her mouth with shaky hands she took a sip to sample its purity. Finding it cool and refreshing, she drank deeply until her thirst had been satisfied. Now that she was no longer thirsty she looked about for something to eat. Spotting an iron skillet resting in the cold ashes of the campfire, she fell to her knees and scooped up the piece of meat in it and bit into it. It was not too tasty and she knew if she were not so hungry she would never have eaten it. She ate quickly, trying to alleviate the hunger pangs that were causing her stomach to growl in protest. After eating her fill, she felt somewhat better, in spite of the slight feeling of nausea that sent her back to the waterskin to sip the cool water.

Circling the camp once again she tried to find anything that would give her a clue to where she was. Once more she had the feeling of not belonging. Suddenly she heard a sound in the bushes, and she clasped her hands tightly together, not knowing whether to run or to stay and face whomever or whatever it was that was walking heavily toward her.

The bushes parted and Mara saw the tall form of a man appear. She held her breath as he walked slowly over to her. Her eyes were wide with apprehension as she studied him. He was an older man, with long red hair and a bushy beard to match. He was a stranger to her. She was sure she had never seen him before. His dress indicated that he was a trapper. He wore buckskin clothing and heavy leather boots, and over his shoulder he carried several small animal pelts. As she was studying him, he was also sizing her up. She lost some of her apprehension when his face eased into a broad grin.

"Well now, little lady, I see that you are up and about. Did you get you something to eat?" His manner was friendly without being too familiar.

Mara nodded an affirmative, still wondering who he was.

"Can you talk?" he asked as he swung the animal pelts over a low-hanging branch. He looked at her with curious interest. She noticed his eyes were a soft blue color. His face she could not tell much about, for so much of it was covered with his beard. She found nothing in his attitude to make her fear him.

"I do not know," she whispered, hearing her own voice for the first time and not recognizing it.

"My name's Zeke Caulfield. Me and my brother, Jake, found you a few days back. You been a mighty sick little gal. Me and my brother were afeared you wouldn't make it, you being so tiny and all." He smiled down at her and chuckled. "You might be small, but you are strong, ain't you? What's your name?"

Mara knitted her brow in confusion. "I . . . I do not know!" Panic encased her mind as she realized she could not remember her own name. "Oh, Zeke, I do not know who I am. Do you not know me?" she said in a pitiful voice.

Zeke covered the distance that separated them in

two long strides. He took her hand awkwardly. "Don't you fret none, little lady, your name will come back to you given time," he said, trying to comfort her, but not knowing how.

"Well, well, so our little princess is awake at last," a second man said as he came up behind them.

Mara spun around to see a man who closely resembled Zeke, although he was an older version. His hair and beard were completely white, but he had the same soft blue eyes as Zeke, and Mara knew he would be the brother Zeke had spoken of.

"She don't recollect who she is, Jake."

The older man shook his head. "Is that a fact? Don't let that worry you none, little princess. A name ain't worth two whoops and a holler. Me and Zeke here aim to take good care of you till we can get you to a settlement where someone will likely know who you are."

Zeke led her over to the shelter and sat her down on the blanket. "What you need is some hot food so you can put some meat on them bones."

"Mr. Caulfield, where did you find me, and under what circumstances."

Jake was slapping a slab of bacon in the iron skillet. He paused to look at her over his shoulder. He gave his brother a warning glance that told him not to upset the little princess in her state of mind.

Zeke read his brother's message and spoke softly. "Why don't you call me Zeke, and my brother Jake? We ain't been called by our last name in many a year. As to how we found you, I will tell you this and no more for now. You was by a river and from the looks of you at the time you looked as if you had

had a good dunking."

"Where are you taking me?"

"Me and Jake got us a cabin, not a far distance from here. We will take you there until you are feeling stronger, then we will take you to the closest white settlement."

Mara leaned back on the blanket. Her head ached and she felt very tired. Her eyes closed and she felt herself drifting off.

By nightfall Mara was still sleeping, so the two brothers decided not to awaken her, thinking she needed the rest more than the food. As they sat by the campfire eating bacon and beans they talked in hushed voices so they would not disturb her sleep.

"Reckon she will ever recollect who she is, Jake?"

Jake looked at the princess to make sure she was asleep and could not overhear him. "It's hard to say. Depends on how long she was a captive of them savages. I heard once of a woman was captured by them red devils who *never* remembered who she was. You recollect when we used to go to that Pawnee camp, where they had that red-haired white girl."

"Yep, she weren't no girl though, she was well past her prime."

"Be that the truth or not, it don't have any bearing on my story. I once tried to talk to her, found her alone by the river. When I tried to find out who she were, she stared at me blankly just as the little princess done."

"You ain't thinking she is like the princess? That redhead was as crazy as a bedbug."

"No, the princess ain't crazy. She sure is a pretty little thing. Don't appear to have been mistreated, least not so as it shows."

"Yeah, well it ain't likely they left her untouched. I 'spect by tomorrow we will have to tell her we took her away from two Injuns. Won't be too long before she will question how she is dressed."

"I reckon the best thing will be to start out for the cabin early tomorrow morning. It ain't good for her being out in this rain."

Mara slept peacefully that night, and when she awoke the next morning her stomach reminded her she had not eaten in a long time. Jake was frying bacon, which smelled heavenly to her. Standing up, she stretched her arms over her head and then walked over to Jake and sat down on a blanket he had placed there for her.

"That smells good, Jake, but how do you happen to have pork?"

"It ain't pork, Princess, leastwise not the kind you mean. This here's wild boar."

"Whatever it is, it makes my mouth water," she told him, smiling brightly.

"You can have all you want, and some nice flapjacks to go along with it," Jake told her as he turned the bacon to brown on the other side and dished up the golden-brown hot cakes for her.

Mara ate every bite of the three hot cakes and six slices of bacon, while Jake looked on like a mother hen.

"Where is Zeke?" Mara wanted to know as she helped Jake clean the cooking pans and handed them to him to pack away in a leather pouch.

"He is loadin' the packhorses, all except one. We want you to ride. It's a far piece to the cabin and you don't look like you could walk it."

"I think I am strong, Jake," she told him lifting the heavy pouch that contained the pots and pans to prove it.

He grinned at her and took the pouch from her and slung it over his shoulder with ease. "You are strong in the only way that counts, princess. You have my respect."

"I am glad, Jake, but what have I done to gain your respect?"

"I know about people, and since I first saw you I knowed you were special, and ain't nothing happened since you woke up to change my mind."

Zeke returned and threw dirt on the campfire. When he was satisfied it was safely out, he gathered up the remnants of the camp and shoved them into a leather bag, then turned to Mara. "We ain't got no lady's saddle, princess. Think you can ride astride?"

"I do not know, but I will try."

When she reached the horse they intended her to ride she walked around the animal speculatively. Jake bent down and laced his fingers together to give her a boost up. Mara placed her foot in his hands, threw her leg over the horse and settled down on its back. "It seems second nature to me, Jake," she said as she urged the horse forward in a walk.

"I reckon the nice ladies of the town wouldn't approve none, but I won't tell them if you don't, princess."

"Jake why do you and Zeke call me princess?" she said, watching him trudge along beisde her. Zeke walked on the other side of her, leading the pack-horse.

"Well, you ain't got no name as far as you know, and it just seemed right that you be called a princess."

Mara frowned, "Is it not strange that I do not know my name? That does not seem like something one would easily forget."

"Give it a day or so, you will remember, or I'll be a cross-eyed mule."

Mara smiled at the vocabulary of the two brothers. They were tough outdoorsmen, and yet with her they had been kind and considerate. She had no fear of them; the only thing she feared was not remembering who she was. It was a lovely day, the sun was shining warmly and the birds were singing. She saw a white-tail deer dart among the trees just ahead of her. When they reached the cabin there would be time enough to ask Jake and Zeke to tell her all they knew about her, and how they had come to find her.

"Zeke, how far is it to your cabin?"

"We should be there by last light tomorrow, barring trouble."

Mara nodded her head. She had no past and no future; for now her whole world revolved around Jake and Zeke. She knew no one else.

They stopped around noon and Mara dismounted and walked around to stretch her legs. Jake offered her a slice of sourdough bread. She hesitated a moment, noticing Zeke was drinking out of the leather skin. She wondered if there would be enough for her to wash her hands in.

"Zeke, would you mind if I washed my hands if I only used a small amount of water?"

Zeke looked taken aback for a moment. It had

been a long while since he had been in the company of a woman, and most of the women he knew were from some Indian tribe or other, and were willing to swap their favors for a pretty trinket. They had never been too clean, and he had not minded overmuch.

Jake's loud laughter boomed out, as he doubled over with mirth. "See, Zeke, I told you there was other uses for water besides drinking."

Zeke gave Mara a lopsided grin. "Take all the water you want for washing, little princess, and don't let Jake goad you into thinking I don't never take a bath. I had me a bath . . ."

"Go ahead, Zeke, tell her when's the last time you took you a bath," his brother challenged, trying to suppress his laughter.

Zeke scratched his beard in thoughtfulness. "Does swimming in the water count as a bath?"

Mara's laughter startled both brothers. The sound of her laughter seemed to dance on the wind, and Jake and Zeke thought they had never heard anything half so nice. She was so beautiful, and they both felt it was their duty to look after her and protect her since they had saved her from the two savages.

"Zeke, I think you could count swimming as a bath without soap," Mara said wiping her eyes. Both men watched as she poured water into her hands and splashed it on her face.

After they had eaten, Jake lifted Mara onto the horse and they renewed their journey. They did not slow their pace the rest of the day, and that night when they set up camp Mara helped Zeke prepare the food, while Jake gathered wood and built a fire.

Soon all three of them sat down to a plate of beans and beef jerky. Once again Mara became nauseated after she had eaten a portion of the food. She tried to hide it from Jake and Zeke, but they noticed she had not eaten half the food on her plate and decided it was because she was overtired. Jake spread the blanket under a tree for her to lie on. Soon after she lay down she felt better and fell asleep.

The two brothers sat by the fire drinking the thick black coffee and talking in hushed tones. Every so often their eyes would wander to the golden-haired girl, who appeared to be sleeping.

"She sure is a sweet little lady," Zeke told his brother.

"Yep, she don't complain and carry on. She is lost and don't know who she is. We are strangers to her, and yet she smiles that sweet smile of hers, and it just melts my heart."

"Jake, she ain't no ordinary woman. You notice how fine she talks?"

"Yeh, she is a lady, born and bred. Someone, somewhere wants her back real bad." Jake scratched his thick white beard. "I intend that she gets back to those that she belongs to, so she will be looked after and cared for."

"Like taking her to the settlement. We can't go till she is stronger."

Jake nodded his head in agreement as he stood up and poured his remaining coffee back into the pot. "Best we get some shut-eye, but be wary. I got a feeling them Injuns weren't alone and they might try to track us to get her back."

"Jake, did you recollect anything strange about

102

them two Injuns we killed?"

"I didn't pay too much mind to them once they was dead. What you mean?"

"They was tall, taller than the Sioux. Thinking back on it, they was different from any redskin I ever saw."

"Your imagination always was a mite farfetched."

"It weren't my imagination this time, Jake. Have you paid any heed to how the princess is dressed?"

Jake shrugged his shoulders. "She ain't dressed too different from any Injun maiden," he stated matter-of-factly.

"I was watching her tonight as she was setting beside the campfire. That beading on her buckskin dress picked up the firelight. Now I have seen gold before, and unless I miss my guess them beads is gold."

"You are crazier than a right-side-up opossum, Zeke, ain't no Injun got no gold. And if he did he wouldn't give it to no woman."

"You just look closely at them beads tomorrow and see if I ain't right. I think you will find I am right, and if I am . . . I don't know what kind of savages we were dealing with." Zeke's observation caused both men to feel uneasy as they drifted off to sleep that night. Each kept a loaded gun by his side and jumped at any noise.

# *Six*

I reach upward like a twisted vine.
I say a silent prayer, help me gracious father,
Find that which is mine.


Mara looked at the cabin sitting in a glen surrounded by dense woods. It did not appear very large, and somehow looked as if it had not been lived in for a very long time. The weeds were knee-high as she walked to the front door. Jake opened the door for her, and Mara was immediately hit with an unpleasant odor. Trying not to show her distaste, she entered and looked about her at the disarray. Reluctantly she walked over to the wide fireplace. There were two small cots, a wooden table and four chairs, and along the wall was a small cupboard and a wooden stand that was stacked with dirty dishes and pots. A huge iron pot hung from a hook over the fireplace, and, from the odor that pervaded the room, she could tell the pot contained spoiled, leftover food. Mara stepped away from the pot so she could put some distance between herself and the offensive smell.

"It ain't much to look at, princess," Jake told

her, looking about him with his hands resting on his hips.

Mara tried to find something positive to reply and she searched the room. "It has nice wood floors, Jake."

She saw the windows were shuttered and walked over to unlatch them. Pushing the shutters wide she breathed in the fresh air.

Zeke entered and placed the animal pelts down in a corner that was already piled high with pelts. "You are to make yourself to home, little lady. It ain't fancy, but me and Jake call it home."

Mara placed her hands on her hips and turned around in a circle. "What it needs is a woman's touch."

"There ain't never been a woman inside this cabin," Jake told her as he unhooked the pot containing the offensive odor and carried it out the door.

Mara eyed the two cots and wondered where she would be sleeping.

Zeke seemed to read her mind and nodded at the wooden ladder that led up to the loft. "We can make you comfortable up there. With a little fixing up, it won't be too bad, I reckon."

Mara nodded her head, then scanned the room, not knowing where to start cleaning first. There was so much to do before the cabin would be clean enough for human habitation, she thought. She did not say this to Zeke, however, not wanting to hurt his feelings. It was too late in the day for her to get much accomplished. If she could only clean the cooking area it would help some, she thought.

"Zeke, would you bring me some water?" she asked, eyeing the pile of dirty dishes.

"You want it for drinking or bathing?"

"I want it for washing dishes," she said as she stacked the dishes together.

By now Jake had returned and both brothers looked about the cabin, as if seeing it for the first time, observing it as it must appear to a fine lady.

"Guess it could do with a bit of sprucing up," Zeke said.

"It won't hurt it none to have a good cleaning," Jake spoke up. "Zeke, do you recollect if we ever had a broom?"

"Nope, I don't think so. Never needed one before."

Mara smiled to herself. Already the two brothers were becoming important to her. They spoke in soft tones, and she could read kindness and concern in their eyes. She could not imagine either of them ever raising his voice in anger. "Zeke, the water," she reminded him.

The light was beginning to fade when Mara finished washing the stack of dirty dishes. Zeke had disappeared up the ladder to the loft where Mara was to sleep, and Jake had broken a small branch of a tree and was trying to sweep the floor with it.

Mara looked at him fondly, thinking that he was stirring up more dust then he would ever sweep out the door with the branch. Opening the door to the lower cupboard, she saw that it was well stocked with a large tin of lard, flour, cornmeal, coffee and sugar. Evidently the brothers liked to eat well when they were in residence, she thought.

She was not aware that Zeke had come up behind her until he spoke. "Ifin you are too tired to cook, I will do it," he volunteered.

She looked at him, total confusion written on her face. "I do not think I know how to prepare food. If I did, I have forgotten."

Zeke picked up her hands and turned them over. He noticed they were delicate and well shaped, soft hands that had never labored. "There ain't no callouses on these hands," he said.

Jake leaned his makeshift broom against the wall and came over to stand beside his brother. He took Mara's hand and inspected it. "You ain't never done no hard work, but that don't surprise me none. I knew when I first heard your voice that you was a real lady. Most probably had servants waiting on you."

Mara felt tears of frustration gathering in her eyes as she tried to remember who she was.

"I do not know, Jake. I do not know who I am."

"It don't make no never mind, little princess. Zeke and me will take care of the cooking, and as far as you knowing who you are, I bet you will wake up one morning and tell us your name and where you live." Jake took her by the shoulders and led her to the table, where he sat her down. "You just rest. Me and Zeke will cook you up something nice and hot to eat."

Mara lowered her head to the table in total misery. She sat there the whole time the brothers were preparing the meal. Every so often they would look at her with concern, but she did not notice. She was searching her mind, trying to remember anything

107

that would tell her who she was. It was frightening—the blank void of her mind would reveal no clue to her past life.

Dinner that night consisted of fried fatback and eggs. Jake told Mara that he had bought the chickens some years back, since he had a fondness for eggs. He had turned them loose in the woods since he and Zeke were gone most of the time and could not tend them properly. The chickens had thrived. They roosted in the trees at night, and to his surprise had multiplied. The only problem was finding the eggs, which the chickens hid in various nests among the underbrush.

Mara found she was hungry and the fresh eggs tasted delicious. Jake and Zeke watched in satisfaction as she ate two eggs.

After dinner she insisted on clearing the table and washing dishes, while Jake brought in more wood and Zeke tended to the horses. By the time Mara had finished the last of the dishes Jake and Zeke were seated by the fireplace. Zeke filled his pipe with tobacco and lit it. The room took on a cheerful glow as Mara sat down on one of the wooden chairs, warmed by the fire that glowed in the fireplace. She had discovered that although the days were hot, the nights could turn quite cool.

Once again Mara's stomach felt queasy, but she tried to ignore it. She was not aware that the two men were watching her as she picked up the fringe on her doeskin dress and studied it in the bright firelight. She frowned. Why was she dressed so strangely? She ran her hand over the soft doeskin, then she studied her moccasins. She was dressed as an Indian!

Looking at her hands she saw that they were white. She picked up a tress of hair and saw it was golden in color. Raising her head to Jake she gave him a questioning look.

"I am not an Indian. How is it that I am dressed as one? Jake how . . . where did you and Zeke find me?" she said, beginning to panic.

The two brothers exchanged glances. "It ain't no use you fretting over anything, little princess. We will talk on it when you are more rested," Zeke told her.

"No, tell me now. I have to know, can you not see? It is as if I have no past. I was born the day you found me. I have to find out who I am."

"Well," Zeke said, taking a puff on his pipe and blowing out a smoke ring and watching as it floated upward. "When me and Jake found you, you were with two big Injun bucks. They were fighting over you. Me and Jake shot and killed them."

Mara swallowed convulsively. "I was a captive of Indians?"

"It would appear so," Jake spoke up, wishing they had not had to tell her how they had found her.

She looked down at her doeskin dress with new understanding. "Is that all you can tell me?"

"Yep," Jake said. "There ain't no more to tell. That's all we know."

"You was in a faint or something and me and Jake took turns carrying you," Zeke added.

Suddenly Mara remembered the golden medallion she had placed in her shoe. The two brothers watched curiously as she removed her moccasin. She held the medallion up to the firelight watching the way it shimmered.

"Do either of you know about this?" she asked.

Zeke reached across and took the medallion. "I ain't never seen the likes of it before. It's gold," he said, handing it to Jake to inspect.

"Yeah, it's gold, all right. Look, it has some kind of markings on it. It ain't English. I can't read, but I know writing when I see it. Can't be no Injun writing. It might be a clue to your past, princess," he said, handing her back the bright object.

Mara held the golden disk closer to the fire so she could see what was written on it. "It is Egyptian hieroglyphics," she said immediately. She strained her eyes to read the tiny markings. "It says: 'I will seek where I belong.' What can it mean?" she asked in a puzzled voice. For some strange reason she feared the medallion. Her hands were shaking and the golden disc dropped to the floor.

"How could I know what was written on it? Why can I read and understand hieroglyphics?

Zeke shook his head and picked up the medallion, handing it back to her. "I don't know, princess. What is this Egypt you speak of?"

"Egypt is a place."

"Is it in the United States?"

"No, it is across the Atlantic Ocean. Do not ask me how I know this, I just do."

"Do you think you are from this Egypt?" Jake asked.

"I do not think so. Do I speak English with an accent?"

Jake grinned. "You speak the language like it was intended to be spoken. You have the accent of the

110

upper class American.''

"This is getting stranger and stranger. Who am I? Where did I come from? How long do you suppose I was with the Indians before you rescued me?'' Her voice was rising hysterically.

Jake stood up and walked over to the corner where he kept his jug of whiskey. Hurrying back to Mara he uncorked the stopper and handed the jug to her.

"Jake, she can't drink out of the jug,'' Zeke said, reaching for a tin cup and holding it out for Jake to pour the whiskey into. Kneeling down, her urged Mara to take a sip. She shook her head, but Zeke persisted until she took a small swallow.

She coughed as the fiery liquid burned a trail down her throat. When she caught her breath she found that she was somewhat calmer.

Jake helped her to stand then led her over to the ladder. "You go on up and have you a good night's sleep. Things will look better for you in the morning. Who knows, you might wake up knowing who you are.''

Mara nodded, clutching the golden medallion. She started up the ladder. Halfway up she paused and looked down at Jake.

"How long do you suppose I was a captive of the Indians?''

"I don't know for sure, princess, but I have been studying on it. All the captives I ever heard of that was took by the Injuns were forced to work like slaves. The women of the tribe live a hard life, they work harder than the men do. It don't appear you was forced to do no work, so you must have recently been captured.''

111

"Then how do you explain how I am dressed?"

"I don't, and you shouldn't try to think about it."

"The memory's a funny thing," Zeke spoke up. "I once knowed a man who got a hard lick on his head. You recall him Jake, Fielder Jack, they called him."

"Yeh, I knowed him."

"He clean forgot who he was for three days. Could be that you got a lick on your head and forgot the same way."

Both men watched as she digested what Zeke had told her. Then she smiled sadly and said, "If you will excuse me, I think I will go to bed. Good night. I thank both of you for rescuing me and treating me with such kindness. To me now, you are the only family I have. I am very fond of you."

Both men watched her, speechless, as she climbed the ladder to the overhead loft.

In the loft Mara discovered that Zeke had placed blankets on a pile of soft leaves to make her bed. As she lay down something flickered in her mind. She pulled a second blanket over her for warmth. It was as if she could remember the touch of a hand caressing her body. Closing her eyes, a face flashed through her mind. A pair of dark eyes looking at her lovingly. The image quickly faded, leaving her to wonder whom she had been thinking of. Closing her eyes she willed herself to sleep, for in sleep she could find peace for her tortured mind.

Zeke leaned back in his chair and combed his fingers through his red beard. "Jake, wouldn't it be nice if we could keep her with us? Something about her makes me want to take care of her, seeing that no one ever does her any harm."

"Yep, me too, Zeke. But you know we can't do that. This ain't no way for a lady like her to live. She needs to be with her own kind."

"I guess, but it's a pity, ain't it."

"Yep."

Palomas opened his eyes. His mind seemed to be in a dense fog, with swirling flashes of lights and pain so intense he almost cried out in agony. The pain was in his chest and seemed to pin him to the fur robe he was lying on. He groaned as his lips formed a word.

"Mara." It was no more than a whisper.

His eyes began to focus on his surroundings and he saw he was lying in a tent. He tried to rise but the pain shot through his body like a sharp-edged knife.

"Mara, the white men took Mara!" he said in a loud voice.

Falon, who was sitting beside him, ran out of the tent to find Jantu.

Moments later Jantu entered the tent and looked grimly at Palomas, who had managed to sit up with considerable effort. Beads of perspiration stood out on his face, indicating that he was in a great deal of pain.

"I am glad that you have awakened, Palomas," Jantu said as he sat down beside him.

"Have you found the queen?" Palomas asked.

Jantu dropped his eyes. "No, there is no clue to her whereabouts. I fear she has drowned, although we could not find . . . her body."

"Why do you say this?"

"There is no other explanation."

"You are a fool, Jantu," Palomas said angrily. "Mara did not drown, she was taken by two white men."

Jantu's eyes widened and he shook his head in disbelief. "I did not know. How can this be?"

"How did you suppose I was wounded? Did not someone remove the white man's bullet from my body? Does it not then stand to reason that your queen would have been seen by the white men, and taken away?" Palomas gave him a disgusted look. "Where is Matio, did you find him?"

"No, there has been no sign of him," Jantu said, feeling like the fool Palomas had called him.

"Matio was also shot. You have wasted time looking for the body of your queen, while she was being taken away by the white men."

Jantu looked Palomas straight in the eye without flinching. "You were unconscious, and I did not know what to do. I saw my duty and did the best I knew how without you to counsel me."

"Great Father, who thought you were ready to command men? Why were you chosen to come with the queen?"

Jantu stood up and folded his arms across his chest. "Garsa was the chosen one, but he broke his arm the day before we left. I took his place."

"On whose orders did you replace Garsa?"

"I was told it was your orders, Palomas," Jantu replied.

Palomas placed his hand over his eyes. He was not thinking clearly. Yes, he remembered replacing

Garsa with Jantu now. "Then the fault lies with me, Jantu. Why are you not searching now?" Palomas demanded.

"I will go now, but I fear there will be no trace to follow."

"How long have I been unconscious?"

"For two weeks."

Palomas tried to stand, but fell back. When Jantu tried to help him, he shoved him away. He tried again to stand and this time succeeded. The pain of his body did not match the pain in his heart. He had to find Mara! Taking a step forward he fell to his knees. He knew he was too weak to search for her.

"Go look for your queen," he commanded as he fell back on his robe.


Matio knew he was burning up with fever. His head wound was throbbing and aching. His teeth chattered, and even though it was a warm day, he felt cold. He had been wandering aimlessly for days, seeking any trace, any clue that would help him find his queen. He sank down on the ground, knowing he could go no further. He managed to make it to the shelter of a tall tree and curled up on a bed of dry leaves. Matio had had very little to eat, only what roots and berries he could find. He was weak from lack of nourishment. Only intending to close his eyes for a short time and then to resume his search, Matio fell into an exhausted sleep.

# Seven

Life is a cycle, each spring is to renew.
Where there is life, there is always hope.
I will always search for you.

Mara made good use of the two days Zeke and Jake had been gone. She scrubbed the wooden floor until it sparkled. The dishes were all clean and stacked neatly in the now gleaming cupboard. She had aired all the bedding, washed the blankets and the dirty clothing she found tossed carelessly in corners or stuffed under beds. The fireplace had been scrubbed and was now gleaming brightly, as was the iron pot that had been returned to its hook over the glowing hot coals.

She had found deer meat hanging in the lean-to at the back of the cabin. Slicing it into nice-sized chunks, she added it to the pot of boiling water. When the meat was almost done she added potatoes and some wild onions she found growing at the edge of the woods. The aroma was delicious, she had to admit. She then mixed up flour and lard, and added some water, thinking she would try her hand at making dumplings. Dropping the flour mixture into the boiling juices, Mara put the lid in place, and hoped for the best. Jake had told her they would be home before sundown today and she wanted to surprise them with a good dinner, since they had been so kind to her.

The door swung open and Jake stood motionless on the threshold, struck dumb by the sight that welcomed him. Zeke came up behind him and both brothers were awestruck. The cabin sparkled with cleanliness, and the smell from the bubbling stew filled their nostrils.

"Wipe your feet before you come in," Mara greeted them, smiling.

They both complied without question.

"My, my, this place do shine, princess. Looks like you have been mighty busy," Zeke said, placing his pack down in the corner.

"This place weren't this clean when it were new," Jake said laughingly.

"Both of you wash, and when you return, dinner will be ready," Mara told them, placing her hands on her hips to assert her authority.

Zeke looked like he might object for a moment, but he was silenced by a look from his brother.

Mara watched, smiling to herself, as the two men disappeared out the door. She had decided that preparing food did not come easy to her, and hoped she would not disgrace herself with the stew and dumplings she had taken such pains with. Removing the lid from the pot, she spooned the mixture into a large bowl.

When Jake and Zeke returned, Mara saw that they had apparently bathed in the nearby stream. Their hair was wet and smoothed down, and each of them grinned at her, awaiting her approval.

"Zeke here were afeared he would melt once he got in the water," Jake told her.

"Is it all right if we set at the table now?" Zeke asked looking undecided.

Mara's laughter was soft and held a note of amusement. "Of course you may sit at the table. This is your home."

"Don't look much like it," Jake admonished as he sat down on one of the wooden chairs and pulled it closer to the table.

Mara spooned up a generous helping of the stew and dumplings and set it before each man. Jake picked up his spoon scooped up a fat puffy dumpling and started to bite into it when Zeke kicked his leg under the table, reminding him of his long forgotten manners. Placing his spoon back in the bowl he folded his hands in his lap and waited for Mara to sit down.

"Eat," she told the brothers, and waited tensely for them to take a bite, hoping against hope that it would taste good.

Zeke scooped up a spoonful and tasted it carefully, noticing the apprehension in Mara's eyes. He grinned broadly. "Best stew and dumplings I ever tasted. Puts me in mind of the dumplings Ma used to make when I was a boy," he told her.

Mara lifted her spoon to her lips and took a bite. Her face lit up as she discovered that it was indeed delicious.

"Tell me about your family," she asked them. "Did either of you ever marry?"

"No," Jake said between mouthfuls, "ain't no woman ever wanted to marry up with the likes of us."

"Did you ever ask a lady if she would marry you, to come to that conclusion?" Mara wanted to know.

Zeke laughed. "We didn't have to ask them to know what they would say."

"You are wrong, both of you. A lady would have been proud to be the wife of such considerate, handsome men as yourselves."

Both brothers looked pleased.

"Ain't no woman would want to live out here. Most of them would think it was too lonesome. Me and Jake are gone for months at a time."

"I suppose some ladies would think it was lonesome out here, but had you found the right ones, they would have lived anywhere, gone anywhere with you. Have you always been trappers?"

Jake laid his spoon aside and his brow creased in thoughtfulness before he answered her.

"Let's see now. We been trapping for nigh on thirty years. Used to move around a lot, but the last ten years we built this cabin and stayed pretty much in one place."

"You have no family?"

Zeke had cleaned his plate and gone back for seconds. He sat down at the table, took a mouthful and swallowed it, then spoke. "We grew up on a small farm in Pennsylvania, where we lived with our Ma and Pa and baby sister. The farm weren't much, but we made a fairly decent living. Pa, Ma, and Rachel was taken by the pox when I was seventeen and Jake were twenty-five. We tried to make a living with the farm after they died, but it weren't no good. Folks kept crowding in on us, so one day we just up and sold everything, and lit out. Ain't never been back and ain't never been sorry."

"Some things I miss though," Jake spoke up, "like the nice little touches a woman can give to a home. Ma was real pretty, and she could read. Every night she would read to us from a book. Ma was born in France, but she could speak English real good. The one thing I really miss is Ma reading to us."

"Why did you never learn to read?"

"Pa didn't hold much with schooling, but he sure liked to hear Ma read."

"I found a book while I was cleaning. It is *The Odyssey,* by Homer. Is that the book your mother read to you?"

"Yeah, that's the only book we ever had."

"But it is written in French!" Mara said.

"Ma would translate it into English when she would read to us. Pa didn't want us to speak in French. He said we was Americans. I sure wish we could read it."

Mara stood up and began clearing the dishes away. "As soon as I have straightened up I will read to you, if you would like."

Jake began shoveling the rest of his food into his mouth and then stood up to help Mara. "Can you read French, princess?"

"I was surprised to find that I am very proficient in French. I did not even realize it until I began reading your book."

"I would be mighty obliged if you would read to

Zeke and me, princess," Jake said excitedly.

Jake was building up the fire. "I'll just get some more wood, and you help the princess with the dishes. Then we can both sit down and listen to her read," Zeke said eagerly, as his blue eyes lit up with excitement.

When all the dishes were cleared away, Mara took the book down from the top of the cupboard where she had placed it the day before. Zeke filled his pipe, and Jake held the chair for her to sit down. Mara opened the green leather-bound book. Its pages were yellow with age, but she could tell it had been well taken care of. She began to read.

*"The Odyssey,* by Homer."

Both pairs of blue eyes were glued to her face expectantly.

"Tell me, muse, of that man, so ready at need, who wandered far and wide, after he had sacked the sacred citadel of Troy."

Mara looked up from her reading and noticed that Jake was mouthing the words along with her.

"And many were the men whose towns he saw and whose mind he learnt, yea, and many the woes he suffered in his heart upon the deep, striving to win his own life and the return of his company."

Mara read until the light had failed and she could no longer see the words on the pages. As she closed the book neither man moved.

She was deeply touched by them. They were rugged, outdoor men, and yet they had been moved by words from a book their mother had read to them as children. Mara doubted that they fully comprehended the complicated story, but it meant a great deal to them. She smiled warmly at them both.

"I shall read to you each night, if you would like."

"I would be powerful grateful if you would," Jake told her.

"You may be a princess," Zeke told her, "but your voice is like an angel's. Even Ma couldn't say the words like you do."

Mara looked at the crackling fire and the warm, friendly glow it lent to the room. She loved these two men who had taken her in, given her a home, and let her feel as if she belonged.

"I wonder if you can guess how grateful I am to the both of you for saving me from the Indians, and bringing me to your home, where you have made me feel a part of your family. I cannot remember my past. I do not know who I am, and in spite of that I am not unhappy, thanks to you Jake, and you Zeke."

"I wish we could keep you here forever, but it ain't no good for you out here. Come first snowfall we will have to take you to a settlement," Zeke said, thinking how lonesome this cabin would seem without the princess.

"I wish . . . I wish it did not have to be so, Zeke, I like living here with you and Jake. I am frightened of leaving." Suddenly Mara felt her stomach churn, and she knew she was going to be sick in front of Jake and Zeke if she did not make it outside. Placing the book on the table she ran for the door, holding her hand over her mouth. Zeke followed and caught up with her just as she reached the woodpile and retched. Jake appeared beside her and handed her a wet cloth, which she used to wipe her face.

"You didn't eat something that didn't agree with you, did you?" Jake asked.

"I do not think so. I have been feeling this way every night after I eat. Tonight it took a little longer to develop, but it seemed worse than the other times."

Mara was not aware of the brothers exchanging glances over her head.

"Most probably it will go away before too many more days." Jake spoke up quickly before Zeke had a chance to mouth what was on both their minds. "Come into the cabin and lie down. Mayhaps you had better turn in for the night."

Mara lay in the loft feeling very foolish. She felt perfectly well now. She was beginning to see that Jake and Zeke had a tendency to pamper her, and she feared after tonight they would be worse than ever. Turning over, her hand hit against the wall and she felt something lodged against her bed and the logs of the outer wall. She picked it up and dangled it above her, feeling the warmth of it against her hand. The medallion! She had forgotten all about it. How strange that it felt warm, she thought. Should not metal feel cool to the touch? Suddenly she heard a sound. It was little more than a whisper: perhaps it was the sound of the wind in the trees, she reasoned. Closing her eyes, she began to feel frightened for some reason.

"Do not put on the medallion," a voice said. It came to her as clearly as if whoever spoke stood right beside her.

Opening her eyes, Mara saw a flash of white. It

seemed to shape itself into the outline of a man. He was dressed in a white robe, and his long hair was white as well. She must be hallucinating, she thought. Perhaps she really was ill. Now she could see him more clearly. He was an Indian!

"Who are you?" she whispered in a voice that shook with fright.

"Do not put the medallion on," he repeated.

Her hand trembled as she threw the golden object across the room and heard it slam against the wall. Closing her eyes tightly she willed the vision to go away. Opening her eyes a crack, she could no longer see the old man. Mara felt relief. She was sick, she told herself. That was what was wrong with her. She would feel better by morning. It was the wee hours of the morning before she could get the incident out of her mind so that she could fall asleep.

# Eight

Do not leave me, he pleaded.
I cannot say, I replied.
I need you, he answered.
I love you I cried.

When Palomas had recovered sufficiently, he searched the place where he had last seen Mara, not expecting to find anything since any clue would have long since been washed away by the rain. They made a wide sweep of the countryside, but found nothing. There was no sign of Matio, and Palomas had thought he would at least find his dead body.

It was with a heavy heart that Palomas turned his horse toward home. He knew how difficult it would be to tell Tajarez that Mara was missing, perhaps dead. He could not ever remember feeling so helpless. He considered sending the others back to the hidden valley to tell Tajarez of Mara's disappearance, so he could continue to search for her. But no, that would be to play the coward. He would face Tajarez. He alone was responsible for Mara. He alone would face the king.

\* \* \*

Matio devoured the last of the rabbit he had killed the day before, and washed it down with a cool drink of water. He almost felt his old self again. His head wound was all but healed. It had proved to be mainly superficial, and now that he had gotten over the fever, he had regained his strength. He was ready to renew his search for his queen.

Matio had no notion how many days had passed since she had been missing. All he knew was that some force seemed to be pushing him onward, guiding his footsteps, giving him the will to find her. Everything was against him, he was not familiar with the territory he was traveling through, and he could not be sure he was even going in the right direction. It did not matter. He would not turn back until he found her, alive or dead.


Zeke had told Mara that it was now June, not that time had any meaning to her. She was perfectly content to let the days pass without notice. Sometimes it bothered her that she still did not remember who she was, but perhaps it was better that way. Since she had been captured by Indians, there was a good chance that some members of her family had been slain, and she did not want to know about that.

Mara was grateful that she no longer became nauseated in the evenings, and she felt that hard work was having a good effect on her. She would work until she was exhausted, and at night she would fall asleep without having the disturbing dreams about the old Indian man. She had hidden the medallion at the bottom of a small chest Zeke had carved for her from a piece of oak, and she had tried to forget about it.

Her cooking had improved; at least she now felt somewhat more confident about serving the food she prepared. Her hands were no longer white and soft, but red and calloused from the hard work she now loved doing.

Mara was aware that the brothers never left her alone at night. One of them would always show up before dark. She felt guilty knowing they were neglecting their trapping because of her. No amount of persuasion on her part would induce them to leave her by herself at night. She had also become accustomed to being called "princess" by the brothers, and she answered to it as if it were her own name.

It was a warm evening and Mara was preparing supper. She removed the deer meat from the roasting spit, taking care not to burn her fingers with the hot juices. Placing it on a platter, she picked up the razor-sharp hunting knife and began slicing the tender meat. Stepping back a pace she admired the meal she had prepared. Jake had taught her how to make spoonbread and the flapjacks he was so fond of.

She could hear him now, chopping wood at the back of the cabin, and she smiled slightly. Sometimes Jake and Zeke reminded her of two overgrown boys, and she had grown accustomed to the way they hovered and fussed over her like two mother hens. Lately she had noticed they would become upset if she lifted anything they considered heavy, insisting that she leave the heavy work for them to do when they got home.

She walked over to the window and called out to Jake. "Will Zeke be home this evening?"

Jake leaned on his ax and grinned at her. "Now that your cooking's so good, can't hardly keep him away at suppertime."

She removed three plates from the cupboard and placed them on the table. She was humming to herself when Jake and Zeke entered the cabin.

After they had eaten, Zeke took his fiddle out of a box he kept under his bed and began playing a snappy tune. Mara finished putting away the dishes, then tapped her foot and curtsied to Jake. She then gave him a coquettish smile.

"Tell me, sir, would you dance with a poor young lady whom no one seems to want to dance with?"

She watched as Jake's face turned red. Taking his hand she urged him to rise.

"I ain't danced in many a long year, princess, I don't recollect how."

Mara cocked her head, and laughter bubbled out of her mouth. "I do not remember if I ever danced, so perhaps we could find out if either of us can dance."

Jake took her hands reluctantly. At first both of them were awkward, but before too many steps, they were dancing around the room, laughing. Zeke tapped his foot as he played the fiddle. Mara was surprised to find how light Jake was on his feet.

"You have been holding out on me, Jake," she said laughing up into his face. "I bet you danced with many a fair maiden."

"It must be my partner that makes me seem to dance well, princess," he teased lightly.

As Zeke finished one tune he went right into another and the cabin rang with laughter and music.

Suddenly Mara felt a pain rip through her side, and she paused to catch her breath.

Zeke put down his fiddle, and Jake turned her to face him. "Princess, are you all right?" he said in concern.

She smiled brightly. "It was no more than a stitch. I want to dance."

Zeke took her firmly by the arm and led her over to a wooden chair and sat her down. "It's time we told her, Jake. We can't let her go on not knowing," Zeke said, giving his brother a troubled glance.

"Yep, she might do harm to herself or the baby," Jake agreed.

Mara looked from one brother to the other. "What are you talking about. What baby?"

Zeke's face reddened and he could not meet her eyes. Jake knelt down beside her and took her hand in his. "Princess, Zeke and me . . . we want to tell you . . . aw, hell! You are going to have a little one," he finally blurted out.

Mara's face lost its color, and her free hand stole up to her stomach. She felt a roundness that was well hidden beneath her doeskin gown. She swallowed convulsively and tried to speak. Jerking her hand free of Jake, she stood up abruptly.

"How can this be? I do not want to have a baby! Say you are mistaken." Tears of helplessness gathered in her green eyes, as the two brothers watched, not knowing how to comfort her. Mara bit her trembling lower lip as the tears spilled down her face.

"Could it be an Indian's baby? Oh God, no, please do not let it be," she cried pitifully.

Jake stood up slowly, feeling distressed at her reaction. "There ain't no reason to think it is an Injun's baby, princess. I bet you are married, and it's your man's baby."

Zeke took Mara's hand. "I bet that's the right of it. It ain't likely that a gal as pretty as you ain't got no husband," he said convincingly.

"That's right," Jake agreed quickly.

Mara's hands fell hopelessly to her side. "Oh, how I want to believe that. If only I could remember!"

Jake sat her back down in the chair and knelt down beside her while Zeke poured her a cup of coffee from the pot that rested among the hot coals of the fireplace. Mara took a sip of the scalding liquid and noticed her hands were trembling.

Jake touched her golden head, feeling pain at her distress. "Don't you fret none, little princess. Me and Zeke are going to take real good care of you. We know a doctor at a trading post not too far from here. We intend to take you to him."

Mara took another sip of the coffee, then stood up and placed the cup on the table. "I want to go to bed now. I do not want to talk about it anymore tonight," she said, as if not talking about it would make the baby go away.

The brothers watched her silently as she climbed the ladder to the loft. When she disappeared at the top, they sat down wearily. Neither spoke for a long time. They just sat staring into the fireplace. Finally

Zeke stood up and stretched his arms over his head and leaned against the table.

"What's going to happen when the baby comes and it's an Injun?"

"I don't know, but remember Pa always said not to go hunting trouble, let it find you. Maybe she is married."

"Maybe. One thing for sure, we will know when the baby comes. There ain't no way you can disguise an Injun baby."

Mara felt the heat of the sultry night as she tossed on her bed. Her hand sought her rounded stomach. Hot tears scalded her eyes. Burying her face in the blanket, she tried to muffle her sobs. She wanted desperately to believe that she was married and carrying her husband's child. But if that was the case, how did she come to be with the Indians? Had they slain her husband? She tried to open her mind to the past, but nothing would come to her.

Her only link with the past seemed to be the medallion, and for some reason she was frightened of it. She did not want to see the old Indian man again. Sitting up, she reached for the wooden chest, realizing that she must overcome her fear. As she lifted the lid she thought her eyes must be playing tricks on her, because the medallion seemed to have an eerie green glow about it.

Her fingertips touched the metal and found it was warm, as she knew it would be. Her fingers closed around the golden chain and she lifted it out of the chest.

"Help me," she whispered.

Mara lay back on the blanket and her fingers tentatively touched the pyramid-shaped object.

"I am frightened," she said in a trembling voice. "Help me." Suddenly it was as if her body were being lifted into the sky. She was no longer lying in the loft but soaring among the stars. She knew she was not dreaming. She was awake! What was happening to her? She was now standing in water. It appeared to be a pond. She could feel the wetness of the water as it gently caressed her body. The night was bright with millions of stars. There was a man beside her, but she could not yet make out his face.

"I am frightened," she told him.

"There is no need to fear, beloved," the man said in a deep voice. "I will never allow anything to harm you."

A feeling of peace and contentment came over her, a sense of belonging. But that feeling did not last long. It was replaced with something else as she looked into the man's face. His dark, liquid brown eyes seemed to burn her with their intensity. She gasped as he touched her face. Her eyes moved from his handsome face to his dark ebony hair, then downward to his wide, muscled chest. He was standing in the water, and her eyes could not see below his trim waist, so they returned to his face. He was magnificent. His powerful shoulders rippled with muscles as he picked her up into his arms. Without her wanting them to, her arms went around his neck. She could almost feel the texture of his long raven-black hair. His face was unbelievably beautiful, if one could call a man beautiful who was so obviously male, so virile looking.

She flinched as his eyes moved over her body, and then when he waded out of the pool and set her on her feet. He had no clothes on! Blushing, she turned her head away, but her eyes were soon drawn back to his magnificent body. His skin was bronze and he was exceedingly tall. Her eyes widened in shock. He was an Indian!

"Come to me, beloved," he said in a deep voice that seemed to vibrate though her body. She took a step backwards hoping to escape his hand as he reached for her. She shivered as his hand came down on her arm, his touch was so gentle as his hand moved up her arm to her cheek. So gentle it felt as though she had been kissed by the soft wind. She could feel her legs begin to tremble, and her stomach seemed to tighten into a knot, but the feeling had nothing to do with fear. Once more he lifted her into his arms, and now he placed her on the sweet-smelling grass that grew beside the pond. Her eyes widened as he ran his hands over her body. *She* had no clothes on! What was she doing with this man she did not know? How had she gotten here?

Looking into his dark face that was now hovering over hers, she let her lips part invitingly. When his head started its slow descent, she thought his lips would never reach hers, and when they did, it was as if the sky came down and touched the ground. She was no longer earthbound but winging her way across the heavens.

Her hands moved down the corded muscles of his shoulders to his tapered waist. Her body came alive with burning desire. Looking into his face she saw an answering desire in his dark eyes. She closed her eyes as his hands moved down her back, across her hips in a stroking motion. She moved closer to him, wanting to feel his body pressed against hers. He allowed her the closeness she craved. She was aware that her breathing had heightened, in fact all her senses were alive to touch, feel, taste, smell. Never had she felt so alive.

"I need you," he said and his voice came out in a passionate growl, which she answered with a low groan.

He took her lips in a burning, savage kiss, ravishing her tender lips.

She knew what his intentions were, they were no different from hers. His lips and his body were stamping his ownership on hers, and for the moment she was his, body and soul, to do with as he wished.

Her fingers entwined in his soft, ebony hair, as his lips blazed a trail of kisses down her throat to her breasts.

Mara cried out as his male hardness entered her body, filling her with its warmth. The pain and the beauty of it was so intense that she felt tears on her cheeks.

He began to fade as she seemed to be lifted into the air. With all her strength, she tried to stay with him.

"Do not leave me, beloved," the Indian cried out in an agonized voice.

"I cannot stay. I am lost," she answered him.

Mara could no longer feel the cool grass beneath her, but she felt instead the roughness of the blanket she lay upon in the loft bedroom. She was breathing hard and she did not know if it was from fear or desire. What had happened to her? Did the medallion have some strange magical power? Tiny whimpers escaped her lips and she clasped her hand over her mouth to stifle them.

"Oh no!" she cried out as she realized her body was wet. Turning her head she buried it in the blanket. Was her body wet from perspiration, or from being in the pond?

"It cannot be," she whimpered.

"Have no fear," a soft voice said to her from the dark shadows of the loft. "Sleep now, be at peace with yourself."

Mara knew it was the voice of the old Indian man. She also realized he spoke to her in some strange language, and she had understood him. The beautiful Indian had also spoken in that language, and she had answered him in kind. She felt herself drifting off as the shadowy form of the old man knelt down beside her.

"Sleep, sleep," he told her. And she did.


Tajarez awoke from his dream and sat up quickly. He had dreamed he had been with Mara in their Eden. The dream had been so real it seemed he could almost smell the sweet scent she always wore. As she had begun to fade he had tried to hold on to her, but the dream had ended with his begging her not to leave him.

It reminded him of the dream he had had before he had ever met Mara. In those dreams he had also begged her not to leave him. He felt real fear in his heart. Was it an omen, a warning? Was Mara in danger?

Standing up he walked over to the balcony and stared out into the night. He wished Sagas would return, then he could tell him about the dream. He shook his head and looked up at the stars that were just beginning to fade, with the first fingers of daylight touching the eastern sky.

He was being foolish, Mara was with her brother David now, and any day she would be on her way home.

# Nine

Why can I not see, why do I not know?
Whom do I seek, when the cold winds blow?


Tajarez crossed the huge anteroom and placed his hand on Jeffery's shoulder. Seeing the worried frown on his brother-in-law's face, he felt inclined to comfort him.

"Vista tells me that your child is being born." Jeffery's face was an ashen color. "Yes, Sasha's pains started last night. I summoned the medicine man. I had no idea having a baby would be so painful. Sasha was very brave, but I could tell she was in agony."

"You are concerned that it is taking too long?"

Jeffery turned back to the window and stared down at the city below without really seeing it. "I am frightened. Sasha is so frail I cannot bear to think of her being in pain."

Tajarez wanted to comfort his brother-in-law, but did not know what to say to him. He loved and respected the golden-haired man as if he were the brother he had never had. Tajarez had made Jeffery the leader of his royal guards, and he had never had cause to regret putting a white man in charge of the fierce Lagonda warriors. Jeffery's even temperament and patience had won him the respect of all of the Lagonda tribe, who had accepted him as one of their own.

"Come sit with me, Jeffery. We shall wait together for the birth of your child."

Jeffery followed Tajarez across the room and they both sat down on cushions.

"Did the medicine man tell you how long it would be before the child would be born?"

"No. He was unsure," Jeffery replied, looking up at the stairs to see if there was any sign of Tabo, the medicine man.

"I wish Mara were here, Jeffery, she would have the words to comfort you, while I do not. Since I was not with her when Hamez and Tamera were born, I do not know how long it should take."

Jeffery glanced at Tajarez. He felt closer to him than to his own brother, David. He thought if Tajarez were not king, he would still be an outstanding man whom other men would follow willingly. He was born to lead, and Jeffery was proud to call him his friend, as well as his king. At times he would be in awe of his powerful brother-in-law, for when he was acting the king, he could be very commanding. Jeffery smiled to himself. There was a very human side to Tajarez that others did not see. It was always apparent when he was with Mara or the twins.

His thoughts were transferred to his own wife, Sasha, who was now in labor and about to give birth to their child. He wished he could be with her, but he knew she would not welcome him. No Lagonda woman would allow her husband to see her in pain.

"It seems like I have been waiting forever, Tajarez," Jeffery said leaning back and closing his eyes.

"I am sure that wait is all but over. It cannot be much longer," Tajarez assured him.

Both Tajarez and Jeffery stood up slowly as they watched Tabo descent the stairs. The medicine man approached them smiling. Jeffery waited for the man to speak while Tajarez gave him a reassuring glance. When Jeffery had first come to the hidden valley he had scoffed at the Indian who had called himself medicine man, having heard tales of the medicine men who chanted and waved sticks about, claiming to cure sicknesses. He had soon discovered that Tabo had knowledge that would surpass that of many doctors of the white world.

"How is my wife? Has she had the baby yet?" he asked nervously.

"She is doing well. At this time she is holding your newborn infant. She asked that I send you to her."

"Is the child a son or a daughter?" Tajarez asked.

"The child is a son, my king. A bit on the small side, but nonetheless healthy, and perfectly formed."

Tajarez grinned broadly at Jeffery and clapped him on the back. "It is good, Jeffery, you are the father of a son."

Jeffery shook his head, and then smiled widely. "I am a father," he said, letting the words sink in.

Jeffery had started toward the stairs when there was a commotion at the main entrance of the anteroom. He paused, as his gaze followed Tajarez's to the door.

Tajarez's eyes narrowed, and he felt as if he could not breathe. His mind could not accept the haggard look he saw on Palomas's face. Where was Mara? Oh no, Great Father, I cannot bear this, he cried on the inside. He knew by the look on Palomas's face that something had happened to Mara. He silently waited for Palomas to approach him, fearing to hear, yet needing to know about his beloved Mara.

Tajarez felt Jeffery beside him. He was aware that Tabo had withdrawn.

Jeffery saw his own fear mirrored in Tajarez's eyes. It was too soon for Mara to have returned, and Palomas would never return alone unless something had happened to her.

"Where is your queen? Why do you stand before me without her?" Tajarez demanded.

Palomas lowered his head, unable to meet Tajarez's piercing gaze. He dropped to his knees as silence descended on the room. The only sound that could be heard was Tajarez's heavy breathing. Slowly Palomas raised his head to look into the face of his king, and he knew he would rather be walking in the spirit world than relay the news about Mara to the king.

"My king, it pains me to tell you that the queen is missing," Palomas said, choosing his words with care.

Tajarez grabbed Palomas by the shoulders and hauled him to his feet. "What do you mean?" Tajarez's voice was spoken with the sharpness of a whiplash.

Palomas could feel the painful grip on his shoulders, but it in no way matched the pain in his heart. Tajarez released him and Palomas sank down on his knees, while he told the king all that had happened, starting with the river crossing and ending with his being shot by the two white men.

Tajarez did not speak immediately. His eyes moved across Palomas's chest, viewing the angry red scar left by the bullet that had entered his body. When he finally spoke his voice was harsh, laced with disbelief and anger.

"If you have not found Mara, why are you here? If she is dead why are you not dead as well? Your one purpose in life was to keep her safe for me. Why have you not done so?"

"I will gladly forfeit my life, my king. It is no more than I deserve," Palomas said, expecting to hear his death was imminent.

Tajarez's hands moved to Palomas's throat. Palomas did not flinch or look away as his king applied pressure.

Jeffery rushed forward and pried Tajarez's hands free of Palomas's throat, and Palomas fell to the floor. "My God, Tajarez, it was not his fault. Can you not see he is as devastated over Mara's disappearance as you and I are?" Jeffery said, trying to mask his own fear for the moment.

Palomas and Jeffery watched as Tajarez raised his face upward, and a savage yell issued from between his lips, a yell that echoed around the high ceilings of the anteroom.

"Mara, beloved! Great Father, I can not bear the pain!"

Jeffery motioned for Palomas to withdraw, then he turned to Tajarez who still had his face turned upward and his fists tightly clenched at his side.

"Tajarez, we have to think Mara is all right, and we will find her."

"No, Jeffery, Mara is dead. I had a dream about her, and in that dream she told me she could not stay with me. Never have I felt such hopelessness. How will I live without her?"

Jeffery gripped Tajarez by the shoulders and felt the tremor that shook his body. Tajarez tried to turn away, but Jeffery did not miss seeing the tears that shone in the depth of Tajarez's dark eyes.

"I will not live one day longer than it takes to find her dead body, Jeffery. This I swear."

Jeffery had never seen Tajarez in such a state before. His own fears for his sister's safety were pushed aside. He knew that he would have to be strong. Tajarez would need him.

"Tajarez, I do not feel Mara is dead. It seems to me that if she was taken by the two trappers, they would not harm her. We shall return to the place where she was last seen and make a wide, sweeping search of the surrounding countryside. I have never known you to give up so easily."

Hope flickered to life in Tajarez's eyes, but it soon faded. "Palomas would never have returned unless he had made a thorough search. He must believe Mara is dead," Tajarez said, hardly above a whisper.

"You can stay here if you want to, believing the worst. As for myself, I am going to look for my sister!"

Tajarez pushed his grief aside and raised his head. "Select ten of your best warriors, Jeffery. We leave before first light in the morning. Stand beside me, my friend. I will need your strength," Tajarez admitted.

Later Tajarez climbed the stairs to the nursery. When he entered the room, Vista was just putting Tamera in bed for the night. Tajarez lifted his daughter in his arms and held her soft little body against him.

"Leave me, Vista," he said harshly.

Vista blinked her eyes, wondering why the king had spoken so gruffly to her, but it was not for her to question. She walked quickly to the door, but before she could leave his voice stopped her.

"Your brother Palomas has returned. He has been badly wounded. You might want to see him. Tell him we leave in the morning, and to be ready to travel."

Vista's mouth gaped open, and she had many questions that went unanswered as he dismissed her with a curt nod.

When Vista had gone Tajarez hugged Tamera tightly. The tears from his eyes fell on her tiny head as she curled up in his arms. His throat was working convulsively as he tried to speak. "I have lost your mother. If it were not for you and your brother . . ." his voice trailed off.

Tamera, not understanding her father's words nor his grief, patted his cheek and jabbered to him in baby talk.

Hamez pulled at his father's tunic, trying to get his attention, so Tajarez sat down on the floor so he could hold both of his offspring in his lap.

Moments passed as he hugged his children in silence. Finally he spoke, hoping he could make them understand that he must go away. "I am going to be away from you for a while. I do not like leaving you since your mother . . . is also away. I promise you that I will find your mother. This I swear. I want each of you to be good and patient while I am away. If the Great Father wills it that your mother is lost to us forever, I shall return to you." Tajarez knew he was talking irrationally and that the twins could not possibly understand all of his words. It did not matter, he felt the words needed to be said.

"I will return to you because your mother would expect it of me," he said more to himself than to his children.

Tajarez had no idea how long he sat there on the floor holding the children, talking soothingly to them. But he did not leave until the tears on his face had dried, and the twins had both fallen asleep. His kissed each of them and then placed them in their beds. Walking quietly across the room he closed the door softly behind him.

Jeffery paused beside the bed and looked down at Sasha. The afternoon sunlight filtered into the room and cast his face into the shadows. Sasha leaned forward so she could see him more clearly. Seeing the look on his face, which he did not try to hide, she frowned.

"Did not Tabo tell you that the baby and I are well?" she asked.

He sat down beside her and moved the blanket

aside so he could see his son.

The infant's head was covered with soft brown hair. He was sleeping, so Jeffery could not see his son's eyes. His skin color was lighter than his father's, since Jeffery was tanned from the sun.

"Yes, I was told that the both of you are in good health," he said as he examined a tiny hand, amazed at the smallness of it. Jeffery felt love and pride in his new son, but it was overshadowed by his fear for Mara's safety.

Looking up at his wife he tried to smile, but did not quite succeed. Instead his face creased into a painful grimace. His green gaze swept Sasha's lovely face to rest on her soft brown eyes. He saw puzzlement in her returned gaze.

"What has happened, Jeffery? I can see that something is wrong," she asked fearing to hear the reason he appeared so upset.

Sasha loved Mara, and he dreaded telling her what had occurred, but he knew he must, and there was no way to soften the blow.

"I have to go away in the morning. I cannot tell you how long I will be gone."

Sasha, who knew her husband well, read the pain in his eyes. "It is Mara, is it not? Has something happened to her?"

Jeffery nodded, and then told her all that Palomas had said to him and Tajarez. Afterwards he held Sasha in his arms, giving and seeking comfort. They held each other, each trying to be strong for the sake of the other.

There was a knock on the door and Jeffery arose to answer it. He was surprised to see Tajarez.

Stepping back he allowed him to enter the room. Jeffery tried to read Tajarez's thoughts, but by this time Tajarez was in command of himself, and his face was a mask.

"I have come to see your son, Jeffery," he said crossing to the bed where Sasha uncovered her baby so her cousin could admire him. She was teary-eyed as Tajarez bent over the infant.

"May I hold him, Sasha?"

Sasha nodded. "Yes, my king."

Tajarez lifted the tiny baby in his arms and smiled slightly. "He is a fine son, Jeffery. Mara would be so proud. I wish she were here to see this child."

Sasha lowered her head hearing the pain in his voice. He was hurting, and he must be half out of his mind over Mara's disappearance; yet he had come to see her new son.

Tajarez handed the baby back to Sasha and turned to Jeffery. "He will be a companion for my son. I will declare that they both receive their training together."

Sasha tried to feel pleasure at the great honor that had just been bestowed upon her son. To be raised as companion to the prince royal was a very high honor indeed, but her happiness was overshadowed by her fear for Mara. She wondered at Tajarez's strength, when she knew what he was feeling on the inside.

"My king, you will find Mara, I know you will."

He touched her face softly. "Pray that it is so, little cousin," he said as he left the room to be alone.

Palomas watched as Tajarez knelt down and

146

examined the ground. "You are sure this was where you and Matio were shot?"

"Yes, there can be no doubt. I was standing here, and when I was wounded, I fell backwards into the water."

Tajarez stood up and looked at Palomas. "I can see now that you could have done no more than you did to help Mara."

Palomas lowered his eyes. He knew it was Tajarez's way of saying he was sorry for the harsh words he had spoken to him. It was as close to an apology as the king would ever come, but it did not lessen the guilt Palomas felt about Mara.

Tajarez turned his back to Palomas, realizing he still resented him for not taking better care of Mara. But knowing how impulsive Mara was, it was not hard for him to visualize her thinking it an adventure to plunge into the river, although Palomas had asked her to wait.

Jeffery swung his body down the overhanging cliff and stood beside Tajarez. "There are no signs, no footprints, nothing. I believe it would be wise for us to split up and comb each side of the river."

"No. To search the river would be a waste of time." Tajarez glanced at Palomas. "You did search this area thoroughly, did you not?"

"It is so, my king."

Tajarez climbed up the embankment and when Jeffery and Palomas joined him, he made a sweeping gaze of the countryside. "We will separate here, and make a wide swing. Look for any clues. An old camp, tracks, perhaps even a cabin. I do not want anything overlooked," Tajarez told them.

"I think that is the wise thing to do," Jeffery agreed. "I will take Palomas with me, since he is better at tracking than I am."

Tajarez raised his eyebrow, knowing Jeffery wanted to keep Palomas away from him, since he blamed Palomas for Mara's disappearance.

"As you wish, Jeffery. Leave a trail that will be easy to follow . . . Carve three notches on a tree and I shall do the same. If either of us finds anything we can easily find the other."

"How far do you want the search to go?" Jeffery asked.

Tajarez placed his hands on his hips and glanced down at the river below him. "We shall not give up until we have found her alive, or I have proof that she is . . . dead."

# Ten

The end of the summer is now drawing nigh.
I seek who I am as the first snowflakes fly.


The passing of time did not have any great significance for Mara. The summer had gone quickly as August gave way to September, and an early frost had turned the trees to a rainbow of autumn colors. It was a breathtaking sight against the backdrop of the bright blue sky.

Mara shaded her eyes and watched the wild geese that flew overhead, their vee formation stretched as far as the eye could see as they winged their way south. Something kept nagging at the back of her mind, as if she remembered that she was supposed to be somewhere at this time. She pushed her thoughts aside and entered the cabin, thinking she would never remember who she was, or where she belonged.

The child she carried within her body was very active, and her stomach was well rounded, but she chose to ignore her condition, as if not thinking about it would make it go away.

For several days now her mind had been troubled.

Jake and Zeke had told her they were going to take her to the doctor at the trading post to have her baby, but she had decided that she did not want to have her child among strangers.

Mara frowned as she heard Jake enter. She looked up from the pie crust she was rolling out and watched him dump an armload of wood in the wood bin.

Jake glanced up at Mara and saw that there was a white streak of flour on her cheek. He could not help smiling at her.

"You attack that dough as if you are mad at it, little princess. You got something on your mind?" he said leaning against the cupboard and folding his arms over his chest.

Mara looked at him from beneath half-closed eyelashes. "I have made a decision, and you and Zeke are not going to like it."

Jake silently watched her shape the pie dough to a pan, and waited for her to speak.

"There is no way you can change my mind, Jake, so do not even make the attempt," she said stubbornly, and had he known her longer, he would have known by the set of her chin that she meant just what she said.

He wiped a streak of flour from her cheek with his finger and gave her a crooked smile. "Care to tell me what you are so all-fired set on?"

Mara began slicing apples into the pie crust, as she avoided looking at Jake. "I was going to tell you and Zeke when you were together, but I will tell you and you can tell him," she told him as she sprinkled sugar over the apple mixture.

150

"Sure, go ahead, can't think what you are so skittish about though."

She placed her hands on her hips and turned to face him, a look of defiance on her beautiful face. "I am not going to the trading post to have this baby, and nothing you or Zeke can say will cause me to change my mind. I have no intentions of allowing you and Zeke to push me off on strangers. You are the only family I have, and if you abandon me, I will have no one."

"You know me and Zeke would never desert you. After the child is born me and Zeke will fetch you home, if that's what you want."

"Jake, I thought friends stood by one another. I want to have the baby here," she said, knowing she was being unreasonable and taking unfair advantage of his love for her. Tears glistened in her eyes, and she watched as all of Jake's resistance crumbled.

Jake was feeling very distressed by her tears, as well as by her attitude. If he had his way she would stay with him for the rest of his life. She had become very important to him and Zeke. Since she had been with them, this old cabin had turned into a home. This was the first time the princess had asked for anything, and he could not find it within him to deny her. But what about the baby? Should she not be with a doctor when her time came to give birth?

"Princess, me and Zeke don't know nothing about bringing a baby into the world, and we can't ask the doctor to come out here. The doctor's wife is a nice lady, and I spect you will need a woman with you when the time comes," he said, using the only excuses he could think of. For, in truth, he did not want her to leave.

Seeing that Jake was weakening, Mara placed her hand on his. "Have you thought how I will be treated if this baby turns out to be . . . fathered by an Indian? Would you want me to be shunned by the good doctor and his wife?" she said, knowing how to reach him and feeling a twinge of guilt for her method. She was playing on his sympathy, and on his love for her.

Mara's tiny hand was dwarfed by Jake's huge one when his fingers closed about hers. He could not stand the thought of anyone's hurting the little princess. His mind was made up. He would not take her to the trading post, even if he had to do battle with his brother when he came home. If the princess wanted to stay at the cabin to have her baby, then be damned, she would remain. Patting her hand awkwardly, he released it and turned his back to her with the pretense of stoking the fire.

"Seeing as how you are so set on having your baby here, I will speak to Zeke about it. I warn you he ain't going to like it none. He thinks you need a doctor when the time comes."

Mara walked around him and smiled up into his face, knowing she had won her point. "Oh, Jake, I just knew you would not abandon me to strangers."

He was startled for a moment when she stood on tiptoes and planted a kiss on his rough cheek.

"I truly love you and Zeke. I know at times I must be a burden to you, but you are my family and I want to stay with you."

"You ain't never been a burden, princess," he said earnestly, in a gruff voice, knowing at that moment that he would give her anything she asked for.

Jake paced back and forth practicing what he would say to his brother when he returned. Every so often his eyes would wander to the loft where the princess slept. In his mind he envisioned the argument that would ensue when he told Zeke that Mara was not going to the trading post to have her baby.

When Zeke arrived, Jake had worked himself into such a state, he hardly gave his brother time to get through the door before he started in on him. Jake's voice boomed out and he slammed his fist into his open palm.

"My mind is made up and you ain't about to change it, Zeke. Being the oldest counts for something, and I want you to reckon with that."

Zeke sat down on his bed and began unlacing his boot. "I reckon age counts for something."

"I'm glad you see it my way, 'cause that's the way it is, and if you got anything else to say, say it now, cause I'm going to bed," Jake said, lying down on his bed and folding his hands behind his head.

"Jake, I only got one thing to say," Zeke said, removing his boots and looking at his brother.

Jake raised up on his elbow. "What is it?"

"What are you talking about?"

"I'm talking about the princess. She don't want to have her baby at the trading post, and I don't want her to go neither. She is afeared folks will treat her bad if the little one turns out to be an Injun."

"But Jake, you and me can't bring no baby into the world!" Zeke said in a disbelieving voice.

"You want her to be shunned when the baby comes and it's an Injun? You know as well as I do that this baby will be a breed."

"But Jake, you said yourself that she had a husband. I remember that clearly."

"I said that so the princess wouldn't be upset. Don't tell me you believed me?"

"Well, if you really believe that, we can't let her go. I swear, Jake, if anyone were to hurt the princess, I would be ready to fight," Zeke said as he crawled under the covers. "What will we do when it's her time? We don't know nothing about babies."

"I spect we'll let nature be our teacher, Zeke. I recollect when we was living with Ma and Pa, I sometimes helped Pa birth the farm animals."

"Good Lord, Jake. The princess ain't no farm animal!"

"No, but having babies can't be too different, can it?"

"I don't know, Jake, but as sure as bears hibernate, we are gonna find out."


The next morning when Jake told Mara she would not be going to the trading post to have her baby, she was ecstatic.

After the two brothers had left the cabin, Mara went outside to enjoy the bright sunshine, knowing it would soon be cold and she would have to spend most of her time inside. She dreaded the time when the child she was carrying would be born. For now

154

she was living in a state of limbo, waiting and not knowing what would happen from one day to the next. Each morning when she awoke, she hoped to remember who she was, but so far the past had kept its secrets from her.

Mara often wondered if she had a family who missed her, and if so, were they searching for her? Was it possible for one to disappear, never to be heard of again? Did she have a husband who loved her? Was this his child she carried? As the days passed and the roundness of her stomach proclaimed her condition, she had half convinced herself that she did indeed have a husband, and when the baby was born, it would be white.

Autumn was short-lived as winter descended upon the land. The red and gold leaves still clung to the trees when the first snow began to fall.

Zeke had lined the walls of the loft with many furs to keep out the cold that had seeped through the cracks in the logs. The room was warm and cozy, and Mara felt quite comfortable now.

Jake had been absent from the cabin for a week, and Mara again could not help feeling guilty knowing that one of the brothers always remained with her because they did not want to leave her alone. By now her doeskin gown fit snugly across her stomach, and Mara was grateful she did not have a mirror to see her reflection. When the weather had been warmer she had gone daily to bathe in the creek that was a short distance from the cabin. She had stared at her reflection in the water, looking at the face of a stranger. She had been surprised to find the girl, or woman, was not bad to look at, in fact she might be considered to be pretty by some. She could not judge very well, since she could not really see clearly in the water.

Cleaning the doeskin gown had proved a bit of a problem. She was finding she liked to be clean, and the gown had been washed many times, which made it stiff. She had to wear it for awhile, then it would become soft again.

Mara entered the cabin after dusting the light snow from her hair. It was early afternoon and Zeke had gone into the woods to hunt for game. She checked the position of the sun through the window and hoped Jake would return before dark. Glancing about the spotlessly clean cabin she saw there was not much for her to do. Jake and Zeke now insisted on helping her with the housework. She smiled, thinking how much neater the two brothers were now, compared to when she had first come to live with them. They picked up after themselves, took care to wipe their feet before entering the cabin, and bathed often. Mara adored the two men who made up her whole world.

Going over to the fireplace she turned the duck that was roasting over the hot coals, so it would brown evenly. Humming to herself, she wondered why Zeke had gone hunting, since the lean-to was filled with meat. Much of the meat had been dried over a slow fire to preserve it. The pork—as she called it, but which was in fact wild boar—had been soaked in brine to keep it fresh. There were wild turkeys salted down and several small game animals that had been cured for future use.

Mara added a bit of flour to the corn chowder to thicken it. She thought how contented she was. She would be happy if her life continued on with the same safe, day-to-day existence. She had no wish to leave this cabin. This was her world and anything that threatened her haven frightened her. The only thing that ever encroached on her peace of mind was the baby she did not want, and the vision of the dark Indian she had seen, and she tried not to think of either of them.

The door opened and a blast of frigid air circulated around the room. She smiled a greeting when she saw Jake, who was loaded down with parcels, kick the door shut with his foot.

"I am glad you made it home for dinner, Jake. What have you got there? I thought you were tending your traps."

"Nope, I ain't been trapping. I been buying presents for a princess," he told her dumping the parcels on the bed.

"For me, Jake? You bought something for me?"

"I surely did. Seeing as how you ain't got no clothes but the ones on your back, me and Zeke wanted to get you some nice things."

The door burst open a second time, and Zeke entered the cabin, puffing as if he were out of breath. "Did you get what you went for, Jake?" he said excitedly.

"Yep, that's them there on the bed," his brother answered.

"You sure took your time," he said, eyeing the bounty on the bed.

"You wouldn't say that if you knew what a fix I been in. I ran into heavy snow that slowed me down, then the horse went lame and I had to walk him slow, the last five miles."

Jake crossed the room and took Mara's arm and led her over to the bed where the packages were scattered. "Go on, princess, open them. They are all for you."

Mara hesitated for a moment. "All of them?"

"Every last one of them," Zeke spoke up.

Mara noticed both brothers were watching her expectantly, waiting for her reaction.

"You should not have spent money on me. I know how hard you work, and I do not want you to feel you must buy me anything," she said, teary-eyed.

"What good is money, if we can't use it to make you happy, princess," Jake said.

"Can I open them now?" Mara smiled expectantly.

"Sure. Open the big one first," Jake told her as he handed her a parcel.

Mara tore the paper apart with enthusiasm. She gasped when she saw several lengths of material. One was blue calico, another was green print, and the last was soft white flannel.

"Oh, Jake, Zeke, these are beautiful," she said running her hand over the flannel, loving the way it felt against her skin.

"I got you needles and thread so you can make you some mighty fine garments."

Mara turned to the two brothers and smiled sweetly. "I do not know what to say. You are both so good to me. How will I ever repay your kindness to me?"

"See what else we got you," Zeke said hurriedly, not knowing how to deal with her gratitude.

Opening the second package, Mara found ribbons and lace, a hairbrush and a comb. She ran the brush through her hair, loving the way it made her golden curls crackle with electricity.

"Mrs. White told me there was enough flannel to make lots of things for the baby. She said that's what all the women use to make baby garments with," Jake said, clearly pleased with himself.

Laughter bubbled from Mara's lips. "I would say there is enough flannel here to make gowns, blankets—and everything *two* babies would ever need. Thank you both, my dearest friends."

Jake looked pleased, but Zeke shifted his feet uncomfortably. "I got you another present. I been working on it out in the lean-to, so it would be a surprise for you."

"What is it, Zeke?" Mara asked.

"You wait right here while I go and fetch it," he told her as he rushed out the door of the cabin.

When he had gone, Jake picked up the white flannel and ran his rough hands over it. "It has not escaped my notice that you never refer to the baby, princess. Don't you think it's time you began to make plans for it?"

Mara sank down on the bed and looked up at him. "I suppose so, Jake. Not thinking about the baby will not make it go away, will it?"

He knelt down beside her and tilted her chin up. "Some facts need to be faced, princess, and this here baby is a fact. Me and Zeke will love your baby no matter what color its skin is, and I'm betting you will too."

159

"You are right. The past is hidden from me and there does not seem to be anything I can do about it. I will no longer hide from the future. Starting tomorrow, I will make plans for the baby's birth."

Zeke returned just then. He kicked on the door and Jake walked over to let him in. Mara's eyes widened as she saw the beautiful wooden cradle he carried. Setting it down in front of her, he straightened up to his full height, proudly waiting for her to examine his handiwork.

Going down on her knees, Mara saw that the cradle was constructed of heavy oak, which had been polished to a bright sheen. Running her hand over it, she admired the tiny rosebuds that had been skillfully carved on both sides.

"Zeke, this is truly beautiful. I had no idea you were such a fine craftsman," Mara told him.

"I always did like to work with my hands. Jake here always liked to poke fun at me, for wanting to make pretty things. I guess you won't laugh now, Jake," he said proudly.

Jake dropped down on his knees to get a better look at his brother's handiwork. "I'd say this is a mighty fine piece of work. I didn't know you could do this kind of thing."

Zeke winked at Mara. "Just 'cause you live with someone most of your life don't mean you know everything about them."

"Well, I think you are both wonderful," Mara said giving each of them a kiss and a hug.

"All we want is for you to be happy, princess. Ain't that right, Zeke?"

Zeke agreed with a nod of his head, while he lifted

the cradle. "I'll just put this up in the loft for the time being."

That night as Mara lay on her soft bed, she allowed herself to think about the child she carried within her body. Jake was right, she could no longer ignore it, for soon it would be born and she needed to start thinking of it as a person. Somehow seeing the cradle tonight had made the baby seem more real to her. Her hand moved down to her swollen stomach, and she wondered about the baby's father. Was he a man she had loved and been married to, or was he an Indian savage, perhaps one of the men Jake and Zeke had killed?

Once more she tried to force herself to remember the past, and once more she was met with a blank wall. Perhaps it was best if she never remembered, especially if she had been ravished by savages. She felt the baby move within her body, but felt no love for it. To her the baby was an unwelcome guest, using her body like a parasite, needing her body to nourish itself and grow. She pushed all thoughts of the baby out of her mind. She would live one day at a time, and when it was time to give birth to the baby, she would then deal with her feelings for it.

Suddenly she thought of the golden medallion. She had not allowed herself to take it from the chest since the night she had seen the strange visions of the Indian. She sat up and reached for the chest, wondering if she dared hold the medallion in her hand once more. Opening the lid, she slowly lifted the shiny object out of the chest. As usual it was warm in her hand. "If you have some strange magical powers, help me remember who I am," she whispered. "I am frightened of your powers."

"Do not be frightened," a raspy voice spoke up from somewhere behind her.

Mara turned quickly, hoping either Jake or Zeke had come into the loft without her being aware of it, but she saw she was alone. Her eyes stared into the darkness, and suddenly she thought she could make out a shadowy mist.

"Who are you? Am I dreaming?" she said in a shaky voice.

For a moment there seemed to be a green glow coming from the dark, shapeless figure. She was on the verge of throwing the medallion across the room as she had done before, when she heard the voice again.

"Have no fear. I will bring you comfort," the voice said.

The mist seemed to clear, and Mara caught a glimpse of the old Indian man. Closing her eyes tightly, she tried to imagine she was dreaming. Either that or the medallion really did have magical powers. Perhaps it was evil. Gathering it in her hand, she sent it flying across the room.

She lay down and turned her back on it. One thing for sure. She was wide awake, and the strange golden medallion did have some strange power, a power that she did not want to know about. Tomorrow she would walk deep into the woods and lose this thing that must be evil.

That night she dreamed of the beautiful Indian man.

When she awoke the next morning, she hurriedly dressed and slipped into her moccasins, then picked up the medallion. She silently descended the ladder, grateful that Jake and Zeke seemed to be sleeping. She walked deep into the woods. Her footsteps seemed to lag and she had the strangest sensation that she must not part with the golden neckpiece. Fearing she would change her mind, she started running, and when she felt she was far enough away from the cabin, she drew back her arm and sent the medallion flying into the air. She did not watch to see where it landed, but hurried back to the safety of the cabin.

It began to snow heavily, and soon the medallion was covered with a thick layer of white.

# Eleven

He with the dark brooding eyes.
Dark as the midnight skies.


Tajarez looked toward the rising sun, as soft snowflakes fell to earth, covering the dismal landscape. His heart was heavy, for there had been no word about Mara. They had questioned several different Indian tribes, but none of them had been of help. Fear gripped his insides as he gave in to total despair. It did not appear they would ever find his beloved. He would not allow his mind to dwell on the fact that she might have been mistreated by the two white men who had taken her. He knew if he thought in that vein he would lose his mind.

The day had begun, and it was time to mount his horse to start another fruitless day of searching. Perhaps Jeffery had found something that would lead them to Mara, he thought, not really daring to hope.

His dark eyes were sad as he called on his warriors to mount their horses. As the snow fell on his ebony-colored hair, his horse moved forward, and the rising sun was soon lost behind the dark snow clouds shrouding the land like a dark omen.

A cheerful fire was burning in the fireplace and Zeke leaned back in his chair, lit his pipe, and studied Mara's face. She wore the dress she had made out of the green print material. Since she found she did not know the first thing about sewing, the gown was made like a smock that gathered at the shoulders and fell in generous folds, hiding her swollen stomach.

Mara's face was creased into a frown as she tried to take small neat stitches on the gown she was making for the baby out of the white flannel. She had no notion of how beautiful she looked to Zeke, as the firelight reflected off her golden hair, giving the illusion of soft spun gold. Her face was so delicate and lovely, Zeke could only stare in wonder.

Feeling Zeke's eyes on her, Mara held up the tiny garment for his inspection. He nodded approvingly.

"Zeke, do you ever have visitors?" she said, frowning as she pricked her finger with the sharp needle.

He took a draw on his pipe, and exhaled slowly. "Yeah, me and Jake knows this trapper go's by the name of Du Lac. If he has any other name no one knows about it. Some years he comes to spend a few weeks with us, if the winter is hard."

"Tell me about him," Mara said, wanting to hear about anyone. To her the only people who existed in the whole world were Jake and Zeke.

"Well, Jake don't like him much, says there's something shifty about him, but I like him well enough. He is a right handsome man, and if he is to be believed, quite a man with the ladies. He is kind of a gentleman, talks all fancy. He told me once he had to leave France, got into some kind of trouble with the law. He don't talk much about himself, but most men you meet out here are closemouthed about their past."

"Will I meet him?"

"Like as not you will. I spect he will show up one day soon."

Mara bit her lip, trying to make a neat row of stitches. "If he is from France, I wonder what he is doing out here trapping?"

"Me and Jake wondered the same thing. But out here you learn to take a man for what he is. You either like a man or you don't. Me, I like Du Lac."

Mara broke off the thread, tied a knot in it, and turned the baby gown over to make a seam on the other side. "Zeke, do you ever wonder if the Indians you rescued me from are searching for me?" she asked thinking of her dream about the old Indian man and the tall handsome one who haunted her dreams.

"Nope. Leastwise not the two we took you from. If they ain't dead they ought to be."

Mara felt a pain in her heart as she thought of the beautiful Indian with the liquid brown eyes. She was not sure if he was real or just a figment of her imagination, but she could not bear to think of him as being one of the Indians Jake and Zeke had killed. She felt deep sadness in her heart, thinking of his beautiful eyes closed in death. It was almost as if she could feel his caressing hands on her body, and she shivered.

"Zeke, tell me what the two Indians looked like that you shot," she said through trembling lips.

He closed his eyes, as if trying to remember, then he smiled at her. "They were different somehow from any other Injuns I have ever seen. They was tall. One of them fell into the river, so I didn't get a good look at him, and the other one was nice-looking, if you could call an Injun good-looking."

Mara felt a tightening in her chest. Oh no, please god, do not let it be the man in my dreams who is dead. She felt such a sadness she was having trouble trying not to cry.

"If you fear some members of the tribe that took you will come looking for you, be at rest. I don't think they could track us here," he said with more confidence than he really felt. He and Jake had discussed the possibility of the Indians' trying to find the princess. It was not likely that they would want to give up one with her beauty so easily. They had decided that the Indians might think she had drowned in the floodwaters, and given up the search.

"I do not think I will ever remember who I am, Zeke. I have about decided that I may spend the rest of my life as someone with no past and no name."

"Me and Jake have been studying on that. We thought once the little one is born, we will take you to see the doctor at the trading post and let him look at you. It might be he can help you."

"What is a doctor doing living at a trading post, Zeke?"

"Doc White is a real doctor, all right. He once treated people in Virginia, till he came out here and found he could make more money selling goods and trading with the Injuns and trappers. He still treats folks when the need arises."

"Do you suppose he can help me?"

"We won't know less we try. He's a good man, and if anyone can help you, he can."

"How far is it to this trading post?"

"No more than three or four days. But don't you fret none, we will bundle the baby up real good, and take a tent for you to sleep in. Me and Jake will take it real slow, so as not to tire you out."

Mara gathered up the tiny garment she had been sewing on and folded it neatly. "I try not to think about the baby," she said softly.

Zeke took her hand in his. "Princess, it won't make no never mind to me and Jake if your baby is . . ." he was red-faced and could not meet her eyes. "Me and Jake will like having a little one around."

"I wish I could feel as you do. I know it is not right to resent this baby, but I cannot help myself."

"You just give yourself time. As my pa used to say, 'don't go borrowing trouble, it will find you on its own.' "

Mara stood up and walked over to the door and opened it a crack to peer out. There was a thick layer of snow covering the ground, and the wind was blowing it into high snowdrifts. Closing the door, she returned to the warmth of the fire.

"I wish Jake were here. I have had the strangest feeling we are being watched. I do not know why, it is just a feeling."

Zeke removed his rifle from the pegs where it hung over the fireplace. "I'll just go out and have a look around if it will make you feel any better," he told her.

Matio looked skyward, and the snow fell on his face like icy fingers. The deerskin wrap he was using for warmth barely reached his knees and did little to keep out the cold winds. He shivered, wondering why he continued to search for his queen, since there had been no sign of encouragement. There was nothing for him to follow, but still some force drove him on, refusing to allow him to turn back. If he could only find something that would tell him he was going in the right direction. Anything to give him hope.

The cold winds intensified, and his body was numb. He knew he would have to find some kind of shelter, or he would freeze to death. He soon found a hollowed-out log. Turning one end of it so it was blocked by the trunk of a tree, he crawled inside hoping to find some protection from the cold. The wind could not reach him now, but he wondered if he would ever feel warm again. Crawling out, he decided he needed to find something to block the other end of the log. He took a step and then cried out in pain. Something sharp had penetrated his moccasin. Feeling around in the snow, he searched for the offending object. When he found it he held it up so he could see what it was. Matio stared at the golden medallion in total disbelief. It was the same neckpiece the queen had worn. There could be no doubt, for he had seen it many times.

Joy leaped into his heart. The Great Father must have been guiding his footsteps, he thought. For the first time in many weeks, there was hope in his heart. The queen must be nearby. He did not question how the medallion came to be in the woods. Some things were not meant for mortals to know. One must merely accept them on faith.

It was beginning to grow dark, and he knew he would have to wait until the morning to renew his search. But now he knew the queen was near, and he would find her. Crawling back into the hollow log he pulled the scant deerskin tightly about him and fell asleep clutching the golden medallion that belonged to his queen.

It was not full light when Matio awoke. Crawling out of the log, he started off at a run, ignoring the hunger pangs, as well as the cold. He felt confident in his heart that he would find some sign of the queen today.

He had hardly gone any distance, when his keen hearing picked up an unfamiliar sound. He dropped quickly to his stomach and peered through the branches of a bush. There was a large clearing just ahead with some crude kind of structure built on it.

Slowly and silently he crept closer until he had a better view of the cabin. There was a man chopping wood with a strange-looking object. The man's hair was red, and to Matio's surprise he saw the man had the same red hair growing on his chin. His eyes moved from the man to the cabin. He watched as the smoke curled from the chimney, rising into the sky to mix with the snow.

He was wondering if the queen could be in the cabin, when the door opened and a woman came out. She was bundled up in warm furs, but there was no mistaking her, even from a distance.

*He had found his queen!*

Matio resisted the urge to call out to her. Not that he feared the man with the flaming hair, but there might be others inside the cabin, and he could not risk the queen's safety.

His heart was drumming inside his chest, and he felt great happiness wash over him. He had to find a way to communicate with her, to let her know he was near, ready to help her escape. Reaching into his leather pouch, he withdrew the medallion. That was what he could use to send her his message that her rescue was at hand.

All day Matio stayed at his vantage point. The queen did not reappear, but the man with the flaming hair came out of the cabin several times.

As night began to creep over the land the snowfall intensified. Matio crept out of his hiding place and moved cautiously toward the cabin. The windows were boarded up so he could see nothing that was going on inside the small structure. Looking about he tried to find someplace to put the medallion so she might find it. Seeing the strange handle on the door, he hung the chain over it, and then faded into the darkness, knowing the heavy snowfall would soon cover his tracks. The queen did not appear to be in any danger, so he would wait and watch, hoping to find her alone.


Mara was tired, and her back had been bothering her all day, so she had decided she would go to bed early. She and Zeke had been expecting Jake home,

171

but he had not appeared before dinner. Mara and Zeke had eaten together and she had left Jake's dinner warming in case he did return.

She was halfway up the ladder when the front door opened and Jake entered. She watched as he shook the snow from his hooded jacket.

"You are late. We began to think you would not return tonight," she told him.

Jake looked up to her and grinned broadly. "Did you misplace something, princess?" he asked removing his glove and holding something out to her.

Mara gasped as she saw the medallion. "Where did you find it, Jake?" she said in a weak voice.

"It was hanging on the doorknob. You ought to be more careful with it. Unless I miss my guess, it is very valuable."

Mara climbed down the ladder on shaky legs. When she reached the floor, she stood as if paralyzed. Finally, she reached for the medallion and it felt warm in her hand, as she knew it would.

"Jake, did the medallion feel warm to you?" she asked.

He looked taken aback for a moment, not understanding her question. "No, of course not, it's cold as ice. It's been hanging outside in the snow. Why do you ask?"

Mara merely shook her head, knowing she could never tell Jake about the strange effect the medallion had on her. Nor would she tell him she had thrown it away in the woods. Climbing up the ladder, she lay down on the soft furs. Clutching the golden chain, she closed her eyes. How was it possible that the medallion had been found, and by whom? She no longer doubted that it had some strange power, nor would she resist it any longer. She was frightened, but she would try to find out tonight what the medallion was trying to show her.

Inside the cave, high among the mountains of the hidden valley, Sagas the wise watched as the flames from the fire he had built, leapt higher and higher, as it gave off a silver-blue glow.

"Very good, Matio. Now she has the medallion. You were easy to control. When you wanted to give up, I urged you onward. Mara, you are a bit harder to control. You keep trying to resist. Now that you have the medallion, it will not be so difficult. You must not put it on until you are with me. It would be too dangerous. Keep it with you and I will help you find your way home."

Mara held the strange, mysterious object above her head. "What do you want of me?" she asked, thinking if anyone could hear her talking to the medallion, they would think her crazed.

She wondered what would happen if she were to slip it over her head. Raising it, she was in the process of putting it on when the chain became entangled in her hair and she cried out in pain. The more she tried to untangle it the more tangled it became. Tears of pain moistened her eyes, and with a final yank she dislodged it from her hair, but not without pulling several strands of golden hair out by the roots.

She saw a faint movement against the far wall. It appeared the same as before, a smoky mist without form. Her eyes widened as the mist formed itself into the shape of the old Indian.

"Who are you? What do you want of me?" she asked in a soft whisper.

"Do not again attempt to put the medallion on. Had you done as I asked you to and not taken it off, you would know who I am."

"W . . . what do you want with me?"

"Merely to show you the way home."

"I am frightened!"

"I know, but you have nothing to fear. You are seeking who you are."

"Who am I? If you know, please show me."

"Close your eyes, rest, come with me on a journey. A journey where you will find that which you seek."

Mara closed her eyes, soothed by the sound of the old man's voice. She was in total darkness, and she felt as if her body were being lifted into the air, but she knew that she had not moved, for she could feel the soft fur beneath her. Time had no meaning, and she felt neither hot nor cold. She felt only movement, as if her body were being transported to another place.

She was in a woods. It was snowing, and yet she walked barefoot through the snow without feeling cold.

There was some kind of tent just ahead, not the usual kind of Indian teepee, but a huge white tent. She ran toward it wanting to see what was on the inside. Pushing the flap aside, she entered. Her eyes searched the interior—searching for what? She saw a man lying on a white fur robe. It was he! The beautiful Indian! She moved closer to him, but he did not appear to see her.

"Can you tell me who I am?" she asked, but he did not answer. His dark eyes moved past her as if he did not see her.

"I know I am dreaming. That is why you cannot see me."

If he could not see her, she could venture closer. She could even touch him and he would not know it. Going down on her knees beside him, she touched his face shyly. He did not respond, and yet she could feel the warmth of his skin. Sliding her hand downward, she felt the mighty strength of his muscled chest, which was bare. He wore nothing but a white loincloth, and her eyes traveled over his chest to his flat stomach. She saw his long, powerful legs. Surely there had never been a man to match this one in power or handsomeness. Raising her head, she looked into eyes that were as black as the night, soft magnetic eyes that seemed to pull at her heart.

She drew in her breath when she saw that the dark eyes looked sad and misty. She felt such pain in her heart, and a tear formed at the corner of the dark orbs and rolled down his bronze cheek. He was sad, and it tore at her. She wanted to comfort him. With a trembling hand, she wiped a tear from his cheek, and found it felt wet to her fingertip.

"Why do you cry? Who has hurt you?" she whispered, feeling his heartache as if it were her own.

His dark eyes shifted and it seemed he was staring right at her. She drew in her breath thinking he had seen her at last.

"I wish . . . I wish I could help ease your pain," she said tenderly.

He closed his eyes, and she resented the fact that he had not seen her at all. With shaking fingers, she touched his long ebony hair and found it to be soft. Her hand drifted down his face to his strong chin, then she tentatively touched his sensitive lips. Strong feelings of desire were fanned to life within her body as she lowered her head to kiss his warm lips. She hesitated at her own daring. Feeling his warm breath on her lips, she kissed him softly. There was no response, so she raised her head.

Opening his eyes he spoke for the first time: "Let me die. I feel such pain and hopelessness. I no longer want to live."

"No!" She screamed. "No! You must not say that! I do not want anything to happen to you." She could feel her body being pulled away from him, and she grabbed on to his arm, not wanting to leave him. "Do not take me back. Let me remain with him," she pleaded, but even as she spoke the mist was swirling about her, and she felt herself being transported into the night skies.

She struggled, trying to return to the Indian, but it was useless. She felt a pain rip through her body and she was falling, falling. There was another pain and she bit her lip to keep from crying out. Suddenly the mist disappeared and she was back in her room in the loft. Nothing seemed real to her but the pain . . . and it was all too real! She placed her hand on her stomach and felt it contract. Just when she thought she could no longer stand the pain, it subsided. She was breathing in short gasps. Her body arched as the next pain caught her unaware, and she cried out. The child she did not want was fighting to be born.

Mara became aware that Jake was kneeling beside her. "Is the baby coming, princess?" he asked in a voice filled with fear.

Mara nodded, unable to speak. Jake ran to the ladder and called down to his brother. "Boil some water, the baby is coming!"

The hours that followed were like a living nightmare. Mara tried to be brave and not scream, but sometimes she could not stop herself. She was hardly aware that Jake was beside her, speaking to her soothingly.

Each time a pain would rip her body she became rigid. She squeezed her hand tightly into a fist and felt the medallion. She heard the old Indian's voice as plainly as if he were standing right beside her, but Jake did not seem to hear him at all.

"Do not fight against the child, it will be born with or without your help. It will go better for you if you give in," the old Indian said to her.

He was right, she thought. The child would be born and nothing she could do would stop it. When the next pain came, she allowed herself to bear down, with all her strength. When the first rays of sunlight covered the land, Mara heard the first cry of her baby.

## Twelve

In a world of whiteness, in a world of snow,
I seek that which evades me, that which I do not know.


She felt overpowering love for the tiny infant who had been born into the white world with no one to care for him but her. He would be scorned and ridiculed for the color of his skin, but when she looked at him she saw how beautiful he was. It did not matter to her now that she must have been brutally raped by one of the Indians Jake and Zeke had killed. This was her son, and she loved him. She knew at that moment she would protect him with her life, if need be. She felt no shame when she looked into the dark eyes, but only strong maternal love.

Zeke had joined his brother in the loft, and both men stared at the tiny infant, then they looked inquiringly at Mara. When she smiled at them, they both knew she had accepted the baby.

"He is a fine-looking boy, princess," Jake said seriously.

Zeke reached out his hand and touched the dark hair, amazed at how soft it felt. "I can't ever recollect seeing a newborn baby," he said in an awed

178

voice. "He is a handsome boy, for sure."

Mara smiled at both of them through her tears. "I know that you are wondering if I will accept my son, since we all know what his father was. I want the both of you to know that I love him, and I will fight anyone who would ever want to hurt him."

Jake grinned broadly. "I reckon that makes three of us, don't it, Zeke?"

"Yep. Ain't no one ever going to hurt this little tyke, with ole Zeke around to watch over him."

"Thank you both so much, I love you for many things, but most of all I love you for loving my son."

Zeke became red-faced at her words, because he felt so deeply for the beautiful golden-haired girl who had come into his life. Unable to show how he felt, he changed the subject. "When he gets older, I will teach him to hunt and fish."

Jake stood up. "He is a mite too young now, Zeke. We best go below and let them both get some sleep." He turned to Mara and smiled. "Princess, you and the little one there has a home with me and Zeke for as long as you want it."

Mara smiled contentedly as both men disappeared down the ladder. Already she had started to nod off.

Jake eased his body down on his bed and stared at the loft where the princess lay. "She took it right well, about the baby being Injun."

"Yep, our princess has got a lot of grit. She don't let nothing throw her for very long. The baby sure were cute, weren't he, Jake?"

"What did you think he would be with a ma like the princess?"

"You think she will let me hold him sometime?"

"Sure. She is going to need a lot of care, until she gets over birthing the baby. You and me will have to help her," Jake told him covering a yawn.

"Jake, you go on to sleep, and I'll take the first watch. If the baby cries, I'll be up that ladder like a shot out of a gun."

"That's fine, Zeke. Now, will you let me get some sleep? I'm damned near tuckered out."

"Jake, it were nice to help bring a baby into the world, weren't it?"

"Yeh."

"It's kind of like we are his uncles, or something, ain't it?" But his brother did not answer. He had fallen asleep. Zeke put a pot of strong coffee in the hot coals of the fireplace, thinking he would drink several cups so he would be alert in case the baby woke up.

Matio awoke, feeling as though a heavy weight was pressing down on his chest. When he tried to sit up he was besieged by a fit of coughing. His head was aching, and he realized he was feverish. He found he was too weak to crawl out of the hollow log. Throughout the long day he had felt burning hot, and then shivered with the chills. He knew it was not a mild sickness, but the more serious lung sickness that could be fatal, if one did not get the proper help. He knew it would be bad for him, being out in the open as he was. He would have to find more warmth. He could not allow himself to die, he was the only one who knew where to find the queen.

After nightfall he managed to crawl out of the log

and stumble toward the cabin. There was no moon and the snow was falling heavily, erasing his footprints. He had noticed the shed that stood in back of the cabin, and had decided on his previous visits that the shed was used for storage. Perhaps he would find what he needed there.

He staggered and fell many times before he reached the shed. It took him a few moments to discover how to open the door, which was held together by a leather strap that hooked over a wooden peg. When he unfastened it, the door swung open noisily. Matio stood silently, waiting to see if the noise had carried to the cabin. When no one came to investigate, he cautiously entered the darkened shed. Feeling around in the darkness he discovered many animal pelts that would be beneficial to him. There was dried meat hanging from a hook in the ceiling. If he took some of the meat, he could eat without having to hunt in his weakened condition.

Loaded down with fur pelts and dried meat, he started the long, slow progress back to his shelter in the hollowed-out log. Many times he fell to his knees in a fit of coughing, but he always pulled himself up by sheer strength of will.

Once he reached his shelter, he crawled inside and covered himself with the warm furs, using one of them to block the wind out. He had used up all his strength, and he soon fell into an exhausted sleep. His last conscious thought was of the queen. How would she ever reach the king, if he were to die?

Matio's fever raged on for many days. Much of the time he was delirious and could not remember where he was. He was too weak to take nourishment, other than the snow he used to ease his thirst.

While Mara had been recovering from the birth of her son, Zeke had made her a rocking chair, which she now sat in rocking the baby. There was a warm fire blazing in the fireplace, and she hummed softly and smiled lovingly down at Andrew. She had liked the name Andrew, and when Jake and Zeke voiced their approval, she decided it was a good choice.

Andrew was such a good baby, he was content to lie in his cradle and look about the room, waving his little arms aimlessly in the air.

Mara noticed Jake was punching holes in a bear-skin and lacing a leather strap through it. "What are you making, Jake?" she asked.

He looked up and grinned at her. "It's sort of like what the Injuns carry their babies in. When we make the trek to the trading post for you to see the doctor, me and Zeke will take turns carrying little Andrew on our backs. He will be all warm and cozy, and you won't have to worry about him becoming too cold."

Jake and Zeke adored Andrew, almost to the point of being foolish over him. They were full of plans for him when he grew older. Sometimes she would see them standing over the cradle just watching Andrew sleep. She felt fortunate that they had come into her life. Mara knew if she never remembered who she was, it would not matter. She would be content to stay here forever. She did not delude herself about the kind of treatment Andrew would receive, should she ever return to civilization.

But here with Jake and Zeke he would grow up knowing only love and a sense of belonging.

Lately the two brothers had been talking about giving up trapping, and settling down to clear the land and try farming. She knew they would never be happy as farmers, and she had no intentions of allowing them to give up the trapping they both loved on her and Andrew's account.

There was a loud rap on the door and Jake rushed across the room, took his rifle down from over the fireplace and aimed it at the door. He and Zeke had not wanted to upset Mara, but several weeks ago they had discovered footprints in the lean-to. There had been no doubt in their minds that the prints had been made by a pair of moccasins, and, judging by the size of the man's feet, he was tall, like the Indians Mara had been abducted by. Nothing had been stolen but a few pelts and some dried meat, but Jake did not trust the Indian's motives. It could be that he was waiting to find Mara alone so he could take her away with him. Jake doubted that there were more than the one man. But he could always call on reinforcements.

"Who's there?" Jake asked in a booming voice.

"It is I, Du Lac, you grizzly old trapper. Let me in before I freeze to death," a heavily French-accented voice called from the other side of the door.

Jake propped his gun against the wall and opened the door. "I thought the Indians might have scalped you, you crazy Frenchman," Jake said in a cool voice, that plainly told Mara he was not happy to see the man. She surmised it must be the Frenchman Zeke had told her about.

The Frenchman laughed. "Only the Indian maidens are interested in Du Lac's hair, no."

His eyes were drawn to the woman who sat by the fire, and he stared at her, first in astonishment, and then in open admiration. He could not ever remember having seen any female who was so beautiful. She now smiled at him. She was almost too lovely to be real. Her hair was a mass of riotous golden curls. Her face was perfect, her mouth enticing, and her eyes were a color of green that he had never before seen.

"Tell me, my friend, Jake. Am I dead and dreaming, or is that an angel I see?"

Jake closed the door and gave Mara a look of apology. "This here's the princess," Jake said as he stepped between Du Lac and Mara. "You ain't to try any of your pretty words on her, or me and Zeke will save the Indians the trouble of scalping you," Jake said, in a voice that plainly showed that he meant what he said.

"Ah, princess, since Jake will not introduce us, may I present myself. I am known as Du Lac, and I am your willing subject," he said, sweeping her an exaggerated bow.

"I am pleased to meet you Monsieur Du Lac," she answered, smiling at the charming French man.

"No, no, not monsieur, just Du Lac. What name do you answer to other than princess?" he asked.

Mara looked at Jake for help, she did not know how to explain herself to a stranger.

Just then Du Lac's eyes fell on the baby in her arms, and he, too, looked at Jake. He had seen the dark hair and skin and knew the baby was of the

184

Indian race.

Jake's face turned red with anger. He was not at all pleased that the princess was being made to feel uncomfortable. "Are you planning to stay long?" Jake asked sourly.

"For the moment I am only passing through, but now that I have seen the princess, I will be returning." Du Lac answered arrogantly. He removed his jacket and tossed it carelessly on a nearby chair. Mara now saw that he was a handsome man, with sandy-colored hair and bright blue eyes. He was broad of shoulder, and Mara thought Zeke had been right, the ladies must surely love Du Lac, but to her he was no more than a friend of Jake and Zeke's. He in no way compared to the tall Indian she dreamed about, but then, no man could be expected to come up to her dream love.

"Has anyone ever told you of your loveliness, princess?" the Frenchman asked, with a twinkle in his eyes. He smiled, showing a mouth full of flashing white teeth, and Mara thought that he was out of place in the woods—he would fit every young girl's fantasy of a dashing pirate.

"I warn you, monsieur, I do not fall for pretty speeches. I have been warned about you by Zeke," she told him lightly.

"Oh, princess, you wound Du Lac. Now that I have seen you, I would never be satisfied with any other."

He turned to Jake. "I think I have lost my heart to this angel, this goddess."

"More than likely you will lose your head, if you do not watch your step," Jake said, bending over

185

Mara and picking Andrew up in his arms.

"But what are you doing with an Indian baby? Do you have a particular liking for Indians?" Du Lac asked.

Mara stood up and raised her head proudly. She looked straight into his eyes without flinching. "Andrew is my son," she told him.

Jake cleared his throat as he saw shock register on Du Lac's face. He handed the baby to Mara and motioned for the Frenchman to follow him outside. "Come with me and we will stow your gear in the lean-to," he said, walking toward the door, leaving Du Lac no choice but to follow him.

When both men left, Mara hugged Andrew tightly. She had just received a small sampling of what Andrew would have to contend with in the white world. Her heart was heavy for her son's sake. She loved him so much and could not bear to think what the future held for him.

When Jake felt he and Du Lac were far enough away from the cabin so they could not be overheard, he spun Du Lac around and glared at him. "I am giving you fair warning, Frenchman, you had better keep your hands off the princess. And I don't want you making anything about the baby, either. She has suffered a great deal, and I won't have the likes of you hurting her more."

"Jake, I did not know about the baby being hers. I still do not know what happened to her. Perhaps you would explain it to me."

Jake grabbed Du Lac by the shirtfront, and drew him closer. "It ain't none of your affair. All you need to know is that I would kill you if you was to touch her.''

Du Lac tried to loosen Jake's grip, but was unsuccessful. "I do not believe you like me, Jake, and I know you do not trust me.''

"I don't trust you the least bit, and I like you even less.''

"But why? I have never done anything to you.''

"Let's just say I have a gut feeling about you and let it go at that.''

"Your brother Zeke does not share your distrust of me,'' Du Lac said.

"That's the only reason you are allowed to come around. You step one foot out of line and you will be lying under the dirt before you can count three.''

"I will be moving on, Jake, but I will be back. Say good-bye to the princess for me, will you?''

Jake watched the Frenchman, not trusting his intentions. He was not sure whom he mistrusted most, the Indian who had brazenly gone into the lean-to, or Du Lac, whom he suspected would sneak behind a man's back to do his skullduggery.

"You will stay to supper, and then stay the night. I do not want the princess to think you left on her account. Just think on what I said to you, and you can be gone first thing in the morning.''

Dinner that night was an uncomfortable affair as far as Mara was concerned. The conversation was stiff and polite. She would often feel the Frenchman's eyes on her, but when she looked at him, he would glance at Jake.

She was glad when the meal was over and she could clean the table, while Jake and Du Lac talked in mumbled tones.

Du Lac could not keep his eyes from straying to the lovely golden-haired woman. He found himself wondering what it would feel like to touch her soft skin. She had a grace and elegance about her that was out of place in the crude cabin. He could easily imagine her dressed in silks and satins. Her speech was cultured, refined, and he found he wanted to know more about her. He noticed her firmly rounded breasts, and the way her hips swayed gracefully as she walked. He could tell she felt uncomfortable in his presence. He thought that when he returned he would try to gain her trust and approval. He already knew how that could be accomplished. He would reach her through the child.

Mara had finished washing the dishes, and little Andrew had been tucked snugly in his cradle in the loft. She would have liked nothing better than to excuse herself and retreat to the loft, but she did not want to appear rude, so she sat down in the rocking chair.

"Did you say this Indian broke into your lean-to?" Du Lac asked.

Mara could feel her heartbeat stop. "What Indian? Jake, what are the two of you talking about?" she cried, knowing her voice sounded hysterical.

Jake had tried to stop Du Lac before he spoke, but it was too late now, there was nothing to do but tell the princess the truth, he thought grimly. "There ain't nothing to be upset about, just some Injun broke into the lean-to and took some furs and food."

"But Jake, you said he was bigger than the

Indians around here," Du Lac said.

Jake cursed the Frenchman silently when he saw Mara's face whiten.

"Jake, I can tell you are trying to keep something from me. I think it would be best for you to be honest with me," Mara told him.

"All right," Jake said, sighing heavily. "This Injun was big, and me and Zeke think he might be from the tribe that took you. There don't seem to be more than the one and he ain't been around lately. Chances are, he went back to wherever he came from."

"But suppose you are wrong and he is watching the cabin, waiting for a chance to . . . oh, Jake I am frightened."

"No reason to be, me and Zeke ain't going to let nothing harm you and little Andrew."

Mara tried to push her fear aside, but she was not entirely successful.

As she lay in her bed that night she jumped at each noise. She wished Zeke would return. Was this nightmare ever to be over? Would she spend the rest of her life looking over her shoulder, wondering if some Indian would be hiding somewhere, ready to pounce on her?

The next morning at breakfast, Mara felt tired and tense. She had not slept well at all, and there were dark circles under her eyes.

Du Lac prepared to leave after he had eaten. He was stiff and polite as he told Mara goodbye under the watchful eye of Jake.

Mara felt relief after he had gone, there was something about him that made her feel uneasy. It was nothing she could put her finger on. It was something in the way he watched her. He would stare at her with something in his eyes that she could not put a name to.

The next few days Jake never left her side for any length of time. She knew he was more concerned about the Indian who had raided the lean-to than he would admit.

Mara tried never to think about the medallion. She stayed busy in the daytime. But at night she would often think about the tall, dark Indian who invaded her dreams. Sometimes he was very real to her, and at other times she would be frightened of her feelings for him. She was beginning to love him. It was foolish; he could not be real, and yet, to her, he was very real indeed.

Finally, the day came when Jake thought Mara was recovered enough to make the trip to the trading post to see the doctor. Zeke had returned a few days before, and they loaded their animal pelts onto the packhorses.

Jake lifted Mara onto the back of a horse, and she was surprised to see the lady's side-saddle. Zeke told her it had been their mother's, and they had kept it all these years, never knowing it would come in handy. He had replaced the cinch and stirrups, and Mara could find no fault with it. She smiled to herself, thinking how the brothers had kept remnants and mementos from their childhood. A lady's side-saddle was certainly not what one would expect two tough, grizzly trappers to cherish.

As they started out, Mara thought how strange they would appear to anyone who saw them. Two trappers, Jake with Andrew strapped to his back, and her, dressed in a homemade green print gown and bundled up in furs for warmth.

The weather was cold and crisp, and Mara was enjoying being out in the open after being cooped up for so long.

At night they all slept in a small tent, and Mara was aware of the extra precaution that Jake was taking. The two men slept with loaded guns beside them and were alert to every noise. The first night Mara had been a bit apprehensive, thinking the Indian might be following them, but Zeke had doubled back many times and assured her they were not being trailed.

Matio lay on his stomach peering through the thick growth of a bush. He could see the cabin clearly from his vantage point. He noticed that no smoke came from the chimney, and there did not seem to be anyone around. He was still weak from his sickness, and today was the first day he had been up to crawling out of the log in many suns.

The day passed slowly, and still he waited. It was almost sundown when he decided the cabin was empty. He stood up and walked silently toward the cabin. When he reached the door, he listened for a moment, but no sound came from inside.

He unsheathed his knife and fumbled with the

door, trying to see how to open it. He was relieved when he slipped a wooden bar sideways and the door swung open. He knew he would find no one inside since the door had been bolted from the outside.

The interior of the cabin was dark, and it took a moment for his eyes to adjust as he entered quietly. His senses were trained to pick up any sound that might spell danger. His hand tightened on the hilt of his knife as his eyes made a quick sweep around the room. He looked for something, anything that would show him that the queen still abided in the cabin.

Bending down he examined the ashes of the fireplace. They were cold. The fire had not been lit for at least two days. He stood up and dusted the ashes from his hands. The cabin was clean, and his sweeping gaze took in the two beds, the table and chairs, and the cupboard with its crude wooden dishes. He picked up a pot that was made of some heavy metal, and knew it was used for cooking. Seeing a loaf of some kind of white bread, he picked it up and tasted it. He found it not bad, but it could not compare with the sweet breads his mother made. However, he was hungry, and he ate without stopping, until the bread was all gone. He circled the room, looking for anything that would belong to the queen, but could see nothing. He felt fear and disappointment. Suppose while he had been sick they had taken her away. Spying the ladder that led up to the loft, he climbed it cautiously. When he reached the small room, the ceiling was so low he had to duck his head to stand up.

He looked at the bed covered with warm furs, and

then his eyes moved to the baby cradle. He had not been aware that there was a baby in the cabin.

He searched the room frantically. Opening a small chest he found the doeskin dress that belonged to the queen, and, wrapped inside of it, the golden medallion.

Wherever the two men had taken the queen, she would be back. It did not appear that the queen had been mistreated. But the men must be forcing her to stay with them, otherwise she would have gotten away and tried to return to the Seven Cities.

He did not understand many things, least of all the baby cradle.

He must devise a plan to rescue her, with as little danger to her as possible. If only he had not become ill, they would now be on their way home.

He needed to leave her a sign that he had been here. She had the medallion, so she would have guessed he had put it on the door, but he needed to leave something else to give her hope. Reaching up to his arm, he unclasped his silver and turquoise armband and placed it on her bed. When she returned she would see the armband and know she was safe.

# Thirteen

The past is lost and still I yearn.
That which is lost will not return.

Mara looked about the trading post with interest. The pungent smell of the many fur pelts that were stacked against the wall was the dominant odor. There were bolts of material, tins of coffee, sugar, flour, and many other staples needed by trappers who frequented the trading post. Mara had been dreading meeting the doctor's wife, since she knew many questions would come up about the birth of Andrew, but she found, to her relief, that Mrs. White had gone to visit her daughter.

Zeke was tending the horses and unloading the furs, while Jake was with the doctor in the back room. She knew he would be telling the doctor all about her condition. She sighed and looked down at Andrew, who was beginning to wake up. He saw his mother and gave her a sweet smile that tugged at her heart. How she loved her little dark-skinned baby. He was so sweet and always seemed to be smiling.

Jake entered through the door that led to the back room. "I spoke to the doctor and he wants to see you and Andrew now," he told her.

Mara entered the back room hesitantly. To her surprise, the room really looked like a doctor's office. There were medical books stacked neatly on a shelf, along with jars and bottles of pills and liquids. There were several sharp-looking instruments lying on a white cloth.

The man who smiled down at her from behind bushy white eyebrows looked more like a trapper than a doctor. He was dressed in buckskin shirt and trousers. His hair was laced with gray, and his hazel eyes twinkled as he offered her a chair.

"So, you are Jake and Zeke Cawfield's lost princess!" he said, as he pulled up a chair and sat down in front of her.

Mara nodded. She watched silently as the doctor checked Andrew over from head to toe. When he had completed his examination of the baby, he smiled and told her the baby was in excellent health. The doctor made no reference to Andrew's dark skin, and Mara knew Jake had cautioned him against it.

She began to feel more at ease as the doctor chucked Andrew on the chin and was rewarded with a winsome smile from the baby, which brought an answering smile from the doctor.

"Now, princess," the doctor said, turning his attention to her. "Tell me what is the first thing you can remember?"

"I can remember nothing past the day I awoke to meet Jake and Zeke. Everything before that is a blank."

"I see," he said.

"I assume Jake told you that I was captured by Indians."

"Yes, he told me." He studied her closely. He had been watching her manner since she had entered the room. She was well educated, and came from a well-to-do family. Her manner of speaking was cultured. Some things could not be faked, the way she walked, the way she spoke, as if she had been taught from birth to speak every word correctly. Dr. White had seen many beautiful women in his lifetime. His own wife was considered to be nice-looking, but this girl was lovely.

"Jake told me he and Zeke found you in June."

"Yes, that is correct."

"That is a very long time to live without a memory," he said in a sympathetic voice.

She reached out and took his hand. "You are a doctor, can you not help me? It is very upsetting not knowing who I am, or where I come from."

"I will do all I can to help you, but in your case, it may not be enough." He patted her hand. "Why did you not come to me sooner, then we could have begun a search for your family?"

"Jake did not think I should make the trip until . . ." She withdrew her hand and raised her head proudly, meeting his eyes squarely. The doctor drew in his breath at how lovely she looked at that moment.

"You waited until your baby was born," he finished for her.

"Yes."

"I see," he said. Reaching for his instrument bag, he made a thorough examination of her ears, eyes, and throat, just as he had with Andrew moments before.

"Nice teeth," he joked lightly, trying to put her at ease.

She gave him a half-smile, and he looked away quickly. My God, he thought, she is too lovely to be real. When he looked back at her she was watching him, waiting for him to say he would help her.

"I find nothing physically wrong with you. When you first woke up after Jake had found you, did you have a bump or a knot on your head?"

"No, there was nothing like that."

"If your loss of memory was not caused by a blow to the head, then it must be mental."

A smile lit her face. "Yes, perhaps I am a mental case."

He laughed. "That was not what I was implying. What I was saying is that your loss of memory must be from witnessing something so horrible you did not want to remember, so your mind simply shut it out."

"I do not understand."

"This has often happened to soldiers in war. They witness so much death and dying that their minds retreat behind a protective wall."

Mara's hand trembled as she covered her face. "Perhaps I saw my family murdered by the Indians," she whispered.

"Maybe not. It could have happened when you were attacked by the Indians."

"Sometimes I want to remember so badly, and at other times I am terrified at what I will remember."

He leaned back in his chair. "Do not try to rush it. The mind is a strange thing. We doctors know less about it than any other part of the human body. Perhaps, given time, you will remember everything.''

"Is it possible that I will never remember who I am?"

"Possible, but highly unlikely. What name do you go by?"

Mara favored him with a smile. "I have no name, so as you know, Jake and Zeke call me princess. *That's* highly unlikely, do you not think?"

He studied her lovely face. It did not seem so wrong to call her princess. She would rival any fairy-tale princess in grace and beauty. "Perhaps you *are* a lost princess," he said lightly. "Who can say."

Mara looked at him in astonishment. "I saw my reflection in the water, and I thought I might be pretty, but not beautiful.''

"Ah, I have found a lovely girl who does not know she is beautiful. A rare and wonderful combination.''

"Doctor, I believe you are teasing me."

He laughed deeply. "Has it ever occurred to you that you have something most women would give anything for?''

"What is that?''

"You do not know how old you are, so therefore you do not have to lie about your age. You can just pull an age out of the air, and use it as your own.''

She knitted her brow in thoughtfulness. "I tried to judge my age, by my reflection in the stream, but it was difficult. I think I must be around twenty-five, or even thirty, perhaps.''

For the moment the doctor was speechless, he could not believe she had so badly misjudged her own age. He took her by the hand and led her through the door to his own private living quarters. He stood her in front of a mirror that hung on the wall, and Mara stared at the stranger that was her own image. She was taken completely by surprise. The golden-haired girl who stared back at her was nowhere near as old as she felt. She swallowed a lump in her throat. She was pretty. The doctor stood just behind her, and she looked up at his reflection.

"How old would you say I am?"

"I would place you on the sunny side of twenty, Perhaps seventeen, or eighteen."

He watched as she smiled and turned to face him. "I find it a pleasant surprise, to know I am younger than I thought."

His smile creased the tiny laugh lines about his hazel eyes. "Not many women are handed the gift of youth."

Mara realized that she was taking up too much of the doctor's time. She shifted Andrew up to her shoulder and extended her hand to the doctor. "I want to thank you for seeing me."

"I am sorry I could not be more help to you. Try not to worry. Perhaps, one day when you least expect it, you will remember."

She crossed the room and his voice stopped her at the door.

"Send Jake and Zeke to me. I would like to speak to them about something."

When Mara reached the main room of the trading post, she saw Du Lac leaning against one of the counters. He stared at her, and she tried to smile, wondering why he made her feel so uncomfortable.

"Where are Jake and Zeke?" she asked, seeing they were not in the room.

"I do not care where they are, princess. At last, I have you to myself."

Mara looked past him and was grateful when she saw the two brothers entering the trading post. She rushed forward to relay the doctor's message to them, then watched as they disappeared into the office.

Du Lac walked casually over to her. She was a bit unsettled by the look in his eyes. Remembering her image in the mirror, she thought he might think her pretty. She wanted to draw away when his hand moved to her cheek, but she stood her ground.

"Oh, lovely princess, I have thought of little else since I last saw you. Are you an enchantress that you get inside a man's head and cause him to think all other women are plain compared to you?"

Andrew chose that time to awaken, and she was grateful she could turn her attention to him and try to block out the disturbing Frenchman.

Du Lac was not to be put off, however. He pushed a golden strand of hair from her face and stared at her long and hard. "Does it not matter to you that I have lost my heart to you?"

Looking up, she frowned. "I suspect a man such as yourself, has lost his heart many times."

"Not so, princess. I have never lost my heart . . . until now."

Mara walked away from him without answering. She did not want him to think she was rude, but she wanted some privacy to feed Andrew, and she was not at all sure she liked the Frenchman very much.

The doctor waited for the two brothers to be seated before he spoke. "I want to talk to you about the princess."

"She ain't sick, is she?" Zeke asked.

"No, her health is good, but I want to warn you about a few things. There is no way of knowing for sure if she will ever recover her memory. I could tell by talking to her that she comes from a very prominent social background. Chances are, her family is at this very moment searching for her. I want to caution you in case some member of her family should find her. She should not be told everything about her past at once. It could be too great a shock to her. Should anyone come to your cabin claiming to be her family, send them to me so I can warn them about her condition."

"Why?" Jake wanted to know.

"I once knew of a case like hers, where this woman was taken by the Indians. Years later she was found and returned to her husband. She could not adjust and finally took her own life. You do not want that to happen to the princess, do you?"

"No!" Zeke said, in a booming voice.

Dr. White nodded. "When spring comes, I am going to make the trek to St. Louis to pick up supplies. Now here's what I think I should do. I will put an ad in the papers, and post a notice asking if anyone has a wife, daughter, or sister missing that fits her description. I will leave word that they can get in touch with me here at the trading post. Does that meet with your approval?"

Zeke was undecided. He wished they could keep

the princess and little Andrew with them. But his good sense prevailed and he nodded his agreement, as did his brother. The princess did not belong with him and Jake, not if she had a family somewhere.

The two brothers stood up and shook the doctor's hand, and both of them left with heavy hearts.

It snowed on the travelers all the way home. Du Lac had accompanied them to the cabin. Mara noticed that Jake and Zeke never left her alone with the Frenchman, and she was glad.

Andrew had proved to be no trouble at all. He was either strapped to Jake or Zeke's back, with nothing showing but his little face. He seemed very alert for one so young, but Mara thought that might just be a proud mother's observation.

When they reached the cabin, Zeke laid a fire in the fireplace, while Jake climbed the ladder to the loft, so he could bring Andrew's cradle down and place it beside the warmth of the now roaring fire.

He lifted the cradle up and was about to leave the loft when he saw something shiny lying on the princess's bed. Setting Andrew's bed down, he picked up the object to examine it closely. Frowning, he turned it over in his hand. He had never seen it before, and he was almost certain it did not belong to the princess. It resembled an Indian armband, yet they were usually made of brightly colored beads, while this one was silver and turquoise. Jake was troubled by his discovery. He hated showing it to the princess. If it was hers, there was nothing to be concerned about, but if she had never seen it before, it could only mean that her presence had been discovered by the Indians, and this was their way of letting her know.

Pushing it into his pocket, he picked up the cradle and climbed down the ladder. Once below, he took Andrew from the princess and laid him in the cradle. He then took the armband from his pocket and held it out to her.

"What is that, Jake? It is very lovely."

"Look at it. Have you ever seen it before?"

By now, Zeke and Du Lac had gathered closer and they all stared at the armband.

Mara reached for it and turned it over in her hand. "This is very valuable. I have never seen it before."

Jake looked at his brother. "I found it lying in her bed in the loft."

Du Lac took the armband and studied it. "The craftsmanship is extraordinary. This would bring a lot of money."

Mara could feel her knees began to tremble, and she reached for Jake's hand. "Oh, dear God, Jake. They have found me, and this is their way of letting me know." Her voice was becoming hysterical. "What shall I do! Where can I hide?"

Jake hugged her protectively in his arms, while Zeke patted her arm. "Don't you worry. Me and Jake ain't gonna let no one, least of all no Injuns, take you."

"I am so frightened," she sobbed against Jake's wide chest.

Du Lac looked puzzled, "Why should you think that this armband belongs to an Indian? I have seen many different tribes, and none of them would be able to craft a thing of beauty such as this."

"You don't know the kind of Indians we are dealing with," Jake told him, "These ain't no ordinary Injuns like the ones we are used to."

"How is it that I do not know of this tribe?" the Frenchman asked.

Zeke shook his head. "Me and Jake killed us two of them, and we knew there was something different about them, but I am just now figgering out how different they really are."

Jake set Mara down in the rocking chair and took his rifle down from the rack. "I have been studying on it. At first when I saw the footprints in the lean-to, I figured there was only one man. But now I'm not so sure."

"How you figure that, Jake?" his brother asked.

"Cause this Injun ain't got no fear. He comes in here and leaves his calling card, to let us know he's out there watching us."

Zeke walked over and shot the bolt on the door, then checked to make sure the window was securely fastened. "We have to make sure the princess ain't never left alone, 'cause if I know Injuns, and I do, they will be watching and waiting."

"Why have they not attempted to rush us and take her by force?" Du Lac asked, as he checked his rifle to make sure it was loaded.

"Cause they must want her back real bad, but they don't want her to get hurt in an all-out fight," Jake said.

Mara buried her face in her hands. She felt fear so strong it left a bitter taste in her mouth.

When she climbed the ladder to her room she was

in a real state. Her secret fear had been realized. Mara was sure at any moment she would hear a wild whoop, and the Indians would surround the cabin, overcome them, and take her away.

She felt she needed comfort from her fear, so she removed the medallion from the chest. Holding it up in the dim candlelight she read the inscription. *I will seek who I am.* She expected to see the old Indian man as she had on previous occasions. But he did not appear. Checking to see that Andrew was covered, she blew out the candle and lay down on the bed, still clutching the medallion.

"Who am I?" she wondered aloud.

"You are called Mara," a voice beside her spoke up.

Turning her head she was not surprised to see the shadowy form of the old man. Suddenly her fear seemed to ebb, and she felt at peace. "Should I fear?" she asked.

"Have no fear, Mara. Soon you will be on your way home. Close your eyes. Sleep, Mara."

Her eyelids grew heavy, and she felt sleep overtake her. She closed her eyes and slept peacefully all night.

The next morning the three men were surprised to find Mara so cheerful, knowing the night before she had been on the verge of hysteria. She smiled brightly as she prepared breakfast, and greeted each of them warmly as she poured them a cup of steaming hot coffee. They looked at her baffled when she sat down, propped her elbows on the table, and laughed out loud.

"I know my name. I know who I am!"

Jake halted his spoon halfway to his mouth. "What!"

She lifted her cup of coffee to her mouth and took a sip, while three sets of eyes watched her. "My name is Mara."

"What else do you remember?" Du Lac spoke up.

"Nothing else, only my name."

"But how can you recall your name and nothing else?" Du Lac asked. "Do you know what your last name is?"

"No, all I know is my name is Mara. It is a strange name, is it not?"

"If you know your name, it won't be long before you recollect more about yourself," Zeke said around a mouthful of corn mush.

Mara stood up and spun around in a circle. "Is it not a glorious day?"

"Shows you ain't been outside," Jake told her. "It's snowing and the wind is whipping up a blizzard."

"I do not mean the weather. I mean life in general."

Jake and Zeke watched her as if she had taken leave of her senses. Du Lac watched her thinking that somehow, some way, he had to have her.

He was beginning to have crazy fantasies about her. Thought of settling down in one place, building a cabin, raising a family. He could almost envision himself returning to her at the end of each day. She would set a well prepared meal before him, and afterwards . . . he would take her in his arms, and remove her clothing one thing at a time, until she lay naked in his arms. Du Lac could almost feel the silkiness of her skin.

Good Lord! he thought, was he losing his mind? He had made himself a promise ten years ago when he had fled France, because of a woman, that he would never again become involved with the fair sex, and so far he had kept that promise. He had used women, yes, but they had not been important to him, merely objects. Something to be used for his pleasure and then tossed aside.

Thinking back, he tried to recall what Monique had looked like, but he could not remember her face. She had been blond and beautiful, and at the time he had thought he loved her.

Du Lac had been twenty-one years old that summer. He and the fair Monique had spent many happy hours in bed together. Their little affair had ended abruptly one night, when her husband, a wealthy merchant, had returned home unexpectedly and caught him and Monique in a very compromising situation.

Two days later, Du Lac and Monique's enraged husband had faced each other on a field of honor. It had been pistols at twenty paces.

Du Lac did not like to think of himself as a coward, but many witnesses that day had seen him fire his pistol early, killing his opponent instantly. He had fled the country, with the law not far behind him. He could never return to France. To do so would mean his arrest and imprisonment or even death.

Watching Mara's lovely face, now all he could

think of was making love to her. He was a man in love. He thought of all the women who had loved him, and how he had used them, only to toss them aside when he began to tire of them, but Mara was different from all other women.

He had to find a way to get her alone. If she wished it, he would build her a cabin close by, where she could be near Jake and Zeke.

He looked at the cradle where Andrew was sleeping. He was not too fond of the idea of raising another man's child, but Mara loved the baby, so he would allow her to keep him.

He was beginning to feel confident that she would consent to become his wife. After all, she could not remember who she was, and she needed a man to look after her.

"Mara," Du Lac said, testing her name out loud.

"Yes," she answered.

"I am glad to see you no longer fear the Indians. I will never let them harm you." He said confidently.

Mara thought of the armband that had been left on her bed where she would be sure to find it. She had begun to wonder if the man who had left it might be the tall Indian she had dreamed of so often. She found herself hoping he was real and not someone she had imagined. Mara wondered what she would do if he were to come to her and ask her to go away with him. She was beginning to wonder if he might not be Andrew's father.

"No I am not frightened of the Indians any longer," she said.

Du Lac tested the tip of his hunting knife, then slipped it into the sheath about his waist. "That is

208

good, Mara. But do not ever underestimate the Indians. They always seem to strike when least expected.''


As night fell, the winds died down and the clouds moved away, leaving a deep blanket of snow bathed in the bright moonlight, giving the illusion of daylight.

Andrew was sleeping peacefully beside a warm fire, and Jake and Zeke were cleaning their guns.

Mara felt restless, and she was on the point of being annoyed with the way the three men watched her every move. She had decided she could not live with the threat of Indians hanging over her head. Pulling a warm wrap about her shoulders, she walked to the door.

''Where do you think you are going?'' Jake said standing up abruptly.

''I am going out for a breath of fresh air. I do not intend to spend the rest of my life shut away in this cabin.''

Jake was beginning to know her moods very well, and when she got that stubborn set to her chin it meant she would have her own way, or there would be all hell to pay.

Du Lac had been waiting for the opportunity to get her alone, so he picked up his rifle and walked over to her.

''I will go with her,'' he told Jake. Seeing doubt in Jake's eyes he patted his rifle. ''Do not worry, we shall stay near the cabin.''

Outside, Mara took a deep breath of fresh air. ''It

is almost like an enchanted world," she said breathlessly. "The stars appear so close, I have the feeling I could reach out and touch them."

Matio watched from his hiding place, where he had been waiting all day. When he saw the queen, he almost called out to her, but then his eyes moved to the white man with the gun. He remembered very well how it felt to be hit with the fire from the weapon, and he did not want to feel the fire enter his body again.

"Mara," Du Lac said lightly, not knowing how to tell her what was on her mind. He decided it would be best to lead up to it slowly. "There are two schools of thought about the stars. I wonder which one you subscribe to?"

"What are my choices?"

He smiled down at her. "One theory is that each star is a giant ball of fire, and, should one come within thousands of leagues of a star, he would be burned to ashes in the flickering of an eyelash. The other theory is that the stars are cold, and if you were to get too close to them you would freeze."

"I do not want to believe either of your theories. I would like to think that each star is a world, very much like this one, with people who are similar to ourselves. I would like to think there is a place somewhere where the people live without fear and hunger, apart from the rest of the world. A special place . . . an Eden." Mara frowned, as something flickered in her mind, but it was a fleeting thought, nothing she could hold on to.

"I wish there were a place that was cut off from the rest of the world, where there was no greed, and no ugliness," she went on. When she saw how strangely Du Lac looked at her, she laughed nervously. "Of course there is no such place, is there?"

Du Lac turned her around so she was facing him. He touched her golden hair lightly. "What a strange, exciting woman you are. Are you a witch who has come to earth from one of those faraway stars, to entrap poor mortals such as I in your enchanted web?"

Matio could not understand the white man's words, but he could tell by his tone of voice that the man desired the queen. He waited to hear Mara rebuke the man, but when she spoke, her voice was soft.

"I am nothing more than a woman who has lost her identity. I neither seek to ensnare a man nor would I welcome any show of affection from one."

He tilted her chin up and stared into her green eyes. "Whether you set out to entrap me or not. I am indeed trapped. I myself did not see it coming. One day I walked into this cabin and there you were. When first I laid eyes on you I knew that I was a man who had lost his heart."

He lowered his head, and Mara knew he was going to kiss her. At first she wanted to pull away, but she remembered her dreams where the tall Indian had kissed her, and she wondered if Du Lac's kiss would feel the same. When his lips touched hers it was no more to her than his warm lips pressed against her cold ones.

Du Lac, however, was not having the same reaction to her. The feel of her soft lips caused his pulse to quicken and his heart to race.

Anger burned in Matio's heart as he witnessed the kiss. He could not believe the queen he had loved and worshipped would allow anyone other than the king to kiss her. He wanted to rush forward and tear her out of the white man's arms. In his anger he wanted to drive his knife into the man's heart. He might very well have done that very thing, had not the sound of the queen's voice stopped him.

Mara pushed Du Lac away from her, wishing she had not allowed him to kiss her. She was almost repelled by his touch. When he tried to pull her into his arms once more, she slipped away from him.

"Do not again attempt to kiss me. You are no more than a stranger to me. I do not think I like being kissed very much," she said, thinking she was being unfair to Du Lac. She had been comparing him to the man in her dreams, and no one could compare with him.

"I think you are only frightened of me. I have not been known for my patience in the past, but with you I am prepared to be very patient. I want you to be my wife."

"No! You must not say this to me. I do not even know who I am. I do not want to hurt you, but I do not like you well enough to marry you, even if I did remember who I am," she told him, hoping he would not say anything more about marriage.

"What about Andrew? He will need a father, and I am prepared to take on that role for him."

"I am cold," Mara said, not wanting to talk to the Frenchman any longer. How could he expect she would marry him? She did not even know him. "I am going in now."

Du Lac's eyes burned with anger. How dare she—a little nobody who did not even know who she was, who had given birth to an Indian brat—reject him. She would find out that he was not a man to say no to. He could do nothing for now, but the time would come when he would have her. He had offered her marriage, something he had offered no other woman. Now he would take her without benefit of a wedding.

Matio stood up as he watched the door close. His heart was heavy. He felt his king had been betrayed, and, in some way, that he too had been betrayed. He was not yet ready to give up. He would watch until he found her alone, then he would go to her and see if she would return to the Seven Cities with him.

## *Fourteen*

A glimmer of hope, from a bright golden sky.
Will I find my love with the dark, brooding eyes?

For the next week the weather remained clear. Jake had told Mara it was only temporary. It was the end of January and the winter had not yet released its hold on the land.

Since the night Du Lac had asked Mara to marry him and she had refused, he had not attempted to approach her. She hoped he had forgotten all about the incident, but sometimes she would catch him watching her and would feel fear.

Zeke and Du Lac had ridden out early that morning to check on their traps. Jake was at the back of the cabin chopping wood, and Andrew was asleep in his cradle.

Mara folded a white flannel blanket and added it to the stack of clean clothes she had taken from the makeshift clothesline Jake had strung across the cabin.

She heard Andrew stirring and bent over the cradle to smile down at him. "So, at last you are awake. You must be hungry." She lifted him in her arms, and unfastened her gown to nurse him. Andrew nursed hungrily, while Mara smiled down at him. Her heart overflowed with love for her dark-skinned son.

"You are such . . ." The door opened, and her heart stopped. She could still hear Jake chopping wood at the back, and she knew Zeke and Du Lac would not return until dark. Her hand went to her throat as she saw the Indian. He was not much older than herself, and he was tall and handsome, but he was not the one she had dreamed of so often. She tried to show a brave face. Zeke had told her that Indians respected bravery. She felt at that moment she must be the worst coward that had ever drawn a breath, because her legs were shaking and she felt like she might choke on her fear.

"W . . . what do you want?" she said clutching Andrew tightly in her arms.

"I do not understand when you speak in the white man's tongue," the Indian said, advancing toward her.

He had spoken to her in another language and she had understood him clearly. Mara took a step backwards and came up against the cradle, unable to retreat any further.

"What do you want?" she asked him, in the language he had spoken to her in.

"I have come for you."

She saw his dark eyes move to Andrew and she drew the blanket over his face, not wanting the man to see that her son was Indian. Her heart was drumming so loudly she was sure he could hear it. "Go away! I will not go with you. If you try to force me, I will scream, and I warn you, Jake will drive you away."

Slowly, he stepped closer. She could not guess his intentions, but she could see he was not worried about her threat. There was something in his eyes, though. Was it sadness or disbelief?

"Who does the baby belong to?" he asked. "I saw you with the white man."

Mara frowned. Why should he want to know about the baby unless . . . unless he thought it might be his. She searched her mind to think of something to say to him that would make him go away. "My son is . . . the son of the white man," she said, fearing that if he discovered Andrew was of Indian blood he would force both of them to go away with him.

He stepped in front of her and looked into her eyes. "Leave the child, then, come with me. We must hasten before the man with the flaming hair returns."

"No, I will not leave my baby, and I will not come with you."

The young Indian's eyes narrowed. "Do they hold you here by force?" Matio asked, not understanding why she was not happy to see him.

"No, I stay of my own free will. I wish you would go."

"Is it your command that I leave?"

"Yes, if it will make you go away, I command it."

"What do I say to the k . . ."

Just then the front door burst open and Jake stood with his rifle aimed at the Indian's chest. "Back away from her, Injun," he said in an ominous voice.

"Wait, Jake, he does not speak English, do not hurt him. He is just leaving," Mara cried.

"I can overcome the man, and get you safely away," Matio said, giving her one more chance. "Do you come with me?"

"Please go away, and do not come near me again," she said in a pleading voice.

Matio did not understand what had happened to his queen. Why would she not return home with him? Did she no longer love the king? He backed away from her, keeping his eyes on Jake and the rifle that was still aimed at him. When Matio reached the door, he looked at Mara. "I go because you command it. I will not trouble you again."

"I do not wish to ever see you again," she told him.

His eyes became sad, and he disappeared out the door. Jake followed, his rifle still poised. Fearing he might shoot, Mara flew across the room and grabbed his arm.

"Do not shoot. He will not trouble us again."

Jake lowered the gun and looked at her strangely. "You were speaking to him in his tongue?"

She stood on her tip-toes and peered over his shoulder, trying to see the Indian, but he had already disappeared. "I did not know I could speak in the language of the Indian. Oh Jake, what does it mean?"

Jake closed the door, and shot the bolt. He then took Andrew from her and laid him in the cradle. Mara watched him as if she were in a daze. Taking her hand, Jake sat her down beside the fire.

"We got some talking to do. I haven't understood half of what happened here today."

"Jake, I myself do not know what happened."

"Tell me what the Injun said to you?"

"He wanted to take me with him. He seemed to think I was being held here against my will. When I told him to go away, he said he would if I commanded him to."

"Sounds mighty strange to me. Did you see his headband?"

"No, I was too frightened to notice much about him."

"It was like the armband we found. I ain't sure, but I think he was one of the Injuns me and Zeke shot."

"But you said you killed those two."

"Well, I guess I was wrong."

"Jake, I would have been with the Indians a long time to learn to speak with them."

"I heard me lots of Injun talk, but I ain't heard nothing like the two of you were saying."

"Jake, there was something else. He asked me who Andrew belonged to. I told him his father was a white man. I was afraid he might be the father, and if he knew about Andrew he would force us to go with him."

"I sure wish you could remember who you are, princess. I got me a powerful curiosity, about the kind of tribe we are dealing with here."

Andrew began to fuss, so Mara picked him up. As she rocked him, her mind was troubled. Who was the Indian? Why had he left when she said she would not go with him? She knew he was not afraid of Jake.

Thinking back, she began to remember other things about him. His eyes had been sad at times, and she knew he would not have harmed her or Andrew.


Palomas was the first to hear the rider. He motioned for Jeffery to follow him into the woods, where they hid behind some bushes.

Jeffery tried to check his horse, but the high-spirited animal pranced around, turning sideways. Dismounting, he grabbed the reins and tried to soothe his horse by running his hand over its long, sleek neck.

They did not have to wait long for the rider to draw even with them. Palomas immediately recognized Matio and called out to him, but the thunder of Matio's horse's hoofs drowned out his voice, so he urged his horse forward into a gallop, hoping to catch the young warrior before he had gone too far.

Matio, hearing his name being called, reined in his horse and looked back over his shoulder. When he saw Palomas, he vaulted to the ground, and ran back down the trail. His face showed his happiness, as Palomas dismounted and grabbed him, and they greeted each other in Lagonda fashion, by clasping wrists. By now Jeffery had joined them, and he too greeted Matio.

"I thought you were among the spirits," Palomas said.

"I also thought that you walked with the dead," Matio replied.

"Where have you been all this time?" Jeffery asked.

"I have been searching for the queen, my captain."

"As we all have, Matio, without any success, I fear," Jeffery said, and his voice showed how weary he was.

Matio looked into the green eyes of his captain, hating to be the one to tell him about his sister. "I have just been with the queen," he said, lowering his head.

Jeffery grabbed him by the shoulders and shook him in his excitement. "You have seen Mara! Is she well?"

Palomas read disillusionment in the young warrior's eyes, and he waited for Matio to speak.

"I do not know how to tell you this, but the queen is with three white men and she ordered me to leave her. She did not want to come away with me."

Jeffery looked astounded. "Was she being held against her will?"

"No, my captain. I made sure that was not the case. She stays with the white men because she desires to." Matio could not bring himself to tell the queen's brother about the baby.

"Tell me how I can find my sister," Jeffery said.

Matio bent down and picked up a stick and began drawing directions to the cabin in the snow.

Palomas stood silently as Jeffery stood up and put his hand on Matio's shoulder. "Have you searched for the queen all this time, Matio?"

"Yes, my captain."

"You have done well. I am sure the king will reward you for your loyalty."

"It was no more than any other would have done

in my place," Matio said, trying not to show how proud he was to receive praise from his captain. "Do I return to the cabin with you?" he said, changing the subject.

"No. I want you to ride as quickly as you can to the king. Tell him that you have found my sister and for him to wait by the river where she was abducted, and I shall bring her to him."

"Where do I find the king?"

Jeffery picked up the stick and drew three marks in the snow. "Follow the trail of the three marks, and you will find your king."

"My captain, suppose the queen will not come with you?"

Jeffery frowned. "There is something wrong here, Matio, but rest easy. When we meet at the river, my sister will be with me. I will bid you farewell, for now. Make haste and find your king. He has been very worried about the queen."

Matio nodded. He thought the king would not be well pleased when he heard all he must tell him about the queen. "I will find the king and tell him to wait for you," Matio said.

Matio mounted his horse and looked at Palomas, wishing he could ask his advice on telling the king about the baby.

Palomas ran his hand over the sleek neck of the horse Matio was riding. "This is a fine-looking animal. How did you come by him? The last time I saw you, you had no horse."

"I found this one, Palomas. Apparently someone had lost him." Matio said with a straight face.

"Where did you find him?" Palomas wanted to know.

Matio grinned. "I found him in a white man's barn."

Palomas drew back his hand and slapped the horse on the rump. The animal charged forward, and Palomas had to yell to be heard. "I charge you with the task of telling the king one of his warriors has turned thief."

Jeffery stood silently watching the young warrior disappear down the trail. "He has done well, Palomas."

"Yes, he found Mara where others failed. He has done more to protect her than I, who am her protector."

"You are still stinging from Tajarez's anger," Jeffery observed.

"I will never forget that my king was displeased with me, and with good reason."

"Let us not dwell on that just now. I believe I shall change clothes, since I am to go calling." Jeffery removed his trousers, shirt, and boots from his saddle bag and began changing from his fringed buckskins into the clothing of a well-dressed gentleman.


Palomas pushed the undergrowth aside to get a better view of the cabin. Smoke was drifting skyward from the chimney, and he could smell the aroma of roasting deer meat.

"Shall we invite ourselves to dinner, Palomas?"

"I think it would be better if you would go alone, Jeffery. I will wait here and watch for any sign of trouble."

"I suppose that would be best. I am not sure how I will be received."

"If you should need me, I will come to you at once," Palomas said.

"Pray that I find Mara well."

"That is my desire."

Palomas watched Jeffery approach the cabin. He then led the horses a short distance into the woods, secured their reins to a tree, and returned to his vantage point just as Jeffery rapped on the door.

Mara had gone to bed early and had fallen asleep almost instantly. Du Lac was running his trap line and was not expected back until later. Jake and Zeke were sitting at the table eating a late supper when they heard the knock on the door.

Jake looked at his brother questioningly. "Must be Du Lac."

The knock came again. "Is anyone here?" a muffled voice called out.

"It's a stranger," Zeke said, grabbing up his rifle and aiming it at the door, while Jake crossed the room and jerked the door open. His mouth gaped open when he saw Jeffery.

"We don't get no callers out here. What you want?"

Jeffery looked at the huge trapper. He did not seem very friendly, and he could see the second man, who was aiming a gun at his chest. He decided not to reveal the reason for his visit until he was sure what the situation was.

"It is a cold night. If you would allow me to come

in and warm myself I would appreciate it."

Jake looked at the stranger suspiciously. He could not see much of his face since he was bundled up in a hooded fur jacket. He was sure a fancy talker though, and Jake wondered what the likes of him was doing at his door.

"If you got any weapons, leave them outside."

Jeffery reached inside his jacket and unbuckled the belt around his waist and let it drop to the ground.

"This knife is the only weapon I have on me," he told Jake.

"Step in, then. You got a name?"

Jeffery pushed the hood of his jacket off his head, an offered his hand to Jake. "My name is Jeffery Golden, lately of St. Louis."

"I heard tell of some Goldens lived at St. Louis. They lived in a fancy house overlooking the Mississippi River. They any kin of yours?" Zeke asked, lowering his rifle.

"Yes. My father and mother died three years past, but my brother David still lives in St. Louis. Have you not heard of me?" Jeffery asked, thinking surely Mara would have told the men about him.

Jake looked at him closely. There was something vaguely familiar about him, but he could not say what it was. "Why should you think we know about you?"

"I just thought you might know someone who would have mentioned me."

"Nope," Jake said, still not trusting the stranger. "Take your jacket off. If you of a mind to, you can eat a bite with us."

224

Jeffery removed his heavy jacket and made a sweeping glance of the cabin. There was no sign of Mara. His eyes moved to the ladder that led up to the loft, wondering if she would be up there. If she was, she must be asleep, otherwise she would have heard his voice.

Jeffery became aware the two trappers were looking him over. "I would be pleased to dine with you. I am rather famished."

Zeke motioned for him to sit at the table, while Jake sliced a generous slice of venison steak, put it on a plate and handed it to Jeffery

"You a trapper?" Zeke asked, knowing the answer before he asked the question. This fancy-talking gentleman wouldn't know the first thing about trapping, he thought.

Jeffery took a bite of the meat and found it to be palatable.

"No, I am not a trapper." He had decided not to divulge too much information about himself just yet.

"You on your way to Mitchel?" Jake asked.

"Never heard of it."

"It's a town about three weeks from here."

"I see." Jeffery looked from one man to the other, deciding he would turn the tables and ask the questions.

"You two trappers?"

"It's a living." Zeke volunteered.

"Have you lived out here long?"

"Off and on for ten years."

"The deer meat is very good. Thank you for allowing me to share it with you."

"You are a fancy-talking fellow. Don't look like

225

you belong in the backwoods," Jake said at last.

Jeffery pushed his plate aside, tired of playing questions and answers.

"Let's quit dancing and start talking," Jeffery said, leaning forward. "You both know I am not from around here. His eyes fastened on the face of the man with the red beard, watching his reaction to his next words.

"I am searching for someone." Jeffery saw the look that passed between the two men.

"Who you looking for?" the man with the red beard wanted to know.

"I am searching for my sister." His words fell heavy on the room that had suddenly become silent. "Perhaps you have heard of her. Her name is Mara. She has hair the same color as mine, and the same green eyes. Some say we look like twins, but in truth I am several years older than she."

Jake and Zeke looked at the blond man with new understanding. He did bear a striking resemblance to the princess, and he had called her by her name.

The look Jake gave his brother warned him not to say anything until they knew more about the man's intentions toward Mara.

"If you lost your sister, shouldn't you have taken better care of her?"

"It was through no fault of mine that she was lost. I love her, and she has a husband who is out of his mind with worry for her safety, as well as a twin son and daughter."

"You say she is married?" Jake said, giving Zeke a guarded look.

"Yes, her husband is a powerful, influential man.

226

He has great wealth and is willing to pay much to get her back," Jeffery said, wondering why Mara had not told the two men that she was married. He could tell they had been surprised to learn she had a husband.

"Zeke and me don't have no use for gold. We got all we need right here."

"If you do not care for gold, perhaps you would help me find her, so she can be reunited with a man who loves her more than his own life, and has been in despair, fearing for her safety." Jeffery realized that the two men knew more than they were saying, and wondered why they were being so secretive.

"How come this husband allowed her to be taken by Injuns if he loves her so much?" Jake asked.

Jeffery's eyes narrowed to icy green pinpoints. These were the two men who had shot Palomas and Matio, he thought. Good God, they thought they had *rescued* her! He was puzzled. Why had Mara not told them the truth? What were these men trying to hide? He decided it was best not to tell them that Mara was married to an Indian. If she had not told them about Tajarez she must have her reasons.

"Her husband was not with her when she was . . . taken," he said. "He is at this time scouring the countryside searching for her."

"I want to hear more about what your sister looks like," Zeke said, already convinced that the man spoke the truth.

"As I told you, she is of the same coloring as myself. The last time she was seen, she wore a doe-skin dress, with gold beading. Oh yes, she was also wearing a golden medallion about her neck."

Jake jumped to his feet, a broad grin lighting his face. "There ain't no use you looking no further. I know where your sister is. She is at this moment sleeping up in the loft."

Jeffery stood up slowly. "I want to see her."

"Not yet," Zeke said in a hushed tone. "There are some things we need to tell you about your sister."

"Is her health good?" Jeffery asked quickly.

"Yep, me and Jake took her to a doctor. He said she was fine, 'cept for one thing."

"What is that?"

"She ain't got no memory. She clean forgot who she is. She don't know nothing about having a brother, nor a husband and babies, for that matter."

"My God," Jeffery said, sinking down onto the chair. That explained why she had not told them about Tajarez. "How did this happen to her?"

"We don't rightly know," Jake said, "when we found her, she didn't know who she was."

"This explains many things," Jeffery said beneath his breath, thinking about Matio's telling him Mara did not want to go away with him. She had not known who Matio was.

"You had better brace yourself, Mr. Golden," Jake said in an uneven voice. "Mara done had a baby, and it ain't her husband's. It's an Injun baby. The Injuns who took her must have . . . well you know what I mean."

Jeffery tried to control his facial muscles, to keep from smiling. Of course the baby would look like an Indian, since Mara's husband was Indian. He could not say this to the two men, however.

"Is the baby well?"

Jake looked relieved, he had not expected the princess's brother to take the news about the baby so well. "The baby is in good health. It don't matter to you that your sister had some Injun's baby?"

"I love my sister a great deal, therefore any child she would have I shall love also."

"That's easy for you to say, but what about her husband? How will he treat Andrew?"

"Andrew?"

"Yep, that's the baby's name. Me and Zeke here don't want the princess to be hurt. She loves that baby, and if her man can't accept Andrew, it will hurt her."

"You have my word that her husband is an extraordinary man. You need not be concerned. Andrew will be well loved."

"Tell me," Zeke spoke up, "does she have a good marriage? Me and my brother have become attached to her. We wouldn't like to see her returned to a man who ain't good to her."

"You have my word, theirs was a love match. I have seldom, if ever, seen two people who love as deeply as Mara and her husband. If my sister had not lost her memory she would tell you this for herself."

"I think I should tell you, the doctor warned us against telling her too much about her past at one time. He said it could be dangerous for her," Jake said in a quiet tone.

"Where did she see a doctor?"

"At the trading post. The doctor said she might get worse if she gets a shock."

"I am glad you told me this," Jeffery replied, thinking how much of a shock it could be for Mara to learn that she was married to an Indian, since she thought she had been captured and ravished by one.

Jeffery stood up and smiled. "I told you my name when I came in, but you failed to tell me yours."

Jake extended his hand. "I would be Jake Cawfield, and this here's my brother Zeke."

Jeffery shook hands with both men. "I am glad to make your acquaintance. It seems that I owe you a great debt for taking care of my sister." Jeffery knew he could not tell the two brothers that it was because of them that Mara had been separated from her family. They would never understand, nor believe she was married to the mighty king of the Lagonda tribe.

The three men turned their attention to the front door as Du Lac entered the cabin. As he removed his outer jacket he stared at Jeffery. The man looked out of place, he thought. His dress was that of a gentleman. Du Lac immediately saw that the stranger bore a remarkable resemblance to Mara.

Jake leaned toward Jeffery and spoke in a quiet tone so only Jeffery and Zeke could hear. "Don't say nothing to him about the princess having a husband, he might let it slip to her."

Du Lac ambled over to Jeffery and looked him up and down in an insulting manner. "You are a long way from a fancy drawing room are you not?" he said, with a heavy French accent.

Jeffery's green gaze seemed to pin the Frenchman with its intensity. "I am Jeffery Golden. You are a long way from France, are you not?" he said in an equally insulting tone.

Jake smiled to himself, glad that the Frenchman

had received better than he gave.

"You have come for Mara?" Du Lac asked.

"Mara is my sister. I have come to take her home," Jeffery said, not liking the newcomer in the least.

"I had hoped her family would never find her."

Jeffery raised his eyebrow. "A strange desire. I wonder why you would hope that?"

The Frenchman bowed slightly. "I am known as Du Lac, and I had hoped to convince your sister to become my bride."

"What was my sister's answer to that?"

"She said no the first time I asked her, but I think when her memory returns she would say yes."

It was Jeffery's turn to look Du Lac over. His expression plainly showed what he thought of the man as a suitor for his sister's hand. "You reach high, Du Lac."

The insult did not go over Du Lac's head. Jake was enjoying himself. He had never liked the Frenchman, and now Mara's brother was cutting him down to size. Zeke, who had liked Du Lac in the past had come to see him as the pompous fool he was, and he grinned broadly.

"I would have thought you would like to see your sister married, since she gave birth to a savage's brat," Du Lac said angrily.

Jeffery towered over the man, wishing he dared teach him the lesson he deserved. He would have liked to have knocked the Frenchman to the floor, but instead, he would beat him with words.

"You must think highly of yourself. I can assure you my sister's lowest servant outclasses you."

"Do not let Jake and Zeke's pet name for your sister go to your head, monsieur. She is not really a princess," Du Lac said, through clenched teeth.

"You are right, monsieur, Mara is not a princess. She is a queen."

"Now it is you who reaches high. Do you think me a complete fool?"

Jeffery decided he had sparred enough with the Frenchman. He turned to Jake. "I would like to see my sister now."

"Is the princess a real live queen?" Zeke asked.

Jeffery looked the red-headed man in the eyes. "I had not intended to reveal her identity, but I can assure you, in all honesty, that Mara is indeed a queen."

Du Lac's eyes widened. "Of what country is your sister queen? How is it that Jake and Zeke found her among the Indians?"

Jeffery ignored Du Lac and spoke instead to Zeke. "I am sure you will understand the need for secrecy. I am sure also that the two of you will not say anything to my sister about this."

The brothers nodded, as if in a state of shock. It was hard for them to think of their princess as being real royalty.

Du Lac sat down in one of the chairs and propped his feet on the table. "I do not believe you. How do we know you are who you say you are?" he said lazily.

Fire leaped into Jeffery's eyes, and again he resisted the urge to throw a punch at the Frenchman.

"Du Lac, why don't you shut up," Zeke said angrily. "This ain't none of your affair."

"Don't pay him no mind," Jake told Jeffery. "He thinks the good Lord put him on earth to service all women."

Du Lac lifted his feet from the table and stood up. "I can see that I am not welcome here, so I will leave." He grabbed up his jacket on his way to the door and threw it over his shoulder. "I will be back," he said between clenched teeth. There was anger in his heart, and he knew Mara had not seen the last of him.

"Will you go up and awaken my sister now?" Jeffery asked Jake. "I am anxious to see her."

"I'll do it," Jake volunteererd. "Give me time alone with her to tell her about you."

"Thank you, Jake. Tell her I would like to see Andrew also."

# Fifteen

How will it end, how will I know?
Where do I flee, where do I go?

Mara was awakened from a sound sleep as someone shook her gently by the shoulders.

"Mara, wake up, I want to talk to you," Jake told her.

Blinking her eyes, she sat up slowly. "Is something wrong?" She was not yet fully awake, and she glanced at the cradle to see that Andrew was still asleep.

"No, there ain't nothing wrong. I got good news to tell you." He pulled a blanket about her shoulders and tucked it beneath her chin before he spoke again. "There is a man below who says he is your brother."

Mara fumbled around in the half-light for the candle. Seeing her intentions, Jake found the candle and lit it for her. He could see her eyes were full of disbelief and uncertainty.

"Are you sure he is my brother, Jake? Could there be a mistake?"

"I am sure he is your brother, princess. He is the

spittin' image of you. He says the two of you could pass for twins. 'Course you are the pretty one,'' he said teasingly, trying to ease her fright.

"What is he like? Will he like me, do you think?"

"As to what he is like, he's a gentleman, talks all fancy, like you do. I liked him, and as to if he will like you, he said he loved you and had been searching for you real hard.''

Mara's hand trembled as she tried to smooth the tangles from her hair by running her fingers through the golden curls.

"Jake, did you tell him about Andrew?''

"I told him and he didn't seem to mind. He said to have you bring Andrew below so he could see him.''


Jeffery watched as Mara climbed down the ladder. When she reached the bottom, she turned to face him. He searched her face for any sign of recognition, but the green eyes that looked back at him were wide with apprehension.

Mara stared at the handsome stranger who claimed to be her brother. His dress stated that he was a gentleman. His face eased into a smile and she waited for him to speak, not knowing how to react to him.

He walked slowly toward her, then reached out and took her hand and squeezed it, trying to reassure her. He could hardly stand to look into her beautiful eyes and know that she viewed him as a stranger, but he knew he could not let her see his distress.

"Hello, Mara. I am sure Jake explained to you

that I am your brother."

"I . . . can see that you and I are of the same coloring. Are you sure I am your sister?" she said frowning.

The smile he flashed her lit his whole face. "I can assure you that you are my sister."

Jake, who had been standing behind her, handed Andrew to her and motioned for Zeke to follow him outside, so the brother and sister could be alone.

"I am embarrassed that I do not know you. What is your name?"

"My name is Jeffery, Jeffery Golden."

"I am Mara Golden?"

He hesitated a moment. "You were born Mara Golden." He took her arm and led her over to the warm fire and sat her down in the rocking chair. "Mara, may I see Andrew?" he asked, sitting down in the chair beside her. He held out his arms, and she handed him her son, reluctantly. She wanted to look away when he took Andrew and pulled the blanket aside, fearing what his reaction would be to her baby.

Jeffery smiled down at his tiny nephew, who could only be Tajarez's son. Jeffery thought Andrew looked more like his father than the prince royal did. "He is a very handsome boy." Lowering his head he kissed the baby on his smooth cheek, a tender gesture that startled Mara.

"Well, Andrew, I am your Uncle Jeffery. You and I are going to become very good friends."

"You do not mind that he is an Indian?" Mara blurted out, almost loving the tall blond man who was so kind to her son.

"He is your son, Mara, therefore I shall love him."

Her green eyes became misty. "I did not expect you to be so understanding . . . and loving."

"Mara, you do not remember this but you and I were closer than most brothers and sisters," he told her gently. "I am just so happy that I found you. At times I feared you were lost to me forever."

"I am sorry I do not remember. I can imagine liking you a great deal," she said earnestly. "Do we have any other brothers and sisters?"

"We have a brother David who lives in St. Louis; he is married to Linda. You are the only sister David and I have." His face eased into a grin. "Who would need another sister when I have you to bully me? You have a sassy mouth, and if you do not agree with something, your temper can flare, scorching everything in your path."

Mara laughed. "I sound simply horrid. I am surprised you should search for me at all."

"Not so, Mara. I lived in fear that I would never find you," he said in all sincerity.

"Jeffery, I think I am going to like being your sister. It is wonderful knowing I belong to someone. For so long now I have been lost. Jake and Zeke have been so good to me and I love them, but it is not the same as having one's own family."

His hand covered hers, and he looked deeply into her eyes. "Honey, I know you have lived through hell, but it is all but over. I have come to take you and Andrew home."

Just hearing the word home gladdened Mara's heart. She was not lost anymore. She belonged to someone.

"When will we leave?"

Andrew awoke and Jeffery could not help smiling down at the beautiful baby boy. "I was told by Jake that there is a trading post not far from here. I will ride there and get all the supplies we will need for the homeward journey. I will purchase a tent and warm clothing for you and Andrew. Can you think of anything else you will need?"

"Have you much money?"

He grinned. "Would it surprise you if I told you we are extremely wealthy?"

"No, I guess I never gave money much thought. I only meant, I would need a horse and side-saddle."

Jeffery knew now was not the time to tell Mara she had not ridden side-saddle in a long time. He supposed she would be shocked to learn she rode as any Indian maiden would.

"Let us hope we will be able to find a lady's side-saddle at the trading post."

Her forehead creased into a frown. "Yes, it would be awful if I could not ride a horse."

Jeffery reached for his jacket and withdrew something from the pocket and handed it to Mara. "I want you to give this to Jake and Zeke, as payment for looking after you."

"It feels heavy."

"It contains a great deal of gold."

"Are you sure we can afford such a large sum of money?"

He laughed. "I can assure you we can." He handed Andrew to her and stood up. "I will leave you now. Try and get plenty of rest, we have a long journey ahead of us."

Jeffery, I am sure Jake and Zeke would expect you to stay here for the night," Mara said not wanting him to leave. She liked him very much, and was almost certain he would not return for her and Andrew.

He seemed to read her thoughts. "Mara, I will return within a week's time. I would not have come all this way searching for you, to abandon you now that I have found you."

"Jeffery, I really am glad you are my brother. I think you are very handsome."

He laughed and kissed her on the forehead, seeing a trace of the sister he loved so well. "I will remind you that you said that when you get your memory back."

Mara felt as if the cabin was strangely empty after Jeffery had gone. He had given her something she could not define, a sense of belonging. He had a magnetic personality that seemed to draw her to him. She wished more than ever she could remember the past, and what she and her brother had meant to each other.

The door opened and Jake and Zeke entered the cabin. It hit Mara hard that she would have to leave her two best friends. For so long now they had been her only family. It would be a sad day when she had to ride away and leave them.

Jake saw the tears in her eyes and bent down beside her. "Don't cry, little princess. We always knew the day would come when your family would find you and you would have to go away."

"It is not that I do not want to go with my

brother. I just do not want to leave the two of you."

Zeke knelt down beside his brother and wiped a tear from Mara's cheek. "It was good we got to keep you for a while, but we always knowed that you didn't belong with us. You belong with your family."

Mara leaned her head on Zeke's shoulder. "Oh Zeke, I love you and Jake so much. I will think of you often."

When she looked up she saw tears swimming in Zeke's eyes and knew she must retreat up the ladder before she broke down completely. Clutching Andrew tightly in her arms she moved hurriedly across the room.

"There is something my brother left for you on the table," she said climbing the ladder.

Mara had disappeared into the loft when the door opened and Du Lac entered.

"I saw Mara's brother leave, so I decided to return. I did not like that man."

"He didn't think too highly of you, either," Jake snorted.

Zeke picked up the leather pouch from the table and emptied the contents into his hand. All three men stared at the gold in silence. Du Lac reached out and lifted a gold nugget. Whistling through his teeth, he looked at the brothers.

"Where did this come from?"

"Jeffery Golden left it for me and Zeke."

"We ain't going to keep it, are we Jake?"

"Nope."

"I think you are both crazy. If you do not want the gold, I will take it," Du Lac said.

Jake returned the gold to the pouch and tucked it in his belt. "This goes back to the princess's brother."

Du Lac's eyes glazed over with greed. What would happen, he wondered, if he took Mara away? How much would her brother pay to get her back.

The brothers did not see the greed on the Frenchman's face, nor did they know how much he desired Mara. His eyes flamed passionately as he looked up the ladder to the loft where she slept.

Palomas watched as Jeffery approached him, trying to read his face, but Jeffery's face gave nothing away. Jeffery untied his horse and mounted solemnly.

"Do you stay here all night, Palomas, or do you ride with me to buy Mara a horse, so we can take her home?"

Palomas could not hide his joy. "You have seen her, she is well?"

"Yes, my friend I have seen her, and her health is good. She has one slight problem, though. I think you should know she has lost all memory of the past. She did not even know me."

Palomas mounted his horse and looked toward the cabin. "How can such a thing happen?"

"I am not sure, but there is a doctor at the trading post. He has seen Mara, and I want to talk to him."

"Mara will not know me?" Palomas asked.

"No, I did not even mention you to her, nor did I tell her about Tajarez. There is more to tell you."

"Not more bad news, I hope."

"No, this is good news. Tajarez has a newborn son!"

"She does not know Tajarez is the baby's father?"

"No, I did not tell her," Jeffery said, urging his horse forward. He was anxious to reach the trading post and return to his sister.

Jeffery tapped his fingers on the arm of the chair he was sitting in while he looked at Dr. White.

"You think it would be harmful to her to tell her about her husband?"

"One can never be sure in these cases, but I would advise against telling her until she gets to know the man, and to trust him."

Jeffery leaned forward. "I will tell this to her husband, I am sure I can convince him it is in Mara's best interest to be patient." He sounded more confident than he felt. Tajarez was not long on patience, but he did love Mara, and in the end he hoped Tajarez would see that Mara needed time.

Jeffery stood up and shook the doctor's hand. "I thank you for seeing me."

"I am glad you have found your sister. She is a beautiful little lady, it is good to know she will soon be reunited with her family. One thing though before you go: How will her husband take to the child?"

Jeffery smiled. "Take my word for it Doctor, he will treat Andrew as if he were his own son."

Jeffery had been gone for over a week, and Mara

found time weighing heavily on her. She moved about the spotlessly clean cabin looking for something to do to make the time pass more quickly. Zeke and Du Lac had been gone for two days. Jake was in the woods somewhere, and she did not expect him back until dinnertime. She checked on Andrew and found him sleeping. Picking up the broom Zeke had made for her, she started sweeping the already clean floor. She was so deep in thought she did not hear the cabin door open, nor did she see Du Lac until he stood in the path of her broom.

"You startled me, I did not hear you come in," she said side-stepping him.

"It is much too nice a day to spend indoors. Come for a ride with me. It is the last chance I will have to talk to you alone," he said taking the broom from her and standing it against the wall.

"No, I do not want to wake Andrew, and I cannot leave him alone. Jake is in the woods."

Du Lac grabbed her by the arm and swung her around. "Come with me, Mara, I do not have time to play games."

She looked at him quickly, hearing the urgency in his voice. "I do not know what you mean." Just then she saw the leather pouch tucked in his belt and recognized it as the gold her brother had given Jake and Zeke. She had seen the pouch attached to Jake's belt this very morning before he went into the woods.

"What are you doing with that pouch, Du Lac? Where is Jake?" she asked, feeling that something was dreadfully wrong.

He lifted her into his arms, and she tried to squirm

free. "Be still, Mara, I am much too strong for you. I tried to be nice, but you would not come with me. No matter, one way or another, it is all the same to me." He grabbed her fur wrap from the hook where she always kept it and carried her out the door.

"You had better put me down. Jake will return any time and he will make you sorry you ever touched me."

Du Lac mounted his horse with Mara in his arms. "I would not expect any help from Jake, he is unable to help anyone now."

"What are you saying, what have you done to Jake?"

"Let us hope that he will have no more than a headache when he regains consciousness," he said urging his horse forward.

Mara could not believe she had heard him correctly. "Have you injured Jake?"

"Keep quiet, and sit still," he ordered.

Mara began to struggle, but he struck her across the face so hard her eyes stung. "Why are you doing this? I thought you liked me."

"You are a blind fool, Mara. Did I not tell you that I loved you?"

"Is this the way you treat the ones you love?" she had to yell to make herself heard. She was beginning to feel real fear now.

"Your brother would have taken you away and I would never have seen you again. I asked you to marry me, remember. You thought you were too high and mighty for Du Lac. I will have you now though, with or without benefit of marriage."

"Zeke will come after you, Du Lac. He will discover what you have done and he will not rest until he finds you!'' she said, grasping for something to believe in. She knew if she gave in to the terror she was feeling she would be lost.

Ugly laughter issued from Du Lac's lips. "I put a burr under Zeke's saddle, his horse will not stop running for a week, and Zeke has a long way to walk before he reaches the cabin. We will be a long ways from here by then."

"Have you forgotten my brother? He could come back at any time."

"Pugh, your brother, the fancy gentleman, would not know the first thing about tracking anyone. I doubt he can function outside a drawing room."

Mara looked over her shoulder. The cabin was lost from sight. She wondered what Andrew would do when he awoke alone and hungry. She hoped Jake had not been too badly hurt. Everything looked hopeless to her at the moment. Du Lac was a madman. And she was completely at his mercy.


Jeffery and Palomas rode down the trail single file. Jeffery's eyes scanned the horizon in the direction of the cabin. They reached a point where the trail widened, and Palomas drew even with him.

"Something's strange, Palomas. It is a clear day and the cabin is just off to our right, and yet there is no smoke coming from the chimney."

Palomas's eyes scanned the skies. "You are right, Jeffery there is something worng."

Palomas was leading two packhorses, and Jeffery had the horse he had purchased for Mara on a tight rein. Both men nudged their horses into a run. When they reached the cabin, Jeffery vaulted from his saddle. The door was standing wide open and he could hear Andrew crying at the top of his lungs.

Running inside, he made a quick survey. The room was cold. The fire in the fireplace had been out for many hours.

"Is anyone here?" he called loudly, not expecting an answer, and not receiving one. He rushed over to Andrew and picked him up, finding he was soaking wet. He had obviously been crying for a long time.

Palomas appeared at his side. "There is something wrong here," Jeffery said. "You look around outside while I tend the baby."

Jeffery found all he needed to change the baby's clothing, then he wrapped him in a warm blanket he stripped from one of the beds. Andrew felt very cold. He had not been changed for a long time, and he had kicked his covers off. Jeffery knew if he did not get him warm soon he would become ill.

What had happened here? There was no sign of a struggle. Mara would never have left her baby, unless she had been forced to.

Laying Andrew down, Jeffery closed the door and added wood to the fireplace and started a fire. Now that Andrew was warm he drifted off to sleep, but Jeffery knew he must be hungry and would soon awake wanting something to eat. Crossing the room he opened the door, just in time to admit Palomas carrying Jake's body.

"Lay him on the bed," Jeffery directed. He went down on his knees and examined the gash on Jake's head.

"I found him in the woods. He is not dead, but that is a bad wound."

"He has to wake up. We have to know what happened to Mara."

"I saw horse tracks leading off toward the setting sun, the horse appeared to be carrying double. I will track it," Palomas said.

"No, you stay with Jake and Andrew, I will search for my sister."

"Jeffery, it is my place to find Mara," Palomas said opening the door, leaving Jeffery no choice but to tend the baby and Jake.

Palomas mounted the horse they had brought for Mara since it would be fresher than his, which had been ridden all day. He was grateful there had been no fresh snow, so the tracks were easy to follow. The man was a fool, he thought. He made a clumsy attempt to cover his tracks, but any Indian could easily pick up his trail.

Palomas rode for several hours before he dismounted to rest the horse. He bent down and examined the tracks, he could see the man's horse was tiring. He saw where the man had dismounted to walk the animal. It was easy to recognize Mara's small footprints. He saw a place where she had broken away from the man, and the place where the man had overtaken her. He was grim-faced when he saw blood on the snow. Hatred burned in his heart for the unknown man who had hurt Mara. He mounted once more, and urged his horse forward at a run. He would catch up with them before nightfall.

\* \* \*

Mara huddled near the fire, watching Du Lac unsaddle the horse. She wished she dare try to run away again. She reached up and tested her swollen lip, where Du Lac had struck her the last time she tried to get away from him. Picking up a handful of snow she used it to wash the worst of the blood from her face.

Du Lac threw her a fugitive glance as he tossed the saddle to the ground. When he approached her, Mara cringed.

"There is no reason for you to fear me, Mara. I will not harm you," he said sitting down beside her.

She turned away from him, and when he reached out to touch her she batted his hand away.

"I am not as bad as you believe me to be, Mara. You have bewitched me. I never wanted a woman as I want you. I would do anything to have you."

"Does that include betraying Jake and Zeke, who befriended you?" she said bitterly.

"Mara," he whispered as he drew her into his arms. "Never has there been a woman such as yourself. I love you. Ask what you will of me and I will gladly grant it."

"Let me return to my baby."

She saw the dangerous glint in his eyes. "I cannot see what you could find to love in that Indian baby. If it is a child you want, I will fill you with my baby."

Mara shivered in disgust. "I would kill myself before I would ever allow you to touch me."

His hands fell heavily on her shoulders, and she could feel his fingers dig into her skin. "You would deny me your body, and yet you love a baby that was fathered by an Indian savage!"

"Remove your hands from me, it is you who are savage."

He applied pressure to her shoulders and lowered her to the ground. "Why do you do this?" she said as she felt his hand slide up her leg, raising her gown.

He lowered his head and rested his lips against her ear. "I do not know. Ever since I first saw you I knew I must have you." His lips covered hers, and Mara tried to turn her head away. She tried to fight him but he was too strong. She felt his hands move bruisingly across her breast, and she wanted to cry you. Finally she tore her mouth away from his and screamed, knowing there was no one to hear her and come to her aid.

Looking around frantically, she tried to see something she could defend herself with. Her eyes fell on a pair of moccasin-clad feet. Before she could react, Du Lac was jerked into the air and dangled from the tall Indian's arms like a limp puppet. She watched as the Indian withdrew his knife from its sheath and plunged it into the heart of the terrified Du Lac. Mara whimpered as she saw the blood flowing from Du Lac's chest. She knew he was dead.

Mara scrambled to her feet, never taking her eyes off the Indian. Was she to be his next victim? She was not sorry Du Lac was dead, in fact she had wanted to slay him herself, but what was to be her fate at the hands of the fierce-looking Indian?

She took a step backward, with the intention of fleeing into the woods. Turning her back she ran as fast as she could, but she knew she was not fast enough. She could hear him right behind her. She felt his arms go around her waist and she was lifted into his arms.

Staring into the dark eyes she saw the puzzled expression on his face. Her eyes took in his silver and turquoise headband, and she felt even more afraid. She did not struggle, but lay passive in his arms knowing she would never be able to escape this powerful Indian.

"Do not fear me, Mara. I would never cause you harm." He spoke to her in the same dialect the other Indian had used and she understood him. He had called her by name.

"W . . . who are you? How do you know me?"

He looked at her with such sadness that she knew in that moment she had nothing to fear from him. "I am called Palomas."

"You killed Du Lac."

"He deserved to die."

"I . . . suppose I should thank you for saving me. What are you going to do with me?"

"I will take you to your brother, Jeffery."

"You know my brother?"

Palomas nodded. He strolled to his horse and placed Mara on the animal's back. He was about to mount behind her when she remembered that Du Lac had Jake's gold.

"Wait, I must get the gold and return it to Jake and Zeke."

"I will get it," he told her.

Mara looked away as Palomas rolled the dead Frenchman over and removed the bag of gold from his belt.

"Do we just ride off and leave him like this?" she

asked thinking they should at least bury him.

"Let his body be food for the wolf," Palomas said as he mounted the horse behind Mara.

"His horse?"

"The animal will follow."

As the horse moved forward, Mara tried to hold herself stiff so she would not come in contact with the Indian, but she soon began to tire and leaned back against him. Something about this man inspired trust in her. He said he would take her to Jeffery and she believed him. She shuddered to think what would have been her fate had he not come along when he had.

Mara felt herself getting sleepy. She closed her eyes. There were many questions that she did not know the answers to, but they would keep until tomorrow. Her head relaxed against his shoulder, and she was aware that he shifted her body crossways across the horse so she would be more comfortable.

"Palomas," she said sleepily.

"Go to sleep, Mara, nothing can harm you now."

She felt comforted. Nothing would hurt her now. She drifted off to sleep.

Palomas lowered his head and rested his face against her golden hair. His love ran deep for the woman who was his queen. She was safe, his heart cried out in joy.

Mara sighed as she snuggled into his arms seeking his warmth.

If she had seen the soft look on the fierce warrior's face at that moment she would not have understood it. This time belonged to him. He could hold her while she slept, taking nothing away from the king.

Shortly before dawn he halted the horse. "Mara," he called softly. "It is time to awake." He watched as her eyes opened. She smiled.

"I forgot, what did you say your name is?"

"I am Palomas," he reminded her. Lifting her to the ground he pointed to the cabin.

"Will I see you again?"

"Yes," he told her, and then he rode away.

# Sixteen

I feel this great fear as I seek the past.
How long, I cry out, will this darkness last?

Jeffery was pacing the floor with a screaming Andrew in his arms. He had tried to feed the baby some watered-down mush, but Andrew protested loudly. It had been a long night for Jeffery, with a hungry baby and an injured man to tend to. He was worried about Mara. Jake had regained consciousness, and told him that it was the Frenchman who had attacked him.

His face lit up when the door opened and Mara herself entered. "Thank God you are safe," he said, sinking down in a chair.

"How is Jake?" she asked.

Jake raised up on his elbow and gave her a lopsided grin. "Takes more than a crazy Frenchman to kill me."

She smiled brightly at him and rushed over to take Andrew from her brother.

"I tried to feed him, but he did not like the diet I offered him," her brother told her, gladly relinquishing the baby into her care.

Sitting down in the rocking chair, Mara unfastened her gown and fed Andrew. She dropped a blanket over her shoulder for modesty's sake.

"What happened, Mara?" Jeffery asked.

"Do you know a man named Palomas?"

"Yes, he is traveling with me."

"I did not know him before last night, and yet I owe him so much. He saved me from Du Lac."

"How, what happened?" Jake asked sitting up weakly.

"You must rest, Jake, you are still not well. All you need to know for now is that Du Lac forced me to go away with him. He is now dead." Jake lay back and closed his eyes. Mara was right, he did not feel at all well. His head throbbed painfully, and when he tried to sit up he felt dizzy.

Mara watched him with a worried frown on her face. "Jeffery, will Jake be all right?"

"He will be fine by tomorrow, Mara. That was a nasty blow Du Lac gave him, but it not life threatening."

"Tell me about Palomas. How is it that he knows me? How did he find me last night?"

"It is a long story, Mara, and I am a bit weary now," Jeffery said, standing up and stretching his arms over his head. "Right now that bed looks mighty tempting to me," he said, walking over to Zeke's bed and sinking down on it. It was not long before he was fast asleep.

Mara tiptoed about the cabin so she would not disturb Jeffery and Jake. She knew when they awoke she would have to tell them all about Du Lac and the man Palomas.

Surprisingly, Mara felt rested after her long ordeal of the day before. Of course she had slept all night in the arms of the Indian. She wondered where he had disappeared to after he had brought her back to the cabin.

Late that afternoon, Zeke returned. He was very tired and half frozen. He told Mara he had walked over twenty miles, after Du Lac had driven his horse away. When Jake awoke Mara spoonfed him some broth, while she told all three men about what had happened to her the day before.

Zeke went to bed early, and Mara and her brother sat beside the warm fire, talking in hushed tone so they would not disturb Jake and Zeke.

"Jeffery, I want to thank you for taking care of Andrew and Jake. It was so kind of you."

"Jake was no problem." A smile brightened his handsome features. "I merely had to clean his wound, and prevent him from going in search of you. I assured him that the best tracker I knew was on your trail. Andrew was a little more difficult to deal with. He was hungry, and all I knew to feed him was watered-down mush, which he showed me in a very vocal way was not to his liking."

Mara laughed. "Have you not been around babies much?"

Jeffery though of his own son who had been born the day before he had set out to search for Mara. "No, but with a little luck, my nephew will have no bad after-effects from my care."

"Jeffery, you are a fine man. I wish I could remember our life together. We must have had such fun."

He looked into her beautiful face, feeling pain that she could not remember the past. Leaning forward, he cupped her chin in his hand. "Mara, I cannot tell you the hue and cry that has gone out over your disappearance. You would be astounded if you knew how many lives your absence has affected."

"No, I cannot imagine. It is wonderful to have a family." She caught her lower lip between her teeth. "I want to go home with you, but I wish I did not have to be separated from Jake and Zeke. They have been so kind to me. I will miss them so much. Perhaps they could come to visit me sometime."

Jeffery had no answer to give her. He knew Tajarez would not be inclined to forgive the two men, who, by thinking they were rescuing Mara, had caused so much grief. He doubted that they would ever be allowed to enter the hidden valley.

"Jeffery, will the others in our family accept Andrew? I could not bear it if he were to be shamed."

"Have no fear, Mara. I give you my word he will be welcomed with love."

"You said you would tell me about Palomas. Did you know I was able to converse with him."

Jeffery hedged. "Palomas is a very good friend of mine. He helped me search for you."

"There was another Indian, who was dressed very much like Palomas, he came here and tried to get me to go away with him."

"Yes. His name is Matio. It was he who told me where to find you. Mara, you need not fear Palomas. He would never harm you."

"As strange as it sounds, I do not fear him, but I have many questions to ask you. How did I learn to speak the language of the Indians? Will you help me

256

to sort out these things in my mind?"

"Mara, I consulted with the doctor at the trading post. He said I must go slowly in revealing your past. Will you understand and accept this?" He hoped that would put her off for a while. Tonight was not the time to tell her about the Seven Cities, the Lagonda tribe, or Tajarez.

Two days later, Mara said a tearful good-bye to Jake and Zeke. It was very painful leaving them. It was as though she was leaving all that was dear and familiar to her, going off into the great unknown.

Jeffery was being very mysterious about their destination, and when Mara asked him about it, he put her off by saying he would tell her when they were under way.

When Mara kissed Jake and Zeke, the sorrow in their eyes mirrored her own sadness. They had refused the gold, as she knew they would, so she had left it lying on her bed, knowing they would find it when she had gone.

As she and Jeffery rode away from the cabin, Mara looked back at the only home she could remember. She was blinded by tears when they entered the woods and the cabin was lost from view.

It was a bright clear day, but off to the north there were dark snow clouds building up. Jeffery carried Andrew strapped to his back in the leather pouch Jake had made for him. He could see Mara's unhappiness, so he decided to distract her.

"Mara, Palomas will be joining us shortly. I do not want you to be frightened by him."

"I do not think Zeke believed me when I told him how I had been rescued by Palomas, since he and Jake never saw him," Mara said.

"Perhaps it is better if they believe Palomas was a figment of your imagination. Some things are not easy to explain to outsiders," Jeffery told her, moving his horse ahead before Mara could question his last remark.

They rode until noon, then stopped to rest the horses and to eat. Mara sat down on a huge rock that had been warmed by the sun. Jeffery handed Andrew to her so she could feed him. Once Andrew's stomach was full he fell asleep once more. Mara was hesitant to remount until Jeffery explained some things to her. She watched as he tightened the cinch on her saddle.

"Jeffery, are we going to St. Louis? Is that where we live?"

He turned to her and smiled. "I can see why you would be confused. You do not remember the past, and I, your brother, who could fill in the void for you, have been very secretive."

"Is St. Louis a long way, Jeffery?" she asked pointedly, since he still seemed to be avoiding her questions.

He took her by the arm, led her back to the rock where she had been sitting earlier, and sat her down. There was a serious frown on his face as he knelt down beside her.

"Mara, we are not going to St. Louis."

"Yes, but you let Jake and Zeke think that . . ."

"Hear me out, Mara," he said interrupting her. "The place I am taking you is far to the West." He saw the confusion in her eyes and decided it was time to tell her about the Lagonda Indians. He would start with himself and Sasha, perhaps she would not question him further. "Mara, I am married to an Indian princess, of a tribe called Lagonda. Before you were taken by Jake and Zeke, you and I lived with these Indians."

Mara stood up slowly, her eyes wild with fright. "I do not understand what you are saying to me. Why would I live with Indians? Jake and Zeke rescued me from two Indians!"

Jeffery stood up and put his arm around her. "Honey, Jake and Zeke thought they were rescuing you, but in truth you were in no danger from the two Indians that they shot."

Mara felt her body begin to tremble, not understanding what her brother was telling her. "Andrew is an Indian, I must have been attacked by one of the men!"

"No, you were not attacked, Mara."

She lowered her head, feeling shame at what he implied. "Are you saying that I allowed an Indian to . . . no, I would never do that." Suddenly Mara remembered her dreams about the beautiful Indian and wondered if he did really exist. Could he be the father of her son?

Jeffery forced her face up to his. "Mara, there are some things that I cannot tell you, you will have to discover those for yourself. Trust me when I say to you that you did nothing wrong."

"You keep asking me to trust you, and yet you are secretive, and you are deliberately keeping things from me. What am I to believe?"

"Mara, I must do as the doctor said. I can tell you many things about our childhood, and growing up in Philadelphia and St. Louis. However, I must omit the last three years."

"Was it so terrible you cannot tell me about it?"

"Not at all, you were extremely happy."

"If you tell me to trust you again, I will scream. I am not a china figurine. I will not break so easily. I will not be coddled and treated as if I have no mind of my own."

He grinned down at her. "Now that is the old Mara, that I know and love. I was beginning to think you had become docile and tame."

Her chin jutted out stubbornly. "Are you trying to be funny?"

He laughed deeply as he hugged her to him. "Perhaps, but it would seem my humor is lost on you."

She could not suppress the smile that tugged at her mouth. "I will go with you to this Indian village, Jeffery, but be warned, if I do not like it there, I will insist on leaving. Agreed?"

He nodded, thinking it did not matter what he agreed to. Tajarez would be the one Mara would have to reckon with.

He felt pride in her as he helped her mount her horse. She did not remember who she was, but still she had all of the qualities she had always had. Bravery had always been one of her strongest points. And he knew she was calling on that quality now.

As they rode away, Palomas suddenly joined them. He seemed to have come from out of nowhere. When he pulled his horse alongside Mara's, she looked into his face. He was anything but handsome, with his fierce-looking eyes and his irregular features, but she did not fear him; after all, she owed him a great deal.

"I am glad to see you looking well, Mara," he said in the tongue of the Lagonda.

"Thanks to you, Palomas," she answered him, in the same language.

It was like a physical pain in Palomas's heart that Mara did not know him, but he hid his feelings behind the mask he had learned to perform behind.

They rode hard for the rest of the day. Andrew was proving to be a good traveler, he slept all afternoon, safely strapped to Jeffery's back.

That night when they set up camp, Palomas erected the tent, while Jeffery built the campfire. After they had eaten and Andrew had been tucked all warm and cozy inside the tent, Mara joined Palomas and Jeffery beside the fire.

Palomas handed Mara a cup of coffee, but she noticed he did not drink coffee himself.

"Jeffery, tell me how I came to speak his language so well?" she asked, looking at Palomas's silver and turquoise headband. She suddenly noticed that Jeffery was now dressed in buckskin trousers, and he too wore the silver-and-turquoise-beaded headband.

"You will understand when you reach the city," he answered, in the same English she had spoken to him in.

"The city? You mean the Indian village?"

Jeffery leaned back against the saddle he would no longer need. He had become accustomed to riding in the Indian fashion, and he now found the saddle

261

to be uncomfortable. Also, it only added extra weight to the horse.

"I will now begin to explain some things to you. The best place to start is at the beginning. You were born in Philadelphia, as Mara Golden. Our mother and father traveled abroad for most of our childhood, so we lived with our grandparents. Our father was an expert on ancient Egypt, where he and our mother lived for many years. He was able to translate Egyptian hieroglyphics which he taught you. You are very good at translating them."

"Did my father give me a golden medallion with hieroglyphics carved on it?"

"No, that was given to you by an Indian called Sagas, but that would be getting ahead of my story. Our mother and father moved us to St. Louis when they returned to the United States to live. That is where you spent most of your growing-up years." He paused. "Our parents are now dead."

"Oh," Mara said, waiting to feel grief that her mother and father were dead. She could not picture what they had looked like, it was as if she were hearing about the death of two strangers.

"How did you meet your Indian princess, and why did I go with you to this city you speak of?"

Jeffery knew that, leaving out the part about Tajarez, he would only be telling half-truths, but he would follow the doctor's orders until such time as he handed Mara over to Tajarez. It would then be up to her husband to tell her what he wanted her to know.

"Mara, when we first journeyed to the Cities, you were very excited. I will tell you something about them, and perhaps you will better understand why I have been so secretive. They are rightly called the Seven Cities of Gold. They are inhabited by a highly advanced and intelligent tribe of Indians. The Lagonda are ruled by a mighty king, who lives in a magnificent palace. No one outside the tribe knows the location of the Cities, with the exception of yourself and me."

Mara looked unsure. "I cannot credit what you are telling me, Jeffery, and yet, if Palomas is an example of the Lagonda Indians, I can almost imagine how different they are from all other tribes. Even Jake and Zeke pointed out the difference."

"I know it is hard to believe, for if I had never been there, and you were sitting here telling me about the Cities, I would not believe you."

Mara took a sip of her coffee and found it cold. Her eyes moved across the campfire, to where Palomas sat. She did not know if he could speak English. His eyes kept moving to the tent where Andrew slept, and she wondered what he was thinking.

"Tell me more about this wondrous place, Jeffery."

He took her cup, emptied the cold coffee, and filled the cup from the pot before he spoke.

"There is sheeting on the walls of the anteroom of the palace, with ancient hieroglyphics carved on it. Before you were . . . lost you had been transcribing them. You had discovered that the Lagonda tribe is descended from a pharoah and his family who fled Egypt under fear of death, thousands of years ago. They landed in the new world, and eventually found

263

their way to the hidden valley, where they built the great Cities. The king, whom you will meet shortly, is a descendant of that Pharoah. Of course, over the years there was much intermarriage with the Lagonda tribe and that is the most prominent heritage of the king.''

"How extraordinary. I am excited to see this place! This king you speak of, he must be the father of your wife.''

"No, the king is Sasha's cousin.''

"Is there a queen?''

Jeffery took a deep breath. "Yes, there is a queen, and she and the king have twins. A prince and princess.''

"I must admit to being anxious to see this place. Do I live with you and your wife.''

"We all live at the palace," Jeffery said without hesitation.

"You spoke of an Indian man who gave me the medallion. Tell me about him.'' She was beginning to think that the man who had given her the medallion might be Andrew's father.

"His name is Sagas the wise, and if I told you of his powers, you would think me mad. He is well over a hundred years old, and he can foretell the future, although he does it reluctantly.''

Mara drew in her breath. She did not think him mad. She thought of the old man who had come to her in the visions. For some reason she did not want to tell her brother about him, he was too closely related to the beautiful Indian man of her dreams. She began to wonder if that man also existed, and if she would see him when she reached the Seven Cities.

"Tell me about your wife," she said changing the subject.

"Sasha is lovely. You and she were very good friends. She and I just had a son . . . actually it's six months ago now. The day after he was born, I left to search for you."

"You left your wife and newborn son because of me?"

"Of course. You are my sister. There was a wide search made for you. Tajarez ordered that no one return until there was some word of your whereabouts."

"Tajarez?"

"Tajarez is the king. He and a group of warriors are also searching for you, although Matio would have told Tajarez that you have been found by now."

Mara laughed. "Am I so important that the king himself searched for me?"

"You are very important to the Lagonda."

"Because I can translate the hieroglyphics?"

"The past is very important to the king and his people," Jeffery told her, thinking it would do no harm if she thought the Lagonda tribe wanted her back to finish revealing the past for them.

# Seventeen

My heart reaches toward him, my body declines.
It is he the dark Indian, whom my heart sought
   to find.


Matio jumped from his horse and walked toward the big white tent. Many of the warriors called out to him, but he paid them no heed. He must first see the king and tell the queen had been found. Stopping at the tent opening, he did not enter. No one approached the king without first seeking permission.

"It is Matio, my king, I wish to speak to you on a matter of great importance."

The tent flap was thrown aside and the king himself stood just inside. "I heard you were dead."

"I was no more than wounded, my king."

"Enter, Matio. Where have you been? Why did you not return to the Seven Cities?"

"I was trying to find the queen."

Tajarez sank down wearily on a fur robe. "We have all tried to find her, Matio, but without success."

"But my king, I have located her. She is alive."

Tajarez stood up slowly. "Where is she? Is she

with you?"

"No, she would not return with me," Matio said, wishing he did not have to report the information he had.

"What do you mean she would not come with you? Tell me where to find her and I will go to her."

"I have a message from Jeffery. He said to tell you to wait by the river where she was taken and he would bring her to you."

"Sit down, Matio, I would hear all you have to tell."

Matio complied, and he began telling Tajarez of his long, fruitless search, and how he finally found the queen with the white man. He told him about seeing Mara in the white man's arms.

"You lie!" Tajarez hissed. "Mara would never betray me. Why do you say these false things about your queen? The men were obviously holding her against her will. Why did you not see this for yourself, slay the men and bring her to me?"

"I would have, had I thought she was being forced to stay with them, but she told me to leave." Matio lowered his head. "There is more, my king, there is a child."

"What are you saying, what child?"

"The queen's child," Matio said.

Tajarez swallowed convulsively. Standing up, he turned his back. Mara loved him, he knew that, but if she loved him, why had she not come back with Matio? A child! Had he been betrayed by her? He spoke in an uneven voice. "You are sure the child was hers?"

"Yes, my king. The child suckled at her breast."

"What did the child look like? How old was it?" Tajarez asked in a calm-sounding voice, his mind racing backwards, trying to calculate if the child was his. But no, not unless the child had been conceived the last week they were together.

"I did not see the baby very well, my king, but she told me it was the white man's child."

"Leave me now. And tell the others I do not want to be disturbed." Tajorez said in a voice that shook with emotion.

"Yes, my king," Matio replied, bowing.

Tajarez waited until he heard Matio leave, and then his broad shoulders drooped. There had to be some explanation. Mara would not betray him, he felt it in his heart. She had not wanted to leave him; it had been his decision for her to go. She would never desert Tamera and Hamez, she loved them too much. But why would Matio say it if it were not so? Matio had said that Jeffery would bring Mara to him. Tajarez remembered the law that if ever the king or queen sought out another to lie with they would forfeit their life. Questions with no answers whirled around in his mind.

If Jeffery brought Mara to him he had better not bring the child. But suppose it was his child? No, if Mara had borne his child, she would have returned with Matio. He was heartsick. "I would rather have found your dead body, Mara, than to have had you betray me," he said to the empty tent.

During the next weeks Tajarez's mind was troubled. At times he would convince himself that Mara loved him, and that the child was his. At other times his old hatred for the white race returned, and he swore that they were deceitful and unreliable. He was angry that his body still craved Mara. The long months of separation had been hard on him, for he was by nature a very passionate man. If only he were not king, he would find a woman, any woman! He would hurt Mara as she was now hurting him.

Weeks passed, and all signs of civilization disappeared. Jeffery and Palomas kept a watchful eye on Mara, who had become strangely silent the last week. They were able to travel faster now, and Jeffery's fear that Mara might not be able to keep up the strenuous pace—since she had so recently given birth—disappeared as she easily kept up with him and Palomas. Jeffery and Palomas took turns carrying little Andrew, and one day around noon they finally reached the river where they were to meet Tajarez.

Jeffery wanted a chance to talk to Tajarez alone before he saw Mara, so he and Palomas pitched the tent on the far side of the river.

Leaving Palomas to guard Mara and the baby, Jeffery made his way across the icy river, knowing he would find Tajarez waiting on the other side.

As he urged his horse up the steep embankment he was met by two of his warriors.

"The king awaits you, my captain," one of the men told him. "He is in his tent."

Jeffery stopped at the tent opening. "Tajarez, it is Jeffery. May I enter?"

"Enter."

No torch burned to lend its light to the darkness

inside the tent. When Jeffery's eyes became accustomed to the faint light, he saw Tajarez reclining on a fur robe.

"I have word that Mara is camped on the other side of the river. Was she afraid to come to me?"

"She was a bit apprehensive."

"I am told she has the child with her."

"Of course."

"Did she send you to plead for her life?" Tajarez said, throwing the golden goblet he had been clenching in his hand across the tent and watching as its contents spilled on the white fur rug.

"Tajarez, what are you talking about?"

"I know about the child. I also know about the white men she was living with. Did you think Matio would not tell me?"

"I have no idea what Matio told you. Perhaps you would care to enlighten me."

Tajarez rose abruptly and towered over Jeffery. The look on his face was murderous, and his dark eyes sparkled dangerously. "Do not take me for a fool, Jeffery. You would have done better had you not brought your deceitful sister to me. But no matter, had you not, I would have found her myself."

"You had better explain that remark. Mara is not deceitful," Jeffery said, unafraid. He had always spoken his mind where Tajarez was concerned.

"You should have left the child with its father." Suddenly Tajarez's voice broke, and he looked at the ceiling of the tent. "You are a fool, Jeffery. Did you not know I will have to order her death once we get back to the city? Why did you bring her to me?"

Jeffery frowned. "I think I am beginning to see what you are saying. My God, what did Matio tell you?"

"The truth, Jeffery. He told me the truth."

Jeffery went over to the tent opening and threw it aside. "All right, if you want to shed blood, you can start with the child, Gaord, go to the other side of the river and tell Palomas I want you to bring the child to me."

"Right away, my captain," came the quick reply.

"You dare bring that child to me?" Tajarez said, grabbing Jeffery by the shoulders and whirling him around.

"Apparently you do not love my sister as you have claimed you do. I will show you the child, and then if you want his life, you can take it."

"Do not think that because he is a baby I will hesitate, Jeffery. I can assure you I could drive my knife into his heart as easily as I could through the heart of my worst enemy."

"I do not doubt it. You have no faith, do you, Tajarez? It must be lonely for you sometimes in your kingly world, suspecting those that you claim to love. I wish I had not brought my sister back. Had I known your reaction, I would have hidden her where you would never have found her," Jeffery said angrily. He could not believe that Tajarez thought Andrew belonged to a white man. Only Matio could have planted that thought in his mind.

"You forget to whom you are speaking, Jeffery," Tajarez said in an ominous voice.

"I am angry, Tajarez. I will wait outside, and when Gaord returns, I will bring you the child."

"I have not dismissed you."

Jeffery stood up to his full height. "I will wait until you do so."

"You act like Mara is the one who has been betrayed. Your loyalty to your sister does you credit, but what she did is unforgivable. You are dismissed, but do not bring the child into my presence."

A muscle twitched in Jeffery's jaw, and he quickly withdrew. He walked to the river's edge. He could already see Gaord returning with the infant in his arms. He waited impatiently for him to reach shore, and when he finally did, Jeffery took the child from him and walked purposefully toward the big white tent.

He threw open the flap.

Tajarez, hearing him enter, whirled around to face him. His dark eyes went to the bundle Jeffery carried in his arms. He watched silently as Jeffery laid the child down on the white fur, withdrew his knife and handed it to Tajarez.

"I give you the weapon to end this child's life."

Tajarez's anger was unbounded. His dark eyes narrowed and he grabbed the knife from Jeffery. "I will do it, Jeffery. I will kill the white man's child, and you cannot stop me."

"Did I say I would stop you? Did I not give you the knife to do the deed with? What are you waiting for?"

Tajarez dropped to his knees and pulled the blanket aside. The hand that clenched the knife wavered and the knife fell onto the robe.

"Great Father!" Tajarez cried out. "This is my child." With trembling hands, he picked up the baby, whose skin was as dark as his own. Long black hair covered the child's head. Black eyes wandered aimlessly across Tajarez's face.

"Damn right, he is your son," Jeffery said in English. "Do you no longer wish for the child's death?"

Tajarez held his son against his face, too overcome with emotion to speak. "I . . . am confused."

"What you are is a bastard, Tajarez. You were ready to believe the worst about Mara, condemning her without ever giving her a chance to defend herself."

"Matio said Mara told him this child belonged to the white man. He said Mara ordered him to leave, that she would not return to me. What was I to believe?"

"How about believing in Mara?"

"Do not go too far, Jeffery. You have said more to me today than any man has ever dared, and you are still alive. But do not push me more."

"I left Mara on the other side of the river so I could explain some things to you. Right now I do not much care if you hear the truth, since you are so willing to believe a lie."

"I will have Matio's death."

"He is innocent, Tajarez. He told you what he saw. He could not know what had happened to Mara."

"What are you saying? She is well, is she not?"

"Physically, yes, but she does have a problem. After what I have witnessed here today I fear to tell you, thinking you will not understand. She needs gentleness and understanding."

273

Tajarez looked down at his sleeping child. "You are frightening me, Jeffery. What is wrong with Mara?"

"She has lost her memory. She does not remember me; she will not know you. She did not recognize Matio when he tried to get her to go away with him."

Tajarez looked at Jeffery suspiciously. "I have never heard of this happening to anyone. Mara would not forget me and our children."

"A moment ago you were willing to believe she had betrayed you. Why is the truth so hard to believe?"

"How could this happen?"

"The doctor says it was apparently something that happened to make her want to forget. I suspect it was when she thought Palomas and Matio had been killed right before her eyes."

"It could explain many things if she has lost her memory. I want to see her."

"In a moment. I want to tell you what the doctor told me first. He thinks it would not be wise to tell her that you are her husband just yet. He said it could be very dangerous for her if she were to become unduly upset."

"She will know me when she sees me," Tajarez said confidently. "You watch the child. I will go to her."

Tajarez handed his son to Jeffery and left before he could dissuade him.


Palomas stood guard outside Mara's tent. Tajarez

clasped his arms in greeting. "It is good to see you, Palomas."

Palomas suppressed a happy smile, knowing this was Tajarez's way of saying he was forgiven for allowing Mara to be taken.

"Is Mara inside the tent?"

"Yes, my king, but she is sleeping."

Tajarez opened the flap and stepped inside. His eyes softened as they fell on his golden-haired wife. She was even more beautiful than he remembered. Her eyes were closed, and he watched the even rise and fall of her breasts that were swollen with milk for his son.

He felt pain in his heart that he had doubted her. She moved slightly, and he knelt down beside her and took her hand. "Mara," he whispered. "Awaken."

Mara opened her eyes slowly, and they collided with soft brown ones. She sat up quickly. This was the beautiful Indian she had dreamed of. "Am I dreaming?" she asked.

Dark eyes that seemed to go to the very depth of her soul drew her gaze with such an intensity she could not look away. If she was dreaming, this time he could also see her.

"Mara, if you dream, I share the dream with you." His hand slipped up her arm to frame her lovely face.

"Who are you?"

His hand froze, and his eyes narrowed. She did not know him. Jeffery spoke the truth. There was no recognition in her eyes, only uncertainty and fear. He had seen that look before. The first day he had ever seen her she had worn that expression.

"You do not remember me?" he said, and the words came out as a painful question.

"My brother told me we would be meeting up with a tribe of Lagonda warriors. Are you of that tribe?"

Tajarez swallowed convulsively as his hand dropped away from her face, and he stood up. "I have come to take you across the river."

"But where is my brother? Is my son with him?"

He reached for her and lifted her into his arms. He then picked up a fur robe and wrapped it about her to keep her warm. "I will take you to your son."

As he carried her out of the tent he set her on her feet for a moment and took Palomas off to the side so he could speak to him without Mara's overhearing. "Ride ahead of us and tell Jeffery to order all the warriors not to treat Mara as their queen. No one is to let her know I am her husband."

"I am glad you have seen the wisdom of this, my king. Jeffery told me the medical man advised against revealing too much to her at once."

"Go, I will bring her shortly."

Tajarez walked back to Mara and pulled the fur that had slipped off her shoulder tightly about her throat. He noticed she flinched at his touch, so he withdrew his hand. It tore at his heart that she was frightened of him, even though she tried to hide her fear. He knew her so well. It would not be wise for her to learn that the man she feared was her husband.

"Mara, I saw your son. He is a beautiful child."

She smiled nervously. "I thank you for saying so. As his mother, I welcome all compliments on his behalf." She saw Palomas ride away and enter the frozen river water. Over the weeks she had grown accustomed to having him around, and she felt like calling after him not to leave her alone with this man whom she feared, for some unknown reason. Tajarez, seeing her fear, took a step backward. "Mara," he said, thinking to draw her thoughts away from her fear, "By what name do you call your son?"

"I named him Andrew," she said, avoiding his magnetic eyes. She suppressed a shudder. The man she had dreamed of was real flesh and blood! She hoped he could not see her confusion.

"Andrew, I like the sound of that, but it is not an Indian name."

"I know my son is an Indian. You need not remind me. I have been wondering all afternoon if I might meet the man who is his father and not recognize him as such."

Tajarez swallowed hard. "What makes you think Andrew's father is among the Lagonda tribe?"

"I hope it is not so. I do not think I am ready to meet the man. I do not think it is proper that we are having this conversation. I do not even know your name."

"I am called Tajarez," he said, watching her face for some sign of recognition.

"I know you, you are Jeffery's wife's cousin!" Her face whitened. "Oh, I am sorry, you are the . . . you are the king. I am so embarrassed! I do not know how to address you."

"You may call me Tajarez," he said in a dull voice.

She smiled impishly. "It seems only fair, since you call me Mara."

He wanted to tell her he had often called her another name . . . he had called her "beloved." He wanted to reach out and take her slight body in his arms. He wanted to carry her into the tent and strip all her clothing off and make love to her. He wanted to tell her how proud he was of his son, who was dark like himself, and looked more like his son than the prince royal did. Oh, he wanted so many things as he stood there looking into her eyes.

"Come, Mara. I will take you across the river now." He lifted her into his arms and mounted his horse. The horse balked at the river crossing and reared up on its hind legs. Tajarez easily controlled the animal, but the movement sent Mara crashing against his hard, lean body. As he reached around her to get a tighter rein on the horse, his lips brushed against her cheek, and she drew in her breath. With his knees he urged the horse forward and it entered the icy stream. He smiled down at her and her heart fluttered. She wondered why she was having such a strong reaction to this man of whom she had dreamed so often. Her face reddened as she remembered how intimate they had been in one of her dreams. He misread her reaction as one of fright. "Have no fear, I will not let you fall into the icy water," he assured her. He shifted her weight so her head was resting against his shoulder and she could observe his face better. His face was so beautiful and noble, yet it was a male face, one that could cause many a young maiden to lose her heart. Mara thought of his queen and wondered what she would be like. "Why are you being so kind to me?" she could not help asking.

He looked down at her with a warm gaze. "You were lost to us. There will be many who will welcome your return, Mara."

She wanted to reach up and touch his ebony hair to see if it was as soft as she remembered in her dreams. Her eyes widened. What was the matter with her? She was beginning to covet another woman's husband. They had reached the other side of the river, and Tajarez handed Mara into Jeffery's arms.

The look Jeffery gave him plainly told him how grateful he was that Tajarez had not revealed to Mara that he was her husband.

"It is good to have your sister back with us, Jeffery. It is cold. I think you should take her into the tent with her child."

"Which tent do you wish her to occupy?" Jeffery asked, hoping Tajarez would not want her to share his tent.

"Put her in my tent. I will seek shelter elsewhere tonight," Tajarez said, as he nudged his mount forward and rode away.

Mara noticed the other Indians as Jeffery set her on her feet and steered her toward the big white tent. The men seemed to be ignoring her; it seemed to make little difference to them that Jeffery had found his sister. Upon entering the tent, she took in the luxury in one glance. The white skins that covered the floor could only be ermine. There were white deerskin cushions to sit on. Golden plates and goblets stood on a low table.

"This is magnificent! I could not be more

surprised. I am beginning to see that some of the things you told me about the Lagonda tribe are true. I expected to find a camp with the usual Indian teepees,'' she said, bending over Andrew and discovering he was sleeping soundly.

"You will find they differ in many ways from what you would expect of Indians. I think you should rest now. The trip from here on out will be a grueling one. Tajarez covers many miles in a day. Should you need anything, you have only to call out.''

Tajarez was standing near the river's edge, looking across to the opposite shore. A light snow had begun to fall, and the dying light from the sun was shrouded behind dark clouds. He heard footsteps and recognized them as Jeffery's. He did not turn around, but spoke softly: "I feel like the lowest creature for ever doubting Mara. It pains me to think I had so little faith in her. I pray she never learns how I doubted her.''

"She will not hear of it from me.''

"She does not remember the times we laughed, talked, and loved,'' Tajarez said, as if speaking to himself. "I did not think you spoke the truth when you told me of her condition, but when I looked into her eyes, I saw that I was a stranger to her. She does not know of the times she came willingly into my arms and I held her. She cannot guess how I wanted to die when I thought she was dead. I had to hide the joy in my heart at seeing her again. Nor can I tell her Andrew is my son. I want to go to her and tell her of this great love I have for her, to feel her body close to mine. But I must play the part of a polite stranger, instead of an ardent husband.''

"Perhaps when we reach the Cities, the medicine man can cure her. Or Sagas may know what must be done,'' Jeffery told him.

Tajarez turned to face him. "It is a long way to the Seven Cities, Jeffery. It will take many weeks to get there, as you know.''

"You will be called upon to exercise patience and understanding. Knowing you and how impatient you can be, I wonder if you can remain a polite stranger.''

"Jeffery, I wish to apologize to you for the way I spoke to you earlier. It seems I have had much to apologize for lately, Palomas has felt the sting of my tongue and he, too, did not deserve it.''

"As for myself, I accept your apology, and I know Palomas thinks he deserves all you said to him,'' Jeffery said, knowing how hard it was for Tajarez to admit he was wrong. There had been a time when he would never have admitted erring, but that was before Mara had mellowed him.

Tajarez sighed. "Since I would most probably say it all wrong, I would like you to tell Matio about Mara. I still feel very angry with him, and if I spoke to him, he would also feel the sting of my tongue. He was very steadfast in his search for Mara and should be rewarded for his devotion, while I would want to point out his faults.''

"I will talk to him for you,'' Jeffery laughed, "but he may also feel the sting of *my* tongue. I myself am not well pleased with his assessment of Mara's situation, although I suspect by this time he knows of his misconception, and nothing I could say would make him feel any worse."

"In the morning I want every man to be shown my son, so there will be no doubt in their minds that he is my son."

"I agree."

Tajarez raised a dark eyebrow. "At least, something we agree on. Get some sleep, Jeffery. Tomorrow we start for home, and *you* can see *your* son!"

# Eighteen

I am seeking, I am searching for that which is lost
   to me.
If I find him will I know it? If I love him should I
   show it?


Mara slept peacefully, awakening only once to
feed a hungry Andrew. When she rose the next
morning she fed her son, and Jeffery brought her
some corncakes and roasted rabbit. He held little
Andrew while she ate.

"Mara, Tajarez wants you to ride without your
side-saddle. He thinks it will be too dangerous with
the rough terrain we will be traveling through."

Mara popped the last bit of corncake into her
mouth and stood up. "Am I subject to this Tajarez's
orders? I am a good rider and it is not likely that I
will be unseated. Besides, I do not think it proper to
ride without a saddle."

"I would not advise you to go against him. It was
not a request, but more of an order." Jeffery could
not tell her she had once fallen from her horse while
riding side-saddle, and Tajarez did not want to risk
its happening a second time. Looking into his sister's

face and seeing the stubborn set of her chin, he knew she was preparing to do battle.

"Jeffery, either you saddle my horse or I will! I will not allow this man to tell me what to do. I am not one of his subjects who must obey his orders. I am a good rider, and I would be more likely to take a spill from my horse riding like an Indian than I would riding side-saddle."

A smile spread over Jeffery's face. This was Mara as she used to be. There would be trouble, because she was willful and set on having her own way. She and Tajarez would clash many times before they reached their journey's end, but he welcomed it. It did the mighty king of the Lagondas' good to come up against the one person who did not always blindly obey him. He saw no need to tell Mara that she had often ridden bareback in the past.

"I will saddle your horse. Be sure to dress warmly. It is bitterly cold," he said. "I will take Andrew outside with me while you dress."

Many Lagonda warriors came forward to see the new prince. Matio looked down at the dark-skinned baby and felt shame that he had wronged his queen.

When Mara came out of the tent the warriors went back to breaking camp.

They had ridden hard all morning, and Mara had no trouble keeping pace. Palomas rode to her left holding Andrew, and Jeffery was at her right. Six other Lagonda warriors surrounded her.

The snow clouds had moved away, revealing a bright sun that began melting the snow, causing it to turn to slush. But Mara preferred that to the slick icy ground she had ridden on yesterday. She had not seen Tajarez so far today, and she thought it was just as well, because if he said anything about her side-saddle, she would give him a piece of her mind. No lady would ride like a man! It was unheard of. She had made up her mind that even though she was among the Indians she would act like a lady. Looking about her, she assessed the way the warriors were dressed. They all had leather headbands interwoven with silver and turquoise. They were a strange band of Indians. None of them spoke to her, but every so often she would catch them watching her with a strange expression on their faces.

She recognized the young man who had come to the cabin that day and asked her to go away with him, but he, more than the others, seemed to avoid eye contact with her.

When they stopped around noon Mara took little Andrew from Palomas and walked away from the group so she could have privacy while she fed him. He was wrapped in a warm cocoon of fur, with only his little face visible. Touching his soft cheek, she smiled lovingly down at him while she unfastened her gown to nurse him. He was such a good baby, and once his hunger had been satisfied and she changed him, he fell asleep once more.

Standing up with the intention of returning to the others, she felt her eyes drawn to a hillside a short distance across the valley. She saw a rider and immediately identified him as Tajarez. He and the black horse he rode seemed as one. The horse's hooves kicked up the snow and sent it swirling into the air.

285

The man's dark ebony shoulder-length hair was tousled by the wind. From the speed he was traveling, she knew he would soon reach the point where she was standing, though she doubted he had seen her. He was so magnificent, like some young god out of an ancient Greek tale.

She felt a tightening in her throat, wishing she could continue watching the beautiful Indian. What kind of man was he? Surely like no other she had ever known.

Gathering Andrew tightly against her, Mara made her way back to camp, hoping the Indian Tajarez would not discover she had been watching him.

Jeffery offered her a piece of dried meat, but she refused, not feeling hungry. Moments later Tajarez entered the camp and halted his horse beside Mara. The animal tried to rear up on its hind legs, but the pure strength of the man prevented it.

"How is the child, Mara?" When he spoke her name it was almost like a caress.

Before she could reply, Tajarez's face darkened in anger, and Mara followed his eyes to the object of his fury. She gasped when she saw he was staring at her mount with the side-saddle, and felt a prickle of fear run down her spine when he turned his dark eyes on her.

"Did your brother not tell you that I ordered your side-saddle removed?" he said in an angry voice.

Mara tried twice to speak before she finally succeeded. "Yes, but I cannot ride without it."

He dismounted and walked over to her horse, many dark eyes watching him as he took his knife and cut the strap that secured the saddle to the horse.

He then lifted the offensive object and threw it to the ground. Then he turned back to Mara. "Now you will have to ride bareback, will you not?"

Hot anger shot through Mara's veins like wildfire. How dare he try to assert his authority over her! He shamed her in front of the others. She would not stand idly by and take such treatment!

"You have destroyed my saddle and you had no right," Mara said angrily, in English.

The other Indians seemed to fade into the distance, out of earshot, as Tajarez gave her a smile with no humor in it.

"You always did lapse into English when you became angry, Mara. Perhaps it is just as well. I would not like my warriors to know how you speak to their king."

"What right do you have dictating to me how I should ride? I am a lady, and I will not ride like some man, or like an Indian!"

"It seems you have no choice. Your saddle cannot be repaired. Had you obeyed my order in the first place, you would not know my anger."

Her hands went to her hips, and she stamped her foot.

"You have no right to speak to me in this manner. I do not care what an illustrious person you are, you have no say in what I do." She turned to Jeffery. "Are you going to allow him to treat me in this fashion?"

Jeffery merely shrugged his shoulders. "He is my king; I am bound by his orders."

Tajarez raised his eyebrow. "You, like your sister, obey me when it is what you want to do."

"I will never submit to your orders. You have destroyed a saddle that must have cost my brother a great deal of money."

"It was not your brother's gold that bought the saddle, but mine. Now, I do not intend to stand here conversing with a woman who acts like a child."

He took Andrew from her and handed him to Jeffery, picked her up, and, before she could protest, plopped her onto the horse. "I will carry the baby," he said as he took the baby from Jeffery. "And Mara, you might try to pull your gown down. I do not like for my warriors to see your legs." With that he nudged his horse in the flanks and rode away, leaving her to stew in her own anger.

When she looked at Jeffery for some sympathy, she found him smiling, his eyes glued to Tajarez's back. Mara yanked at the skirt of her gown to cover her legs and kicked her horse in the flanks harder than was necessary. As the animal started off in a lope, she discovered that she could indeed ride very well astride, and remembered that she had done so when she first met Jake and Zeke, but the knowledge did not serve to cool her heated temper.

Tajarez's temper, however, cooled almost immediately as he remembered Mara's flashing green eyes and the creamy white leg he had glimpsed when he put her on the horse. He looked down at the baby and saw that he was awake. His heart swelled with love and pride in his tiny son. He looked to his right and saw Matio riding beside him. "Have you seen my son, Matio?" he said meaningfully.

"Only from a distance, until Jeffery showed him to me this morning," Matio said, shamefaced.

"Take two men and scout ahead, Matio. I am not ready to forgive what you charged against your queen," Tajarez said in a deadly calm voice.

For the first time in his life, Matio wished he could cry. He had done the queen a great injustice, and he doubted that the king would ever forgive him. In fact, he waited to hear at any time that he was no longer a member of the royal guard. He made no reply as he dropped back to select two men to accompany him.

It was early March. Weeks passed, with the same pattern repeated each day. The cold weather continued and the snow fell intermittently, piling up in a thick, heavy blanket, making forward progress difficult; but still they pushed on, ever westward. Mara was beginning to think the mysterious Seven Cities were a myth and they would never reach them.

One morning they awoke to see that there had been a fierce blizzard with strong winds that had whipped the down-falling snow into a world of whiteness, making it impossible for them to travel. Everyone remained in their tents, and the wind howled and pushed against the shelters. Inside the tent Mara occupied it was warm and cozy, with all the white robes she needed to cover herself with. Jeffery had told Mara the tent had been treated with some kind of oil that repelled cold and moisture. She hummed softly as she nursed Andrew. He was a greedy eater, as his chubby little body attested.

A sudden gust of wind engulfed Mara as the tent flap was pushed aside, and she looked up to see

Tajarez enter. The fur wrap he wore was covered with snow, and he removed it and dropped it to the fur rug. He stood silently watching her, his dark eyes resting on the gentle swell of her creamy white breast.

Mara would have covered herself against his intense stare, but her heart was pounding against her ribs, and she seemed unable to move even when he dropped down beside her and touched the dark hair of her son.

He spoke no words as he looked into her eyes, and she could not speak for the way her throat had suddenly closed off, making it hard for her to breathe.

She watched as he lowered his head and kissed Andrew on his chubby little cheek, and then she gasped as she felt his warm breath against her sensitive breast. She closed her eyes as she felt his mouth move from her son's cheek to lightly touch her exposed skin.

When he raised his head, his hand slid around the back of her neck, and she could see the passion reflected in his dark, haunting eyes.

It struck a chord in her heart. Raising her head with gentle pressure, his lips descended slowly. Mara waited in torment for the touch of his mouth on hers, and when his lips did touch hers, a small groan escaped her, only to be smothered by his kiss.

Her body and her mind worked against each other. Her mind cried out that it was wrong, but her body denied that.

His lips were at first soft and searching, but they soon became hungry and devouring. When he raised his head, her eyes were full of wonder at the beautiful thing that had just happened between them. She did not protest when he took the child from her and laid him on the fur rug. Nor did she object when he pulled her into his arms and drew her body down beside him. Drawing the fur rug over them both he sought and found her lips. This time as he kissed her, he skillfully undressed her.

Mara saw it all in a haze of raging passion. She did not know how it had been accomplished, but soon neither of them had anything on, and instead of feeling shame and embarrassment as she knew she should, her body sought to touch his. Tentatively at first, her hand slid to his broad chest, feeling the mighty strength beneath her fingertips.

She raised her face to him and parted her lips.

"Mara, beloved," he whispered, glorying in the feel of her soft, silky body pressed against his hard, muscled one. He lowered his head for a taste of her soft honeyed lips while his hands roamed seductively over her body. He had the advantage. He knew all her likes, and what points to touch her on to make her almost mindless. He kissed her closed eyelids, the lobes of her delicate ears, her throat, murmuring her name over and over.

Mara's hand slid up his back to entwine in his ebony hair. Ebony hair mingled with golden hair, as the hard, bronzed body covered the soft white one. The weight of his body caused her momentary fear, but not fear of him, never of him.

"Someone may come in," she whispered.

"No one will enter, Mara, trust me," he said in a deep, husky voice, knowing she was at the point of surrender. His hand gently spread her legs apart as he sought and found the entrance to her body. He saw her eyes widen and flame into green fire.

"I have needed this for so long, Mara. Feel how my body trembles with wanting you."

How could she feel his body tremble, she wondered, when her own body would not stop shaking.

"This is wrong," she said, in a puny effort to justify allowing him to take her body.

"No, not wrong, Mara. I have tried to stay away from you, but I cannot. Touch me, beloved; let me have what belongs to me."

Words were not necessary as she arched her hips in invitation. With a strangled groan he thrust forward, and soon they were locked in furious lovemaking. So long had they been apart that Tajarez, who was usually gentle with her, was almost at the point of being brutal. He was aware of what he was doing, and the fact that he might be hurting her, but his body and not his mind had the upper hand.

Mara felt as if her body was not hers, but an instrument that belonged to Tajarez to do with as he wished. When she was sure she could not stand the beauty and the pain of it for a moment longer, her body seemed to explode, and she was making little whimpering sounds. But that was not to be the end, for many times Tajarez took her to the point of total exhaustion, only to find her strength renewed. It could have been minutes, and it could have been hours, as he mastered her body. At last he saw her strength was all but spent. His desire, which he had been trying to hold in check so he could satisfy her, erupted simultaneously with hers, and they lay in each other's arms, his mouth covering hers in a long, drugging kiss.

As Mara's desire began to wane, her body felt totally relaxed. She closed her eyes and fell asleep.

Tajarez raised his head and stared down at his sleeping wife. He had aroused her passion, but she had not remembered that he was her husband, he thought sadly. He kissed her eyelids, which were framed by long, silky lashes. "Where do we go from here, beloved?" he asked softly, but Mara did not hear, nor did he expect her to.

He got up and dressed, his eyes never leaving her silky body. He picked up his sleeping son, placed him beside Mara, pulled the robe over them both, and left quietly.

He had all but forgotten his purpose in coming to Mara's tent, which had been to make peace with her. She had not forgiven him for the incident involving her saddle and had hardly spoken to him in many days. Her anger toward him had been like a pain in his heart, and he had thought to appease her, but when he had seen her nursing his son, all thoughts had left his mind, and he had been driven by his unbridled passion. Their lovemaking had been as beautiful as it always was, but something was missing; she had not said she loved him; she had not known that he loved her.

# Nineteen

Give me your hand: take what I offer you, says he.
I asked, what do you want of me.
He answered, immortality.

Mara awoke during the night and reached out her
hand, hoping to find Tajarez lying beside her, but
she was alone with little Andrew. When she became
fully awake, she was appalled by her wanton
behavior.

Dear Lord, she thought frantically, what sort of
woman was she that she would let a man take her the
way she had allowed Tajarez to? There was a name
for women such as herself. He was a married man
and had two children. A terrifying thought came to
her. Had she allowed him to make love to her in the
past?

She sat up quickly. Was Andrew his son? She
remembered him kissing Andrew last night. Oh, no,
please not that. How would she ever face him again?

Did Jeffery know about her and Tajarez? Did the
others?

The wind pushed against the tent, and she felt its

icy cold touch her naked body. Fumbling around in the darkness she found her nightgown and slipped it over her head. Then she snuggled down in the warm fur rug. She tried to push all thoughts of Tajarez's lovemaking and her response to him out of her mind. One thing was certain—tomorrow she would demand to know if Andrew was his son.

She vowed she would never allow him to make love to her again. She lay awake, tortured by her troubled thoughts, and when the sun made its appearance, she was awake to greet it.

Much to her relief, Tajarez was not among the warriors who surrounded her, nor was her brother, and she was grateful for the absence of both, for she was afraid her brother would read the guilt in her face, and Tajarez, of course, already knew of it.

When they stopped at noon for her to feed Andrew, Tajarez and Jeffery had not yet appeared, and when they set up camp for the night there was still no sign of either of them.

"I do not see why you are so concerened. After all, Mara is your wife. You were married to her in two different ceremonies. I know of no one who is more married than you and my sister," Jeffery said as he and Tajarez rode into the darkened camp.

Tajarez dismounted, and one of his warriors rushed forward to take his mount. He waited for Jeffery to dismount before he spoke again. He lowered his voice so only Jeffery could hear him speak.

"You do not seem to understand. This could get out of hand. I almost told Mara last night that I was her husband, and I am not sure it would have been a bad thing, either. Knowing Mara as I do, I am sure she has started having recriminations for what happened between us last night. Would it not be better for her to know she is my wife, than to think that I took her out of lust and not love?"

"I do not know. All I know is what the doctor said. We are no more than a week from home. Could you not wait until you talk to the medicine man? A week is not so long to wait."

Tajarez's eyes sought Mara's tent. "I do not think I can wait that long to hold her again. When I am near her all my good intentions go for naught."

Jeffery had long ago become accustomed to the easy manner in which the Lagonda viewed the act of love. Not that they talked about the intimate details of what took place between a husband and wife, but they had a healthy attitude toward sex, and never talked of it in hushed tones as if it were something to be ashamed of. Their attitude made it seem beautiful, the ultimate experience between two people who loved each other. When Jeffery had courted Sasha she had been shy and untouched, but on the night of their wedding she had come into his arms without hesitation, and she had given herself as trustingly and as openly as if she were not the inexperienced virgin that he had found her to be.

"You could always ride on ahead and greet her when she entered the Cities. By that time you could have spoken to the medicine man, and he might advise you to tell her that you are her husband."

"No! I will not leave her until she is safely inside the hidden valley. Too many things have happened to her in the past. I will stay with her. I will go and speak to her now, and perhaps try to justify what happened between us last night."

Andrew was sleeping peacefully and Mara was dressed in her long white gown and was braiding her hair into a long golden rope when the tent flap was pulled aside and Tajarez entered. Even though her back was to him she knew it was Tajarez. When he was near her there seemed to be a charge of electricity in the air. Turning slowly to face him, she raised her head proudly.

"I am glad you have come," she said, giving the illusion of feeling much more calm than she actually did. At the sight of his handsome face, her insides seemed to turn to mush.

As he had done the night before, he removed the outer wrap that he wore for warmth and let it fall to the robe that covered the ground. The evening before he had worn a fringed shirt with long sleeves, but tonight he wore no more than a beaded vest, and around his upper arm he wore an armband of the purest gold.

"You want to speak to me about last night?" he asked as he sat down at a safe distance from her and motioned for her to do the same.

She reached for a robe and pulled it in front of her modestly. Tajarez smiled inwardly at her gesture, thinking he knew her body better than she did.

"Yes, I have some questions I would like for you

to answer for me. This is very hard for me, so I will try to be brief.''

He nodded, but said nothing.

''First of all, I would like to ask if you and I have ever before been together as we were last night?''

Tajarez was silent for a moment, trying to decide how to answer her. Then he said, ''I have been with no woman but my queen in over two years, by the way you measure time.''

''I see. That answers my second question, then. Andrew could not be your son.''

Tajarez wanted to shout at her and tell her that Andrew was not only his son, but that he had fathered two other children by her. But he did not.

Mara lowered her head and tried to suppress a sob. If he was not Andrew's father, then she had been with another man, maybe more than one. She was a more despicable woman than she had thought at first. No wonder Jeffery kept her in the place he sometimes referred to as the hidden valley. He could not allow her to live among decent people.

''I will never allow you to come near me again. I would kill myself before I would let you touch me as you did last night,'' she finally said.

''You are assuming that I would want to touch you.''

Mara's head snapped back as if he had delivered a mortal blow to her. So deeply did his harshly spoken words wound her that tears gathered in her eyes.

''I cannot blame you. You must despise me for what I am.''

Tajarez closed his eyes against the horror he heard in her voice. ''What do you think you are?''

"I know there is a word for women like me, but I do not know what it is. Please go."

"If that is what you want."

He stood up, willing his legs to take him out of the tent. Mara hoped she could keep from breaking down in front of him. The blast of frigid air told her he had opened the tent flap. When she no longer felt the intense cold she knew he had departed, and she opened her eyes.

Sobs that she had tried to smother broke the silence of the tent, and she threw herself down on the fur robe and cried brokenheartedly. She knew why she felt as if her heart had been ripped to shreds and why she felt like the lowest form of life. She was in love with another woman's husband, and she had just been rejected by him.

The pain was so intense she could not stop crying. She was not aware that the tent flap had been jerked open and that Tajarez knelt down beside her. He lifted her into his arms.

She buried her face against his shoulder, loving the feel of his strong hands that ran up and down her back soothingly. She did not mean for him to see her cry, but she could not seem to stop. All the months of not knowing who she was and not knowing where she belonged, coupled with her discovery that she was a wanton female, made her tears fall all the more freely.

In her misery she lifted her face to tell him how sorry she was about her tears, but the words never issued from her mouth.

"I was going to be strong for both of us, Mara, but I cannot. I want you," he whispered against her lips.

There was no denial in the kiss Mara gave him. Her lips clung to his hungrily as she became limp and pliant in his arms.

As before, she found herself lying naked in his arms. She knew what she was doing was wrong, but she could not stop the raging fire within her body. She felt herself being pushed back against the soft fur and tried not to think how wantonly she was behaving.

"I cannot be around you without wanting to love you, Mara," he said softly in her ear. "You are to me as food is to a man dying of starvation." He made love to her slowly, lingeringly, and when they lay in each other's arms afterwards, he kissed her softly.

She curled up contentedly. So much for her decision not to let him make love to her again, she thought, knowing she would never be able to resist him. At that moment it did not concern her overmuch. She wanted only to stay in his arms and hear him murmur lovely words in her ear.

This time he did not leave her as he had before, and she was glad. She fell asleep, and he picked Andrew up when he began to fuss and laid him between them. Mara awoke, and he watched as his son nursed hungrily at her breast, feeling a great love for his wife and the tiny infant.

When Andrew fell asleep, Tajarez moved him to the other side of Mara and pulled her into his arms. Words of love tumbled to his lips. He did not voice them, but his hands became intimate, and Mara clung to him.

They made love again, and this time when she fell

asleep, he left her quietly.

Now he came to her nightly. They would make love, and when she fell asleep, he would leave her. Mara knew he was being thoughtful by leaving, wanting to spare her any embarrassment she might feel if the others knew he spent his nights with her.

She no longer tried to resist him. When he came to her tent she would run into his arms in a way that delighted him. He waited for her to say she loved him, but she did not.

One night, after they had made love, she lay quietly in his arms, and he wanted to know what she was thinking.

"Why are you so quiet?"

"I was wondering about the woman who is your queen."

"Are you asking me to tell you about her?"

"Yes, what is she like?"

He hid a smile against her golden hair. "She is the loveliest of women. Her hair is indescribably beautiful. Her eyes are haunting, and show her feelings. I can read her thoughts through her eyes; they speak if she is happy, sad, or angry."

Mara closed her eyes, not really wanting to hear any more, but curious all the same. "You love her very much?"

"I adore her."

"Then why do you come to me each night?" she asked, not really wanting him to tell her it was purely physical.

"You are a very lovely, desirable woman. I cannot

301

seem to stay away."

Pain knifed through her heart at his words. He had told her what she already knew, he loved his queen, but he desired her. "Do you know who is the father of my baby?"

"Does it matter so much?"

"Not to you, but I would hate it if one of the Lagonda warriors who ride beside me each day was Andrew's father and I was not aware of it."

"He is not one of my warriors."

"I have come not to like myself very much lately. At times I feel remorse for allowing another woman's husband to make love to me, and at other times I try not to think of it at all."

"You are saying that your mind is ruled by your body?"

"Yes. I wonder what my brother would say if he knew about you and me?"

His hand slipped underneath her chin, and he stared down at her. "Mara, is it just that I hold your body, or is it possible that I hold your heart?" he said, changing the subject.

Mara considered telling him that she loved him deeply, but saying the words out loud would make it too real. Once they reached his home they could no longer meet like this, and if he knew of her love, it would only arouse his pity. The words he had spoken about his wife had been beautiful. There was no doubt that he loved her. Some sixth sense told her that men did not like clinging females, especially when they had a wife they loved.

"I doubt that I know what true love is, Tajarez. If you want love, you should seek your wife."

His hand tangled in her hair and he jerked her forward painfully. In a strange way he felt as if he was his own rival, competing with himself for her love.

"And if I do not seek love, I can always come to you," he said savagely as his mouth ground into hers with a punishing force. He was hurting her and he knew it, but he was angry with her and she did not know why. Pitiful whimpers were escaping her throat as she fought against him. She twisted and turned in his arms, trying to get away from him. She could hardly breathe, and his hands were cruel as they untangled from her hair and ran roughly over her body.

"If lust is all you want, I will give you lust," he growled. He took her brutally. Her fists pounded at his chest with no more effect than a leaf blowing in a strong wind.

After he had finished with her he shoved her away from him. "Do not think you can ever keep me from taking what I desire, Mara. I can have you any time I want."

Mara was humiliated by the thing he had just done to her body and the words he had spoken. She was nothing to him but a body, someone he could use until he was with his queen again. She turned her head away so he would not see the tears that scalded her eyes. She would never submit to him willingly again, she told herself. He might take her body, but never again would he reach her heart, and never again would she let his lovemaking render her mindless. All she would have to do when he came near her in the future was remember the cruel words he had spoken to her tonight, and it would be the shield she needed to save herself from him.

She was beginning to realize that behind her outer facade was a strong-willed person. He might have more outward strength than she, but he would be no match for her inner self. If it was possible, she would leave and seek Jake and Zeke. They would take her and little Andrew back, but she had no idea where to find her two friends, and with Andrew to think about, she could not afford to be irrational. Perhaps she could ask her brother to take her away. She was so deep in thought that she did not hear Tajarez leave.

Sitting up clutching the robe about her, she noticed she was alone except for Andrew, and he was sleeping. She slipped her nightgown over her head and lay down once more, to ponder her future. She could tell Jeffery that Tajarez had made love to her, and perhaps he would help her. But what could she say to him? "Jeffery, your king made love to me and I welcomed it?" She began to feel hatred for the man who had used her for his own pleasure while he claimed to love the woman who was his wife. Mara no longer envied the queen. She had a faithless husband in Tajarez. How many other women had he made tremble at his touch while professing to love his wife?

Her sleep was troubled, and she dreamed that Tajarez was taking her body against her will and afterwards he mocked her.

The next morning she found her Indian gown and moccasins and dressed herself in them. She braided her hair in one single plait that hung down her back to her waist. Then she woke Andrew, fed him and dressed him warmly, and left the tent in search for her brother.

Her mind was made up. She would ask him to take her back to Jake and Zeke. She would beg him if she had to. She found her brother shaving a day's growth of beard from his face, something that the Indians did not have to contend with since they had no facial hair. Jeffery watched her approach through the mirror he had hung from the branch of a tree.

"Good morning, little sister. I am glad to see you wearing the Indian garb. It is much more sensible than the gowns you have been wearing."

"Jeffery, I want to talk to you," she said, not knowing quite how to broach the subject of her leaving.

He wiped his face on a cloth and turned to her. "You have about five minutes before we have to leave.

"That is what I want to talk to you about. I do not want to go with you to this city."

He placed his razor back in its brown leather case and placed it in his satchel. "I was wondering when you would get around to that," he said, unruffled by her announcement.

"Would you consent to taking me back to Jake and Zeke?" she said, her hopes rising.

"What would you do stuck in an obscure cabin in the wilderness with no one for company but two grizzly old trappers?"

"They are like family to me. In fact, I know them far better than I do you, who are my own brother. I want you to take me and little Andrew where we will be safe. Please, if you love me, do this for me," she said clutching at his arm. "I do not belong with you and your Indian friends. I felt safe only when I was with Jake and Zeke."

"What has happened to make you feel unsafe? I can assure you each man you see here would give his life to protect you. What could be safer than that?"

She wanted to tell him that what she feared was the man he called his king. She was frightened of what he might turn her into with his dark eyes that drew her to him like a magnet and his lips that could make her surrender all of her principles and cause her to sacrifice all she felt was right and decent. But she could not tell him this.

"You said I had been on my way to visit our brother David when Jake and Zeke found me. Could you not take me to St. Louis, where you said he lives?" she said, clutching at straws.

He could see how distressed she was, and he did not want to tell her that Tajarez would never allow her to leave.

"I could talk to Tajarez and see if he would allow you to visit David perhaps next spring," he said, trying to put her off. If she would only remember who she was, she would not want to leave.

Mara's eyes narrowed, and he had been on the receiving end of her temper far too often not to recognize her anger now.

"I am not one of your mighty king's subjects! I am not governed by his laws, as you seem to be. I can leave any time I please, and not you, he, or anyone else can stop me!"

"Mara, be reasonable. I cannot take you back. It

s impossible at this time," he said, hoping he could make her see reason.

"Very well, if you will not help me, I shall just go by myself."

"You are being childish now, Mara. You know as well as I do that you could not survive past the first day in the wilderness. Besides, what about Andrew? What would become of him should you lose your way? There are wild animals, hostile Indians, and the weather that would all be against you."

"You are a coward. I am ashamed to call you my brother. I believe you are frightened of this man, this king, whom I detest."

Mara did not hear Tajarez come up behind her. Jeffery tried to warn her with a glance, but she misread him and continued. "Yes, I can see the fear on your face. This king is only a man, not some god who seems to rule you and his warriors with some strange power. I hate him and I do not like you very well, either," she raged.

"Hate is a very powerful emotion, Mara," a deep voice said behind her. She spun around to face Tajarez, not in the least sorry he had overheard her.

"You can add sneaking up on people to listen to private conversations to your other sins, oh mighty king. I believe an eavesdropper never hears anything good said about himself."

Tajarez stared at her blankly for a moment, then he looked past her to Jeffery. "Had you not better get the men together? We are already late starting out."

Jeffery nodded and took Mara's hand, but she pulled away from him, her angry eyes defying him to say anything more to her. He shrugged his shoulders and walked away from her.

"Should you not mount your horse, Mara? I do not like being held up by a woman's temper tantrums."

"I know what you can do, Tajarez. You can go right straight to the devil."

"Ah, but the devil is a white man's demon. He would not be interested in a mere Indian."

"I think you are wrong. I would suggest you are his disciple."

"If that is the truth, then, should you not fear me? Perhaps I seek your soul."

Her eyes went to the golden cobra that spanned his upper arm. "Do you know what the cobra the pharoahs of ancient Egypt wore represented?" she asked, not knowing where her knowledge came from. "It meant they had the power of vengeance, a grim reminder to anyone who disobeyed them that punishment could be swift and deadly. Do you practice that?"

He looked at her, astounded for the moment. "You never told me that before now. . . ."

"Was there ever any reason for me to? Did I have your ear in the past?" she said testily.

"I do not wish to continue this conversation. Either you get on that horse, or I will forcibly put you on it."

"I will do it, but I want to warn you. The first chance that presents itself, I will get away from you. It will be impossible for you to watch me all the time. Once you let your guard down, I shall be gone."

Before she knew what he was doing, he took

Andrew from her arms.

"In that case, I will see that you are not left alone with the baby. Knowing you as I do, I know you might try to leave, but you would not go without Andrew."

"If you know me as well as you say you do, tell me what I am that would have made me behave as I have. What kind of woman am I that I would allow you to touch me, and to have another man's child without benefit of marriage?" The anger seemed to drain out of her as she waited for him to tell her the answers that eluded her.

"It would not be a fair assessment were I to tell you what you seek to know. I confess to being blinded in the way I see you. I cannot help you open your past, Mara. You are alone in a hell you did not create. If it were possible I would walk in your aloneness with you and point out the way." He motioned for Palomas to come to him, and when the tall craggy-faced Indian approached, he handed Andrew to him.

"She is not to be left alone with the baby, under any circumstances. See to him," Tajarez ordered.

Palomas's dark eyes went from Tajarez to Mara, assessing the situation with a clarity that would have surprised Mara had she known of it.

Mara wanted to protest, but now was not the time. It would serve no purpose to make a scene before everyone. Her mind rejected the fact that Tajarez seemed to view her as someone who was subservient to his wishes. He would find out different, she thought, as she mounted her horse in mock submission. She would bide her time until she was alone with the king of the Lagonda tribe, then she would tell him she would not tolerate his high-handed treatment of her.

# Twenty

I saw the sadness in his dark eyes.
A sadness that he did not try to disguise.

It snowed most of the day, and the temperature dropped to below freezing. The snow made a crunching sound beneath the horses' hooves. The weary travelers plodded onward, always moving in a westerly direction.

Mara was glad when they made camp for the night. Andrew had been changed and fed, and Mara held him gently in her arms, loving the feel of his warm little body. He gave her a bright smile, and she kissed his soft cheek.

Palomas had carried out Tajarez's orders, and Mara was never allowed to be alone with her son except when she was in the tent at night. The only time she was allowed to hold him in the daytime was to feed him, and then Palomas was always near by, with his back discreetly turned to her. Sometimes she would see Palomas looking at her with what looked like sympathy, but she could not be sure.

She watched as Andrew drifted off to sleep. She was like a wild filly chafing at the bit as she paced the length of the tent and back again. Laying Andrew down and pulling the covers around him, she thought that if she did not get away from Tajarez she would lose her mind. She was so angry with him for the way he tried to run her life. He was not her king. She owed him nothing.

She pushed the tent flap aside and felt the cold wind blast her in the face with its icy fingers. Seeing that the Indian Matio was stationed just in front of her tent, her anger rose to a new height. Tajarez would do well not to trust her, she thought, for should he be lax and let his guard down, she would find some way to take Andrew and escape.

She jerked the flap together and continued her pacing. She hoped Tajarez would come, and she was almost certain he would. She had a few choice words to say to him. She expected him to come so he could gloat over the fact that she was little more than his prisoner.

When Tajarez did come, it was with his usual silence that gave her no warning so she could prepare herself. A blast of cold air was the only thing that warned her of his presence.

Mara whirled around to face him and watched as he dropped his fur-lined wrap onto the robe and looked at her with melting ebony eyes.

"Surely you do not intend to stay here with me. I told you I would never allow you to touch me again," she said angrily. Her ire was boundless as he looked past her to the sleeping infant and dropped to his knees, regarding her discomfort with a smile playing on his lips.

"It would be too much to hope you would

welcome me into your . . . bed as you did before, but nonetheless you will suffer my presence. After the threat you made today, did you think I would not come?''

"Oh, I knew you would come." Mara sank down on the fur robe and clutched her nightgown tightly across her heaving breasts. "Does my brother think so little of my virtue that he would allow you to come here in broad daylight, so all the camp will know you are spending the night with me? If you are worried that I will flee into the night you could always order Jeffery to share my tent. It would be far more appropriate. He seems only too willing to carry out your slightest command.''

"I wonder which is bothering you the most. Is it the fact that my warriors will know I will be staying the night with you, or that your brother will allow it?''

"Take your choice. I have become very disillusioned with my brother, and as to what your warriors think of me, they seem to treat me as if I am not even here.''

"I wonder if you are being unfair to your brother as well as to my men.''

"What does it matter.''

"Mara, would you prefer if I came to you by cover of night, as I did before?'' he asked, as his eyes were drawn to her breasts, which were thrust forward with every breath she took.

Seeing where his eyes were resting, she grabbed a fur robe and pulled it about her shoulders, pulling it up under her chin with shaking fingers. She was disturbed by the warmth that spread through her body like wildfire.

"I would prefer it if you would not come to my tent at all," she said, horrified by the fact that her voice came out in a throaty whisper.

Tajarez began unfastening his fringed shirt, and Mara turned away quickly, not wanting to be reminded of the broad expanse of his shoulders.

"W . . . what are you doing?" she asked, scrambling to her feet.

"It has never been my habit to sleep with anything on. However, I shall retain some of my clothing for your sake," he said smiling in amusement at her shyness after all that had transpired between them.

She turned her back, more upset by her own feelings toward him than by any fear of what he might do. "I will never allow you to force your unwanted attentions on me again. I will fight you with every ounce of strength I possess," she challenged him.

She had not heard him come up to her until he spoke just behind her, and she almost jumped out of her skin.

"I grow weary of this game we play, Mara." She felt his hand at the nape of her neck, and his touch sent her heartbeat soaring. "I would not need force to get you to submit to me."

No, she thought, he would not have to take her by force. All he had to do was touch her and she fell apart. She moved away from him, hoping she would never again allow him to make love to her. She turned slowly to face him, and she felt her stomach tighten into knots. He wore nothing but the white breechcloth. Against her will her eyes moved over his

314

magnificently proportioned body. His long, powerful legs were spread slightly apart in an arrogant
stance. After a sweeping assessment of his body, she
lifted her eyes to his face, and found he was watching her closely. She expected some remark or even a
smug look, but she read only sadness in his dark
eyes. She had seen that look in his eyes once before,
in her dreams, and that knowledge brought her no
comfort. He was hurting; he was sad, and she needed
to know the reason why. All other thoughts were
pushed out of her mind as she silently watched him.

"Why are you sad? Who has caused you pain?"
she asked, wanting to reach out and touch him, to
give him comfort.

A mask seem to fall into place, and the look of
pain was replaced with one of indifference.

"You are mistaken. Why should I be sad?"

Mara was not to be put off by his disarming
remark. "You have the most expressive eyes. They
speak a language of their own. I have seen the sadness, and I would like to help you if you would allow
me to."

"Why? Did I not hear you say today that you
loathed me?"

"I think I do not like you very well. I find you a
man without honor, but still I do not like to think of
anyone suffering, if I can help in any way. I can
sense about you a very deep sadness, and it touches a
chord of pity in my heart." And it did touch her
heart more than she was willing to admit. For a man
such as Tajarez, with such obvious power and
strength, it was almost unthinkable.

"I have been called many things in my life, Mara,

but never was I told that I had no honor. Would you explain that to me?"

"Perhaps among your people it is not considered dishonorable to make love to one woman while you have a wife, but to me it is very wrong."

"But, Mara, what about you, who willingly returned my lovemaking, all the time thinking you were allowing another woman's husband to make love to you?"

"I am no less guilty than you. I have not the right to condemn you."

"What did you mean when you said you would like to comfort me? Would you come into my arms, and grant me a moment of forgetfulness?" he challenged her in a passionate voice.

Her green eyes glinted dangerously, and she tossed her golden hair defiantly. "Is that all it would take for you to be happy? I am beginning to wonder if you ever have anything else on your mind. Perhaps you should consider having a harem; I understand it works quite well in some uncivilized countries."

His eyes sparkled in silent mirth. "I do not think my queen would condone a harem. Still, it is not an unpleasing thought, if I could enlist you as my favorite."

She stepped away from him, but her foot became entangled in her long nightgown and she would have fallen had he not steadied her with a hand on her shoulder.

"You do not need to rush into my arms. I will give you time to consider being my concubine," he said lapsing into English, since there was no word for concubine in the Lagonda language.

316

"Your ego is exceeded only by your audacity. You are no better than a Frenchman called Du Lac, who tried to force me to go away with him. At least he did offer me marriage first, so Andrew would have a father."

Mara drew in her breath at the fire she saw leap into his eyes. She saw the anger distort his face, and when he spoke his voice as hardly above a whisper, but it had the intensity of a whiplash.

"Why was I not told about this? What man do you speak of?"

His hand fell heavily on her shoulder, and she felt his fingers bite into her tender skin. "Speak, Mara. I demand to hear all about this man."

"I beg your pardon. Who do you think you are to demand anything from me? I will tell you nothing!" she said defiantly.

He twisted her around and lifted her into his arms. "Will you not, Mara?" He set her down hard on the fur robe and walked over to the tent flap and threw it open.

"Tell Jeffery to come to me at once," he told whomever it was he spoke to.

Mara would have risen, but he swung around and pinned her with a look that made her change her mind. Why was he acting so strangely? What happened to her was not his affair. She had never seen him so enraged. His eyes were dark and forboding, and the look he gave her told her not to say a word.

Jeffery entered the tent looking first at Mara and then Tajarez.

"Tell your king that what I do is none of his business, and he has no right to treat me as one of

317

his lowly subjects," Mara dared to say, now that her brother was present to stand between her and Tajarez's unreasonable anger.

"What is she talking about, Tajarez?" Jeffery asked wondering what was amiss now.

"Why did you not tell me about the Frenchman?" Tajarez demanded.

Jeffery looked uncomfortable for a moment. "Palomas and I discussed it and decided not to say anything to you, hoping Mara would regain her memory and tell you herself."

"You and Palomas dared to take it upon yourself not to tell me. This time you have gone too far, Jeffery."

Mara stood up slowly. "Do not talk about me as if I were not here," she said coldly. "It was not my brother's place to tell you anything, or to keep anything from you. We are discussing me. If you are so anxious to hear about Du Lac, I will tell you, although I fail to see that it is any of your affair," she finished haughtily.

Tajarez turned to face her. "I am glad you have come to your senses." He sat down and motioned for Mara and Jeffery to do the same.

Mara gathered the fur robe tightly about her and sat down beside her brother, somehow needing to be close to him.

"Who is Du Lac?" Tajarez demanded.

"He was a Frenchman," Mara replied.

"Was?"

"Yes, was. Palomas killed him."

Tajarez's eyes narrowed. "Perhaps you had better start at the beginning."

"I do not see . . ."

"Do as he says, Mara," her brother interrupted.

Mara sighed. Once again she would get no help from her brother. "Du Lac was a friend of Zeke's, Jake did not like him very well."

"I am not interested in the Frenchman's relationship with the trappers. Tell me about you and him."

Mara looked at him defiantly, but the murderous look in his dark eyes made her suddenly fearful. "Du Lac asked me to marry him. I suppose because I allowed him to kiss me, he felt encouraged to ask for my hand."

"You allowed him to touch you?" Tajarez snapped. "Why?"

Mara wondered why he was looking at her so accusingly. "I wanted to see . . . what it would feel like to be kissed by him." She could have said she wanted to compare Du Lac's kiss to the ones Tajarez had given her in her dreams, but she did not dare.

Tajarez closed his eyes. He could not bear to think of any man's touching Mara, let alone kissing her.

"And did you like the kiss?" he asked in an uneven voice.

Jeffery stood up. "I do not think you want me here, Tajarez."

Mara blinked her eyes. Would Jeffery desert her now when she needed him?

"Sit down Jeffery. You will stay," Tajarez said.

Mara jumped to her feet. "My brother can stay here and be insulted by you, but I assure you I will not."

Tajarez stood up and towered over Mara. "Perhaps it is best for you to leave, Jeffery, this no

319

longer concerns you," he said reaching out to take Mara by the arm.

"Jeffery, do not leave me," Mara cried.

"Tajarez, let her go. She does not understand," Jeffery said.

"I said, leave, Jeffery."

"Tajarez, think. Mara does not know. . . ."

"Leave now, Jeffery," Tajarez repeated. His voice was not above a whisper, and his eyes never left Mara's face. She shivered as she heard her brother leave.

"I am not frightened of you," she said in a choked voice, knowing full well that she had seldom been more frightened.

"Answer my question now, Mara. Did you enjoy the Frenchman's kiss?"

"No!" she shouted. "I was repelled by him, is that what you want to hear?"

"Only if it is the truth."

"I did not like him touching me." She found she could no longer look into Tajarez's eyes, but stared at a point just behind him. "It was like a nightmare. He forced me to go away with him. He was talking crazy, saying I bewitched him. He . . . he put his hands on me. It was horrible."

He tilted her chin up to him, and she saw his throat muscles working convulsively. "What did he do to you?"

"Nothing," she whispered, remembering the dreadful ordeal. "Palomas found me just in time. He killed Du Lac."

Tajarez's hand strayed to her mouth, and he touched her lips gently. "I cannot bear to think that another man . . ." He lowered his head and his lips fused with hers.

Mara tried to pull away, but he would not release her. Holding her in a vise-grip, his lips ravished her. There was no passion in his kiss, she sensed only anger. She was making whimpering noises as he ground his mouth against hers. Mara was never to know what would have happened had Andrew not chosen that moment to awaken. When Tajarez heard the baby crying he released her, and she fell backwards, landing on the soft fur robe that did little to cushion her fall.

"See to your son," he said as he turned away from her and lay down on the fur robe. Great Father, he thought, he had wanted to punish her, to make her feel the pain he was feeling.

Mara gathered Andrew into her arms and lay down across the tent from Tajarez. She had not understood anything that had happened tonight. Why had Tajarez reacted so strangely about Du Lac? It was not as if he really cared about her. Perhaps he was one of those men who was jealous of any woman he became intimate with—but that did not make sense. What happened between her and Du Lac had happened before she and Tajarez had ever made love.

"I pity your poor wife," Mara said as she looked at Tajarez's rigid back. "Does she have any idea how you pursue other women?"

He rolled over to face her, and she was surprised to see he had a look of amusement on his face.

"I do not pursue other women, Mara, only you."

"How do you think your wife would feel about me?"

"That remains to be seen. You could always ask her."

Mara's face burned red, and she looked away from him. It was hard to think she would soon have to face the woman she had wronged. "I wish you would go away and leave me in peace. I feel defiled by you." Her voice came out louder than she intended it to, and she blinked as his eyes became swirling, dark storm centers. He rolled to his feet and advanced on her. She was lying down and there was no way she could get away from him. He lowered his body down beside her, and, moving Andrew over, pinned her body to the fur robe with the weight of his own.

"So you feel defiled by me, do you?" The tone of his voice sent tiny shivers of fear climbing up her spine to prickle at the nerve center at the back of her neck.

"Yes! Yes!" she cried.

The dark look on his face was enough to convince her that she faced death at his mighty hands. She gasped as his hands moved upward to play with the nerve that was pulsing madly in her throat. Then he circled her delicate neck.

"If you feel degraded by my touch, perhaps you should remember our conversation earlier. I did not force you to lie with me. You were all too willing for me to take you. Do you resent the fact that you allowed an Indian to penetrate your white body?"

Mara shook her head no. She had not thought of him as anything but a man she loved. Oh God, how she loved him. She was being torn apart inside loving him and wanting him to make love to her, knowing it was wrong. Perhaps his jealousy tonight had been because he cared for her a little.

His dark eyes roved over her lovely face. "All right, then, do you resent the fact that I desire you, and you wanted me to make love to you?"

"No, yes, I suppose I do. I am tortured by the fact that I have evidently been so free with my favors."

"I am saddened that you are suffering so needlessly over this, Mara." He wanted to tell her the truth. She was his wife, and he had every right to make love to her, and she need not feel guilty about her feelings for him. He wanted to tell her that no man had ever entered her body with the exception of him. He wanted to shout to her that Andrew was his son. He felt guilty that he had been unable to wait to make love to her until they reached the Cities. If he had been stronger, Mara would not be living in torment. He thought of the Frenchman who had wanted her, and became eaten up again with jealousy.

"Mara." His mouth circled her lips, and he did not miss the moan that escaped her throat. "Did you not feel desire when the man Du Lac kissed you?" His voice was deep and raspy.

"No."

"I am jealous of every word that man spoke to you. I do not like the thought that he touched your lips with his mouth." Tajarez's mouth settled on hers, as if, by sheer force of his will, his lips would burn his ownership onto her, erasing all traces of another man kissing the sweet lips that should only know his kiss.

Mara's body craved closer contact with his. He

was lying on top of the fur robe, and she resented that there was anything between them. As if he read her thoughts, he slipped underneath the covers with her. She remembered her promise to herself and pulled away from him.

"No, Mara," he growled in her ear. "Do not fight me. You know you want me as I want you. To deny me is to lend a lie to your true feelings."

"You will take all I have and leave me with nothing," came her weak protest.

"All I take from you I shall return a hundred fold. I will take the pleasure of your body, but I shall also give pleasure back to you," he said gruffly.

So much for her restraint, she thought. His hands and body were wreaking havoc with her mind. She was no match for his seductive powers. Would any woman be, she wondered. Her hands moved over his back and she felt a scar. She had noticed before that there was a twin scar on the front of his chest, as if his body had been penetrated by some sharp instrument that had entered either the back or the front and come out the other side. She tried to concentrate on the scar instead of on his hands, which were now moving over her hips to her thigh.

"What happened?" she said, rolling her head from side to side as his hands parted her legs.

His lips brushed hers and she gasped. "What happened?" he questioned.

She could feel his hard maleness against her, and she tried to remember the question. "The scar, on your back and chest," she said breathlessly.

He was silent for so long she thought he chose not to answer or was ignoring her question.

He nibbled at her ear, and his warm breath stirred her hair. "I was near-mortally wounded by the Kiowa." His hand had moved up to her waist and he raised his head to look at her.

"From the extent of the scar, it must have been very bad," she said, beginning to regain some of her control.

His eyes seemed to move lovingly over her face. "Yes, I would have died had not someone very brave intervened and saved my life."

"One of your warriors?"

"No, the woman who is now my queen. She drove a knife into the Kiowa chief who was about to end my life, with no fear for her own safety."

Mara wished she had kept her curiosity to herself. She struggled out of Tajarez's arms and moved away from him, turning her back. She did not want to hear about the woman who was so virtuous, beautiful, and now brave as well. She had seen the way Tajarez's eyes had become soft when he spoke of his wife. It was like a sharp knife in her heart.

Tajarez turned her over to face him, and she closed her eyes.

"I am very tired. I want to go to sleep," she told him.

"Mara." He did not fail to see the tiny teardrops that escaped from her tightly closed eyes. It had been a mistake for him to try to make love to her. He must be strong for her sake. Her heart ached for what she was suffering. He could only imagine what it must be like for her not to know who she was and to be thrown into a world with people she did not fully understand. He brushed a golden curl from her face.

Andrew began to stir and Tajarez reached for him and placed him into Mara's waiting arms. He envied his tiny son as he began to nurse at his mother's breast.

# Twenty-One

As a glimmer of my past unfolds.
I wonder what the future holds.

Mara could see the tall, majestic mountains in the distance. They were blanketed with snow, taking on the appearance of a winter fantasy land. As she stood there viewing the countryside, she felt that she was witnessing a virgin land, one untouched by man. She was awed by the beauty of it.

Jeffery rode up beside her and handed Andrew into her arms. He noticed her preoccupation with the surroundings, and remembered what it had felt like to be witnessing it for the first time. When he and Mara had first come to this place, they had stared in wonder at the beauty of it.

He dismounted and then lifted Mara from her horse. "It is beautiful, is it not?" he said, leading her over the deep snow to a place of solitude behind a pine tree where she could nurse her son in privacy.

Mara waited as he dusted the heavy snow from a large rock so she could sit down. She was still angry with him. "Yes it is lovely. I can imagine nowhere on earth that rivals this place in beauty," she said at last. She opened her gown so Andrew could nurse. "You must be anxious to see your wife and son. I am sorry that you had to leave them because of me."

"Mara, I am grateful that we found you unharmed, and we could bring you home."

"This is not my home, and make no mistake about it. I do not intend to remain here one day longer than I have to."

"Mara, about the other night, I . . ."

"I do not want to talk about it," she cut him off.

Jeffery looked at her not knowing what to say. She had built a wall about her every bit as impregnable as the wall that blocked her memory. He knew the hell she must be living through, but he could not help her. He would be glad when they reached the city, so the medicine man could examine her. It was hard now to be met with her disdain toward him. He decided to try to talk to her despite her coldness to him.

"Mara, sometimes appearances can be deceiving. Observe the mountains you see in the distance. They seem to rise out of the wilderness, untouched by the hand of man, and yet inside those mountains lives a civilization that existed long before any white man set foot on this continent—a civilization that will astound you. There is wealth in the Seven Cities the likes of which the world has never known. The people of the Lagonda tribe are intelligent, loyal, and outgoing, but to their enemies they are fierce and deadly. To each other they are kind and loving, and if you will allow it, you will find a welcome that has never been offered to anyone else from the white race. Have you not been shown every courtesy on this journey? Has not your well-being and comfort been the prime concern of the Lagonda warriors who looked after you?''

Andrew had finished nursing and was pulling at a golden lock of Mara's hair. She stood up and glared at her brother.

"I did not ask to be brought here. You may belong to these people, since you are married to one of them and have fathered a child by her, but I feel no such ties to the people of the Lagonda tribe. I only want to return to . . .''

"Return to what, Mara?"

She looked at him in such a lost way that it tugged at his heart.

"I do not know. I only know I cannot go on much longer the way I have been. I do not know what lies behind me any more than I know what I will face when I reach this city. I am frightened of many things, but most of all I am afraid of the man you call king.''

"Mara, there is nothing for you to fear from Tajarez. He would never do you harm.''

Mara's eyes sparkled like green fire. "I would like for you to define harm to me," she said, looking at him in contempt. He thought Tajarez could do no wrong. Well, she would just tell him about his mighty king. She wanted to hurt her brother for allowing Tajarez to assert his authority over her.

"Do you call not harming me, making love to me? Do you think Tajarez's queen will show me this welcome you spoke of?'' she said, hoping to shock him.

Jeffery met her level gaze. "You are thinking that

as your brother I should have stopped what happened between you and Tajarez. Had I known what your reaction would be, I would have spoken to him on your behalf.''

Mara's mouth flew open. ''Spoken to him! Not demanded that he leave your sister alone? Am I such an immoral person that even my own brother turns his head while I . . . oh, God, what kind of a woman am I? You are not even shocked by my behavior!''

Jeffery reached out his hand to her, but Mara spun away from him. ''Do not touch me; I am not fit for a decent man to come in contact with.''

''Mara, please.''

''It is time to remount.'' A deep voice spoke up just behind Mara.

She turned to Tajarez and scalded him with a glance. ''I am sick to death of the way you Indians sneak up on a person. It would behoove you to announce to someone that you are eavesdropping on their conversation,'' she stormed, venting her anger and frustration on the man she felt had contributed to her downfall.

Tajarez took Andrew from her and turned and walked away before she could say another word.

''Come, Mara. Tomorrow we will be home, then you can rest. Things are not always as black as they appear,'' Jeffery told her.

That night they camped in the foothills of the giant mountain. Tajarez was in Jeffery's tent, speaking to him and the other warriors.

''I have decided that should the people see Mara, they would confuse her with their reaction. I had hoped that before we reached the City her memory

would have returned, but as you know it has not."
He turned to Matio. "I want you to ride to the City
and spread the word. Say that it is my command that
the streets leading to the palace are to be blocked off
by sundown. I want no one to witness the queen's
entrance into the City. Palomas and myself shall
abide here with the queen until we can enter the city
in total darkness. Do not alert the people that Mara
has been found. I shall let them know in due time
that she has returned, but is ill. You may all
withdraw now, with the exception of Jeffery. All of
you but Palomas will leave at first light.

Tajarez waited until the others had gone before he
spoke again. "Jeffery I know you are anxious to see
your wife and son. I give you leave to go to them
now."

"I am not sure I should leave. Mara is very
distressed."

"An understatement," Tajarez said, without
humor. "Mara is my responsibility. What I want you
to do is have the medicine man ready to examine her
tomorrow night. Tell everyone at the palace that I do
not want them to show by thought or deed that Mara
is their queen. I want no one to see her tomorrow,
with the exception of Tabo, and Falon, her serving
girl. Have Falon prepare a room for Mara off of the
anteroom. I think we should try to make things
appear as normal as possible."

"I am glad you are going to be reasonable."

Tajarez raised his eyebrow. "What is that
supposed to mean?"

"I was half afraid you would insist Mara move
into your bedroom."

Tajarez stared for a moment at his brother-in-law. "I am not as insensitive as you believe me to be. I can see the harm I have done Mara by not staying away from her, until such time as Tabo tells me she is able to handle the truth. Go to your wife, Jeffery and leave me to look after mine.

Tajarez saw Mara leaning against a tree, gazing in the direction of the mountains. He was about to join her when he heard Andrew crying from inside Mara's tent. Slipping silently into the tent, he went down on his knees and smiled at the tiny miniature of himself. Andrew had kicked his covers off, and when Tajarez touched him he saw that he was cold. Wrapping the warm blanket about his tiny body, Tajarez lifted him into his arms. Andrew immediately stopped crying and began to coo happily. Love and pride were in Tajarez's eyes as he held his son to his face. He had wanted to show his affection for his son openly, but he had been forced by circumstances not to show too much interest in him, fearing that Mara would come to suspect Andrew was his son.

"My son, my son," he said, kissing the smooth bronzed cheek. "How proud I am of you. I do not ignore you from lack of love, but from necessity."

Andrew gave him a smile that melted his heart. "You are my son," Tajarez said softly as he laid his cheek against the baby's ebony hair. His keen hearing picked up the sound of Mara's returning footsteps. He placed Andrew down on the fur robe, stood up, and backed away, just as the tent flap opened and Mara entered.

"Oh, I did not know you were here," she said, walking past Tajarez and scooping Andrew up into her arms. "You are such a good boy," she said, ignoring Tajarez and smiling down at her son.

"You love your son a great deal," Tajarez said, coming up beside her.

"Of course. Andrew has no one but me to love him?"

"It does not matter to you that he has the dark skin?"

Mara picked up one of Andrew's tiny hands, which looked very dark beside his mother's pale hand. "I would have him no different from what he is. Do you not think him handsome?"

"Exceptionally so, even though he bears no mark that would show you are his mother. Do you yet wonder about the man who is his father?"

"You assured me his father was not among your warriors, so I try not to think about it any longer. Andrew is my son; he does not need a father."

"So you are content to let the identity of the man who planted his seed in you remain a mystery?"

Andrew had fallen asleep, so Mara laid him down and tucked the covers tightly about him. Standing up she faced Tajarez. "I have come to hope that I was an unwilling participant in the accident that gave Andrew to me."

Tajarez's heart cried out to tell her he was Andrew's father. "Why is that?"

She looked past Tajarez. "It is the only way I can live with myself. I have come to suspect that I was attacked and taken against my will, because no one has come forward to admit to being Andrew's father."

Again Tajarez had the feeling of being betrayed, and did not know why. "You have a neat little mind that likes to put all the facts into place. What you cannot analyze, you seek to put aside."

"Is this wrong?" she asked frowning.

Tajarez raised his head and stared at the top of the tent as it moved with the motion of the wind. "I am weary of this pretense. I like only truth. Anything less is repugnant to me."

"I wonder if you would recognize the truth, Tajarez. Will you tell your wife the truth about me? I think not."

Tajarez took a deep breath, and his eyes rested on her golden head. "She knows about you, up to a point."

"But you will not tell her what happened between us. I suspect you only like truth when it is not directed at you."

"You have formed a very low opinion of me, Mara. My wife will know all about you and me in due time."

Mara sank down heavily on a white cushion. "I was looking at the mountain earlier," she said, wanting to change the conversation. She did not really want to talk about his wife. "Jeffery told me I would be entering the City tomorrow night. The mountain looks ominous to me. I could see no way to get past the stone and rock."

"Tomorrow night the mountain will yield its secret to you."

"Why do you wait until dark to enter the mountain?"

"Because I say so," he said curtly. "I am weary of

playing questions and answers with you."

"Could I ask you one more question?" She wondered how she dared, for at the moment he was the arrogant king. "My question has nothing to do with your city. I was wondering how it is that you speak English so well?"

Tajarez lay down and regarded her with dark, brooding eyes. "I was taught to speak English when I was a small boy."

"I know Palomas and Matio do not speak English. Are you among a select few who know the language?"

He looked at her wearily. "My cousin Sasha, your brother's wife, speaks your language well."

"Does your wife speak English?"

"She speaks as well as you do."

"I begin to think there is nothing your queen cannot do."

"Sometimes she talks too much," Tajarez said, turning his back to her.

Mara knew he was indicating that she also talked too much. She lay down as far away as she could get from Tajarez and drew Andrew tightly against her. She found she did not like to be ignored by Tajarez—and yet, had she not asked him to leave her alone? He was for sure leaving her alone. Perhaps he had no use for her now. Tomorrow night he would be with his wife, she thought bitterly.

She had fought hard not to love this dark, mysterious man, but she had been doomed to love him, for she knew she had first fallen in love with him in a dream. There was no joy in her heart at the thought of entering the Seven Cities tomorrow night. She knew the first chance she got she would make her escape. Mara was learning something about herself. She was a realist. She could recognize when something was beyond her capability. At the moment escape was impossible, but she would bide her time and soon she would get her chance. It was becoming apparent that she was little less than a prisoner. For some reason that she did not fully understand. Tajarez was the one who would not allow her to leave. She did not delude herself into thinking he cared about her. When he made love to her he had spoken no words of love, in fact, he had made it plain to her that his only love was the woman he was married to.

Mara's thoughts were troubled and she did not think she could easily fall asleep, but she was mistaken.

Tajarez listened to her even breathing and knew she slept. Great Father, he prayed silently, let there be an end to this farce, this torture.

He felt angry that Mara had begun to view him in an unfavorable light, thinking he only wanted to use her body, while in truth he wanted all of her. He wanted things to be as they once were between them. He wanted her to look at him with love and recognition sparkling in her green eyes. He wanted her to know he was the father of Andrew, and he wanted the right to take her body without feeling guilty.

Mara could not understand why everyone had left the camp. Palomas told her that Jeffery had departed the night before, and the rest of the warriors had entered the mountain early in the morning. To her it seemed that the sensible thing was to make the journey up the rocky hillside with the aid of daylight.

Andrew was fretful, almost as if he could sense his mother's restlessness, so she held him until he fell asleep.

Time weighed heavily on her hands, and the day seemed to drag on forever.

Laying Andrew down she walked over to the tent opening and threw the flap aside. Only one tent besides hers still remained, and she knew Tajarez and Palomas were inside of it. Glancing up at the sun, she saw there was not much more daylight left. Tajarez had left her alone all day. She knew he was still in camp though, because Palomas had told her so when he brought her her food.

How different Tajarez was now from the man whose arms she had lain in during the first part of the trip. Most of the time he seemed angry and brooding. Mara sighed heavily and pulled the tent flap together. Glancing at Andrew to make sure he was covered, she sat down and rested her head on her folded arms. Would this day never end, she wondered.

As the tent began to darken with the dying rays of the sun, Palomas called to her from outside. "Mara, it is time to prepare to enter the hidden valley. You must bundle Andrew up warmly."

Mara pulled on her fur wrap and bundled Andrew up, then walked outside. She noticed that there were two warriors starting to dismantle the tent. Tajarez was not in sight. There would only be Palomas to escort her into the city. What did she expect, she scolded herself, a brass band and trumpets? Her brother was with his wife and baby, and Tajarez would be with his queen.

As they rode into the darkened night an icy wind blew down the mountainside with a punishing force. Palomas was carrying Andrew, and Mara rode just behind him.

She tried to push her fear aside. She thought this was what it must feel like to be led to the guillotine. In spite of her fear, she urged her horse to follow Palomas's. They rode single file up to the seemingly unyielding mountain. Suddenly Mara saw a ribbon of light pierce the darkness. When she rode closer, she saw the light came from a tunnel. As they entered the tunnel Mara noticed torches hung on the walls. Halfway through she halted her mount and noticed that someone was extinguishing the torches as she and Palomas passed. There was no going back. Mara felt her fate was being sealed just as the entrance to the cave would soon be sealed.

Seeing Palomas had halted his mount and was patiently waiting for her, she moved forward to join him. The length of the cave seemed endless. The silence was shattered only by the sound of the plodding horses, which seemed to echo and re-echo through the long tunnel. After what seemed like hours, but had, in fact, been only minutes, Palomas led Mara out of the cave into the inky-black night.

From somewhere up above a lone sentinel called down to them. "Who enters the hidden valley?"

"It is I, Palomas."

"Pass in safety, and welcome home," came the reply.

# Twenty-Two

I feel this web unbroken.
My love's voice has not yet spoken.


Mara looked down into what could only be a deep valley. She could see many lights twinkling in the distance. The lights seemed to beckon to her, like a lighthouse sending out its beacon to an oceangoing vessel, showing the way to a safe harbor. Which of her conflicting emotions should she trust, she wondered. Her fear, or the promise of a haven from the storm?

At one point the lights towered over the rest of the City, and Mara did not need to be told that she was viewing the palace and her destination.

She paid little heed to the punishing winds nor to the snow that had begun to fall, but set her eyes on the distant lights, and rode toward that goal. As they reached the outskirts of the City, the streets appeared to be deserted. How strange, Mara thought. The hour was not late, and yet there was no sign of life. When they reached what could only be the palace, Palomas halted his horse, dismounted, and helped Mara down. With Andrew in one arm, and the other about Mara's shoulder, Palomas led the way up the wide steps.

Mara wished it was not such a dark night. She would have liked to be able to see her surroundings. Even in the dark she could tell it was a great city, with paved streets and stone buildings. For sure, it was no obscure Indian village.

She paused when they reached the top step and looked at the huge doors. She gasped when she saw the doorway was inlaid with gold and turquoise. There were two warriors standing guard, one of them opened the door and then stood aside so Mara and Palomas could enter. It did not escape Mara's notice that neither of the guards had even looked at her.

On entering the room, Mara stared in awe. She could not believe her eyes. The room was huge, with very high ceilings that rose at least twenty feet into the air. The floor was of highly polished marble. There were many white leather couches scattered about the room. The tables were made of polished wood and had gold edging. A raised dais was at the end of the room, with two golden chairs that had a crimson-colored canopy above it. The room was dimly lit, only a few torches burned from golden wall sconces. Mara noticed a wide stone staircase that led up to the second floor. There was a guard stationed at the bottom to prevent anyone who did not belong from climbing the stairs. No doubt they led to Tajarez's living quarters, Mara thought.

Mara had half hoped her brother and his wife would welcome her on her arrival. She knew Tajarez would not be there to greet her. She was alone, with the exception of Andrew and Palomas, and the guard, who seemed to ignore their presence.

"Come, you will be quartered in the room off of the anteroom," Palomas said as he led her forward.

Mara looked about her as Palomas steered her through the huge anteroom. Jeffery had been right, there was great wealth in this city. Gold, silver, and precious stones were in evidence everywhere she looked. Eyeing the gold sheeting on the wall, she saw that it had something engraved on it, but the room was too dimly lit for her to see it in detail. That would be the hieroglyphics Jeffery had told her about, she thought.

They left the great room and Mara followed Palomas down a corridor. He stopped before a door and opened it, allowing her to pass before him.

Mara was stunned into silence as she glimpsed the lovely room. There was a wide bed covered with white ermine skins. Silver sheeting ran the length of one wall, polished mirror-bright. Soft Indian rugs covered the white marble floor. At the foot of Mara's bed was a large cradle, with a royal cobra carved into the wooden surface.

What a contrast to the loft room she had occupied at the cabin with Jake and Zeke! Suddenly she wished she was back in that loft. There had been no impressive furnishings there. She had felt loved and wanted in that cabin.

A young Indian girl rushed in and smiled nervously at Mara. Mara noticed that the girl watched her closely. Perhaps she should know her, perhaps she was Jeffery's wife, come to welcome her, after all.

"You must be Sasha," Mara said, smiling brightly.

The young girl bowed her head. "Oh no, I am Falon. It is my duty to wait upon you."

"I am pleased to know you, Falon. My name is Mara."

Falon looked at her as if undecided for a moment. Palomas handed Andrew to her, and gave her a guarded glance.

"Did you not hear her, Falon—she said her name is Mara," he said quickly.

"I have a message to you from my king, M . . . Mara. He told me to bid you welcome, and to inform you that the medicine man will shortly call on you and your son, to make sure the long journey was not harmful to either of you."

Palomas walked to the door, then turned to her before he left. "Mara, I shall be across the hall from you. Should you need me, you have only to call and I will hear you."

"Thank you," Mara said, somehow comforted by the fact that Palomas would be nearby. She had become accustomed to his presence and was glad he was not abandoning her as everyone else had.

When Palomas had gone, Mara looked at Falon. "Will my brother come to see me tonight?"

"I was told that no one will disturb you tonight but the medicine man. The king thinks it best if you rest, since you have had such a long journey."

"How kind," Mara said sarcastically, but Falon did not seem to notice the bite in her tone. She was staring at Andrew.

"Your son is truly wonderful. I did not know if you wanted me to put his bed in my room, which is just next door, or if you would prefer to have him in the room with you. The king said you would want him with you.''

"The king was right, Falon. I would not like to have Andrew anywhere but with me," Mara said, taking her baby and laying him down in the cradle.

"Mara, I took the liberty of having a bath prepared for you," Falon said, opening a door that led to a small room just beyond the bedroom.

"That sounds wonderful," Mara said, removing the heavy wrap she wore.

Falon took the wrap from her, and when Mara entered the room where her bath was waiting she saw the tub was made of solid gold.

"I have brought all of your clothes and hung them up for you, and here are many things that Vista sent for Andrew."

"Who is Vista?" Mara said, eyeing the golden bathtub in disbelief.

Falon felt the sting of tears in her eyes. Oh, the poor queen, she did not even know the woman who looked after her twins. She had been told what to expect, but it hurt her to see her queen look at her through the eyes of a stranger.

"Vista is the woman who looks after the royal prince and princess."

Mara glanced over her shoulder at Falon and could feel her temper flaring. "What kind of things did Vista send for my son?"

"Merely some clothing the royal prince had outgrown. She thought they might be useful to you."

Mara clamped her mouth tightly together, not wanting to vent her anger on this gentle Indian girl.

How dare this woman send her son the cast-off clothing of Tajarez's son? She did not want Andrew wearing anything that had belonged to his son. There was no reason to make an issue of it, she thought bitterly. It would be childish for her to send them back. She would simply not use them.

As Mara reclined in the warm, scented bath, she felt her body begin to relax. How good it felt to close her eyes and let the soothing water wash the soreness from her body!

Evidently she was to be pampered as a guest in the palace. At the moment she was too weary to offer any resistance. How good it would feel to awaken in the morning and know she would not have to mount a horse and ride all day in the cold.

When she stepped out of the bath, she saw a white cotton nightgown and robe. It was lovely, she thought, as she slipped into it. There was lace at the wrists and collar, and it had evidently cost a great deal of money. Walking into the bedroom she saw Falon turning the covers down.

"Falon, who does this belong to?" she asked, indicating the gown and robe she wore.

"They belong to you, Mara. You left them behind when you went to visit your brother. There are many others for you to choose from if this one is not to your liking."

"No, this one will be fine." Mara climbed into the soft bed, and Falon set a tray across her lap.

"Mara, I have seen to it that Camdon, the cook, prepared your favorite honey cakes. Knowing you do not like to eat a heavy meal at night, I told him to prepare something light."

"Falon, as I am sure you have been told, I have lost my memory. I do not remember you, nor do I know why you know all my likes and dislikes. Are . . . were you and I good friends?"

Falon bowed her head, and when she raised it to look at Mara, Mara saw sadness in the young girl's eyes. "I am saddened that you have this forgetfulness, Mara. I was your servant girl before you went away, as was a maiden called Minet."

"I am sorry, I did not know. Where is Minet?"

"Her parents live in one of the other Cities, and her father is gravely ill. The king gave her leave to be with him."

Mara looked down at the tray and tried to remember that the food it contained was supposed to be her favorite. She picked up the honey cake and took a small bite. It was indeed delicious. She was surprised to see that there was a cup of hot tea, and, taking a sip, she found it to be very much to her liking. Seeing that Falon still stood beside her, she smiled at the girl.

"Sit beside me Falon. I have many questions to ask you."

Falon pulled up a stool and sat down, folding her hands in her lap. "I will try to answer some of your questions, if I can," she said, remembering the king had said Mara was to be told nothing about her life as queen.

"Is this the room I occupied before?" Mara asked, taking another sip of the hot tea.

"Yes, you did sleep in this room at one time."

"Do my brother and his wife have quarters nearby?"

"No, they reside on the third floor," Falon answered, fearing Mara would ask her a question she had been forbidden to reply to. Standing up she picked up the tray, since Mara had pushed it away from her, indicating she was finished with eating.

"I will remove the tray and send the medicine man, Tabo, to you now," Falon said as she left the room.

Mara conjured up a mental picture of the medicine man. Perhaps he would have feathers in his hair and even a ring through his nose, and would be waving a stick about and screeching incantations.

There was a light tap on the door, and Mara called for the man to enter, preparing himself to face him. She was speechless when she saw the tall, distinguished gray-haired man in a pale blue robe. He smiled at her kindly.

He sat down on the stool and took her hand. Falon had returned and stood at the front of the bed with her hands folded in front of her.

"I cannot tell you of the happiness I feel, that you are back with us again, Mara," Tabo said kindly. "I am told that you have suffered a memory loss, so I would like to ask you a few questions."

Mara nodded her head. She had still not spoken to the man.

"When you first awoke, and did not recall who you were, had you received a bump on your head?"

"No, nothing like that," Mara replied, thinking that this man was asking her the same questions Dr. White had asked her.

"Have you had any flashbacks, any thoughts of your past life?"

"No, nothing, it is as if I was born the day I was found by the two trappers."

"I see," he said, examining her eyes. He stood up and smiled at her reassuringly. "Try not to let it upset you unduly. Sometimes these things take time."

"Tabo, I wish you could help me. Sometimes I am very frightened."

"I will do all I can, Mara. Let's just give it more time."

"Time seems to be the one thing I have plenty of, Tabo."

He smiled and patted her hand. "Mara, the mind is one thing that has stumped the medicine man of the Lagonda for a very long time. I am capable of treating many parts of the human body with great success, but the mind must cure itself." He looked over to the cradle where Andrew lay. "I was told by the king to examine your son. I hope you will not object, Mara."

"No, of course not," she said, biting her lower lip. Even if she wanted Andrew to be examined, she resented the fact that the order came from Tajarez.

Mara watched as Tabo poked and prodded her son. He was very thorough, examining every part of Andrew's body, while the baby gurgled and cooed at the man.

"He is in fine health, and no worse for the long journey he has made. A fine boy. You must be very proud of him."

"Yes, I have great pride in him," she replied.

Tabo smiled warmly at Mara. "I will see you tomorrow. I must now go to report to the king.

347

There is no need for my skills here; there are no sick people in this room."

"Tabo, are you certain there is nothing you can do to help my memory return?"

"Mara, I cannot say when or even if your memory will ever return. I do not want you to be unduly distressed. Should your memory return, it will happen without anyone's help." He folded his hands in a hopeless gesture. "I must caution you against becoming too upset. I want to observe you for a few days, then I may have some suggestions."

Mara sighed and sank down beneath the soft fur. It seemed that no one could help her. She watched silently as Tabo withdrew. Falon bowed her head slightly and left also.

The warmth of the fur robes was seeping into Mara's cold body. Her mind could not deal with all the wondrous things she had seen tonight. Glancing at Andrew, she saw he was drifting off to sleep. And Mara, too, fell asleep.


Tajarez stood up slowly and turned to face Tabo. "I do not see the harm of telling Mara she is my wife. I have been patient long enough. You cannot imagine what it is like to have my own wife look at me with contempt."

"You must give me a few days to study her. What is a few days when you will have a whole lifetime with Mara?"

"How easily you speak of waiting, Tabo. I have never been long on patience. Would it not be better for Mara to know I am her husband? I told you I have already been with her on the journey home. You cannot imagine what she thinks of me, whom she believes to be married to another, while seeking to pleasure myself with her.''

"This will all pass. Give me the few days I ask for,'' Tabo said, knowing full well his king was not a patient man.

Tajarez nodded grimly. "I will give you a little more time, but do not make it too long. You said my son was in good health?'' Tajarez said, deciding to change the subject.

"Yes. He reminds me of you when you were his age.''

"I want him moved to the nursery, where he can come to know his brother and sister. It is not good for him to be kept from them.''

"Mara would object strongly should you take the baby from her at this time. I suggest you wait.''

Tajarez glared at Tabo. "Is this all you can say to me: wait? I do not like to treat my own son as if he meant nothing to me.'' Tajarez's eyes blazed dangerously. "I am sick of waiting. I have hidden my feelings, trying not to let Mara see that the heart inside of me felt every pain she was feeling. I have stood by while she accused me of being faithless, and I could not defend myself to her.'' Tajarez walked away from Tabo and climbed the stairs that led to his bedroom. Halfway up the stairs he turned to the medicine man. "Make it soon, Tabo.''

Jeffery watched Sasha from a reclining position on the bed. She tucked the covers about his son, whom they had named John, after Jeffery's father. When Sasha turned to him, he could read the sadness in her eyes. He held out his arms to her and she rushed into them.

"Do not be sad, Sasha. You will see Mara tomorrow," he said, lying her down beside him.

"I do not see the harm it would have done to see her tonight. It must have been frightening for her arriving here where everything is strange to her, with no one to greet her."

"Tajarez thought it would be difficult for her if she had to face strangers."

"I cannot bear to think Mara will think of me as a stranger," Sasha said, hiding her face against Jeffery's broad chest.

"Sasha, even I, her own brother, am a stranger to her. At the moment she does not think too highly of me, thinking I betrayed her for the sake of my king."

Sasha looked into the handsome face she loved so dearly. "I am glad you are home, I have missed you so badly."

Jeffery smiled as he began to loosen the laces that held her dress together. "Show me how much you welcome me, Sasha," he whispered.


Andrew woke Mara the next morning before the sun made its appearance. She fed and bathed him, dressing him in one of the white flannel gowns she had made for him, which was almost too small for him now. He was growing so fast. She looked at the huge stack of neatly folded baby clothes that had been sent to her for Andrew's use. Even if she had to dress her son in rags, she thought bitterly, she would not let him wear the cast-offs of Tajarez's son.

She had just placed Andrew in the cradle when the door opened and Falon entered carrying a tray. "Good morning, Mara. I hope you slept well."

"Yes, I did not awaken all night," Mara said, sitting down on the bed. Falon placed the tray across Mara's lap. There was a white napkin covering the food, and Falon removed it.

Mara tasted the meat, which was seasoned with some kind of spice, and found it to be very delicious. She ate almost all of the meat, and two honey cakes, finishing it off with a cup of coffee.

"Falon, last night I had tea, and today coffee. Where does it come from?"

"I am told that the king has it brought in. Mara, the king will be so glad when I tell him that you ate so well. He is concerned that you are too thin."

Mara felt her temper rising, and she did not attempt to stem the angry words that tumbled from her lips. "I was not aware that your king took an interest in my diet. Has he nothing better to do with his time than to worry about my weight?"

Falon looked distressed. "I am sorry. I did not mean to upset you. The king said no one was to cause you distress," Falon said, not knowing she was adding fuel to Mara's already rising ire.

"The only thing that distresses me, Falon, *is* your king. I am not one of his subjects, and I will not tolerate his interfering in my life."

Falon's eyes widened in horror. The poor queen was indeed very ill. She would *never* have spoken thus of the king if she were herself. Falon, like all of the people, loved her beautiful queen, and she felt tears in her eyes.

"I will take the tray, Mara." It was very difficult for Falon to call the queen by her name, but the king had ordered her to do so.

"Falon, forgive me for speaking to you so harshly. You must understand I am not angry with you. It is your king I am not happy with," Mara said in a kind voice, seeing she had upset the girl, who, it seemed, wanted only to please her.

Not knowing what to reply, Falon set the tray on a low table and walked across the room, pulling the silver sheeting aside to reveal a closet where many gowns were hung.

"Would you like to dress now, Mara?"

Mara stood up and walked over to the closet, looking at the many different-colored gowns. "You said that this clothing belonged to me?" Mara asked, looking at the obviously expensive wardrobe. There were shoes, boots, petticoats, and bonnets. Mara knew instinctively that the gowns came straight from Paris, France.

"Where did I get these gowns, Falon?"

"I am told you brought them with you when you first came to the city."

Mara felt her heart lighten as she ran her hand down the front of a green gauze gown that was embroidered with gold thread—another link to her past. She chose a plain blue gown.

"Evidently I was well clothed, before I came here," she said, more to herself than to Falon. She was glad she could now abandon the gowns she had made herself, as well as the doeskin dress. She would have more confidence when she was well gowned, she thought.

The blue gown fit perfectly. Falon had brushed Mara's hair until it crackled, and it now framed her face in riotous curls. Studying her reflection in the silver sheeting, Mara was pleased with what she saw.

"Am I permitted to leave this room, Falon?"

"Of course. If you would like to look around, I will look after Andrew for you."

Mara looked up and down the long hallway, trying to remember in which direction the huge anteroom was located. If there was no one about she wanted to get a close look at the gold sheeting on the wall. Surprisingly, she found the palace warm, owing to the thick walls, she supposed. It did not take her long to find the anteroom, and to her relief she found it empty.

She gazed about the room in stunned silence. It was magnificent. There were twelve windows that ran from floor to ceiling. They were inlaid with diamond-bright windowpanes that resembled glass. The bright sunlight fell on the gold sheeting that adorned one whole wall. She stood beneath the gold sheeting and drew in her breath. There were the images of a great pharoah and his family carved into the gold. There were rows of hieroglyphics, and Mara knew this was what Jeffery had told her she had been translating.

Reaching out her hand, she touched the wall. The gold felt cold to her fingertips, and she shivered.

What manner of people were these people of the Lagonda tribe? How had they survived, for perhaps thousands of years, in this valley? Theirs appeared to be a civilization that would rival any in the world. How was it they had gone undetected? Her mind could not grasp the magnitude of what the discovery of the Seven Cities would mean to the rest of the world. She found herself hoping no one would ever find this valley.

Hearing voices, Mara stepped back into the shadows, not wanting to be discovered. Perhaps she was not supposed to be here. She could see two people descending the great staircase, and her eyes widened in disbelief.

Tajarez was dressed in a white toga-type wrap. Golden sandles were crisscrossed up his powerful legs to his knees. Around his neck was a golden neckpiece that hung to his waist. Atop his raven-black hair was a golden crown in the shape of two intertwined cobras. He looked like a god, a king, a pharoah!

Mara's eyes shifted to the person at his side, and she felt pain in her heart as she looked at the beautiful Indian woman. She was dressed in tan-colored doeskin that was ornamented with silver. She wanted to hate this woman, whom she thought to be the queen. Jealousy burned in her heart, and she wanted to cry out in pain. Backing farther against the wall so they would not see her, Mara bumped into a table, and a golden dish clattered to the floor, making a loud noise that seemed to echo around the room.

Pressing her hand over her heart, Mara watched as Tajarez and his queen walked slowly toward her.

There was a frown on Tajarez's face, and Mara thought she was about to face his anger for coming uninvited to the anteroom. Mara looked away from him to the woman who gave her a smile that lit her whole face. Stopping in front of her, the woman spoke.

"Mara, I am so happy to see you," Sasha said. She wanted to hug Mara and tell her there was no need to be frightened, for she read fright in the green eyes. Tajarez had warned her about Mara's condition, but seeing no recognition in her eyes was a painful experience to each person who encountered it for the first time.

"Forgive me if I am intruding," Mara blurted out and watched as Tajarez's face became a mask. Did he think she would tell his queen that he had committed an indiscretion with her? She smiled inwardly, thinking it would serve him right to squirm. Mara noticed Tajarez's hand went up to rest protectively on his queen's shoulder. She met his eyes, hoping he could not see how she was hurting at the sight of his hand touching the other woman.

"I will withdraw now," Mara said. "Please excuse me," she said, inching sideways. She could not get past them unless they moved aside to allow her to leave, she thought in a panic. She saw sadness in the woman's face, and squared her shoulders and raised her head proudly. She did not want pity from Tajarez's queen. Taking a step forward she came up against the solid wall of Tajarez's body, and he did not seem inclined to move aside.

"Excuse me, please, I would like to pass," she said, meeting his steady gaze.

"Did you pass a restful night, Mara?" he asked, not bothering to move out of her way.

"Will you please move aside so I can pass?" she said, hating the panic she heard in her own voice.

"Not just yet, Mara. There is someone who wishes to be presented to you."

Mara swallowed hard, but her eyes did not flinch as she looked at the lovely woman. On close inspection, Mara could find no flaw in the woman. Her skin was lightly bronzed. Her face was delicate and lovely. Her eyes were soft brown. Mara could easily see why Tajarez loved her.

"You do not need to tell me who this is. I have already determined that she is your wife."

Tajarez's eyes became dark storm centers.

"No!" Sasha said. "Oh Mara, you do not know me!"

"I am sorry," Mara said, totally confused. "You will have to forgive my lack of memory. If you are not the queen, then who are you?"

Tears sparkled in the soft doelike eyes as the woman reached out and took Mara's hand. "Mara, I am Jeffery's wife, Sasha, your sister-in-law."

Mara could not have been more astounded if the woman had told her she was the queen of England. "I am terribly embarrassed. Please forgive me. I feel so f . . . foolish," she stammered.

Sasha's arms went around Mara's shoulders comfortingly. "There is no reason for you to be concerned about me, Mara. You and I were best friends. Although you cannot remember, I certainly do."

Mara moved slightly away from Sasha. "I believe

you have a son," she said, trying to bring some substance of sanity into her conversation.

"Yes, he is named after your father, Mara."

"I am sorry," Mara said, again feeling at a disadvantage. "You see, I do not remember my father's name."

"Your father's name was John, and that is your brother's son's name," Sasha informed her. "I am told you have a very handsome son, called Andrew. I wonder if you would allow me to see him?"

"Yes, of course," Mara said gratefully, glad for any excuse that would take her away from the dark, brooding Tajarez. How different he seemed in his regal apparel. It was hard to think of him as the man who had held her naked body in his arms and whispered passionate words in her ear. Her eyes moved to rest on the crown with the double cobra that encircled his head. When she looked into his eyes, she could not read the expression she saw there.

"I will excuse the both of you, since I have pressing business to attend to," Tajarez said, moving away from them.

Mara breathed a sigh of relief, and she felt her tension ebb once she was relieved of his ominous presence.

Sasha played with little Andrew until he fell asleep, then she and Mara had lunch together. Mara was beginning to feel relaxed with her, and she thought they must have been good friends, because she was beginning to like her very much.

When Andrew awoke, Mara accompanied Sasha

to the third floor, where her apartments were located. As they passed the second floor on their way up the stairs, Mara looked at the imposing sentinel who guarded the second floor. He seemed to look right past her.

"Sasha, where is the queen?"

They had reached Sasha's apartment and she pushed the door open, allowing Mara to enter and giving her time to think what to say to her.

"The queen is not here for now, Mara."

Mara looked about the spacious room and thought it felt warm and welcoming, like Sasha herself.

"When will she return?"

"I am not sure," Sasha replied avoiding Mara's eyes. "I hope it will be soon."

Mara sensed that Sasha did not want to talk about the queen, so she asked no more questions.

She was delighted with little John. He had much lighter skin than Andrew, and his hair was a deep, rich brown with golden highlights. His brown eyes had green flecks in them.

Mara was finding it easy to talk to Sasha, and she seemed to be learning more about her past from her than she had from anyone else. Sasha had been to her home in St. Louis, so she described it to Mara in great detail. She told about Tess, the serving woman, who had a gruff manner, but was in truth very kind. The afternoon passed quickly, and Mara was almost sorry to leave. Sasha had invited her to take dinner with herself and Jeffery, but Mara declined, not wanting to see her brother.

Sasha escorted Mara downstairs to her own bedroom, and, with a final hug, told her she would see her the next day.

Mara ate a solitary meal in her bedroom. She then played with Andrew until he became fussy. Dressing him in a clean gown, she fed him and put him in the cradle. Time now hung heavily on her hands. It was still early, so she decided she would go into the anteroom again, if no one was about. She definitely did not want to see Tajarez again.

Falon readily agreed to watch Andrew, and Mara pulled a light shawl about her shoulders and made her way to the anteroom. Unlike the night before it was brightly lit, but there did not seem to be anyone about. Mara crossed the floor cautiously, her soft shoes hardly making any noise. When she reached the windows that looked out into the City, she let her gaze wander. It was hard to see anything but the lights. She wished she could view it in the daylight hours. Turning her attention to the gold sheeting, she crossed the room and stood staring up at what she knew would be seen as a great discovery by the scientific world. Soon she was so engrossed in the ancient carvings she did not hear the light footsteps, nor did she know Tajarez stood just behind her.

"I see you are drawn back to the ancient writings, Mara."

Mara jumped guiltly. "I hope you will not think I am intruding. I am fascinated by the hieroglyphics."

"I can assure you that you are welcome to come into the anteroom when it is not being used, which would be early in the morning or in the evenings. I would caution you, though. Do not attempt to leave the palace."

"Am I a prisoner, then?"

"Not at all. It is very cold out, and I would not like you to catch a chill."

"I am not in the least pleased with your interest in my health, and I do not believe your reasons. I just made a trip in extreme cold weather, and I did not become ill. I think you are trying to hold me here against my will. I do not yet know the reason for it, and I do not suppose you will tell me," she said, turning her back to him.

"Let us just say I do not want you to venture past the safety of the palace, and let it go at that."

"Let's not let it go at that. Give me a reason. I like to think I am a reasonable person. If someone gives me a good reason for not doing something, I will try to understand."

He seemed to loom above her. "Knowing you as I do, if I tell you not to do something, that is the very thing you will do," he said, without humor. He could not tell her one of his people might see her, and, by word or deed, reveal who she was. He had taken the precaution of placing a guard at the front entrance, to prevent her leaving.

"Why are you doing this?"

"For your own good."

"Would I be stoned if I went into the streets as a scarlet woman?" she said angrily.

"Mara, do not fight me on this. I grow weary of your sharp tongue."

"I will bid you a good night, then," she said, stinging from his words. Gathering up her swirling skirt she tried to step around him, but he barred her exit. He placed a hand on her shoulder.

"Do I have your word that you will not try to

leave by the front entrance?"

"Would you trust my word?"

"I have never had cause to doubt your honesty."

"Then I give you my word I will not try to go outside tomorrow."

Tajarez was not pacified into believing she would not attempt to go out that night. He could almost see her mind working. He had an advantage she was not aware of—he knew her.

Mara held her head high as she walked away from him. She would show him he could not dictate to her. When she reached her bedroom door she did not enter, but stood outside it, waiting for time to pass. When she felt she had waited long enough, she made her way back to the anteroom. Peering into the room, she felt that it was empty, but she would not venture forth until she was sure. Many of the torches had been extinguished and the room was in shadows. Gathering up her courage, she rushed across the floor. The door seemed a long way off, and she expected to be discovered at any moment. Glancing at the stairs, she saw no one.

When she reached the massive front door, she had trouble opening it. She pulled and tugged at the golden handles and decided that they must be locked. With a final turn, she pushed with all her strength and felt the door open. A blast of frigid air hit her in the face, and she chided herself for not bringing a cloak. She considered going back to get something warm to put on, but decided against it. She might not find the anteroom empty when she returned. She felt elated as she stepped out into the cold night air. She would stand at the top of the steps and view the city below. It felt good to know she was doing something that Tajarez disapproved of.

Hugging her arms about her for warmth, she suddenly came face to face with a fierce-looking warrior. He did not attempt to touch her, but stood with his arms folded across his chest barring her way.

"Stand aside," she said in an authoritative voice, and just for a moment she thought the man would obey her. She saw indecision on his face, but it was soon replaced by a stern look.

"My orders are not to let you pass," he said.

"I do not care about your orders. I say stand aside!"

The guard looked uneasy now, but he did not move out of her path. Mara was on the verge of pushing past him when she felt a fur cape being placed about her shoulders. Its warmth immediately embraced her cold body. She did not need to look up to know who stood behind her.

The guard bowed his head in a salute to the king and moved aside as Tajarez led Mara forward.

Mara could not suppress a shudder, wondering what her punishment would be at Tajarez's hands after she had deliberately disobeyed him.

## Twenty-Three

I cry out to a darkened sky.
I have this love that will not die.

"Do you find it necessary to terrorize my guard?" he said in a voice laced with humor. "I should be angry with you."

"If anyone should be angry, it should be me. How dare you order your guards not to let me pass?"

"My guards obey me without question. You would do well to take a lesson from them."

Mara whirled around to face him. "You . . . you are . . ."

"Insufferable?" he supplied.

"Insufferable," she repeated.

"An egotist?" he offered.

"Yes, that too! And arrogant."

"Hmmm, you forgot irritating."

Mara realized he was toying with her and her anger reached its zenith. She had the strongest urge to fly at him and pound him with her fists. He arched an eyebrow at her as if to say he knew what she was thinking.

Taking both her hands in his he swung her around

to face him. His hands moved up to rest on her shoulder. "Now it is my turn. I have had to stand here and suffer your arrows, and verbal assassination. I will now tell you what I think of you."

She stared at him haughtily. "I do not want to hear what you think of me."

His arms slid from her shoulders to her back, pulling her closer to him.

"Nonetheless, you will hear me out. You are rebellious, disobedient, and totally adorable and enchanting."

Mara wanted to run, to flee into the safety of the palace. She could stand his anger better than she could the soft tone in his voice. In spite of her anger, she felt tiny shivers of delight race down her spine. His voice was deep and husky, and she could feel his warm breath on her face.

"Release me," she said through trembling lips.

He stared at her so long she thought she could not stand it a moment longer. Her heart was racing as she stared back into his liquid brown eyes. She was frightened that he would try to kiss her, and she was afraid he would not. Dear God, she thought, how could he have such power over her? Why did she love him with her whole being?

She heard him take a deep breath and let it out slowly. "You came out here to see the city. Let me show it to you. Off to your right you will see the marketplace. If one is of a mind to, he can purchase foodstuff, clothing, household items, fine jewelry. Although you cannot see it from this vantage point, to your left is the temple. Behind that is a building, which you would call a school, where the young men of the Lagonda receive their education. Behind the palace are the stables, where all of my horses are kept. Perhaps one day I shall take you there."

In spite of her resolve not to listen to him, he had piqued her interest.

"Are your girls educated?"

"Yes, but not in the same way as the males."

"Do they read and write?"

"We have a written language, yes."

"Would it be anything like the hieroglyphics on the wall of the anteroom?"

"No. No one but yourself can read the carvings on the wall."

"I think I am beginning to see why I was brought back here and why I am not allowed to leave. You will not allow me to leave until I have completed translating the hieroglyphics."

Tajarez looked down at her and their eyes locked. Again Mara felt her heart drumming. Did he also feel this strong current that ran between them like a bolt of lightning? she wondered.

"Finish the translating, and then we shall talk about your leaving."

"Why do I have the feeling you will never allow me to leave?" Her eyes looked past him to the City below. She could see many people milling about. Her eyes were drawn to the mountains in the distance. Whether Tajarez would admit it or not, she *was* a prisoner, held captive no more by the forboding mountains than by the tall Indian who stood beside her.

"I must find a way to leave. I do not belong here," she said, looking back to Tajarez who had been watching her intently.

"Mara, what you seek will not be found beyond the mountains. What is lost to you may be much closer to you than you think."

"How can you know what I seek, when I myself do not know?"

He looked upward trying to gain control over his emotions. When he finally looked down at her, his eyes were fierce, and his voice harsh. "I know better than you do what you have lost."

"If you know this, then tell me so that I may know it also!"

Tajarez opened his mouth to speak, then reconsidered. He took her hand and led her back into the palace.

"Do not again attempt to leave the palace, Mara. There is no way you can escape."

"At last you are admitting I am your prisoner!" she cried, jerking her hand free of his grasp. "What do you want of me? Tell me so I can give it to you. I will do anything to gain my freedom."

"I am king. I need no reason to keep you. If I say you stay, you stay."

"But why?" she pleaded.

He moved forward and captured her arm before she suspected his intentions, and drew her to him. "Great Father, can you not see that I . . . want you?" he said in a passionate voice. "I lay in my bed alone last night, and thought of you alone in your bed. I wanted to come to you and beg you on my knees, if need be, to give yourself to me." His hands moved up to cup her face. He brushed a stray curl from her face. His eyes were bright and Mara was hypnotized by them.

"I am not a king with you, Mara, but a beggar. Do you want me to grovel at your feet, Mara? I can assure you I will if you ask it of me."

Mara shook her head. She could not believe the things he was saying to her. It was some kind of trick, she thought. His finger traced the outline of her face, and she closed her eyes, aching from his touch.

"Did you not like the way I made your body respond to me when we made love? Do you not want to feel that way again? Say the words and I will take you to my room. There is denial on your lips, Mara, but I see desire in your eyes." His finger lightly touched her trembling lips. "You want to say yes; I want you to say yes. Come with me now," he whispered, resting his cheek against hers.

Mara turned her face away. Oh, she wanted to say yes, but she would never consent to let him make love to her in the same bed he had shared with his queen. That thought alone gave her the courage to say no.

"I think perhaps you misjudge me, Tajarez. Even I have more thought for your queen than you do. I suggest you wait until she returns. She will give you what you cannot have from me. I do not want you to touch me."

His hands dropped away from her, and when she looked at him, his face seemed to have lost some of its color and his jaw clamped tightly. Mara was never to know what he would have said to her, for at that moment she saw Jeffery enter the anteroom, and she ran toward him.

Jeffery saw the frightened look on his sister's face and put his arms about her. "What has occurred? You seem overly distressed."

"If you have any love for me you will protect me from the man you call king!"

Jeffery's eyes shifted to Tajarez, who had come up behind Mara. "What is the meaning of this, Tajarez? What have you done to my sister?"

It was the first time Mara had heard Jeffery raise his voice to Tajarez, and her spirits rose. Perhaps her brother would now help her to get away from this hell.

Tajarez was still smarting from Mara's words, and it did not help his temper any that she had run to her brother to be protected from him.

"I merely tried to induce your sister to come to my bed. Do you have any objections?"

Mara's eyes moved from one man to the other. Surely Jeffery would not take such an insult directed at his own sister. Tajarez would not be so arrogant once her brother took her side against him. She watched, horrified, as she read indecision on Jeffery's face.

"I wish you would not talk so plainly in front of Mara. I do not like to see her embarrassed," Jeffery said.

"Embarrassed!" Mara screamed. "What about honor, pride, brother-sister love? What about the insult to one of your own blood?" Mara's voice was high-pitched, and she was on the verge of hysteria. "Would you stand by while your sister is held prisoner and humiliated by this man? Are you such a coward that you will not help me?"

Jeffery looked into the eyes of his sister and saw fear. He knew how he must appear in her eyes. But he was helpless to do anything. What could he say against her own husband? Was this nightmare ever going to end?

"Tajarez, I am going to move my sister into my apartment with Sasha and myself. I think she would feel better there," Jeffery finally said.

"Mara stays where she is, Jeffery. Are you forgetting who I am?"

Mara gathered up the skirts of her gown and fled to her room.

"Damnit, Tajarez, can you not control your ardor until Mara remembers who she is? You are making her suffer needlessly. Heaven only knows what she thinks of me, and I cannot even go to her and offer her comfort," Jeffery said angrily.

"I do not have to answer to you, Jeffery. I have tried to stay away from her, but in spite of my good intentions, I cannot leave her alone."

"In the future you might consider her feelings and try a little harder," Jeffery said dryly, as he turned on his heels to leave.

Tajarez watched him depart, and he then walked up the stairs, feeling as if he carried the weight of the world on his broad shoulders.

When Mara reached her room, she found Andrew awake and hungry. She dismissed Falon so she could be alone with her son. Here, in this room, was the only place she felt safe. Looking at the door she saw there was no lock on it. Suppose Tajarez were to come to her here?

Oh God, what was she to do? It seemed as if the

walls were beginning to close in on her. She must find a way to escape! There was no one she could turn to. No one would help her. She had to think rationally. If she did not get away, it would be only a matter of time before Tajarez broke down her defenses and she submitted to him again. He seemed to have a strange power over her. She loved him and wanted nothing more than to be with him.

Andrew's hunger was satisfied, and he fell asleep. Laying him in his cradle, Mara undressed and climbed into bed. Her life had been one upheaval after another since she had first awakened with Jake and Zeke.

Rolling over to her side, Mara tried to fall asleep, but she kept remembering the things Tajarez had said to her tonight. "Why do I love you!" she cried. I do not want to love you. She knew she would never be able to endure another day like today. She prayed for sleep, but it was a long time coming.

The next morning when Falon entered carrying Mara's breakfast tray, she found Mara dressing Andrew. She placed the tray down on a table and smiled at the little prince.

"Mara, if you will allow me to finish dressing Andrew, you can eat your meal while it is hot."

Mara nodded her consent. She sighed as she picked up one of the corncakes spread with honey. Taking a bite she wondered how she would pass the long hours of the day that seemed to yawn before her. She thought about going into the anteroom and studying the gold sheeting on the walls, but quickly rejected that idea, fearing she might encounter Tajarez.

Falon had finished dressing Andrew and lifted him into her arms. "I have a message for you from the king, Mara."

Mara took a sip of the steaming hot coffee and looked at Falon. She wanted to tell the girl that she did not want to hear anything that her king had to say, but she thought better of it. Falon was a sweet girl and Mara knew it would not be right to take out her anger on her.

"What did he ask you to tell me?" Mara asked, trying to disguise the anger in her voice, but not entirely succeeding.

"My king said to tell you that if you wish it, Palomas will accompany you into the garden. He said the fresh air will do you good." Falon frowned. "I do not fully understand the rest of the message."

"What more did he have to say?"

"My king said that you were not to worry, he would not trouble you again."

Mara was immediately suspicious of Tajarez's motives. "Has the queen returned?"

Falon looked down at little Andrew so she would not have to meet Mara's eyes. "My queen is not yet with us. I am told that the king is leaving the City to search for Sagas, the wise."

Mara pushed the breakfast tray aside, feeling somewhat relieved. If Tajarez was out of the City she would not have to worry about running into him. Perhaps with him gone she could search for a way to leave the valley.

The days passed slowly. Winter seemed reluctant

to loosen its grip on the land. Fresh snow fell almost daily. The skies were bleak and overcast. The season suited Mara's mood. She now spent a great deal of time with Sasha, glad that her brother had gone away with Tajarez and she would not have to see him.

Mara felt that she and Sasha were forming a strong bond of friendship. They had much in common in their small sons. Mara was finding out that Sasha had a kind and loving nature, and she could see why her brother had married her and chosen to live in the hidden valley, instead of in the white world he had grown up in.

It was from Sasha that Mara learned of her first long journey from St. Louis to the hidden valley. She was surprised to learn that Tajarez had accompanied her and Jeffery on that journey. Mara began to suspect that Sasha knew about her and Tajarez, for any time Mara tried to ask questions about the king, Sasha would tactfully change the subject.

Suddenly Mara needed to know if she and Tajarez had been together on her first trip to this valley. "Sasha, on the journey from St. Louis, did . . . were Tajarez and I lovers?" she asked, her face flaming red.

"Oh no, Mara, Tajarez did not touch you then!"

"How can you be sure?"

"You must trust me that I am telling you the truth in this, Mara. My king did not dishonor you at that time."

"Sasha, do you know who is the father of Andrew? The answer to who his father is seems to plague me more than anything else. Why does the man not come forth to claim his son?"

"Mara, only you can answer that question. I pray each night that you will find that part of your life that you have lost, then you yourself will know the truth about Andrew's father."

That night Jeffery returned to the City, but Sasha told Mara that Tajarez was still away.

Mara tried to avoid encountering her brother. She did not like him very much and did not want to see him. If she was visiting Sasha and Jeffery came in, she would make an excuse to leave. She remembered when Jeffery had come to the cabin to take her home. She had trusted him blindly, and now she was living to rue the day he had taken her away from Jake and Zeke. Somehow, some way, she would find a way to leave this valley. Nothing was impossible. If one wanted something badly enough, one could make anything happen.

Palomas came to Mara daily and accompanied her on a walk in the garden. She felt comfortable with him and began to look forward to their daily walks. For some reason that Mara could not understand, she had been barred from the anteroom, and there were times when she was forbidden access to the garden. When she questioned Palomas about the reason, he told her that when the royal prince and princess were in the garden she would be unable to go there.

Mara did not know that Tajarez had taken precautions so she would not see Hamez and Tamera. He did not want her to find out they were her son and daugher while he was away looking for Sagas. One look at their green eyes and she might guess that she was their mother.

Mara and Palomas were walking in the garden. It was a warm day and the wind had died down, so she had bundled Andrew up warmly, thinking the fresh air would do him good. Palomas was carrying him, and Mara noticed the loving expression on Palomas's face as he smiled at Andrew. She was suddenly struck with a horrible thought. Palomas was Andrew's father! Why had she not seen it before? Why else would he be so devoted to her and Andrew? He was always near, watching over them.

Looking up, Palomas saw the color drain from Mara's face. "What is the matter, Mara? Are you ill?" he asked in a concerned voice. He took her hand and led her to a bench and sat her down on it.

Mara shook her head in disbelief. "Why did you not tell me? Why did you let me wonder who was the father of my son?" she whispered.

"If you would tell me what you are asking, perhaps I could answer you, Mara," he said, hoping at long last that she was beginning to remember her past life.

"You are the father of Andrew!" she cried.

Palomas looked dumbfounded that she could have drawn such a wrong conclusion. "You think I fathered your son?" His face eased into a smile, as if he were amused by her declaration.

"You could have told me, although it was there for me to see all the time. I wonder why I did not see it before now."

Palomas placed Andrew in Mara's lap and then

knelt down beside her. "Mara, if you place any value on my life, you would not make such a rash statement. Never say this while in the presence of others." His voice still sounded as if he were amused.

"What do you mean?"

He laughed out loud, and she was startled by his humor. Palomas rarely ever smiled, and she did not see anything to be amused about now.

"What I am saying to you, Mara, is that I could not have fathered Andrew, nor any other child, for that matter."

"Oh," she said, not understanding, and ducking her head in shame.

"Mara, look at me," he said, raising her chin. "As the queen's protector, I had to go through a ceremony that rendered me impotent. I cannot lie with a woman, therefore, I could not be the father of your son."

Mara's face reddened, and she tried to hide her horror. "What kind of monster is this queen that she would ask for the manhood of a warrior such as yourself? I did not like her before, I could easily hate her now."

Palomas still seemed amused. "Mara, what was done to me was not of the queen's doing. I allowed the operation of my own free will. I find it a great honor to serve my queen, as would any man I know. There are countless men who would gladly exchange places with me. I have heard it said that when the queen heard of my operation, she was as horrified as you are at this moment."

"I think it is inhuman, no matter how you try to

375

convince me otherwise. Why is she so important that you would give up so much to serve her?"

Palomas stood up to his full height, unwilling to discuss the matter further. "Mara, should you not take Andrew inside? The wind seems to have come up suddenly."

"In other words," she said standing up and looking at him angrily, "you do not want to hear me criticize your precious queen."

Her led her toward the palace. "I do not like to hear anything said against her," he admitted.

Mara stopped their progress and looked up at Palomas. "What is there about this woman that inspires such devotion from so many?" she wanted to know.

"She is the queen," Palomas said, as if that would explain everything.


The days seem to drag by slowly, and the elusive queen did not appear, nor did Tajarez return.

Mara found herself wishing she were allowed to enter the anteroom. If she could only study the drawings on the wall, it would help time pass more quickly. It seemed as if time was holding its breath, waiting for something to happen. Endless hours followed endless hours. One morning Mara was told that the king had returned, and it seemed he was keeping his word to her, for he had not sought her out.

Andrew was growing rapidly. He liked to crawl around on the floor putting everything he could find into his mouth. Sasha had given Mara John's outgrown clothing, and Mara had ordered Falon to get rid of the things Vista had sent her for her son.

Spring was gradually winning over winter. Most of the days were warm and sunny, and the moisture that fell from the skies was now in the form of spring rains instead of winter snows. The garden was beginning to come to life. There were tiny green buds on the trees, and Mara felt the time was fast approaching for her to try to leave this valley. She needed to have a plan and to watch for the right opportunity.

She now accepted the fact that her memory was never going to return. The past was dead, the future unsure. Many times at night when Mara was alone she would cry out in her despair.

# Twenty-Four

On my bed at night I toss and turn
As this jealousy inside me begins to burn.

Mara and Palomas were strolling in the garden. Palomas carried Andrew on his shoulders, and the baby squealed with delight at each new discovery he made. He seemed pleased with the brightly colored butterflies that had made the garden their home. Mara loved the tiny dark-skinned baby who seemed to infect everyone with his laughter and sweet smile.

Palomas lifted Andrew from his shoulders and tossed him into the air. Andrew's eyes grew bright and he laughed in gleeful delight.

Mara was not aware that other eyes watched them. Jealous eyes. Tajarez was not at all pleased that his own son knew Palomas better than he did his own father. Mara seemed to enjoy being with the fierce warrior, and when Mara smiled at Palomas it was like daggers in Tajarez's heart. He had come up behind them silently, and Mara was startled when he spoke.

"Hello, Mara, do you mind if I join you?"

Spinning around to face him. Mara could feel her

heart skip a beat. She had not seen him in such a long time, and she had hoped she had gotten over her feelings for him. But one look into his dark eyes and she knew she still felt the same.

"This is your garden, Tajarez," she said trying to sound normal.

Tajarez's eyes moved to the child in Palomas's arms. "It seems your son thrives. He has grown since last I saw him."

"Yes. The medicine man assures me that Andrew is a healthy boy."

"Yes, Tabo has said the same thing to me." He looked back to Mara. "He also told me that you have not regained any of your memory."

Palomas handed Andrew to Mara and withdrew a few paces.

"I have accepted the fact that I will never remember the past. It no longer seems as important to me as it once did," she answered him, trying to avoid his dark eyes, which seemed to be pulling at her heart.

Andrew took an interest in the stranger. Seeing the bright, shiny crown on Tajarez's head, he reached out his arms to him. Mara grabbed Andrew's hands and tried to distract him, but Andrew was not easily swayed from his quest. Jerking his hands free of his mother's grasp, he leaned toward Tajarez.

Tajarez took the tiny boy in his arms and smoothed his dark silky hair from his face. His eyes wandered lovingly over the face of the son he could not acknowledge.

"I am sorry, Tajarez. Andrew is a very loving child, and he seems to have a mind of his own."

"He is a beautiful child," Tajarez said in an unsteady voice.

"Thank you. I am pleased when anyone admires Andrew."

"I wonder if you would allow Falon to bring Andrew to the nursery today, so Hamez and Tamera might see him?" Tajarez asked.

Mara looked undecided for a moment. "I do not know. Why would you want Andrew to be with your children?"

"I think they would enjoy seeing him. It would please me if you were to say yes."

"I suppose it would do no harm," she said, puzzled by his request. "I have been told by Sasha that your children are very beautiful."

"Yes, they are, but no more so than Andrew," Tajarez told her as he handed her son back to her. He started to walk away from her when Mara spoke.

"Please, do not go yet. There is something of great importance I wish to ask you."

He paused and waited for her to speak, nodding his dark head.

"It is spring, and I was wondering if you would allow me to visit my brother David, in St. Louis?"

His face seemed to freeze and his eyes narrowed. "I had hoped you would not be content to abide with us. I have kept my word to you and stayed away from you."

"Why can you not see, I do not want to stay here? This is not my home. Please allow me to leave."

"What if I were to give you the freedom to go where you wished in the City, would you then consider staying with me . . . with us?"

380

"No, I need to leave here; I feel if I do not get away, I will lose what little of my sanity I have left."

He sat down on a bench and looked at the golden hair that framed her lovely face. Great Father, how he hated to play the heavy-handed king with her, when all he really wanted to do was give her anything that would make her smile again. "Have you thought that life would be like for your son in the white man's world? Andrew would never be accepted, the other children would taunt and ridicule him, and their mothers and fathers would forbid them to play with him. Would it not be far better for you and Andrew to remain here with us?" he said, knowing he was taking unfair advantage of her love for her child.

"I have thought about what you are saying, but I cannot bring myself to leave him, and I cannot stay."

"Mara, I have seen to it that you are given everything within reason that you ask for. You have someone to see to your every need. If there is anything you desire, I will see that you have it, but . . . do not ask me to let you leave."

"You cannot see how I feel. How many times must I tell you, I want to be free! I do not want any of the things you offer. Freedom to me would be more precious than life!"

Tajarez reached out his hand and touched her soft cheek. "Oh, Mara, I have kept my word to stay away from you. Never has it been so hard for me to keep my word. I want to hold you and help you to be rid of all your fears. Come with me now, and I will do no more than you will allow."

Tears welled up in her eyes, and he pulled her head to rest against his broad shoulder. "Please keep your word to me, for you are far stronger than I. I fear I would give you all you asked," she admitted, surprising not only herself, but Tajarez as well.

Tajarez pushed her away from him and stood up. "Great Father, this whole thing begins to tell on me. You once told me you detested me, now you admit you are drawn to me. What are your true feelings?"

"I do not know, all I am certain of is what I want to get away."

"I will never allow you to leave, Mara. Never!"

Mara looked at Palomas, who was standing at a discreet distance from them. "I will find a way to leave, Tajarez. You can put guards on me but they cannot watch me every moment. You have my word, before too many more days have passed, I will be gone."

Tajarez's face creased into a frown and his dark eyes became piercing. Before Mara suspected his intentions, he reached for Andrew and called out to Palomas.

"Take the child to the royal nursery," he told Palomas, handing Andrew to him.

"No, you cannot do this!" Mara cried out reaching for her son, but Tajarez grabbed her about the waist, restraining her, while Palomas gave her a sympathetic glance. "Palomas, do not take my baby away from me!"

Palomas turned his back on her and walked toward the palace. He thought he had never before wanted to disobey his king as he did at that moment.

"I do not think I will need a guard to keep you

here, Mara. You would never leave without Andrew, and he will remain in the nursery with Hamez and Tamera.''

As Mara struggled to be free of him, Tajarez's grip tightened about her waist.

"Are you such a monster that you would take a baby who is not yet weaned from his mother!" she screamed.

"Do not fear, Vista will find a suitable woman to feed your son. I suggest you go to your room now," he said, in a voice of authority.

Mara jerked free of him and raised her head proudly. She would not beg and grovel at his feet. The mighty king of the Seven Cities had just overstepped his bounds. She was not beaten, and if he thought she was, then he was a bigger fool than she thought him to be.

Tajarez watched as she walked away from him, her back straight and her head high. He had never loved her more, nor trusted her less, than he did at that moment.


Tajarez entered the nursery and was greeted by a beaming Vista, who was holding Andrew in her arms. "He is wonderful, my king. I am glad to get to hold him at last. He looks very much like you."

"Do you think so?" he said, pleased at her observation.

"It is so, my king."

He entered a second room, where the twins were playing on the floor. Vista handed Andrew into his arms and then withdrew to give him privacy with his three children.

Tajarez sat down on the floor and held Andrew out for Tamera and Hamez's inspection. "I have a surprise for you. Someone special has come to see you. You must be very patient and gentle with him, for he is but a baby."

"I like babies," Hamez said, looking with interest at the child in his father's arms.

"Can I hold him?" Tamera said, moving to her father's side.

"Yes, you may hold him, for, you see, this baby belongs to you and your brother. He is my son as Hamez is my son, and he is brother to each of you."

"Brother," Hamez said.

"Yes. His name is Andrew, and he is your brother."

Tamera clapped her hands delightedly, but Hamez merely looked puzzled. "Can this brother play with me?"

"No, not until he grows bigger. He is very small."

Tamera peered down at her newly acquired brother. "Oh," she said in an awed voice, as she reached out her hand to touch Andrew's soft cheek. Andrew blessed her with a winsome smile and Tamera clapped her hands in delight.

Hamez looked down at his brother and nodded his approval. "I like him," he announced.

Tajarez lifted Andrew to his face and held him against his cheek. There was no one who could deny him the right to his son. In the privacy of the nursery he could show him the love he had kept secret.

A smile creased Tajarez's face as Andrew began to snuggle close to him. "I love you, my son; Forgive me for the neglect. I will make it all up to you now."

"Tamera hold baby," his daughter said, holding out her arms.

Tajarez placed Andrew in her small, willing arms. "You must hold him secure, Tamera." Tajarez urged as he helped her support her brother.

"I love him," she said as she placed a kiss on his bronzed cheek.

"I want him to play with me," Hamez said, touching the soft, silky hair that covered the baby's head.

"I told you, Hamez, Andrew is too small to play with you now. You must be patient until he grows."

"He is very nice," Hamez said, giving his approval again.

"You are his father?" Tamera wanted to know.

"Yes, just as I am your father."

"Can we keep him?" Hamez wanted to know.

Tajarez looked into the faces of the twins and saw their eagerness: "Yes, Andrew will be staying with you."

The eyes of the tiny prince royal lit up. "How long will it take for him to grow up?"

Tajarez smiled. "Hardly any time at all, Hamez. Before you know it, Andrew will be big enough to play with you."


Mara lay dry-eyed across her bed. She had sent Falon to the nursery to bring Andrew back to her. She heard the door open and rolled over to see Falon with a dejected frown on her face.

"Where is my son, Falon?" Mara demanded.

"Mara, I was told that Andrew would be staying in the royal nursery with the twins," Falon told her, distressed by the look on her queen's face, and not understanding why the king had taken Andrew away.

"For how long, Falon?"

Falon ducked her head. "Vista told me the king said Andrew would be staying in the nursery permanently."

Mara had not really believed that Tajarez would follow through with his threat. After she had had time to think about it, she had decided he would merely use Andrew to make her submissive to his will.

"Your king oversteps his authority. I will go to the nursery and get my son." Mara said raising from the bed and placing her hands on her hips.

"Mara, the guard at the stairs will not allow you to climb to the second floor where the nursery is."

"Where is Tajarez?"

"I am told that he is in the small chamber just off the anteroom," Falon said, wondering what Mara would do to get her son back.

"I will go to him and demand that he return my son to me," Mara said as she stormed to the door and pushed past Falon.

"Mara, the king's word is law," Falon cried in a futile attempt to stop Mara from being hurt any more than she had already been.

"Perhaps for you his word is law, but not for me," Mara said pushing the door open and slamming it behind her.

Falon covered her face with her hands, wondering

what would happen when the queen encountered the king.

Mara burst into the room where she had been told she would find Tajarez. He had been talking to Palomas and when Mara entered both men looked up at her. Both of them knew her well, and they knew by the look on her face that she had come to do battle. Palomas looked at Tajarez and walked to the door, leaving Mara to face his king alone.

"Come in, Mara I have been expecting you." He gave her a mock bow. "Would you care to sit down?"

She ignored his offer to sit. "I do not care if you are king, I will not tolerate your taking my baby from me. Andrew belongs with me. You have had your fun at my expense, you have made me squirm, now you just go and get Andrew and bring him to me," she demanded.

"Sit down, Mara, I want to talk to you."

"I do not want to talk to you. I have said all I came to say. I will be waiting in my room for the return of my baby."

"Why do you always revert to English when you are angry, Mara?"

"I meant what I said, Tajarez," she said, ignoring his barb.

His dark eyes scanned her face with such intensity that Mara closed her eyes against them. "Mara, Andrew will remain in the nursery."

"You only took him as a weapon to use against me. I do not know why you are doing this to me. What have I ever done to you to make you want to treat me so cruelly?"

"Mara, the last thing I would ever want to do is to cause you pain. I have done everything others have told me to do, without knowing what was right. I will now make a decision on my own."

"I do not understand what you are trying to say."

"Great Father, I cannot stand much more of this. Can you not see? Are you so blind that you do not know that Andrew is my son!"

# Twenty-Five

Why do I covet that which is not mine?
Why do I grow bolder with the passing of time?

Mara's face whitened, and she could feel her body begin to tremble. Her hands were shaking so badly she tried to clasp them together to steady them. Seeing her reaction, Tajarez began to fear she could not handle any more. He was glad he had not blurted out that she was his wife.

She backed away from him shaking her head. "No! You lie! Oh, dear God no. Why are you saying this to me? You said before that Andrew was *not* your son."

He reached out and drew her unwilling body into his arms. "No, Mara, I never denied that Andrew was my son."

She searched her mind trying to remember. "But you implied that he was not your son, that is the same thing." She tried to pull away from him, but he held her firmly.

"Mara, Andrew is the son of my flesh. You and I have loved each other many times in the past," he said, resting his face against hers. "I want to make love to you at this moment."

His warm breath stirred her hair, and she felt a weakness in the pit of her stomach. Try as she might, she could not find it in her to resent that he was her son's father. It seemed only right that Tajarez had fathered her son.

"I cannot stand by day after day, wanting to make love to you, yet not being allowed to. If you only knew the torment I have been living through, Mara."

His mouth was only a hairs-breadth away from hers, and his hands were drawing her tightly against his body, Mara's pulse quickened and she closed her eyes as his lips settled on hers. Someone somewhere was moaning, and it took Mara seconds before she realized it was she.

His lips left hers to start the slow mind-destroying trip down the curve of her neck. Nothing and no one mattered at that moment but the feelings Tajarez awakened in her starving body. His hands moved up over her breasts and Mara gasped as his mouth nibbled at the lobe of her ear.

"Mara, beloved," he cried out in his agony, as he crushed her in his arms. "Allow me to carry you to my room. I want to love you; do not deny me."

Everywhere his hands touched her flesh they seemed to sear her skin, as well as her mind. She could feel his hard body pressed tightly against hers, and she knew that the last thing she wanted to do was to deny his slightest wish. Everything but the feelings he had aroused in her body was blotted out. She had all but forgotten her reason for seeking him out in this room, but some tiny voice in the back of her mind reminded her she could not go with him to his room. She would not allow him to make love to her in the room where he slept with his queen.

"No. Not in your room," she whispered, groaning as his mouth settled on hers. When he raised his head, Tajarez saw that Mara's eyes were bright with desire. Lifting her in his arms he carried her out the door, across the anteroom and down the hallway to her room. Mara leaned her head against his chest listening to the heavy drumming of his heart. This is wrong, her mind said. It was meant to happen, her heart answered.

Mara saw that he was taking her to the room she occupied, and she hoped Falon would not be waiting for her. But when Tajarez laid her on her bed she saw the room was empty.

Mara thought she could not stand it as Tajarez unfastened the back of her gown slowly, deliberately. When her gown fell to the floor in a heap, he picked her up and placed her on the bed.

"The queen?" Mara whispered, in a last attempt to free her mind.

"I love you," Tajarez said against her lips. "I love only you." His lips came down on hers hungrily, as Mara's heart sang, "He loves me, he loves *me.*"

Mara felt her undergarments being removed. Closing her eyes, she felt the weight of Tajarez's body pinning her into the soft covers.

"Beloved, I have been in torment. I searched for you, not knowing if I would ever find you, and when you returned to me you looked at me with the eyes of a stranger. Hold me, Mara; let me feel alive again!"

Mara's hands ran down his back and settled at his

narrow waist. She could feel the hardness of his body, and she knew he desired her as she desired him. It did not matter what happened tomorrow, this was now, and she could feel the torment he had spoken of. His body trembled as she turned her head and sought his lips. With a strangled groan, he sought entrance to her body, an entrance made easy for him by the arching of her eager body. As he started moving inside of her, Mara thought she would not be able to bear the beauty of it. Her fingers laced into his long ebony hair as her body became a part of his. Sensuous feelings filled her body, and Mara knew that she had been created to give and receive pleasure from Tajarez. If she were to die tomorrow, tonight she was more alive than she had ever been.

Tajarez's breathing had become labored as he took her beautiful body. He had thought in the past that she had given him more pleasure than a man could ever hope for, but never before had he felt this deep love that surpassed mortal love and reached for the immortal. His body was on fire, his mind was attuned to Mara's. It was as if he could feel every sensation she was feeling and know every thought she was thinking. Their bodies were soaring among the heavens, on golden wings. When Tajarez was sure they had reached the highest point anyone had ever attained, their bodies floated softly back to earth. Time seemed to have no meaning as they lay in each other's arms, both overcome with the wonderful thing that had just passed between them.

Mara looked into the dark eyes of Tajarez and was almost blinded by the love she saw reflected there.

"Did I love you before?" she asked as her hand drifted down his arm and her fingers laced through his fingers.

"You said that you did," he told her as he raised her hand and kissed it softly.

Her free hand pushed a strand of dark hair from his handsome face. "It would seem that I fell in love with you twice, then."

Tajarez cupped her face between his hands and looked deeply into her eyes. "Are you saying that you love me now?"

Her voice caught in her throat. "I love you so much it hurts."

"Beloved, I have waited so long to hear you speak those words to me," he said as his hand drifted over her hips.

"I feel as if this is not the first time I have said those words to you. I must have said I love you many times."

"Not nearly enough," he murmured in her ear. Sounds of pleasure issued from her lips as his hands moved over her breasts. "Having babies does no harm to your body, Mara, you are still unblemished.

"I have only had one baby," she whispered, wondering how his stroking hands could awaken her body so easily. "Tajarez, am I . . . was I promiscuous?"

"No." Her soft curves were driving him wild with renewed desire.

"Are you the only man I have ever been with?"

He raised his head and looked at her, a smile playing on his lips. "I am the only lover you have ever had."

"I am glad. I would not like to think I would allow anyone but you to touch me."

"Beloved, I wish you could remember all we shared in the past." His smile deepened. "We shall make new memories."

Mara closed her eyes as his hand rested on her thigh. She remembered when he had told her he loved his wife. Was it possible for a man to love more than one woman? She could not imagine ever loving anyone but Tajarez. The woman who was his queen began to fade from her thoughts as Tajarez pulled her beneath him. She met his forward thrust and soon everything faded from her mind but sensations that seemed to move the very earth. If her mind did not remember Tajarez, her body had not forgotten him, for she obeyed every command his body issued to hers.

Afterwards he rolled over on his back and pulled her on top of him, his hands moving lovingly over her body. Resting her head on his shoulder, Mara closed her eyes. A feeling of peace descended on her. It was as though, after searching for so long to find where she belonged, she had at last come home. She could not think about tomorrow, when she must plan how she could leave. Tonight belonged to her.

"Beloved, do you still not remember?"

"No, I remember nothing."

Moments passed and they were content just to hold each other. Mara was quiet for so long that Tajarez thought she might have fallen asleep, until she raised her head and looked into his face.

"Tajarez, are you permitted to have more than one wife?"

Now was the time to tell her that she was his wife, he thought. But no, Tabo was visiting one of the other Cities, and if Mara should have an extreme reaction to finding out that she was the queen, he wanted Tabo to be present in the palace. He would send for him tomorrow, and by tomorrow night he would tell Mara who she was, even if Tabo objected.

"No, Mara, I am permitted but one wife. Even if my wife were dead I would be unable to remarry."

"Why is that?" she asked with a heavy heart. She would even be willing to share him with another, if he could marry her, she thought.

"Were there not a son to become prince royal and my wife were to die, I would then be required to take another wife."

"I do not understand."

"It is believed that the prince royal should have no rival brothers from a different mother."

"Like Andrew?"

Tajarez chose to misunderstand her. "Mara, brothers of the same mother and father are rarely jealous of one another, not if they are raised properly, but a half-brother could be envious of the prince royal."

"Yes, I can see what you are saying. But what about Andrew?"

"Mara, I want you to know that I love Andrew every bit as much as I do Hamez and Tamera."

"You pointed out to me how Andrew would be treated in the white world. Will he be treated any differently here in this valley, as the illegitimate son of the king?"

"I can assure you that Andrew will be well received."

Mara laid her head back against his shoulder and spoke so softly that he almost did not catch her words.

"Do you have any other illegitimate children?"

His body shook with laughter. "No, I have no children other than Hamez, Tamera, and last, but no less important, Andrew."

"Oh."

"Let us not talk of others, Mara. I want you to think only of me."

Indeed, Mara was unable to think of anything but him as he raised her head and captured her lips.

Mara fell asleep in Tajarez's arms feeling loved and wanted.

The next morning Tajarez arose early and dressed. He moved silently so he would not awaken Mara. There was much to do today, and the most important thing was to send someone to bring Tabo back to the palace.

Mara awoke and reached out her hand for Tajarez but discovered he was gone. She knew she had not dreamed the night before, for her lips were swollen from Tajarez's kisses, and her body was strangely alive. She climbed quickly out of bed and picked up her discarded gown. She needed some answers, and she knew who could supply them for her. She would visit Sasha.

It was only a short time later that Mara stood before Sasha's door rapping softly. The door was opened by Sasha herself, and the Indian woman's face lit up at the sight of Mara.

"Is my brother here?" Mara asked as she stepped into the room.

"No, but I am sure if he knew you wanted to see him, he would come at once," Sasha said, knowing how much Jeffery had suffered because Mara would not talk to him.

"I did not come to see Jeffery. I want to talk to you."

"I will get you a cup of coffee. Would you like breakfast?"

"No, coffee is fine," Mara said, sitting down.

Mara waited impatiently for Sasha to return with the coffee, and when Sasha handed her the steaming brew Mara placed it on the table without tasting it.

"Sasha, I want you to tell me about the queen."

Sasha's eyes widened. "What would you like to know?"

"Anything and everything."

Sasha set tensely on the edge of her seat. "I, like everyone else, love the queen. After Jeffery and John, I love her best in the world. She is kind, and is always thinking of others before herself."

"What does she look like?"

"I think she is by far the most beautiful woman I have ever seen, and many share that opinion, especially the . . ."

"The king," Mara finished, feeling as though a knife had pierced her heart. "Does Tajarez love the queen?"

"Yes, he loves her above all else."

Mara closed her eyes. Was Tajarez a man who loved two women, or had he told her nothing but lies last night?

"If Tajarez loves the queen as you say he does, why would he be unfaithful to her?"

Sasha's face seemed suddenly to be drained of its color, and she leaned forward and spoke in a hushed voice. "You must not say this thing, Mara. The king would never betray the queen, to do so would mean his death!"

"W . . . what are you saying?"

"I am saying that it is forbidden by law for the king to seek pleasure with anyone other than his queen. Should he do so he would be put to death. It is the law."

Mara jumped to her feet and covered her face with her hands. She was sobbing, and Sasha stood up to put a comforting arm around her shoulders.

"Oh, Sasha, what have I done? Had I known, I would never have allowed Tajarez to make love to me!" She pushed Sasha away from her. "Promise me you will say nothing of this to anyone. Oh Sasha, I have condemned him to death, if anyone finds out." She grabbed Sasha's hands and pleaded with her, tears streaming down her face. "I must get away!"

Sasha felt tears in her eyes at what Mara was suffering so needlessly. "I would never betray you or the king," she promised her.

"Sasha, do you hate me, do you feel I have betrayed your queen?"

"No, Mara, I do not feel that way at all." Sasha now thought that keeping Mara's identity from her had been a mistake from the start, and she decided to tell Tajarez that he must tell Mara the truth. "Mara, I think you should tell Tajarez how you feel."

"No, I must not ever see him again," Mara started pacing the floor. She had to find a way to escape.

"Sasha, you must help me get away, there must be some way to leave this place."

"I would do almost anything you asked of me, Mara, but I will not help you in this."

"I must go," Mara said, rushing toward the door. "Tell no one what I have said to you, Sasha."

Sasha watched with heartbreak written on her face as Mara left. She was usually a soft-spoken, kind person, indeed, few had ever heard Sasha raise her voice in anger, but she was now determined to tell Tajarez just how she felt about the way Mara was being made to suffer. She had no fear that Mara would be able to make good her threat to leave the city. Too many people were watching her. But Mara would try, and she would be devastated when she did not succeed.

Mara fled down the stairs and out into the garden. She knew she would never be able to make her escape through the front entrance of the palace. If she were to get away unseen, it could only be through the garden.

# Twenty-Six

A heart that is broken does not easily mend.
How can I leave him? I cried to the wind.


Mara looked about the garden, thankful that no one seemed to be about. Her eyes scanned the high wall and she knew she would never be able to scale the stone structure. Walking the length of the high garden wall, she searched for a gate.

The wind whipped her gown and she could see heavy clouds in the distance. It had grown colder and she thought it would snow again before the day was out.

Mara could not seem to think straight. All that mattered to her now was making her escape. She told herself that Andrew would be well cared for, Tajarez had said he loved him and would not her son be better off here with his own kind than with her in the white world? Mara tried not to think about the night before. Her loving Tajarez had come at a high price if it was going to cost him his life. She was almost frantic now, searching for some means of escape.

Finally, in an obscure corner of the garden, Mara found the gate she had been searching for. It was made of heavy wooden logs and looked as solid as the wall that supported it. She was unaware that tears were streaming down her face as she pushed against the unyielding gate with all her strength.

Mara heard someone calling out her name and turned her head in the direction of the palace. Fearing that whoever it was would discover her at the gate, she rushed toward the big pond. The gate and her escape would have to wait until she could get rid of whomever it was who had called out to her.

When she reached the pond, she sat down on one of the marble benches. Her shoulders slumped and sobs shook her body. Mara surrendered herself to total misery. A familiar shadow detached itself from the background and knelt down beside her. Feeling someone's presence, Mara raised her head and looked at Palomas. His face was full of sadness and compassion.

"Do not weep, Mara. When it seems the night is at its darkest a star will light the sky."

"Everything seems so hopeless, Palomas. The days and nights both are void of any light for me."

"I feel grief that you are sad, Mara."

She wiped her eyes on the back of her hands and tried to smile. "I do not know you very well. Why should you be sad for me?"

"I know you, Mara."

She sighed heavily. "Everyone seems to know me but me."

Palomas reached for her hand, but then thought better of it. "Mara, there are many who know you and wish for your complete recovery."

"Palomas, sit beside me and tell me about your

queen," she said, wanting to change the subject. "Tell me she has a flaw, a fault, or that she is at least human."

Palomas sat beside her on the bench and smiled. "My queen has a temper, and she can become very obstinate when she does not get her way."

"Are you saying she is selfish?" Mara asked hopefully.

"No. She is the most unselfish person I know." Palomas was unaware that his eyes had become soft as he spoke of his queen. "She is very beautiful. When she enters a room all other women seem to pale to nothingness. She is soft-spoken and cares a great deal about others."

"I believe you love her, Palomas."

"Everyone loves her, Mara."

"Yes, but you feel more deeply about her than others. I can sense it."

Palomas studied his fingertips. "I love her, yes, but not in the way you might think. My happiness is in watching over her and seeing that she is safe. When she smiles, which she often does, my heart is gladdened. When she is sad, which she has often been lately, it tears at my heart. I love her not as a woman, but as something rare and lovely."

"Do not tell me any more," Mara said in a whisper. "I fear your queen is becoming an obsession of mine. I am often reminded of her beauty and kindness." Mara looked over her head and saw the dark clouds had all but blocked out the light of the sun. "If it is your duty to protect the queen, why are you not with her now?"

Palomas stood up. "I await the day she returns,

Mara. I have missed her.''

"Palomas, will you do me a favor?"

"I am yours to command," he said softly.

"Will you help me leave this valley?"

He sat down beside her once more, frowning, "Why would you wish to leave?"

"I think you can guess, Palomas."

"Because you love the king."

Mara did not bother to deny the truth. If Palomas knew of her love for Tajarez, how many others had guessed? How long would it be before they learned that she and Tajarez had been lovers? "Please help me, Palomas. I have no one to turn to."

"Mara, I cannot help you in this, in fact, should you try to leave, I would prevent you from going."

"But why? I do not understand."

"The king would never allow you to leave."

"I do not belong to your king; the queen belongs to Tajarez. I tried not to love him, Palomas. I could not seem to stop myself. If you love your queen as you say, help me make my bid for freedom."

Palomas's face darkened and he looked past Mara to the high garden walls. Mara had suffered enough, he thought. He intended to tell Tajarez, to beg him if need be, to tell Mara the truth.

"I cannot help you in this, Mara. Perhaps tomorrow you will feel differently."

Mara stood up and walked slowly toward the palace, aware that Palomas followed. No one would help her, therefore she must help herself.

When Mara entered her bedroom she found Falon waiting for her. "Your brother Jeffery has been searching for you, Mara." Falon told her.

"Did he say what he wanted?"

"He said that he would see you tonight. He seemed to think you were upset about something. He questioned me about your state of mind, but I told him nothing."

"Was there anything to tell?" Mara said, watching Falon closely.

"I know you have been very distressed about Andrew being taken from you, but I did not say this to your brother."

Mara relaxed. Perhaps Falon did not know that Tajarez had spent the night with her. She would have to be very clever today so that the girl did not suspect that she would make an attempt to escape tonight.

"Do you know if Tajarez is in the palace today?"

"Jeffery said he has ridden to one of the lesser Cities to bring Tabo back here."

Mara felt relief. Perhaps Tajarez would not return tonight. The only thing she would have to worry about would be Jeffery and Palomas. It was strange how calm she felt now that she had made the decision to leave tonight. She ate everything on the tray Falon brought her and then dismissed the girl, telling her she would not need her anymore that day.

After Falon had withdrawn, Mara searched through her belongings until she found the doeskin gown and moccasins. She was glad she had not discarded them. When she had dressed herself, she braided her hair and looked at her image in the mirror. No one would be fooled by her appearance. Searching among her belongings, Mara found a fawn-colored doeskin cape that was lined with mink and had a wide hood that would disguise her golden hair.

After she was ready she paced the floor, waiting for the shadows in the room to warn her that night had fallen. Mara knew she was not being rational, but it did not matter. For now all that mattered was getting away from Tajarez. She did not have any food, no weapon, and no horse. She did not have a clue as to where she would go once she was outside this valley. All she knew was that she must escape, that was the driving force in her life. Everything else was secondary. Mara knew that if she allowed herself to think about Andrew she would weaken. She must think only of the danger to Andrew's father should she not make her escape. She wondered for a moment how Tajarez would explain Andrew to his queen, when she returned. He would not be able to tell her Andrew was his son. Had not Tajarez told her the queen knew that he loved her last night? She could not remember.

Mara rose from the bed where she had been sitting. The room was now dark. Night had fallen. Pulling her fur cape about her, she opened the door and peered out. No one seemed to be about, so she stepped into the hallway. Cautiously she made her way to the garden. She was halfway across the anteroom when she heard voices. Flattening herself quickly against the wall, she hid in the shadows, just as Jeffery and Sasha passed in front of her.

"There is no longer any reason for you to be concerned, Sasha. By tomorrow the whole City will know that the queen has returned." Jeffery said.

Mara did not hear Sasha's reply. They had already begun to climb the stairs and their voices did not reach her ears.

Mara stifled a sob behind her hand. So the queen had returned. It had now become imperative that she escape tonight. Tears blinded her eyes as she raced across the room and out into the garden. When she reached the garden she ran to the corner where she had discovered the gate earlier in the day. She tugged on it and pushed against it, but the gate did not yield. Mara became frantic, whimpering sounds issuing from her throat as she pushed against her only escape route. With renewed effort she braced her shoulder against the gate and pushed with all her strength. She was finally rewarded by the sound of splintering wood, which apparently had been rotten, or she would have never have been able to push it open.

Pulling her cape securely about her, she stepped through the gate and into what appeared to be a deserted roadway. The night was dark and cold and snow was beginning to fall. Mara stood still for tense moments, undecided. She could hear the sound of many horses and knew that the royal stables Tajarez had told her about must be nearby. Moving in the direction of the sound keeping well into the shadows, she saw with relief that she had been correct in her assumption. The stable was darkened and there seemed to be no one about, but she knew she must still not take any chances. She inched along the wall, and it seemed to take her an eternity to reach the stable.

She opened the gate to the first stall she came to. Feeling around in the dark she found the leather rein and slipped it over the head of the horse. She could hear one of the horses rearing and kicking against its stall, and she saw it was Tajarez's black stallion. Tajarez was in the palace. He had returned!

Mara led her horse quickly out of the stall and swung herself onto its back. She urged the horse forward, and the animal readily obeyed her command and broke into a gallop.

The back roadway soon led to a main throughfare, and Mara was forced to check her horse's speed. There were many people milling about, and she saw the stalls and shops where the people displayed their crafts and wares.

Fearing to be discovered at any moment. Mara urged her mount on to a faster pace. She had chosen her time well, for the shopkeepers were busy closing for the day and did not seem to notice her as she passed by them.

She fastened her eyes on the tallest mountain peak, remembering that that was where she had entered the valley. She rode straight toward it. When she reached the outskirts of the City, she had no trouble finding the road that led to the mountains. She had passed no one. The cold weather seemed to be working in her favor. No one would want to be abroad on a night like this. Any sane person would be at home with her family, she thought bitterly.

The roadway began to slant upward as she drew closer to the tall mountain. Just ahead of her was the tunnel that meant her freedom.

Mara had no thought any more for her safety, or about what she would do once she was through the tunnel to the outside. She would not think about the fact that she had brought neither food nor water with her. It was bitterly cold and she had no shelter from the night winds, but that did not trouble her. All thoughts were pushed to the back of her mind. Her only aim in life was to escape this valley.

Mara was well within view of the cave now. She could see the light from the torches piercing the darkened night. Dismounting, she led her horse behind a clump of bushes and peered up the mountainside, knowing that somewhere in the dark recesses of that mountain was a sentry who might stand between her and freedom. Deciding her only hope was to ride boldly up to the entrance of the cave, she remounted and urged her horse forward. She wondered momentarily if there was some kind of password that she would need to get through the mountain?

When she had almost reached the cave a voice came to her from somewhere up above.

"Where do you go?"

"I go to meet my husband," she said, voicing the first thought that entered her mind.

"Is he with the advanced hunting party?" The man called down.

"Yes, I ride forward to welcome him."

"Proceed," the man said.

Mara did not hesitate to impel her horse forward, entering the cave at a fast gallop. Leaving the valley had been almost too easy. Evidently they did not concern themselves with the people who left the valley, only the ones who entered.

The sound of the horse's flying hooves made a deafening echo as it reverberated against the walls of the cave. Mara was now concerned with reaching the other side of the entrance before the hunting party the guard had spoken of returned. It would be devastating for her to have come this far only to be discovered and taken back to the City.

She reached the end of the cave, and she had to slow the horse as they climbed down the steep embankment. Once they reached level ground Mara kicked her mount in the flanks and the horse raced onward.

The snow clouds had moved on, and Mara was grateful that a full moon now lit the countryside, enabling her to see where she was going. The snowfall on this side of the mountain must have been heavier than in the valley, for there were several more inches of snow covering the ground than there had been in the City.

She pointed her horse in a northerly direction, and her spirits soared. She was free!

The horse raced forward into the night. Mara could feel the strong muscles of the animal as its powerful legs covered the ground at an astonishing pace. She had chosen her mount well. She could not imagine any horse's being capable of outdistancing this one.

Mara did not know how long she had been racing the horse, but she could feel he was tiring and she slowed him to a walk. Glancing skyward she saw the clouds had moved over the moon again, and a light snow began to fall. She did not mind the snow, for if anyone had discovered she was missing and come after her, he would be unable to track her.

It soon became too dark to try and guide the horse, so Mara gave the animal its head and allowed him to take her where he would. The horse seemed to sense Mara's urgency and renewed his effort. On and on the great horse thundered into the night.

Once again the clouds moved away, giving Mara a clear view of the moon. Judging from its position, she estimated it was somewhere around midnight.

The cold wind whipped at Mara's cape, its icy fingers stinging her cheeks. Pulling the cape more securely about her, she tried to make her mind a blank, but was not entirely successful. She kept remembering the night before, when Tajarez had held her in his arms and whispered love words in her ear. Tonight he would hold his queen in his arms. Would he also murmur words of love to her?

Tajarez opened the door to Mara's room without knocking. He scanned the room, only to find it was empty. He smiled to himself. Tonight would be special for he would tell Mara that she was his wife.

Walking out into the hallway he rapped on Palomas's door. When there was no answer, he was not unduly concerned. Most probably Mara was with Sasha.

Falon came running down the hallway and almost collided with her king. "Palomas has been searching for you, my king, we cannot find the queen anywhere," she said in a voice bordering on hysteria.

"When was she last seen?" Tajarez snapped.

"I served her the noon meal and she told me she would not have need of me anymore today. That was the last anyone saw of her."

"Have you checked with her brother?"

"Yes, he and Palomas searched the palace, but no

trace was found of her."

"Where are Jeffery and Palomas now?"

"Palomas is searching the garden. She could not have left the palace by the main entrance."

"Find Jeffery and tell him to report to me immediately."

Falon did not hesitate, but ran down the hallway to find Jeffery.

Tajarez had just reached the anteroom when Palomas rushed up to him. "I have found no sign of her, my king, but the gate in the garden was open, and one of your horses is missing," he said, grim-faced.

"Great Father, she has done it, she said she would get away, but I did not believe her. Have you sent someone to the cave entrance?"

"Not yet. I waited to report to you first."

"See that three horses are made ready, and try to arouse no suspicion. You, Jeffery, and myself, will ride to the entrance at once."

"I have already had the horses brought around to the front. I anticipated your order, my king. It seems once again I was lax in my duty. I did not think she was this desperate."

Tajarez looked past him to Jeffery, who had just entered the anteroom. "No one is at fault but myself, Palomas. Knowing Mara as I do, I should have seen this coming."

The three men raced to the door and down the steep steps, each fearing that Mara might have made it through the entrance to the valley.

When they reached the cave, Tajarez and Jeffery waited below while Palomas climbed up to question the guard.

"Your sister has made me very angry, Jeffery," Tajarez said grimly.

"You knew the pressure she had on her. Knowing Mara you should have expected something like this."

"My first mistake was in listening to you and Tabo. Had I told Mara the truth of her identity when I wanted to, this could have been avoided."

"Perhaps, who can know?"

Tarjarez's horse was prancing about restlessly, and he restrained it with his powerful leg muscles, and finally brought it under control. "If she has managed to leave this valley, her life is in great danger. Not only could she freeze to death, there are wolf packs that roam the countryside."

Palomas ran down the mountainside and jumped on his horse. "She passed this way hours ago, my king," Palomas told him.

Tajarez jabbed his horse in the flanks, with fear in his heart. Great Father, he prayed silently, let me find her in time!

# Twenty-Seven

I feel as if the very air about me has drawn a breath.
He will come, the wind whispers, he will come.

Mara dismounted and rubbed her hands over the
flanks of the stallion. In spite of the cold the animal
was lathered and sweating from the fast pace at
which they had been traveling.

"I have used you sorely," she said, looking about
for some place where she could find them shelter
from the cold. "You are sure to become ill if I do
not get you out of this wind." She was surprised that
she had spoken to the horse in the Lagonda language, which seemed more familiar to her now than
English.

In the distance she could hear the howling of
wolves, and she shivered from fear. She realized that
she feared the wolves more than any other danger
she could imagine.

Picking up the trailing reins, Mara led the horse
over to two large boulders that came together in a
vee shape, thinking they might offer some protection.

Forcing the animal down to its knees, she sat with

her back to the rock and pulled one edge of her cape over the horse's back, trying to offer him some warmth.

"He will never find me," she said, as she rested her face against the sleek neck of the horse.

It had begun to snow again and Mara huddled closer to the horse, hoping to borrow some of his warmth. She was totally exhausted. She knew she had been foolish not to plan her escape better, but there had been no time. She wished she had at least had the foresight to bring a warm blanket, or a fur robe.

How long could she last without food, she wondered. If the snow melted she knew she would find green grass underneath for the horse to graze on, but what about herself? Perhaps she would be fortunate enough to find a trapper, someone like Jake and Zeke, but she discarded that thought. This was too far west; she doubted there was another white person within hundreds of miles. The only other people she was likely to encounter would be Indians. Mara considered for a moment if she would rather become the captive of some savage tribe of Indians, or be found by a Lagonda warrior who would take her back to Tajarez.

What was Tajarez doing now? Was he lying beside his queen? Was he at this very moment making love to his wife? Tears scalded Mara's eyes. Why could she not put him out of her mind? She thought of Andrew, and was glad he was safe and warm. He would grow up never knowing how much his mother had loved him.

Thinking was too painful. What she needed was

sleep. She closed her eyes, but the image of Tajarez's face flashed before her. I will never see him again, she thought.

The cold seemed to seep into her body, and her hands and feet felt numb, but she tried not to think of her discomfort. Instead she wondered what Tajarez's reaction would be in the morning when he discovered his prisoner had escaped. She almost wished she could be there to witness his anger when he found her missing. Again his face flashed before her, and the look he wore was not one of anger, but of sadness. Mara groaned, "Leave me in peace, Tajarez, I do not want to think of you."

Suddenly the horse raised his head and rolled his eyes wildly. Mara moved out of his way as the animal stumbled to his feet, and whinnied. Mara looked about trying to determine the reason for the animal's fright. It was impossible to see more than a few feet because of the falling snow. The horse reared up on its hind legs and pawed at the air. Mara grabbed at the trailing reins, trying to soothe the frightened animal.

Was it possible that Tajarez had found her already? she wondered. She did not pause to consider, but jumped on the back of the horse. The animal did not need any urging, he leaped over the rock and landed on the other side with a jolt that almost unseated Mara. She hugged the side of the horse's body with her legs, and held tightly to the reins.

Suddenly a new and terrifying sound reached Mara's ears. It was the sound of growling and snarling and it came from close behind her. Looking back over her shoulder, she saw the reason for the horse's fear. They were being pursued by wolves! Mara could not make out their number, all she could see were the menacing eyes that seemed to glow like hot coals in the darkness.

Leaning low over the horse's back, she prayed they could outrun the wolf pack. Her mind was in a frenzy. She wondered what it would feel like to be torn apart by hungry wolves. Did they kill their prey first, or would they eat them while they were still alive? Mara fought against the bile that rose in her throat—the taste of fear!

Why had she been so foolish as to try to run away from Tajarez? Was her only escape from him to be found in death? she wondered. At that moment she wished she could see him.

Would Tajarez be glad that her escape from him had ended in tragedy? Or would he grieve for her? Casting a quick glance over her shoulder she saw that the wolves were gaining on her. They had spread out and were circling the horse. Their eyes gleamed menacingly in the darkness.

Mara could just make out the shadowy shape of the lead wolf, when her mount reared up on its haunches and pawed at the air. Mara gripped the reins tightly, not wanting to be unseated. By now a lone wolf was nipping at the heels of her horse, and the animal kicked out in pain. The horse seemed to sail into the air, and it came down so forcefully that Mara's hands slipped from the reins, and she went flying through the air to land with a thud in a deep snowbank.

She rolled over and over, then down a steep

embankment. By the time she had jumped to her feet, she could hear the agonizing sounds the horse was making and knew it was being torn apart by the wolf pack.

Tears wet her cheeks as she stood helplessly, unable to save the horse that had served her so well.

"Tajarez, Tajarez, come to me," she cried out. "Oh, my love, I am so frightened!"

There was the sound of the wolves fighting among themselves, and Mara knew they were battling for the supremacy over some choice bit of horseflesh. No sound came from the horse and she knew it was dead. She hoped its death had been quick and merciful.

Mara could not see what was happening on the other side of the steep embankment. She strained her eyes in the darkness.

A gasp escaped her lips as she saw a pair of red glowing eyes peering down on her from the top of the embankment. One of the wolves had broken away from the pack and had spotted her.

Taking a step backwards she bumped into the trunk of a tree. Without taking her eyes off the wolf, she groped above her head trying to find a handhold. Her fingers were numb, and she could not seem to hold on to the branch. She could see the wolf more clearly now as it came slinking toward her. Her heart missed a beat as she noticed that a number of snarling wolves were now charging toward her behind the first one.

With renewed strength, Mara grabbed the tree branch and swung herself into the tree just as the first wolf reached its base.

The tree was not a big one and the branch she was on dipped with her weight. Mara feared that the branch would snap and she would fall to be devoured by the snarling beasts below. One of the wolves seemed to be more daring than the others. It leaped into the air, almost reaching Mara's haven.

Reaching over her head Mara grasped a higher branch, but it dipped downward, and she knew it would not support her weight. She could climb no higher. The venturesome wolf seemed to sense her plight and lunged at her with renewed courage and daring. Mara began crying hysterically as she saw the snarling fangs that could easily rip their prey apart.

"Tajarez, help me!" she screamed, knowing it was but a matter of time before the hungry wolves reached her.

Tajarez was the first to hear the wolf pack as they fought over their kill. He did not slacken his pace as he strung his bow and placed a silver-tipped arrow between its rawhide strings. His mind drew a picture of Mara being torn apart by the wolves, and when he came in view of the wolf pack, tearing at the flesh of the dead horse, that fear did not diminish. He released the arrow and it found the heart of one of the wolves with deadly accuracy.

Tajarez was aware that Jeffery and Palomas also fired at the blood-crazed animals. Tajarez had dismounted and was running among the wolves before his horse had come to a halt. Looking around frantically for some sign of Mara, he did not know whether to be relieved or even more fearful when he did not see her.

Jeffery and Palomas had joined him and were driving the angry animals back with flying arrows that never failed to hit their targets. The surviving animals fell on their wounded companions and began to rip them apart, showing no discrimination in their lust for food. They had no qualms about eating one of their own species.

"She is not here," Tajarez yelled. His eyes were wild as he looked at Jeffery. "Great Father am I too late!" he cried out.

"Listen," Palomas said. "I hear more wolves in the gully."

Tajarez stood listening, and he too heard the sound. Leaping across the space to reach the gully he peered into the darkness, but he could see nothing. All he could hear were the ominous sounds of the snarling wolves. Not bothering to arm his bow, he raced down the embankment. Palomas and Jeffery, seeing Tajarez going unarmed among the wolves, followed in close pursuit. Tajarez was unmindful of the danger he was charging into. All he knew was that Mara could be the victim of the hungry wolves. Palomas and Jeffery tried to overtake him so they could cover for him, but he was much too fast for either of them.

At first Tajarez thought he heard only what he wished to hear. He did not pause to think but charged blindly onward.

"Tajarez, help me!"

He heard it clearly now. He felt relief wash over his body as he neared the tree where Mara had sought safety. He prayed that he would reach her before the wolves did.

Mara was trying to press her body tightly against the trunk of the tree. She was back as far as she could get. She closed her eyes expecting to feel the sharp teeth rip into her skin at any moment. The lead wolf had managed to pull itself into the tree. Hearing one of the animals yelp in pain, she opened her eyes to see the wolf sliding down the tree trunk with an arrow in its back from Palomas's bow. She saw Tajarez charging toward her, but between her and him was one over confident wolf. She held her breath as the animal lunged at Tajarez. It was met with Tajarez's knife thrust, which found the animal's heart. Tajarez tossed the dead wolf aside as if it weighed nothing.

Mara was making whimpering sounds as Tajarez leaped into the tree that sagged with the weight of their bodies. He pulled her into his arms and covered her face with kisses, then he just held her against him until her body stopped trembling. He then leaped to the ground with her in his arms. Jeffery and Palomas had driven the wolves back in the meantime.

"See to our horses, Palomas," Tajarez ordered. "We do not want to provide the wolves with another kill." He pulled Mara's cape tightly about her and stared at her with an unreadable expression on his face.

"Is she harmed?" Jeffery asked fearfully, coming up beside them.

Mara laid her head against Tajarez's shoulder. "I . . . I am unharmed," she whispered.

Tajarez could feel her slight body tremble and gathered her tightly against him. "We ride for home at once. Your sister is half frozen."

Jeffery walked beside Tajarez as he climbed the steep incline. "Why is it, Tajarez, that when you are displeased with Mara, she becomes my sister?"

Tajarez gave Jeffery a dark look, but did not bother to answer him.

Tajarez mounted his horse and looked down at Mara as he urged the animal forward. Raising her head Mara could see the scowl on his handsome face. She waited for him to reproach her, but when he did not, she spoke:

"It is because of me that your horse is dead. He was a fine horse."

"Yes, it is your fault. I am not pleased with you, Mara."

"Was he your horse?" she said, hoping to hold his anger at bay.

His dark eyes settled on her lips. "No, Sagine was a present I once gave to my queen."

Mara buried her face against his shoulder. "I am so sorry," she sobbed.

"It is of little importance. I will see that the queen has another to replace the dead one," Tajarez said dryly.

"W . . . what are you going to do with me? Will I be punished?" she asked in a small voice, for she could feel the anger Tajarez was trying to contain like a taut bowstring ready to fly.

He bent his dark head and rested his lips against her forehead. "I should beat you, but I could never harm that which I love," His voice was passionate, as his lips brushed against hers. "I would much rather take you to my bed and drive my ownership into your body. You have been nothing but trouble to me since the first day I saw you."

"I am sorry."

"Are you? I doubt that you are. I was going to talk to you tonight and straighten out some things between us, but when I sought you out, I found you had gone."

"I know what you wanted to say to me."

"Do you?"

"You wanted to tell me that the queen had returned."

"Mara, would you just keep quiet. I am weary of this conversation."

"What will you do with me?"

"Be silent, I am angry with you."

Mara turned her face against his chest and was comforted by the sound of his steady heartbeat. How she loved this man. She had no idea of what she was going back to, but it did not matter, if she could just be near him, see him once in awhile, she thought. She fell asleep in his arms.

# Twenty-Eight

A warm wind is blowing, my love smiles at me.
He loves me, he loves me. At last I am free.

Tajarez laid Mara down on her bed and pulled
the covers over her. Falon entered the room and
Tajarez placed his finger to his lips telling her to be
silent, and nodded for her to accompany him into
the hallway. With one more glance at his sleeping
wife he left the room and found Falon waiting for
him.

"Watch over your queen tonight, or what's left of
the night. Allow her to sleep as long as possible. She
has had a very bad time."

"It will be as you say, my king."

"How is my son Andrew?"

"I am told he thrives on the milk from the woman
Vista found to feed him. My king, I am happy that
you found the queen and that she is unharmed."

"I know you are, Falon," he said smiling at her
kindly.

Falon could see how tired he looked. The past year
had not been kind to her king, and she hoped he and
the queen would soon find each other again. She

watched sadly as he walked away from her. It was not always easy being king, she thought.


Mara awoke and looked about her in confusion. Sitting up slowly, she saw that she was back in her room at the palace. By the position of the light in the room she could see that it was late afternoon.

Falon, who had been quietly waiting for her to awaken, smiled brightly. "Would you like a bath before you dine, Mara?"

Mara swung her legs over the side of the bed. Every muscle in her body seemed to ache.

"Yes, a bath would be nice, Falon."

As Mara relaxed in the warm bath she tried to put the events of the night before out of her mind. By all rights she should be dead at this very moment. Stepping out of the bath she dressed in a warm gray woolen gown.

Falon noticed she was strangely silent as she toyed with the food on her plate. "Mara, my king would like to see you after you have eaten," Falon told her.

That announcement finished off what little appetite Mara had had. She found she could not eat another bite of food. She might have known Tajarez would not let last night pass unnoticed. Pushing the tray aside, she stood up, thinking she might as well face Tajarez and get it over with. Her only hope was that his queen would not be present when he reprimanded her.

"Where am I to see Tajarez, Falon?"

"I will take you there," the girl told her, giving her an encouraging smile.

Falon left Mara outside the door of the room where she had confronted Tajarez the day she had been so angry with him for taking Andrew from her. She wished she had half of the courage she had demonstrated that day. Squaring her shoulders, she tapped lightly on the door.

The door was immediately opened and Tajarez stood towering over her. She could not read anything in his blank expression. Looking past him, she was glad to see that the room was empty but for him.

Tajarez did not speak but inclined his head and motioned for her to be seated. Mara sat down on the edge of the white doeskin cushion and folded her hands demurely in her lap.

Tajarez sat down beside her and picked up one of her hands. "Did you rest well, Mara?"

Mara jerked her hand free of his, fearing someone would enter and find him holding her hand. "I awoke only a short time ago."

"I have been awake for a long time waiting for you," he said pushing a golden curl from her face.

"Do not touch me," she said scooting away from him.

He arched a dark brow at her, but said nothing.

"Are you still angry with me?"

"I should be. But I am too grateful that you were unharmed." He reached out and captured her hand and pulled her closer to him.

"Tajarez stop this, suppose someone were to come in!"

He noted the urgency in her voice and wondered at the cause of it. "No one will enter, but if they did, why should you care?"

"I do not want you to forfeit your life because of me!"

"Mara, what are you talking about?"

She leaned closer to whisper in his ear as if fearing to be overheard. "I would not like for anyone to find out about us. Sasha told me that if you were to . . . to lie with anyone but the queen, you would be put to death."

Tajarez smiled. He now knew why she had acted so strangely. "Sasha was correct, Mara," he said, his smile deepening.

"I do not find any amusement in that, Tajarez. I would not like you to die because of me. Too many people know about us already. Why can you not see the danger to yourself?"

"Would you care so much, Mara?"

"You know I do. How can you even ask after the other night?"

He pulled her into his arms once more and laughed at her puny attempt to free herself. "That night was wonderful, as tonight will be."

"Tajarez, are you mad? Do you not care what could happen to you?"

"Yes, my beloved, I am raving mad. I love you, and if I must die for it, then so be it," he said, unable to resist the temptation to tease her.

Her green eyes sparkled dangerously. "If you do not release me this moment I will . . . hit you!" she said furiously.

"That is what I like to see, my old Mara who was full of fire, and daring anyone, including myself, to cross her."

Mara relaxed against him, knowing that struggle

426

was futile. "I came here expecting to find you angry with me," she said trying to distract him.

"I should be, but I could never be angry with you for very long. Mara, why did you run away from me last night?" He captured her face and forced her to look at him. She closed her eyes, and when she opened them found he was watching her closely.

"I left because I love you, and I could not bear to think of your being with another woman. And when Sasha told me it was *forbidden* for you to be with another woman, I knew I had to get away."

"Mara, I had a talk with Tabo today. We discussed you."

"That must have been dull."

"I told him I was weary of this farce. He agreed with me that it was time for you to be told who you are."

"I know who I am. I am Mara Golden."

"The name Mara is correct, but you are no longer a Golden."

"I am not sure I am following you, Tajarez," she said, a worried frown on her face. "You are not making sense."

"Am I not?"

"Not to me."

"Come with me," he said standing up and leading her out of the room across the anteroom and toward the stairs.

Mara pulled back when she saw he was leading her to the forbidden stairs that led to his own quarters. "I will not go with you to see the queen!" she told him, twisting away from him.

Reaching out for her, Tajarez lifted her into his

arms and ascended the stairs.

"Put me down, what if someone should see!"

"If they do, they will think I take you to my bed," he said laughing down at her.

When they reached the nursery he set her down and opened the door, waiting for her to precede him inside.

Vista was just putting Andrew down for a nap and she looked up startled at the sight of the queen.

"Wait in the hallway, Vista," Tajarez commanded.

Vista lowered her head in a quick bow and left hurriedly.

Mara walked over to Andrew and smoothed his dark hair from his face. He was sleeping and she felt an ache inside wanting to hold him. Tajarez came up beside her and peered down at his son.

"I am sorry, Mara, for taking Andrew away from you, but after today perhaps you can find it within you to forgive me."

She looked up at him. "You did it to force me to stay with you, did you not?"

"I am not sure. Perhaps that was part of it, but inside I think I wanted to punish you for not loving me."

"I do love you."

Tajarez grabbed her and crushed her to him. "Mara, Mara, I want so much for you to remember, but since you cannot, I am going to help you."

Raising her head she kissed his smooth cheek. "How can you help me, Tajarez?"

"Come. I want you to meet my twins," he said, steering her across the room and opening a door that

428

led to still another room.

"No, Tajarez, do not do this to me. I am not yet ready to see the children of your queen," she cried, trying to loosen his grip on her hand.

Tajarez pulled her forward, and Mara looked about the room. There were thick gray rugs on the floor with bright patterns of animals woven in many different colors. There were shelves stacked with toys and two small beds with blue coverlets each embossed with a gold cobra head.

"Why are you doing this to me? Are you so cruel that you do not see what I am feeling?" she cried out. The tiny prince and princess had been playing on floor and Mara closed her eyes, not wanting to see the children Tajarez had fathered by another woman.

"Hamez you will find, is very advanced for his age. Both he and his sister speak very well. Even at their early age they have a teacher who instructs them daily in speech."

"Tajarez, have pity," she said turning her back, wondering why he was insisting on her seeing the twins.

"Tamera is coy and flirtatious," he continued. "She has stolen everyone's heart, as her mother has."

Mara turned around to face him. If this was some cruel game he was playing, she would not let him see how much it was hurting her. She took a deep breath as she saw the tiny girl stand up and toddle toward her father, holding her arms up to him. Mara looked past the girl to the tiny prince royal, who was still sitting on the floor stacking wooden blocks.

"Your children are lovely," she said without really looking at them closely. "Now that I have seen them, can I go?"

"But, Mara, you have not truly seen them," Tajarez persisted reaching down and scooping up his daughter. "Would you like to hold Tamera, Mara?"

"No," she said in a whisper, backing away from him.

"You will notice that Tamera's hair is dark like mine, although her skin is much lighter in color. Look at her eyes, Mara, her eyes are very like her mother's."

Mara shook her head from side to side. "No, I want to leave," she said in a strangled voice.

Before she could run from the room as she wanted to, Tajarez handed his daughter to her and she had no choice but to take the child in her arms. The tiny girl raised her head and Mara could see her sweet face through a blur of tears. Her gaze focused on the child's eyes, and Mara gasped.

Green eyes! Eyes as green as her own looked back at her curiously. Mara's heart was pumping frantically, and she tried to make some sense out of what she was feeling.

"I am confused," she said, hardly above a whisper.

"As I said, her eyes are very like her mother's," Tajarez whispered close to her ear.

"But I did not know that her mother was white. No one told me."

Tajarez scooped up the prince royal and held him out for Mara's inspection. "Hamez also has your eyes, Mara. Is it not a startling combination with his

430

dark skin?"

Mara swallowed convulsively as hot tears scalded her eyes. "I do not understand any of this, Tajarez, unless . . . your queen was barren, and I provided the children for you." She looked into his face pleadingly. "Is that what happened, Tajarez?"

"My queen is not barren, Mara, but very fruitful, providing me with three children to prove it. The last of which is the Prince Andrew."

"Oh dear God!" she cried. "It cannot be. I am your wife! I am your queen! No, it is not possible!"

"I see you need more proof. You always were hard to convince." Crossing the room, he opened the door. "Vista, come to me," he called.

Vista appeared immediately, looking uneasy because she did not know what was going on.

"Vista, who is this woman? Tajarez asked in a commanding voice.

"I was told to say, if I were asked, that her name is Mara, my king," Vista said, misunderstanding his question.

"I do not mean her name, Vista. I give you leave to speak her true identity. Tell Mara who she is," he ordered.

Mara was startled when Vista dropped to her knees and looked up at her with tears running down her face. "You are my queen, and I have been sorely grieved that you do not remember how much you are loved. I am your humble servant, and stand ready to serve you in all ways."

Mara felt as if her body was drained of all its strength. She felt the room spinning around her and aware that she was falling forward. Her last conscious thought was for the safety of the child she was holding. She felt Tajarez take Tamera from her, and she slumped forward in his arms, into blackness.

# Twenty-Nine

In joyful confusion I reach for his hand.
He is my true love, this dark, brooding man.

Mara awoke in a state of total confusion. Looking about her, she saw that she was in a strange room. It was a huge bedroom. The marble floor was covered with white fur rugs, and there was a big golden insignia hanging on the wall, with a cobra whose eyes were set with two huge emeralds. She needed no one to tell her that she was in the bedroom of the king.

Hearing people talking in hushed tones, Mara turned her head and saw Tajarez and Tabo standing near the door. Tabo glanced up and saw that Mara was awake. He walked over to her and smiled.

"How are you feeling, my queen?" he asked.

"I do not know. I am very confused."

"I was afraid something like this might happen," he said bending over her and examining her eyes. He then felt her pulse rate and turned to Tajarez, who had a worried frown on his face.

"She appears to be fine, but just in case you should need me, I will sleep in the palace tonight."

Tajarez nodded as he looked down at Mara.

433

"I would suggest, my king, that you give her something light to eat, such as broth."

Again Tajarez nodded, and he watched as the medicine man departed. He then turned to Mara, who seemed to think she should say something.

"This is a very grand bedroom. It is yours, is it not?" she said, voicing the first thing that popped into her head.

Tajarez sat down beside her and took her hand in his, raising it to his lips. He kissed it softly. "This is the room you and I have shared since the day my father made us husband and wife."

Mara bit her trembling lip. "Tajarez am I truly your wife, and the queen? Am I the woman that I have heard so many kind words spoken about?"

"You and she are one and the same, beloved. Are you pleased that you are my wife?" he asked shifting his position so he was lying down beside her.

"I think so. I am in such a state of confusion. Do you realize I almost grew to hate the woman who was your queen, and all the time she was I, or I was she."

He pulled her into his arms and rested his face against hers. "Were you perhaps jealous."

Mara looked up at him. "Extremely so. I cannot yet think of the queen as myself."

"Try not to think about it. I want you to rest. It has been a great shock to you finding out who you are." He traced the outline of her lovely face and gave her a smile that melted her heart.

"You were so adorable earlier, when you were concerned that I would come to harm for loving you. I could not resist teasing you. Am I forgiven?"

"Yes," she whispered, willing to forgive him anything. He whom she loved above her own life was her husband. Now she could understand why he had said he loved her, but he also loved his queen.

Mara sat up suddenly. "Tajarez, Hamez and Tamera are my babies. You said so, did you not?"

"Yes, they are of your body, just as Andrew is."

She covered her face, trying to hide her tears, "Andrew is not . . . he would not be branded a . . . he has a legal father!"

"Yes, he has a father who loves him very much."

She turned tear-bright eyes to him. "Tajarez, I want to see all three of my babies. I want to hold them in my arms and tell them how much I love them," she said excitedly.

"I want you to rest for now," Tajarez said standing up. "Perhaps later in the day I will have the children brought to you."

"I am not really tired."

"Close your eyes and rest. I must leave you for a time."

"Why?" she asked, not wanting him to leave her.

"It seems Palomas and Sasha are making noises, demanding that I tell you your true identity," he said, bending over and kissing her on the forehead.

When he was gone Mara closed her eyes trying to rest, but her head ached, and she had so many things to think about. It was as if the sky had opened up and she had been handed her fondest wish. She was the wife of the tall, dark Indian she loved so desperately, and he loved her! How was it possible that she was the woman of whom everyone had spoken as being so unselfish and beautiful? She searched the dark recesses of her mind trying to remember the past, but it would not yield its secrets to her.

Mara could not suppress a giggle as she remembered the unkind things she had said to her brother when he would not defend her from her own husband. Oh poor Jeffery, what a trial she must have been for him.

Mara opened her eyes. She had not thought she would be able to sleep with so many things to think about, but apparently she had been wrong. Sitting up and stretching her arms over her head she found she felt very refreshed.

Suddenly the door opened and Tajarez entered the room carrying Hamez, while Sasha carried Tamera, and Vista held Andrew.

Tajarez plumped Hamez on the bed beside Mara. "Hamez, this is your mother," he said to his son.

Hamez fixed his mother with a green gaze and crawled over to her, climbing onto her lap.

Mara gasped as she looked into his eyes. Yes, he did have her eyes! An avalanche of feeling washed over her as she held Hamez's slight body in her arms. She cuddled him closely, not aware that she was crying.

"My son, my beautiful little boy," she said, planting many kisses on his tiny cheek.

Hamez patted her cheek lovingly, "Mother, pretty mother," he said in a clear voice.

Sasha and Vista were crying at the sight of the tears in their queen's eyes.

"My queen," Vista spoke up. "I have not allowed

436

the children to forget their mother. I have spoken to them of you every day.''

"Thank you, Vista,'' Mara said kindly.

Hamez picked up a lock of his mother's golden hair and stared at it in wonder. "Pretty,'' he said, so seriously that Mara laughed and hugged him tightly.

"He always did have a fascination with your hair, Mara, as his father does,'' Tajarez said as he scooped his son up, and motioned for Sasha to hand Tamera to her mother.

Tamera went readily into Mara's outstretched arms and nestled close to her. "I love you,'' the tiny girl said, kissing Mara on the cheek.

"Oh, she is so lovely,'' Mara said, smoothing the dark, silky hair from Tamera's angelic little face. Mara held the tiny girl, loving her with all of her heart.

"You are going to be a heartbreaker when you grow up,'' Mara said, kissing her smooth cheek.

She looked up at Vista. "Are they healthy, Vista?''

"Yes, they have never known a sick day, my queen.''

Tajarez placed Hamez on the floor and took Andrew from Vista and then sat down on the bed beside Mara. "Everyone says Andrew looks like me,'' he said with pride, holding the newest member of his family against his cheek. "Andrew and I have been getting acquainted lately.''

Mara watched as Tajarez kissed Andrew on his chubby little cheek, and her heart swelled with love. Tajarez seemed such a loving, caring, father. Looking over Tajarez's head Mara caught Sasha's eye.

"Sasha, I am glad that I am the queen, and the woman you spoke of as your best friend. I only wish I could remember our friendship."

Sasha smiled sweetly. "I look forward to the day you will know who you really are."

Tajarez exchanged Andrew for his sister. Andrew had fallen asleep and was totally unaware that he was in his mother's arms.

"Hamez and Tamera are delighted to find that they have a baby brother," Tajarez said. "Tamera wants to mother him, while Hamez wants him to get up and play with him. I told him it would be awhile before Andrew would be able to run and play as he does." The Princess Tamera had curled up in her father's arms, and he looked down at her adoringly.

"Oh no, my prince! You must not do that," Vista cried out in distress. All eyes went to the prince royal who had climbed up on a stool and had put his father's crown, with the double cobra, over his head. The crown was so large it had slipped past his head and rested on his shoulders.

"Father's," he said, with a gleam in his green eyes.

Tajarez laughed and rose from the bed. He picked Hamez up and removed the crown from his head. "You must be content with the crown of the single cobra for a time, my son. It is not yet time for you to replace your father."

There was a rap on the door and Sasha opened it, allowing her husband to enter.

"May I join this happy group?" he asked crossing the room to plant a kiss on his sister's cheek.

Mara hugged him tightly and when he stood up

438

she gave him a bright smile and said in English, "I suppose you are expecting me to say I am sorry for all the cruel things I said to you?"

He gave her a lopsided grin. "You were very hard on me, Mara. I will not soon forget your analysis of my character."

"But you will understand and forgive?" she said uncertainly.

His good humor was apparent when he threw his head back and laughed deeply. "Oh, my sister, you have a sharp tongue, and you did wound me sorely. But not without provocation, I might add. I took a good look at myself as I must have appeared in your eyes."

"Did I make you squirm?" she said with an impish smile.

"Extremely so."

"I truly am sorry, Jeffery."

"Do not let it trouble your lovely head. I knew if you would remember who you were you would forgive me all."

"It is now time to leave," Tajarez said in the voice of authority. "Mara needs her rest."

There were sounds of protest from Hamez and his sister, but Tajarez stood firm and ushered everyone out of the room. After they had gone it seemed strangely quiet.

"Andrew seems to be thriving with the wet nurse, but I do miss feeding him," Mara said.

Tajarez sat down beside her and took her hand. "You have been through so much lately, I want you to rest and regain your strength. You are much too thin."

"I feel fine. If it were not for these headaches, I would be well," she corrected him.

"Tabo told me about your headaches. He seems to think they will pass when you have recovered your memory."

"Yes, he has told me this also."

"Mara, what do you think of Hamez and Tamera?"

"They are so wonderful. I wish I could remember about the past. I am missing the best part of my life."

"I think you should not try to make it happen. Just go with each day as it comes. I will see that your life is filled with beautiful memories starting now," he said, giving her the special smile that Mara was learning he reserved for her alone.

"Tell me about the past. I want to learn how we met and how I came to the hidden valley."

"I will tell you later tonight, but for now Falon is waiting with something for you to eat."

"I am not hungry."

"Nevertheless, you will eat," he said, walking to the door and returning with a tray. He sat down beside her and removed the white napkin from the tray. Lifting the golden goblet to her lips, he urged her to drink. The broth was not very good, and Mara wrinkled her nose in distaste.

Tajarez raised an inquiring eyebrow and took a sip from the golden goblet. "I see what you mean, it is not very good—however," he said, lifting the tasteless brew to her lips once more, "you must drink it all. Tomorrow you can have something more substantial to eat."

Mara was moved by his loving care of her. So she obeyed him and drained the goblet. Thinking back she could see that he had been very patient with her. Today she had seen a very human side of him. Not the arrogant king, but a man who was sensitive and caring.

Tajarez, seeing that she had finished the broth, picked up the corncake and spread it with honey and offered it to her.

"Your reward for being a good girl," he said smiling.

Mara took the corncake and bit into it, finding it more to her liking, and soon had eaten it all. "Have you eaten?" she wanted to know.

"Yes I ate with Jeffery, while you were asleep." His eyes went to her lips. "You have honey on your mouth," he whispered. When Mara would have wiped her mouth with the napkin, Tajarez stayed her hand.

"Allow me," he said in a deep voice.

Mara was shaken to the very depth of her body as his tongue traced the outline of her mouth. Tajarez did not stop when the honey had been removed, but covered her lips in a kiss that was so sweet it brought tears to her eyes. She was disappointed when he broke off the kiss.

"I have something to attend to. I will be back later," he said, standing up and taking the tray.

Mara was deeply frustrated as she watched him disappear out the door. Her body was awakened at his touch, and she tried to dismiss her strong craving for him.

Mara found she felt much better after having

eaten. Her headache was gone and she felt rested. She removed her gray gown, and dressed only in her undergarments, slipped under the covers. In spite of all the sleep she had gotten earlier, Mara felt herself getting drowsy and soon drifted off to sleep again.

# Thirty

My heart is now soaring, I care not for the past.
Happily I surrender: I have come home at last.


Tajarez entered the room. Seeing Mara slept, he took care not to make any noise as he undressed and slipped into bed beside her.

It was dark in the room when Mara awoke. She felt the bed shift as Tajarez lay down and pulled her into his arms.

"I did not mean to awaken you, beloved."

Mara snuggled closely to him, loving the feel of his strong body against her soft curves. "You must be very tired yourself, my love. You got little sleep last night."

"I am a man who does not require a lot of sleep, Mara," he said nuzzling her ear.

"I love you, Tajarez."

"You are quite sure?"

"I have never been more sure of anything in my whole life. Through all the dark days I have been through, my love for you was the only stable thing in my life."

"I would like to hear you tell me what you mean."

"I am not sure if I can," she said, lifting her head to rest it on his shoulder. "I am not sure if you will believe me. Sometimes I do not believe it myself."

"What, Mara?"

"I had these dreams about you when I was with Jake and Zeke. One time you and I were swimming in some kind of pond. I was frightened, and you told me that you would not let anything harm me. Later when the dream was gone I was actually wet, as if it had really happened to me." She tried to see his face, but it was too dark in the room.

"Mara, I think I was in that dream with you. Did I beg you not to leave me?"

"Yes."

"Did you have any other dreams about me?"

"Yes. Once I walked through the snow barefoot, to a tent where you were. I knelt beside you and saw that you had such sadness in your eyes. I wanted to comfort you, but you could not see me. I do not blame you if you do not believe any of what I am telling you."

"I do believe you, Mara. I remember one night while I was searching for you. I had begun to think I would never find you. I was alone in my tent, and I cried out for death to release me from my torment."

"That was the night I came to you, Tajarez. I heard you say you did not want to live. What could it all mean?"

"I remember that night I felt a presence. It was as if I could smell the fragrance you always wore in your hair, and after that night I did not feel quite

444

so desperate.''

Mara ran her hand across Tajarez's chest, ''Do you suppose this happened to us because we love so deeply, or was it . . . because of the old man who came to me in a vision?''

Tajarez turned her over and tried to see her face. ''What old man, Mara?''

''I do not know if he really existed or if he was a figment of my imagination. But whenever I put the golden medallion on I would see this old man, and it terrified me at first. Later, I would feel comforted by him.''

''That would be Sagas the wise, Mara.''

''Sagas. That is the man Jeffery said gave me the medallion.''

''Yes. Sagas has the power to do many things, Mara. I believe he was trying to comfort you and me, while striving to bring us together again.''

''How is that possible. No man could have that kind of power.''

''Sagas does, Mara. You once knew about his powers and believed in them. I think Sagas located you through the medallion and sent Matio to find you. Matio said while he was searching for you, many times he wanted to give up, for he had no clue where to look for you. He said some force kept driving him on. That force would have been Sagas.''

Mara shivered. ''It is all so unreal. Why have I not met this Sagas?''

''He is in the mountains. I myself have searched for him, but if Sagas does not want to be found, no one can find him.''

Mara searched her mind to remember what Sagas had looked like. He had been a shadowy figure when he had come to her, and she found she did not know what his face was like.

"Tajarez, tell me about when we first met."

His hand rested against her stomach and he could smell the sweet, clean scent of her hair. "Mara, the first time I saw you was in a dream. I was a young man then, only sixteen summers. When I had that first dream you could have been no more than six summers, but in my dreams you were a woman. When I would awake from dreaming of you, I could never remember what you looked like, although I would try very hard. You see, I hated the white race. I had only seen one white man, his name was O'Malley, and he had been the cause of my mother's and sister's deaths."

"What did he do?"

"My father had found O'Malley half frozen and had brought him to the hidden valley. O'Malley remained with us for six years. I was very small when O'Malley first came to us. He taught me to speak English. He would sit for hours telling me about the wonderful things in the white world, and next to my father, I loved him best. One day O'Malley found my father away from the City. He slew my mother and forced my sister to leave with him. He had laden four pack horses with gold and furs and used my sister Terza as a shield to get past the guard. My father hunted O'Malley down and he died a long and agonizing death. As a result of O'Malley's treachery, I began to hate the white race, and I swore to my father I would never allow any white man to enter the hidden valley.''

"How sad. I am grieved about your mother and sister.''

"Mara, I have come to know that O'Malley served a purpose. He taught me to speak English, so when I met you we could speak to each other.''

"You said you first saw me in a dream?''

"Yes, many times. I grew to love the beautiful woman in my dreams.''

"Tell me about the dreams?''

"The dreams were always the same. I would pick you up in my arms and lay you on the bed beside me. When I would hold you close you would begin to fade, and I would beg you not to leave me.''

"Tajarez, how is it possible to see someone in a dream before you have met them?''

"I do not know, Mara. Perhaps I saw you in the same way you dreamed of me.''

"Do you think Sagas caused your dreams?''

"Yes, I am sure he did.''

"Tell me more. When did we meet?''

"Mara, it is the law of the Lagonda that the prince royal must go on a quest to the outside world, living off the land and not speaking until he returns to the Seven Cities. Hamez will one day have to make that quest, just as I and my father did and his father before him and as far back as the history of the Lagonda is recorded. Before I left on my quest my father had been urging me to take a bride from one of the maidens of the tribe, but I could not find one whom I could love. My heart was filled with love for the woman in my dreams."

"Even though you could not remember what I looked like when you were awake?" Mara asked in amazement.

"Even though I could not remember your face, I knew that I loved you. I felt one day I would meet the woman of my dreams, and I would know her at once."

"Did we meet while you were on your quest?"

"Yes. While I was on my quest I dreamed of you each night. I suppose it was because our meeting was close at hand."

"This is all very unreal, Tajarez."

"I know it must seem that way to you, but sometimes there are happenings that cannot be explained by everyday rules. Our love and our meeting is one of those."

"Tell me about when we first met. Did you know me at once? How did I react to you?"

"You had been abducted by two Indians. When I first saw you, you were fighting for you life. You had one of the men's knife and had stabbed him in the arm. I saw that you were in trouble and I killed both of the men who had held you captive. I could not tell what you looked like, as you were covered in mud, and at first I did not even like you, because you belonged to the race I had sworn to hate."

"What did you do with me?"

"I took you with me because I could not just leave you to die in the wilderness. I did not like even to touch you."

"How strange this all sounds," Mara said, trying

to imagine herself as the girl Tajarez spoke of. "Then what happened, Tajarez?" she urged.

"I made camp that night and was forced to sleep beside you and share my robe with you so you would not freeze to death. The next morning I left you and bathed in the river, wanting to wash every trace of you from my body."

"Did you make love to me?"

Tajarez laughed. "No. I hated even the thought of touching you, and I was on a quest and forbidden to lie with a woman."

"I see, or I think I see. Tell me more."

"Well," he said, trying to think about his story when his mind was shifting to the soft skin that brushed against his body, "when I returned to camp, you too had bathed in the river. When I saw you were the woman of my dreams, I felt as if I had been struck by a lightning bolt from the sky. You were my love, the woman I had dreamed of, and you belonged to the hated white race. I had never seen hair the golden color, nor eyes of green. Can you imagine how I felt? You were my love, and you did not know me."

"Oh Tajarez, what a beautiful story. Did you bring me home with you?"

"I am skipping much of the story. I took you to a fort and left you, although it tore at my heart to do so. It was as if I had left a part of myself behind."

"But how did I get here?"

"It was not until a year later that I found you. I had searched for you, not knowing where to find you in St. Louis."

"You have not said. Did I love you at that time?"

"Yes, you did, beloved. You told me before I took you to the fort that you loved me."

"Why did you leave me and then come back for me? I do not understand."

"When I returned home, Sagas demanded to know where the Golden One was."

"Who is the Golden One?"

"You are the Golden One, Mara."

"I do not understand."

"Mara, there is an old prophecy that was given my people hundreds of years ago. For long years the Lagonda people have waited for you to come. I will quote you the prophecy."

*When the Golden One comes there will be peace
  and plenty*
*The past will be revealed to the few and the
  many*
*One man will die; another shall weep.*
*There will be love where the Golden One sleeps.*

"What does it mean, Tajarez," Mara asked, feeling uneasy about the prophecy.

"Mara, since you have come to us our crops in the fields have been abundant. Never has the hidden valley known such bounty. And you have been helping Sagas reveal the past."

"Do you mean the hieroglyphics?"

"Yes."

"Who was the man who died?"

"That would be my father."

"And the one who wept?"

Tajarez was quiet for a long time. When he spoke, Mara could hear the anguish in his voice.

"I was that man, Mara."

She touched his face softly, "Why did you weep, Tajarez," she asked, unable to imagine him weeping.

"I do not want to speak of it, Mara. I am not proud that I wept like some woman. Loving you has caused this weakness in me."

Mara could hear the pain in his voice, so she decided not to press him. "Tell me how we were married."

"I married you once in your brother David's home in St. Louis, and then again here in the City, where my father made you my wife."

"Tajarez, I married you twice, and I have loved you twice."

"Never stop loving me Mara, for if you do, I could not live."

"Tajarez, I loved you even when I did not know who I was, or who you were."

He kissed her cheek and his hand moved up to her breast. "No more questions tonight, beloved," he whispered. His hand closed over her breasts that were swollen with milk and Mara cried out, since even his gentle touch was painful to her.

"I am sorry, beloved. I should have remembered how painful it was for you when you weaned Hamez and Tamera."

Pushing the strap of her petticoat aside he tenderly brushed her swollen breasts with his lips first one then the other, in such a beautiful gesture that

Mara's heart melted.

"I will let you sleep now, Mara. You must be in pain from the fullness of your breasts."

Mara did not want to sleep. Her body wanted to find a oneness with her husband. She could now allow herself to surrender to him with no feelings of guilt. Her hand traveled over his chest, feeling the tautness beneath her fingers.

"Mara, I would not continue if you wish to find sleep," he said in a raspy voice.

She smiled to herself, feeling a surge of power. She was finding out that she had the power to move this man. Her hand drifted down to his waist, and she turned her head to find his lips. At first his lips were unyielding, until her hand moved over his firm, flat stomach.

"Mara," he groaned as his lips covered hers, devouring her mouth with a savage kiss. "I warned you," he said, rolling her over and covering her body with his.

"I dare to play with fire," she murmured in his ear.

"I will dare to quench your hunger," he said, driving his manhood into her welcoming body. "Beloved, you have the power to make me your slave," he whispered against her lips.

Their lovemaking was frantic as each of them took and gave to the other. Afterwards Tajarez held her tightly in his arms and Mara curled up contentedly.

"Did I cause you pain, beloved?"

"No."

They were quiet for a long time, needing no words

to tell each other what they felt. Time passed as they touched and caressed one another.

"Mara, I will never allow you to leave this valley again, unless I am with you. If your brother David wants to see you, he will have to come here."

"I cannot imagine wanting to leave. I will be content to live with you here for the rest of my life. My one wish is that I might remember the past."

"There are some things I would not mind if you never remembered."

"Such as?"

"I would be a fool to tell you, would I not?"

Mara sighed contentedly and closed her eyes. Let the past stay dead, she thought. She had the future. She had love. She had the heart of the dark, handsome king of the Seven Cities.


The next morning Tajarez made arrangements for Andrew to be presented to the people of the Lagonda tribe. Word had spread throughout the Seven Cities that the queen had been found and that there was a new prince.

By late afternoon a crowd of people was gathered at the steps of the palace, waiting for the king and queen to appear before them.

Mara walked down the steps to stand beside Tajarez, who was holding Andrew in his arms. When the people saw her a loud uproar reached her. Looking down into the sea of faces, she felt nervous and unsure. When Tajarez held up his hand silence moved over the crowd.

"Do not be nervous, Mara. Everyone here loves you," Tajarez said, knowing what she was feeling.

Mara gave him a weak smile, and raised her head proudly.

"My people," Tajarez called out. "I give you the queen, who has been safely returned to us."

The noise from the crowd was deafening, and Mara could see the joy on the faces of the people. Not knowing what to do with such a warm welcome, she raised her hand and smiled. She felt warmed by the love that reached her from the people of the Lagonda tribe.

"See how much you are loved, Mara," Tajarez said near her ear. Once more Tajarez raised his hand for silence. "I know you are all aware that your queen has been missing for many months. I want to assure you she is in good health. She has, however, lost all memory of the past. I am told by Tabo that her memory could return at any time. I tell you this because I know you have been concerned for her."

Tajarez paused. Raising Andrew over his head, he spoke in a commanding voice. "I give you Andrew, my son, and your new prince."

Once again the crowds went wild in their joy. The day was cold, so Tajarez led Mara back into the palace. Andrew was taken to the nursery and Tajarez took Mara's hand and led her up onto the raised dais, and sat her down in one of the chairs.

Mara looked at him, puzzled.

"There is someone who wishes to seek audience with you, Mara."

"What does this mean, Tajarez? What is expected

of me?''

"Falon and Matio seek to petition you. They need permission that only you can give them."

"I do not understand."

"Falon belongs to you and needs your permission before she can marry."

Mara saw Matio and Falon approaching her. She felt as if she were stepping into someone else's place. The golden crown of the double cobra rested on her head, but it did not give her any insight into what her duties as queen were.

Falon and Matio bowed their heads and looked at Mara inquiringly. A heavy silence hung over the anteroom as Mara wondered what to say. Seeing she was going to receive no help from Tajarez, she spoke.

"What would you ask of me, Falon?"

Falon looked into her eyes hesitantly. "I seek permission to marry Matio of the royal guard, my queen."

Mara's gaze moved to the young warrior, whom she recognized as the one who had come to her at the cabin.

"Matio, do you love Falon?"

"It is so, my queen," he said, bowing his dark head.

"Falon, do you love Matio?"

Falon's eyes became soft. "It is so, my queen."

"Do you ask to be released from my service?"

Falon shook her head and blinked her eyes. "No, my queen, I am greatly honored to wait upon you."

"I see. Matio, I give Falon to you as your bride. I

will charge you to care for her, for if you do not you will incur my displeasure."

The young couple looked at their queen with joy on their faces. "I will care for her very well my queen," Matio said.

"I have something to say to you, Matio," Tajarez spoke up. He had been silently watching the proceedings and thought that Mara handled herself very well as the queen she was.

Matio bowed his head, thinking he was about to be reprimanded for the injustice he had charged against his queen. He had been expecting it for a long time, and he dreaded that the time was now.

"I await your displeasure, my king," he said, standing tall and proud.

Tajarez arched an eyebrow. "My displeasure? Nay, Matio, I wish to honor you for your devotion to finding your queen. Without you, I doubt we would ever have located her."

Matio's face lit up and he looked uncertain for a moment. This was not what he had expected. His heart swelled with pride as he looked into the eyes of his king.

"I will state that you are to be honored, Matio. As of this day I am placing twelve warriors under your care. See to their training. I know you will do well."

Matio could hardly contain his joy. "I am honored by your faith in me, my king. I will strive to do my best."

Tajarez smiled at the young warrior. "You have only one flaw to overcome, Matio. I would charge you not to believe in first impressions. Seek deeper for the truth."

Matio's face burned red, but no one but he and the king knew he had received his reprimand, after all. "It is so, my king. I will remember."

# Thirty-One

I remember, I remember, happy days of years
gone by.
I remember, I remember where my future lies.

Tajarez was standing before the window, watching
the City below him. His thoughts were troubled.
When he was with Mara he was aware that she would
try very hard to remember their past life together,
but when he made love to her in the early morning
hours, she did not surrender herself to him
completely as she once had. He still wished for things
to be as they once were between them. What if she
never remembered? He felt another's presence, and
he looked up to see Sagas standing beside him.

"Where is Mara?"

"I am told she is lying down. Where have you
been all these months?" Tajarez demanded sourly.
"I have made inquiries, but no one seemed to know
where you were."

Sagas removed the heavy fur robe he wore and
tossed it on a nearby cushion. His face showed his
hundred and twenty-some-odd years. His usually

immaculate white robe was stained and dirty.

"I have been in the mountains. I told you this before I went away."

"Great Father, you were in the mountains all winter? Have you no care for your health?"

Saga's black eyes snapped. "I was in no danger. I must go where I am called. So, Mara has lost her memory."

"Yes, and you would have known it sooner if you had been here when I brought her back," Tajarez said angrily.

"I knew it before you even found her. If she had heeded my words and worn the medallion, she would not have lost her memory," Sagas said matter-of-factly.

"The medallion! If she were to put it on now, would she remember everything?" Tajarez asked hopefully.

"Of course."

"Then we shall find the medallion and have her put it on."

"It will not be pleasant for her. Are you sure you want to subject her to that?"

"What do you mean?"

"When she starts to remember, her past life will pass before her and it will be as if she is living it."

"Would that be bad?"

"When she remembers her parents' death and your father's it will be as if they just happened. And what about when she almost lost her baby, and when Anias took her?"

"What shall I do?"

Sagas walked toward the door. "I am going to bathe, and when I return I suggest we consult Mara. And if I know her, which I do, she will want to remember."

Mara was standing on the balcony. The cold winds rustled in the trees and gathered the snow and whipped it about in a great white torrent. Hearing the bedroom door open, she turned and saw Tajarez enter with an old man.

The old man stood straight and tall. His hair was as white as the robe he wore. Looking into his eyes, she remembered him as the old man in her dreams. Ignoring Tajarez, she walked over to the old man and took his hand, an instinct that startled her, but the old man simply smiled.

"So long have you been away, Mara, that these old eyes have hungered for the sight of your face."

"I am still not all returned. Help me." Why had she asked him for help? Who was he?

"Where is the medallion now, Mara?"

She put her hand to her face, trying to remember. "I put it with the gowns I brought with me. I do not know where they are."

"I had them taken to the storage room," Tajarez said. He ran into the hall and told one of the guards to fetch the medallion.

"It has been a long way home for you, Mara, but it is almost over," the old man said.

"I dreamed about you. When I was frightened you came to me in a dream. You told me not to despair, that you would be beside me."

"Yes, I know."

"It was a dream, was it not? Thinking back, it seemed so real at the time. It was as if you were in the room with me—and you took me to see . . . Tajarez!"

"It is best if you think of it as a dream."

Tajarez had returned and he handed the medallion to Sagas.

"Mara," the old man said, "I have it within my power to return the past to you. I must warn you, however, that it will be very painful for you. You will relive all that happened to you that was memorable. Some of the experiences will be pleasant; others will hurt you. It is for you to decide."

"I want to get my memory back. I will do anything. How long will it take?"

"Hours, days, who can say? You will be in a trance and must not be disturbed for any reason, for should you awaken before the transition is completed, you will be lost between the two worlds, and not even I can help you."

"I will take the chance."

"No, Mara!" Tajarez cried. "I did not know it would be so dangerous. Your memory is not that important."

"It is important to me. Please, do not try to stop me. I would do anything you asked of me, but this I must do for myself."

Tajarez took her hand. "I could forbid it."

"You could, but you will not," Sagas said. "Clear this whole floor of everyone. Bar the door to the garden and allow no one to enter it. Post guards at the stairs and let no one come up the stairs. There must be absolute quiet," Sagas said with authority.

"I am going to remain with her," Tajarez said.

"I expected you would, as will I," Sagas said.

Tajarez left the room. First he sent a servant to prepare a big meal for Mara. Then he ordered the second floor vacated, and even the nursery was moved downstairs. He then had the garden sealed off and stationed a guard at the gates. Guards were posted at the foot of the stairs, as Sagas had ordered.

After Mara had eaten and the dishes were cleared away, she sat down on the bed and Tajarez sat beside her. "Mara, there is still time to change your mind."

"No, I have made my decision."

The palace seemed as quiet as a tomb as Sagas pulled up a cushion and sat down beside Mara.

"Mara, you will know fear, heartache, and grief. Tajarez and I will be unable to help you in any way."

"I am ready."

Tajarez leaned forward and kissed her lips softly, and then Sagas stood up and slowly placed the golden medallion over her head. As the medallion fell between Mara's breasts, it felt as if it had burned her skin.

She waited for tense moments, but nothing happened. She was about to voice her doubt that the medallion would help her, when she started feeling dizzy. She clutched Tajarez's hand, and a bright red light flashed before her eyes, blocking everything else from view. Then it was as if she were falling down,

down. She opened her mouth to scream, but she could hear no sound.

But Sagas and Tajarez heard her scream over and over again.

Tajarez jumped to his feet. "Stop it, Sagas. I cannot bear to see her like this."

"Remain silent, or leave this room," Sagas said. "It cannot be stopped now. Her mind has reached back to her childhood and will progress slowly forward. If we stop it now, she will have the mind of a child."

Tajarez sat down on the cushion beside Sagas and watched as Mara's face relaxed into a serene expression.

"She is remembering her childhood," Sagas said. "It will be a long process. The hour grows late. If you want to sleep, I will sit with her."

"No, I will stay with her also."

Hours passed and the two men watched over Mara. Sometimes her face would ease into a smile. "It would seem that she had a pleasant childhood," Sagas said, speaking in a hushed tone.

It was in the morning hours when Mara started to moan and turn her head from side to side.

"What is happening?" Tajarez asked, rising to his feet.

Sagas put a restraining hand on Tajarez's arm. "She is apparently reliving something unpleasant. I would caution you not to interfere in any way. I told you if she were to awaken before she has made the transition to the present, it could be very dangerous for her."

Mara started to cry, and Tajarez sat back down on the cushion, knowing she was going through an experience that he could not help her with. All he could do was sit quietly and watch over her.

"Mother, Father, help me. I have been taken by two savages. Help me," Mara cried out. Her body was trembling as if she were cold, and yet tiny drops of perspiration popped out on her skin. "What can they want with me? I am so frightened. Someone, help me, please. Who are you? Why have you saved me? You are also an Indian, yet like no other I have ever seen."

Tajarez knew she was reliving the time she had been abducted by the two Indians and he had rescued her.

"I love you. What is your name? It does not matter that you are an Indian, I will always love you." Her voice went on and on. "Why do you leave me? I want to go with you. Why is it that you will not talk to me?" She tossed on the bed, and Tajarez could hear the pain in her voice. "You spoke to me. Your name is Tajarez."

Sagas glanced at Tajarez questioningly.

Tajarez shrugged his shoulders. "So I broke my vow of silence. It seemed important to her to know my name."

Suddenly Mara screamed and sat up. Her eyes were open and tears flowed freely down her face. "My mother and father are dead and it is because of me," she cried.

Tajarez would have gone to her, but once again Sagas prevented him.

Mara fell back on the bed and seemed to calm down for a while.

All through the night Tajarez and Sagas stayed beside her as she relived her past. Sometimes she would smile or even laugh, and at other times she would cry. All through the next day Mara continued her search of the past to reach the present.

Once she frowned. "Sasha, in what capacity does Tanka serve the prince?"

Sagas smiled at Tajarez's discomfort. "Wish I could have seen you get out of that one."

The experience was emotionally draining for Tajarez, and he knew that it must be hell for Mara. He heard her cry out when his cousin Anias had abducted her, and he knew when she was reliving the Kiowa raid, where he himself had almost lost his life. It was as though he and Sagas were reliving her past and her inner feelings with her. At one point she smiled and parted her lips. "Tajarez, we cannot make love here in the open, someone will see us."

Sagas looked at Tajarez, and Tajarez raised his eyebrow as if daring the old man to comment.

"Interesting," was the only comment Sagas made.

When the dawn came Sagas had Tajarez hang a fur robe over the window so no light would penetrate the room, and hour after hour Mara took Tajarez on the journey into her past. She cried when Tajarez's father died in her arms, and she laughed when something funny occurred.

Tajarez knew when she was dreaming that he was making love to her. Her lips would part and her beautiful body would become soft and yielding

"I think it would not be wise to tell her how vividly she remembered some things," Sagas said, smiling at Tajarez.

"I do not enjoy your knowing about the more intimate details of our marriage," Tajarez whispered in vexation.

"I am much too old to be stirred by the thoughts of passion, yours or any others," Sagas said, smiling. He was enjoying the effects Mara's dreams were having on his young king.

The two men had no way of knowing how old the day was in the darkened room. Tajarez became restless and began to pace the floor. Mara had been silent for some time when she began to moan, and Tajarez returned to her side.

"They will all drown, and it is because of me," she cried as tears spilled down her face. "Oh, no, God, please. Palomas has been shot. He is dead, and so is Matio. I cannot live with the thought that they lost their lives because of me." She screamed, and then became silent.

Sagas stood up and removed the medallion from around her neck. Mara appeared to be sleeping calmly now, and the old man motioned for Tajarez to follow him to the door.

"I will leave you now. Let her sleep. When she awakens she will be as before." The old man looked tired as he left the room.

Tajarez returned to Mara and removed his clothing. He dropped down on the bed beside her and drew her into his arms. He pulled the covers over them both, kissed her cheek, and fell into

466

an exhausted sleep.

Tajarez awoke feeling something soft against his face. Opening his eyes, he saw Mara bending over him, her golden hair spilling across his chest. She was sprinkling kisses over his smooth face.

"I love you, I love you," she whispered. "I remember everything," she said in an elated voice. "I remember being married to you, I remember your father, I remember everything."

His hand crept down her body and he raised his eyebrow, finding she wore nothing. "Do you remember that I love you?" he asked as he rolled her over on top of him.

"Yes, I remember that you said that you did, but I would like you to refresh my memory a bit more," she challenged him seductively.

Fire leaped into his dark eyes as she rubbed her satiny body against him in the most sensous way.

"What would be my queen's pleasure?" he said in a husky voice.

"To please my king," she told him breathlessly.

Warm flesh melted against warm flesh. If Tajarez had any doubt that Mara had regained her memory, it was soon erased as she touched him and in turn responded to his touch. She remembered all the things that pleased him, and his body reacted strongly to her. She had the power to make a begger out of a king.

Mara was left breathless by her tall, dark husband's lovemaking. When they both reached the pinnacle of desire, they lay in each other's arms, holding, touching, feeling. It was as if they were both rediscovering each other, and in doing so, they reached a happiness they had never before experienced.

Nothing would ever come between them in the future. No one could tear them apart. Their love was strong and deep, and the future shone brightly before them.

"I will never let you leave me again, Mara. Never! I have been in the depths of despair without you."

"What about the promise you made to David?"

"I have sent a courier to him, stating that if he wishes to see you he will have to come here."

"Would you allow David to enter the hidden valley?"

"Yes, for it is the only way he will ever see you."

Mara smiled to herself. She could not help teasing Tajarez just a bit. "Suppose I should become discontented and wish to visit the white world?"

His hand slid up her shoulder and fastened in her golden hair. "I shall just have to keep you content so you will not want to leave me," he said, smiling.

"I will never want to leave you, Tajarez. The world outside this valley has no appeal for me. I cannot wait to see our children now that I remember who they are. I want to see Jeffery, Sasha, Palomas, and so many others. I have the best of all possible worlds right here. My days will be full and happy."

"And your nights?" he said, quirking his dark eyebrow.

She frowned, as if considering. "I am not sure.

Could you give me something to judge by?"

His laughter resounded around the room as he bent his head to taste the sweet lips that were sorely tempting him. "I will be generous with the pleasure I will give you, my queen," he said softly as his lips covered hers.

The next morning Mara and Tajarez were eating breakfast in their room when Palomas knocked on the door. "Sagas has asked if you will come to him in the chamber off the anteroom, my king. He would like you to bring the prince, Andrew."

"For what reason?" Tajarez asked.

Mara smiled. "If I know Sagas, you will not know the why of it until he is ready to reveal it to you. I suggest you do as he ask, my husband."

"Yes, perhaps so." Tajarez stood up and left the room to get Andrew as Sagas had requested.

Mara stood up and approached Palomas, who stood staring at her. "Is it true, my queen, that you now remember who you are?"

"Yes, my dear friend, I remember all. I have much to apologize to you for, have I not? I know what a hard time I have given you lately."

"Not so. The queen need never apologize for any reason," he said, bowing to her slightly.

Mara laughed delightedly. "My, my, are you not the formal one now. Would that you always treated me with such respect. I can remember many times you were displeased with me and did not hesitate to tell me so."

A smile eased Palomas's irregular features. "Welcome home, Mara."

As Tajarez entered the chamber, he saw Sagas rise from the cushion where he had been sitting. Tajarez could not help but notice how old Sagas looked. His back was not as straight as he usually carried it, and his face looked ashen.

"Hand me the child," Sagas said in a voice of authority, and Tajarez complied readily.

He watched as Sagas pulled the blanket aside and stared long and hard at Andrew. "He has the look of you about him, Tajarez. He is an exceptional child. I know now why the spirits have chosen him as my successor."

"What are you saying, Sagas? I do not like what you are implying."

Sagas sank down on one of the white cushions, and his hands seemed to tremble as he touched Andrew's face. "I am old, Tajarez. I have not many days left on this earth. It is time for me to transfer my powers to another. Your son is chosen as my successor."

"I do not want to hear such talk. I do not want to think of your leaving me, and I do not think I want Andrew to have your powers. I want him to have a full and happy life, to one day marry and have children. Besides, if anything should happen to Hamez, Andrew would be *my* successor."

"There is nothing you and I can do about the future. I am ready to depart this life, and you have nothing to say about the power being transferred to Andrew. The spirits have chosen him."

"Mara will not like it, Sagas."

"She will accept it."

"When does this take place?"

Sagas laid Andrew across his lap and placed both his hands on either side of the baby's face. Closing his eyes, Sagas raised his head upward. The room was silent, and Tajarez had the strongest urge to take Andrew into his arms and prevent what was about to occur. He knelt down and looked into Andrew's eyes, and it was as if a flame were burning behind the dark circles.

"Andrew, son of the king of the Seven Cities of Gold, I, Sagas, give unto you the power which once was given to me. Use it wisely; never abuse it. It is given to help your people, and you must follow the path that the spirits have chosen for you."

Tajarez blinked his eyes in total disbelief as a blue light seemed to glow about Sagas's head. It grew in intensity and moved slowly downward to encircle the head of his son.

"Take your son," Sagas said in a weak voice.

Tajarez picked Andrew up and stared at Sagas, who had slumped forward. Laying Andrew down, he reached for Sagas and tried to steady him. "I will get the medicine man. You are ill."

"No, help me stand."

"But you are not well."

Sagas drew himself up and looked at Tajarez with a sad expression in his eyes. "I am returning to the mountains. I shall never see you again. Tell Mara for me that it was not I who chose her son as my successor."

Tajarez did not know how to answer. He hated to think that he would never see Sagas again. Sagas had been his boyhood confidant, and lately his wise counsel, as he had been to Tajarez's father when he was king. "What will I do without you?"

"You will do well, as you always have. I do not have much time, so I want to inform you about Andrew," Sagas said as he wavered on his feet and Tajarez steadied him. "Allow Andrew the freedom he will require while he grows to manhood. Do not question him when he goes into the mountains for long periods of time."

Tajarez nodded. "It will be as you say."

"I leave you now. I have loved you well, my king, as I loved your father before you, and his father before him. Have courage, and rule the people with love."

"And I have loved you, Sagas," Tajarez said, knowing there was nothing he could do to stop what must take place. He watched as Sagas walked across the room with his white robe flapping against his legs.

Sagas turned to him at the door and stood up straight and tall. "Tell Mara to finish the writings on the wall. Tell her I also loved her well."

Tajarez nodded, unable to voice the grief he was feeling. He watched as Sagas disappeared out the door, wanting to call him back, but knowing it would be impossible. He picked Andrew up and looked down at his face.

He seemed unchanged, but for his eyes. His eyes held a look of intelligence and understanding that went far beyond his young age.

Tajarez momentarily felt panic as he kissed Andrew's soft cheek. When he looked into the face of his son, Andrew smiled slightly, and Tajarez drew in his breath at the expression on his face. It was the same look he had seen on Sagas's face many times—sagacious, all-knowing, seeing that which others could not see.

As he climbed the stairs to the nursery, he held Andrew tightly against him, fearing what had just happened to his son. When he reached the nursery and laid Andrew down, his son looked deeply into his father's eyes and Tajarez suddenly felt at peace. He had no fear for Andrew. He was indeed fortunate to have been chosen by the spirits to replace Sagas.

"I understand, my son," he said as his hand touched the ebony hair so like his own. "I go now to tell your mother. She will understand also."

# ZEBRA HAS IT ALL!

**PAY THE PRICE** (1234, $3.95)
by Igor Cassini
Christina was every woman's envy and every man's dream. And she was compulsively driven to making it—to the top of the modeling world and to the most powerful peaks of success, where an empire was hers for the taking, if she was willing to PAY THE PRICE.

**PLEASURE DOME** (1134, $3.75)
by Judith Liederman
Though she posed as the perfect society wife, Laina Eastman was harboring a clandestine love. And within an empire of boundless opulence, throughout the decades following World War II, Laina's love would meet the challenges of fate . . .

**DEBORAH'S LEGACY** (1153, $3.75)
by Stephen Marlowe
Deborah was young and innocent. Benton was worldly and experienced. And while the world rumbled with the thunder of battle, together they rose on a whirlwind of passion—daring fate, fear and fury to keep them apart!

**FOUR SISTERS** (1048, $3.75)
by James Fritzhand
From the ghettos of Moscow to the glamor and glitter of the Winter Palace, four elegant beauties are torn between love and sorrow, danger and desire—but will forever be bound together as FOUR SISTERS.

**BYGONES** (1030, $3.75)
by Frank Wilkinson
Once the extraordinary Gwyneth set eyes on the handsome aristocrat Benjamin Whisten, she was determined to foster the illicit love affair that would shape three generations—and win a remarkable woman an unforgettable dynasty!

# BESTSELLING ROMANCES BY JANELLE TAYLOR

**SAVAGE ECSTASY**                                        (824, $3.50)

It was like lightning striking, the first time the Indian brave Gray Eagle looked into the eyes of the beautiful young settler Alisha. And from the moment he saw her, he knew that he must possess her—and make her his slave!

**DEFIANT ECSTASY**                                       (931, $3.50)

When Gray Eagle returned to Fort Pierre's gates with his hundred warriors behind him, Alisha's heart skipped a beat: would Gray Eagle destroy her—or make his destiny her own?

**FORBIDDEN ECSTASY**                                     (1014, $3.50)

Gray Eagle had promised Alisha his heart forever—nothing could keep him from her. But when Alisha woke to find her red-skinned lover gone, she felt abandoned and alone. Lost between two worlds, desperate and fearful of betrayal, Alisha hungered for the return of her FORBIDDEN ECSTASY.

**BRAZEN ECSTASY**                                        (1133, $3.50)

When Alisha is swept down a raging river and out of her savage brave's life, Gray Eagle must rescue his love again. But Alisha has no memory of him at all. And as she fights to recall a past love, another white slave woman in their camp is fighting for Gray Eagle!

**TENDER ECSTASY**                                        (1212, $3.75)

Bright Arrow is committed to kill every white he sees—until he sets his eyes on ravishing Rebecca. And fate demands that he capture her, torment her . . . and soar with her to the dizzying heights of TENDER ECSTASY!

# THE BEST IN HISTORICAL ROMANCE
## by Sylvie F. Sommerfield

**SAVAGE RAPTURE** (1085, $3.50)

Beautiful Snow Blossom waited years for the return of Cade, the handsome halfbreed who had made her a prisoner of his passion. And when Cade finally rides back into the Cheyenne camp, she vows to make him a captive of her heart!

**REBEL PRIDE** (1084, $3.25)

The Jemmisons and the Forresters were happy to wed their children—and by doing so, unite their plantations. But Holly Jemmison's heart cries out for the roguish Adam Gilcrest. She dare not defy her family; does she dare defy her heart?

**TAMARA'S ECSTASY** (998, $3.50)

Tamara knew it was foolish to give her heart to a sailor. But she was a victim of her own desire. Lost in a sea of passion, she ached for his magic touch—and would do anything for it!

**DEANNA'S DESIRE** (906, $3.50)

Amidst the storm of the American Revolution, Matt and Deanna meet—and fall in love. And bound by passion, they risk everything to keep that love alive!

**ERIN'S ECSTASY** (861, $2.50)

Englishman Gregg Cannon rescues Erin from lecherous Charles Duggan—and at once realizes he must wed and protect this beautiful child-woman. But when a dangerous voyage calls Gregg away, their love must be put to the test . . .

**TAZIA'S TORMENT** (882, $2.95)

When tempestuous Fantasia de Montega danced, men were hypnotized. And this was part of her secret revenge—until cruel fate tricked her into loving the man she'd vowed to kill!

**RAPTURE'S ANGEL** (750, $2.75)

When Angelique boarded the *Wayfarer*, she felt like a frightened child. Then Devon—with his captivating touch—reminded her that she was a woman, with a heart that longed to be won!

*Available wherever paperbacks are sold, or order direct from the Publisher. Send cover price plus 50¢ per copy for mailing and handling to Zebra Books, 475 Park Avenue South, New York, N.Y. 10016. DO NOT SEND CASH.*